Greek &
Roman
Myths

Greek & Roman Myths

General Editor: Jake Jackson

Associate Editor: Laura Bulbeck

FLAME TREE PUBLISHING

This is a FLAME TREE Book

FLAME TREE PUBLISHING
6 Melbray Mews
Fulham, London SW6 3NS
United Kingdom
www.flametreepublishing.com

First published 2014

Copyright © 2014 Flame Tree Publishing Ltd

20 22 23 21 19
7 9 8 6

ISBN: 978-0-85775-819-4

Contributors, authors, editors and sources for this series include:
Loren Auerbach, Norman Bancroft-Hunt, E.M. Berens, Katharine
Berry Judson, Laura Bulbeck, Jeremiah Curtin, O.B. Duane, Dr
Ray Dunning, W.W. Gibbings, H. A. Guerber, Jake Jackson, Joseph
Jacobs, Judith John, J.W. Mackail (translator of Virgil's *Aeneid*) Chris
McNab, Professor James Riordan, Rachel Storm, K.E. Sullivan.

A copy of the CIP data for this book is available from the British Library.

Printed and bound in Turkey

Contents

Series Foreword

STRETCHING BACK to the oral traditions of thousands of years ago, tales of heroes and disaster, creation and conquest have been told by many different civilizations in many different ways. Their impact sits deep within our culture even though the detail in the tales themselves are a loose mix of historical record, transformed narrative and the distortions of hundreds of storytellers.

Today the language of mythology lives with us: our mood is jovial, our countenance is saturnine, we are narcissistic and our modern life is hermetically sealed from others. The nuances of myths and legends form part of our daily routines and help us navigate the world around us, with its half truths and biased reported facts.

The nature of a myth is that its story is already known by most of those who hear it, or read it. Every generation brings a new emphasis, but the fundamentals remain the same: a desire to understand and describe the events and relationships of the world. Many of the great stories are archetypes that help us find our own place, equipping us with tools for self-understanding, both individually and as part of a broader culture.

For Western societies it is Greek mythology that speaks to us most clearly. It greatly influenced the mythological heritage of the ancient Roman civilisation and is the lens through which we still see the Celts, the Norse and many of the other great peoples and religions. The Greeks themselves learned much from their neighbours, the Egyptians, an older culture that became weak with age and incestuous leadership.

It is important to understand that what we perceive now as mythology had its own origins in perceptions of the divine and the rituals of the sacred. The earliest civilisations, in the crucible of the Middle East, in the Sumer of the third millennium BC, are the source to which many of the mythic archetypes can be traced. As humankind collected together in cities for the first time, developed writing and industrial scale agriculture, started to irrigate the rivers and attempted to control rather than be at the mercy of its environment, humanity began to write down its tentative explanations of natural events, of floods and plagues, of disease.

Early stories tell of Gods (or god-like animals in the case of tribal societies such as African, Native American or Aboriginal cultures) who are crafty and use their wits to survive, and it is reasonable to suggest that these were the first rulers of the gathering peoples of the earth, later elevated to god-like status with the distance of time. Such tales became more political as cities vied with each other for supremacy, creating new Gods, new hierarchies for their pantheons. The older Gods took on primordial roles and became the preserve of creation and destruction, leaving the new gods to deal with more current, everyday affairs. Empires rose and fell, with Babylon assuming the mantle from Sumeria in the 1800s BC, then in turn to be swept away by the Assyrians of the 1200s BC; then the Assyrians and the Egyptians were subjugated by the Greeks, the Greeks by the Romans and so on, leading to the spread and assimilation of common themes, ideas and stories throughout the world.

The survival of history is dependent on the telling of good tales, but each one must have the 'feeling' of truth, otherwise it will be ignored. Around the firesides, or embedded in a book or a computer, the myths and legends of the past are still the living materials of retold myth, not restricted to an exploration of origins. Now we have devices and global communications that give us unparalleled access to a diversity of traditions. We can find out about Native American, Indian, Chinese and tribal African mythology in a way that was denied to our ancestors, we can find connections, match the archaeology, religion and the mythologies of the world to build a comprehensive image of the human experience that is endlessly fascinating.

The stories in this book provide an introduction to the themes and concerns of the myths and legends of their respective cultures, with a short introduction to provide a linguistic, geographic and political context. This is where the myths have arrived today, but undoubtedly over the next millennia, they will transform again whilst retaining their essential truths and signs.

Jake Jackson
General Editor, London 2014

Greek Myths

Introduction to Greek Myths

THE STORIES OF GREEK MYTHOLOGY forged the common Greek identity and have been a key influence in the development of Western European art, music and literature since their debut in the eighth century BC, via the epic poems of Homer. These poems mark the introduction of the Olympians; divinities with human flaws, who presided over the fortunes of mortal men.

In about 1900 BC, Greek-speaking peoples from the Caucasus migrated to the southern European peninsula known today as Greece (or Hellas). There they found a land of valleys and mountains, one of which, Mount Olympus, was so high (2917 m/9750 ft) it seemed to touch the heavens – it therefore had to be the home of the gods. Since this peninsula was bounded on three sides by seas (the Ionian, Aegean and Mediterranean), the newcomers naturally looked for trade to neighbouring maritime peoples, as far afield as Asia Minor (eastern Turkey) and North Africa. From these ancient cultures, the Greeks took music, poetry and names of exotic deities, like Hera and Athene; they also took their alphabet, probably from the Phoenicians (southern Syria).

Foundation of Greek Mythology

As city-states, like Athens and Sparta, grew and colonization developed, by the fifth century BC hundreds of Greek communities had arisen, lying round the shores of the Mediterranean ('like frogs about a pond', as Plato put it), the Black Sea, southern Italy and North Africa. Small wonder that the Greek imagination peopled the seas with monsters, giants and sirens whom heroes such as Jason, Odysseus, Theseus and Heracles had to overcome.

In 338 BC Greece fell to Philip II of Macedonia and soon became part of Alexander the Great's empire. But less than two centuries later, in 146 BC, the expanding power of Rome saw Greece reduced to a Roman province. That was not the end of Greek culture however, for many of its gods and heroes were adapted by the Romans under different names (Zeus became Jupiter, Aphrodite – Venus, and Heracles – Hercules).

Greek belief in gods reached its peak between 800 BC and 330 BC. Every city of the ancient Greek world possessed its own myths, heroes and festivals. Despite the diversity, there were rites and festivals, such as the Olympic Games, in which all freeborn Greeks could take part. In addition, the great epic poems of Homer, Hesiod and other bards were known throughout the Greek world. Universal themes – of the Argonauts journeying in search of the Golden Fleece, of the 12 tests of Heracles, of Odysseus's adventures on his return from the Trojan War – helped form a sense of nationhood.

The myths were passed on and adapted by the storytelling tradition, from mouth to mouth. So the pantheon of gods was well established by the time the myths were written down in about 750 BC. When Athens became the centre of Greek intellectual life in the fifth century BC, well over half the adult male population of the city could read and write. The level of literacy in all Greek cities of this period was higher than at any period of Western culture before the twentieth century. It is also important to bear in mind two factors. First, for many purposes Greek culture remained an oral culture. Second, literacy did not extend to slaves (who in Athens accounted for a third of the population) or women. Ancient Greece was not a true democracy and the polis was essentially a male association. True, the most powerful figures seen in Greek tragedy are women, and several goddesses (Hera, Athene, Demeter) show more independence than their sisters in other pantheons, but only men were supposedly endowed with reason (logos) and were therefore the decision-makers in the real society.

Myth in Society

For many centuries, Western civilization looked upon mythology as Greek mythology. Only when collections of myths were made from other cultures was it clear how unique Greek myths were and what an important role they played. Over the centuries, faith in the absolute veracity of the old tales gradually faded. But Greeks had never wholly believed in their own interpretations of nature and history, so there is no standard version of a myth or epic.

In the traditional early versions of Jason and the Golden Fleece (of which only fragments remain), Jason's ill-fortune is put down to the wiles of his wife Medea. Yet, later, Apollonius of Rhodes gives us a different version in which Medea is described as a victim of Jason's infidelity and madness. Again, Homer has the beautiful Helen as prize for Paris of Troy; he elopes with her, so causing the Trojan War. Later poets (Stesichorus, Euripides), however, deny that Helen ever went to Troy at all. The historian Herodotus sums it up when he says that, 'Homer knew the story, but it was not such an attractive subject for verse'. In his *Republic*, the philosopher Plato rejects virtually all the old myths, calling them immoral, and suggests new ones.

Each new bard, therefore, had the right to interpret historical tradition in his own way and the audience did not feel obliged to accept any one as received truth. In fact, the very dynamic nature of myth was intended to stimulate discussion of such virtues as truth, morality and ethics.

Greek myth is unusual in other ways. It very rarely involves talking animals, unlike myths from other parts of the world. Mostly the incidents described are no more than an embellishment of everyday life rather than fantasy adventures. The great bulk of Greek tales also features heroes: men and women from a particular time and place. True, they have greater powers than ordinary mortals, but they are not all-powerful. In Homer's *Iliad*, when Diomedes and Patroclus attack the gods, Apollo reminds them: 'Remember who you are! Gods and men can never be equal.' By contrast, for example, Norse and Egyptian mythologies are far more concerned with gods than heroes.

Another quality of the myths is the educational role they played in society. In fifth-century BC Athens, aristocratic boys had as many as 12 years of schooling, divided into literature, music and physical education. The literature element mainly meant learning verse-myth by heart, taking in its moral content and debating issues raised. From Homer to the late tragedies, it is through myths that poets develop their deepest thoughts. The myths also provide a history of the Greek people, as well as contributing rich material for philosophical debates. In addition, they give ample subject matter for all the visual arts, from the great sculptures and statues adorning temples to mosaics and pottery paintings.

Olympian Gods

Ancient Greece had its cosmogonies, myths of how the world began and other stories of the gods. Although the gods travel far and wide, they always return to their homes beyond the clouds on Mount Olympus. Hence they are known as the Olympic gods or Olympians. Each god has his or her own home, although they usually come together in the palace of Zeus, father of the gods. There they feast on ambrosia and nectar, served by the lovely goddess Hebe and entertained by Apollo on his lyre. It is an immortal world of feasting and discussion of the affairs of heaven and earth.

Zeus, though known as the father of the gods, has a beginning. His father and mother are Cronus and Rhea, of the race of Titans, themselves children of heaven/Uranus and earth/Gaea. They, in turn, 'sprang from Chaos ('the yawning abyss'). Zeus and his two brothers, Poseidon and Hades, shared out the world, with Zeus taking the heavens, Poseidon the seas and Hades the underworld.

The lame god Hephaestus was architect, smith and artist for the gods; he even forged thunderbolts which Zeus hurled at his enemies. In gratitude, Zeus gave him Aphrodite, goddess of love and beauty, as his wife. Some myths say that she was born of sea foam and clothed by the seasons. Eros, god of love, is her son; armed with his bow and arrows, he fires his love darts into the hearts of gods and humans. Athene, goddess of wisdom, sprang fully adult from the head of Zeus; it was she who gave her name to the city of Athens and to the most famous of all Greek temples, the Parthenon (built between 447 and 438 BC) or Athene Parthonos (Athene the Virgin).

Hermes, messenger of the gods, is usually seen wearing a winged cap and sandals. He is also the god of trade, wrestling and other sports, even thieving – whatever requires skill and dexterity. Dionysus, god of wine, presides over sacred festivals to mark the grape harvest, wine being sacred and its drinking ritualized. Dionysus is often portrayed with male and female satyrs (horned creatures, half human, half-goat) and maenads (fauns). Since he is also the god of passion, many temples were named after him and festivals held in his name.

The nine Muses, who were daughters of Zeus and Mnemosyne (Memory), were originally goddesses of memory, but later each becomes identified with song, verse, dance, comedy, tragedy, astronomy, history, art and science. The three Graces (also Zeus's daughters) bestow beauty and charm on humans and preside over banquets, dancing and all elegant entertainment.

The three Fates control every person's birth, life and death. Also known as the Cruel Fates, they spend their time spinning the threads of human destiny and cutting them with shears whenever they wish. Finally, the three

Furies punish all transgressors mercilessly, usually with a deadly sting. Greeks preferred to call them the Eumenides (Good-Tempered Ones), as it would have been bad luck to use their proper name.

Origins of Humanity

Early Greek mythology had no agreed account of the origin of humanity. Sometimes humans emerged from clay, stones or ash trees. Much later, Plato claimed that the first man was a round ball with eight limbs but Zeus cut him in half to form the first man and woman. The best-known origin tale is that concerning the Titan Prometheus, who one day made a man out of clay and water in the image of the gods. But he had to pay for his bold deed.

To help men, Prometheus (whose name means 'forethought') stole fire from the sun's chariot and took it to earth hidden in a fennel stalk. Zeus was furious. He ordered Hephaestus to make a woman out of clay and send her down to earth. Her name was Pandora and, being made in heaven, she possessed every possible gift – including curiosity. At the home of Prometheus's brother, the slow-witted Epimetheus (meaning 'afterthought'), was a sealed jar that Pandora was told never to open. Of course, she opened it, so releasing all the suffering and torment that beset human lives to this day. In fear, she replaced the lid, trapping just one thing inside: hope. The jar became known as Pandora's Box.

Zeus then took revenge on Prometheus. He had him chained to a rock on Mount Caucasus where an eagle pecked out his liver. Being immortal, he could not die; the liver grew back in the night, and his torment started again with each new day.

In another myth, Zeus sent a flood to drown all humans. Deucalion, Prometheus's son, and his wife Pyrrha (daughter of Pandora and Epimetheus) built an ark in which they survived the flood, ending up on Mount Parnassus. They prayed at the Oracle of Delphi and were told to throw stones over their shoulders as they walked along. Those tossed by Deucalion turned into men, those by Pyrrha into women. Thus the human race was recreated on earth.

According to Hesiod, in his *Works and Days*, there were five ages of humanity. In the first, the golden age, people lived in peace and plenty.

The earth gave its riches freely, wine flowed from the vine and milk came of its own accord from cows and sheep. Inasmuch as people never grew old, death was no more terrible than falling asleep. In the course of time, the golden age gave way to the silver age. For the first time the year was divided into seasons and people had to build houses to protect themselves from winter wind and autumn rain. Since all sons were subject to their mothers, there was no cause for war.

It was not until the bronze age that evil entered people's hearts and wars started. Fear, greed and hatred ruled the earth. Next came the heroic age, when Zeus restored some human virtues in order to see heroes through the Trojan War and other semi-mythical events of early Greek history. But the worst age of all was the iron age, when weapons of iron helped people destroy each other. Yet people always lived in hope that the ages would be repeated over time: one day Cronus would return and bring back the golden age, and nature would again produce her gifts freely, snake and weed would lose their poison, goat and sheep would come home without need of a shepherd and sheep would grow fleece in different colours.

The Trojan War

The heroic period of myth is not some remote and dateless past. It spanned only two or three generations, focusing on the Trojan War. This can be dated to the twelfth century BC: based on archaeological findings, scholars have calculated that Troy fell around 1190 BC. The reason that the myths of this period are so well known is thanks to the oral storytelling tradition, from which one man, Homer, stands out. Homer's epic poetry, especially his *Iliad* and *Odyssey*, is truly a jewel in the crown of Western literature.

The tales related by storytellers were important to Greeks because they told the story of their ancestors and glorious past. Homer's epics and other verses were widely performed and children learned them in school. They described a heroic age in which gods freely intervened in human affairs, though mortals had to know their limits. But heroes were brave and adventurous, unafraid of self-sacrifice. Thus, when the warrior-hero Achilles is offered a choice by the Fates of a long life of ease or a short one with immortal glory, he naturally chooses the latter.

Troy (called Ilium in antiquity – hence the *Iliad*) was a city located near the coast in Asia Minor (eastern Turkey). Troy was strategically important because it guarded the Hellespont Straits. The story starts with Paris of Troy who is asked to judge a beauty contest between Hera, Athene and Aphrodite. Each promises him a reward: Hera – untold wealth, Athene – wisdom and fame; and Aphrodite – the most beautiful woman in the world. Paris opts for Aphrodite, so earning Paris the eternal enmity of Hera and Athene.

Paris's prize is Helen, wife of Menelaus, King of Sparta. Enchanted by 'the face that launched a thousand ships and burned the topless towers of Ilium' (Christopher Marlowe), Paris elopes with Helen to Troy. Alone among the Trojans, Paris's sister, Cassandra, foretells the destruction of Troy brought by the abduction. With his brother Agamemnon, King of Argos, Menelaus organizes a great fleet to sail to Troy. The Greeks set up camp outside Troy and besiege it for nigh on ten years. It is at this point that Homer takes up the story.

Two of the most famous Greek warriors, Achilles and Odysseus, at first refuse to join the expedition, but are finally tricked into going. Achilles is a typical Greek hero: strong and proud, but also brutal and headstrong, embodying the paradox of the hero, as seen especially in Heracles. Like many other heroes, he was brought up in the hills by the wise tutor Chiron, a centaur. His mother, hoping to make him invincible, dipped the young Achilles into the River Styx; the heel by which she held him remained the only vulnerable part of his body.

During the siege, Achilles falls out with Agamemnon over the king's acceptance of a Trojan priest's daughter, Chryseis, as war spoils. Achilles refuses to fight and lends his armour to his best friend Patroclus, who is killed in battle by the Trojan commander Hector, King Priam of Troy's eldest son. Achilles returns to the fray bent on revenge. He pursues Hector three times round the walls of Troy and finally kills him in a sword fight. Such is Achilles's fury that he mutilates Hector's corpse and refuses to return it to Priam for burial. However, the angry gods force him to hand over the body and, recklessly, he continues fighting, before being killed by an arrow shot in his heel by Paris. In turn, Paris is killed by a Greek archer. The *Iliad* ends with the games held for Hector's funeral.

Creatures and Monsters

Many are the horrifying monsters sent to test the strength and guile of Greek heroes – Jason, Heracles, Odysseus, Perseus, Theseus. They all have to journey to the very edge of known civilization and beyond into realms of fantasy where, time and again, they have to overcome giants, dragons, many-headed serpents, sirens, huge bulls and sea monsters of every sort.

The creatures of Greek myth are the archetypal villains of the European consciousness, rich material for the fertile imagination of artists, poets and children.

Some monsters, notably the giants, differ from men mainly in their size and ugliness. The human giants, such as the Cyclops (with one eye in the middle of their forehead), King Amycus of Bebryces (covered in thick black hair and beaten by the Argonaut Polydeuces in a boxing match) or Antacus (who is defeated by Heracles at wrestling) resemble ordinary mortals in proportions, and join in love and war with them.

Superhuman giants, on the other hand, war even with the gods and are of vastly grander proportions: Typhon, with his 100 arms, makes war on Zeus who slays him with a thunderbolt. He is so huge that it takes Mount Etna to cover the corpse. His brother Enceladus provides the flames of Mount Etna's volcano with his breath. For his part in the war against Zeus, the Titan Atlas has to hold up the heavens on his shoulders. It is Atlas's three daughters, the Hesperides, who bring Heracles the magical golden apples.

It can hardly have been coincidence that many of the monsters who test heroes are female. Oedipus (who has further troubles with women, unwittingly marrying his own mother) has a trial with the Sphinx, which has a woman's head and breasts, a lion's body and a bird's wings. The Harpies, fierce winged creatures with sharp claws, possess women's faces. These filthy beasts snatch food from the blind Phineus during Jason's journey to Colchis. The three Gorgon sisters, led by Medusa, have writhing snakes for hair and can turn their victims to stone with a single glance. With divine aid, Perseus cuts off Medusa's head while looking at her reflection in a polished shield.

Not all female monsters are ugly brutes. Beautiful femmes fatales out to trap unwary heroes include the Sirens, half-women, half-birds, whose song so bewitches sailors that they throw themselves overboard and drown. The

Argonauts escape by having Orpheus drown out their Siren song with his lyre, while Odysseus has himself bound to the mast while his sailors fill their ears with wax.

Dryope and her sister nereids (naiads), the 50 daughters of the sea god Nereus, are lovely nymphs who entice Hylas of the Argonauts down into their pool. The Amazon queen Hippolyte and Heracles's wife Deianeira both meet their end through witchcraft. The abundance of female monsters preying on men stem, it would seem, from the male fear of infidelity by wives and the belief that women are different from men in their predilection for the blacker, more orgiastic and less rational aspects of belief and ritual. Myth is a way of endorsing and defining women's natural role as loyal, obedient wives and mothers and legitimizing the male-dominated patriarchal society.

Human Heroes and Demigods

The distinction between heroes and demigods is unclear. While some heroes, like Jason and Oedipus, are sons of mortal parents, others, like Heracles, Perseus and Achilles, come from the union of gods or goddesses with mortals. Zeus and Alcmene produced Heracles (his name 'Glory to Hera' was meant to appease Zeus's wife, the goddess Hera); Zeus and Danae produced Perseus; Peleus and the sea-nymph Thetis were responsible for Achilles; while rumours of divine intervention surround both Theseus (Poseidon is his putative father) and Odysseus (the putative bastard son of Sisyphus, offspring of Aeolus, god of winds).

Many rival states claimed a hero as their founder and protector, no doubt embellishing their origins: Theseus of Athens, Jason of Iolcus, Ajax of Salamis. Noble families also asserted a hero as their ancestor. Alexander the Great, for example, claimed descent from both Achilles and the Egyptian god Amon (Ammon) and insisted that his own semi-divine status was recognized throughout Greece. The bards, including Homer and Hesiod, who sang for their living, often took care to extol the ancestors of their patrons and audiences.

The catalogue of ships in Homer's *Iliad* leaves no Greek state off the roll of ancient glory; the 50 Argonauts are each attributed to a noble Greek family.

The figure most akin to a national hero is Heracles. He never settled in any one city that could take full credit for his exploits, and his wanderings carried him beyond the bounds of Greece – far into Africa and Asia Minor. He was one of the earliest mythical heroes to be featured in Greek art (dating from the eighth century BC) and on the coins of city states (on which he is usually depicted strangling snakes while in his cradle). As a symbol of national patriotism he is the only hero to be revered throughout Greece; he is also the only hero to be granted immortality.

What makes Greek heroes particularly interesting is their depiction by bards as deeply complex characters. Typically, they follow a common pattern: unnatural birth, return home as prodigal sons after being separated at an early age, exploits against monsters to prove their manhood and subsequent kingship or glorious death. Super strong and courageous they may be, mostly noble and honourable, but all have to contend with a ruthless streak that often outweighs the good. Heracles, for example, hurls his wife and children into a fire in a fit of madness and his uncontrollable lust forces him on King Thespius's 50 daughters in a single night. Nor is he averse to homosexual affairs (with Hylas, for instance), though Greek pederasty is mostly excluded from the myths.

Despite recapturing the Golden Fleece for Greece, Jason never finds contentment; he deserts his wife Medea and dies when the Argo's rotting prow falls on him. Theseus is also disloyal to his wife Ariadne, abandoning her on the island of Naxos; he kills his Amazon wife Antiope and causes the death both of his son Hippolytus and his father Aegeus. Even the noble and fearless Achilles, the Greek hero of the Trojan War, a man who cannot bear dishonourable conduct, violates the dead hero's code by desecrating Hector's corpse and refusing to hand it over to the Trojans.

Like the heroes, therefore, cities that turn their hero's burial places into shrines (and oracles) receive good fortune, but they also risk invoking the hero's unpredictable temper.

Sources of Greek Myth

Greek myth has been passed down principally from song recitals and plays. In ancient Greece, myth dominated the subject matter of both. From generation to generation, professional bards known as rhapsodes committed to memory whole epics which they then passed on. The earliest of these epic poems known to us are the *Iliad* and the *Odyssey*, though both refer to earlier epics now lost. It was not until about 750 BC that the epics were written down for the first time.

In the middle of the eighth century BC, about the same time as the first written epics were made, a wandering minstrel by the name of Homer became the first of his profession to benefit from the new written records. His Iliad and Odyssey are narrative poems, both many hundreds of pages long, which tell the tale of Greek gods and heroes.

The *Iliad* centres on the Trojan War and, besides the warrior heroes like Achilles, Ajax, Hector and Odysseus, it describes the many gods on Mount Olympus and their various responsibilities, habits and foibles. The *Odyssey* is concerned with the hero Odysseus's ten-year journey home from the Trojan War, though the verses concentrate only on the last 40 days. It is a poem of the sea as well as land, and reaches into the realms of fable, even the underworld, introducing us to the lotus-eaters, Cyclops, Sirens, Scylla and Charybdis.

Both the *Iliad* and the *Odyssey* constitute truly great literature and encapsulate virtually all we know of Greek mythology. Ironically, our knowledge of their author is extremely sketchy. The many ancient accounts of the life of 'The Poet', as he was simply known, have him as a blind bard from Chios, born about 750 BC (Herodotus), but there is absolutely no evidence to verify this. We do not even know if he could read or write. All we can say is that, then as now, the epics ascribed to Homer emanate from a unique interaction between tradition and individual talent.

The other great rhapsodist was Hesiod, who was composing poems and winning singing competitions about 50 years after Homer, in 700 BC. Not only was he evidently the first to write his songs down, in his main epics *Theogony* and *Works and Days*, he was the first author of a systematic mythology. It is from Hesiod that we learn of the creation, the beginning of the gods and the world. Although Hesiod gives no account of the creation of humanity, he does tell us of Prometheus and Pandora.

Both Homer and Hesiod were born in Asia Minor, and their interpretations of mythology show many similarities with ancient Sumerian and other Near Eastern civilizations (the Phoenicians, Hurrians and Hittites). Nowhere else, however, have myths attained such a peak of written excellence as in the Greek epics.

Philosophers later challenged a literal belief in mythology. The great philosopher Plato (427–347 BC), an aristocratic Athenian, especially criticizes many of the myths immortalized by Homer and Hesiod for presenting gods and heroes as morally flawed and vengeful characters. Such characters would have had no place in his ideal society, which he describes in the *Republic*. In his work the *Timaeus*, he provides his own cosmology.

What all the epic bards, dramatists and philosophers show is that Greek mythology was ever changing, giving rise to yet more exciting artistic productions in every area of creativity.

The Underworld

The afterlife was of great importance to the ancient Greeks. Beyond the grave or funeral pyre lay a land of shadows, the underworld. It was ruled by Hades, brother of Zeus and Poseidon, who also gave his name to his dark realm. Because the gloomy underworld was opposed to bright heavenly Olympus, Hades was not accepted as an Olympian god, and his servants were never invited to sup in Zeus's palace.

Dead souls are taken by Hermes, messenger of the gods, down through gloomy caves and long, winding, underground paths until they come to five rivers. First they must be ferried by Charon across the black River Styx (hate) to the Gates of Hades, which are guarded by the three-headed hound Cerberus. Once inside they must then cross four more rivers: black Acheron (woe), Phlegethon (fire), salt-teared Cocytus (wailing) and Lethe (oblivion). Unless the soul has money (put in the corpse's mouth) to pay the ferryman, the ghost will be left to wander for 100 years on the far side of the Styx.

Once across the five infernal rivers, the dead go before three stern judges: Minos, Rhadamanthus and Aeacus, who help Hades assess people's lives and determine their fate. Exceptional heroes might find themselves assigned to the blissful Elysian Fields, also known as the Isles of the Blessed, far off in the western seas where they can relive the joys of life without memory of their sins. For those whose crimes are bad enough to warrant a sentence to eternal punishment, there are special torments in the darkest regions of

Erebus and Tartarus, where they are deprived of oblivion, being eternally reminded of their sins. This is true of King Tantalus who stole nectar and ambrosia from the gods: his punishment was to find that food and drink are always just beyond his grasp (hence our word 'tantalise'). Those who have done evil are also handed over to the three merciless Furies (Erinyes) before being led off to their appointed torment.

For the common dead, neither very good or very bad, their sad fate is to dwell forever in shadowy gloom. On occasion they may gain a glimpse of the strange garden of Persephone, queen of the underworld, with its bloomless poppies, pale beds of rushes and green grapes, which she crushes into deadly wine.

Few heroes or gods manage to venture down into Hades and return. Those that do often meet a sad fate. The three best-known figures to achieve this are Heracles, Orpheus and Persephone. Heracles's last test is to bring up the hound Cerberus. He is led by Hermes to a cave near Sparta from where he descends into Hades, passing the Fates and Furies, eventually coming to the gloomy palace of King Hades and Queen Persephone. Hades gives him the hound to see if he can overcome it with his bare hands. He does so, but returns it to Hades having accomplished his mission.

Orpheus, the greatest of all singers, is grief-stricken when his beloved wife Eurydice dies. So he goes with his lyre into the underworld and persuades Hades to let Eurydice return to earth. Hades agrees but there is one condition: Orpheus must not look back as he leads his wife out. Sadly, at the exit, he looks round at her and she has to return to Hades forever. In his grief he pledges never to remarry and a band of women suitors angrily cut him to pieces. Yet even after his death his head and lyre continue to sing and play.

The Beginning

AMONG ALL THE NATIONS scattered over the face of the earth, the Hebrews alone were instructed by God, who gave them not only a full account of the creation of the world and of all living creatures, but also a code of laws to regulate their conduct. All the questions they fain would ask were fully answered, and no room remained for conjecture.

It was not so, however, with the other nations. The Greeks and Romans, for instance, lacking the definite knowledge which we obtain from the Scriptures, and still anxious to know everything, were forced to construct, in part, their own theory. As they looked about them for some clue to serve as guide, they could not help but observe and admire the wonders of nature. The succession of day and night, summer and winter, rain and sunshine; the fact that the tallest trees sprang from tiny seeds, the greatest rivers from diminutive streams, and the most beautiful flowers and delicious fruits from small green buds,—all seemed to tell them of a superior Being, who had fashioned them to serve a definite purpose.

They soon came to the conclusion that a hand mighty enough to call all these wonders into life, could also have created the beautiful Earth whereon they dwelt. These thoughts gave rise to others; suppositions became certainties; and soon the following myth or fable was evolved, to be handed down from generation to generation. 🐦

Chaos and Nyx

❧

A T FIRST, when all things lay in a great confused mass, the Earth did not exist. Land, sea, and air were mixed up together; so that the earth was not solid, the sea was not fluid, nor the air transparent.

Over this shapeless mass reigned a careless deity called Chaos, whose personal appearance could not be described, as there was no light by which he could be seen. He shared his throne with his wife, the dark goddess of Night, named Nyx or Nox, whose black robes, and still blacker countenance, did not tend to enliven the surrounding gloom.

These two divinities wearied of their power in the course of time, and called their son Erebus (Darkness) to their assistance. His first act was to dethrone and supplant Chaos; and then, thinking he would be happier with a helpmeet, he married his own mother, Nyx. Of course, with our present views, this marriage was a heinous sin; but the ancients, who at first had no fixed laws, did not consider this union unsuitable, and recounted how Erebus and Nyx ruled over the chaotic world together, until their two beautiful children, Aether (Light) and Hemera (Day), acting in concert, dethroned them, and seized the supreme power.

Space, illumined for the first time by their radiance, revealed itself in all its uncouthness. Aether and Hemera carefully examined the confusion, saw its innumerable possibilities, and decided to evolve from it a "thing of beauty;" but quite conscious of the magnitude of such an undertaking, and feeling that some assistance would be desirable, they summoned Eros (Amor or Love), their own child, to their aid. By their combined efforts, Pontus (the Sea) and Gaea (Ge, Tellus, Terra), as the Earth was first called, were created.

In the beginning the Earth did not present the beautiful appearance that it does now. No trees waved their leafy branches on the hillsides; no flowers bloomed in the valleys; no grass grew on the plains; no birds flew through the air. All was silent, bare, and motionless. Eros, the first to perceive these deficiencies, seized his life-giving arrows and pierced the cold bosom of the Earth. Immediately the brown surface was covered with luxuriant verdure; birds of many colours flitted through the foliage of the new-born forest trees; animals of all kinds gamboled over the grassy plains; and swift-darting fishes swam in the limpid streams. All was now life, joy, and motion.

Gaea, roused from her apathy, admired all that had already been done for her embellishment, and, resolving to crown and complete the work so well begun, created Uranus (Heaven).

The Egg Myth

THIS VERSION of the creation of the world, although but one of the many current with the Greeks and Romans, was the one most generally adopted; but another, also very popular, stated that the first divinities, Erebus and Nyx, produced a gigantic egg, from which Eros, the god of love, emerged to create the Earth.

The Earth thus created was supposed by the ancients to be a disk, instead of a sphere as science has proved. The Greeks fancied that their country occupied a central position, and that Mount Olympus, a very high mountain, the mythological abode of their gods, was placed in the exact centre. Their Earth was divided into two equal parts by Pontus (the Sea (equivalent to our Mediterranean and Black Seas); and all around it flowed the great river Oceanus in a "steady, equable current," undisturbed by storm, from which the Sea and all the rivers were supposed to derive their waters.

The Greeks also imagined that the portion of the Earth directly north of their country was inhabited by a fortunate race of men, the Hyperboreans, who dwelt in continual bliss, and enjoyed a never-ending springtide. Their homes were said to be "inaccessible by land or by sea." They were "exempt from disease, old age, and death," and were so virtuous that the gods frequently visited them, and even condescended to share their feasts and games. A people thus favoured could not fail to be happy, and many were the songs in praise of their sunny land.

South of Greece, also near the great river Oceanus, dwelt another nation, just as happy and virtuous as the Hyperboreans,—the Ethiopians. They, too, often enjoyed the company of the gods, who shared their innocent pleasures with great delight.

And far away, on the shore of this same marvelous river, according to some mythologists, were the beautiful Isles of the Blest, where mortals who had led virtuous lives, and had thus found favour in the sight of the gods, were transported without tasting of death, and where they enjoyed an eternity of bliss. These islands had sun, moon, and stars of their own, and were never visited by the cold wintry winds that swept down from the north.

The Titans

CHAOS, EREBUS, AND NYX were deprived of their power by Aether and Hemera, who did not long enjoy the possession of the sceptre; for Uranus and Gaea, more powerful than their progenitors, soon forced them to depart, and began to reign in their stead. They had not dwelt long on the summit of Mount Olympus, before they found themselves the parents of twelve gigantic children, the Titans, whose strength was such that their father, Uranus, greatly feared them. To prevent their ever making use of it against him, he seized them immediately after their birth, hurled them down into a dark abyss called Tartarus, and there chained them fast.

This chasm was situated far under the earth; and Uranus knew that his six sons (Oceanus, Coeus, Crius, Hyperion, Iapetus, and Cronus), as well as his six daughters, the Titanides (Ilia, Rhea, Themis, Thetis, Mnemosyne, and Phoebe), could not easily escape from its cavernous depths. The Titans did not long remain sole occupants of Tartarus, for one day the brazen doors were again thrown wide open to admit the Cyclopes,—Brontes (Thunder), Steropes (Lightning), and Arges (Sheet-lightning),—three later-born children of Uranus and Gaea, who helped the Titans to make the darkness hideous with their incessant roaring for freedom. In due time their number was increased by the three terrible Centimani (Hundred-handed), Cottus, Briareus, and Gyes, who were sent thither by Uranus to share their fate.

Greatly dissatisfied with the treatment her children had received at their father's hands, Gaea remonstrated, but all in vain. Uranus would not grant her request to set the giants free, and, whenever their muffled cries reached his ear, he trembled for his own safety. Angry beyond all expression, Gaea swore revenge, and descended into Tartarus, where she urged the Titans to conspire against their father, and attempt to wrest the sceptre from his grasp.

All listened attentively to the words of sedition; but none were courageous enough to carry out her plans, except Cronus, the youngest of the Titans, more familiarly known as Saturn or Time, who found confinement and chains peculiarly galling, and who hated his father for his cruelty. Gaea finally induced him to lay violent hands upon his sire, and, after releasing him from his bonds, gave him a scythe, and bade him be of good cheer and return victorious.

Thus armed and admonished, Cronus set forth, came upon his father unawares, defeated him, thanks to his extraordinary weapon, and, after binding him fast, took possession of the vacant throne, intending to rule the universe forever. Enraged at this insult, Uranus cursed his son, and prophesied that a day would come when he, too, would be supplanted by his children, and would suffer just punishment for his rebellion.

Cronus paid no heed to his father's imprecations, but calmly proceeded to release the Titans, his brothers and sisters, who, in their joy and gratitude to escape the dismal realm of Tartarus, expressed their willingness to be ruled by him. Their satisfaction was complete, however, when he chose his own sister Rhea (Cybele, Ops) for his consort, and assigned to each of the others some portion of the world to govern at will. To Oceanus and Thetis, for example, he gave charge over the ocean and all the rivers upon earth; while to Hyperion and Phoebe he entrusted the direction of the sun and moon, which the ancients supposed were daily driven across the sky in brilliant golden chariots.

Birth of Zeus

PEACE AND SECURITY NOW REIGNED on and around Mount Olympus; and Cronus, with great satisfaction, congratulated himself on the result of his enterprise. One fine morning, however, his equanimity was disturbed by the announcement that a son was born to him. The memory of his father's curse then suddenly returned to his mind. Anxious to avert so great a calamity as the loss of his power, he hastened to his wife, determined to devour the child, and thus prevent him from causing further annoyance. Wholly unsuspicious, Rhea heard him inquire for his son. Gladly she placed him in his extended arms; but imagine her surprise and horror when she beheld her husband swallow the babe!

Time passed, and another child was born, but only to meet with the same cruel fate. One infant after another disappeared down the capacious throat of the voracious Cronus,—a personification of Time, who creates only to destroy. In vain the bereaved mother besought the life of one little one: the selfish, hard-hearted father would not relent. As her prayers seemed unavailing, Rhea finally resolved to obtain by stratagem the boon her husband denied; and as soon as her youngest son, Zeus, was born, she concealed him.

Cronus, aware of his birth, soon made his appearance, determined to dispose of him in the usual summary manner. For some time Rhea pleaded with him, but at last pretended to yield to his commands. Hastily wrapping a large stone in swaddling clothes, she handed it to Cronus, simulating intense grief. Cronus was evidently not of a very inquiring turn of mind, for he swallowed the whole without investigating the real contents of the shapeless bundle.

Ignorant of the deception practiced upon him, Cronus then took leave, and the overjoyed mother clasped her rescued treasure to her breast. It was not sufficient, however, to have saved young Zeus from imminent death: it was also necessary that his father should remain unconscious of his existence.

To ensure this, Rhea entrusted her babe to the tender care of the Melian nymphs, who bore him off to a cave on Mount Ida. There a goat, Amalthea, was procured to act as nurse, and fulfilled her office so acceptably that she was eventually placed in the heavens as a constellation, a brilliant reward for her kind ministrations. To prevent Zeus's cries being heard in Olympus, the Curetes (Corybantes), Rhea's priests, uttered piercing screams, clashed their weapons, executed fierce dances, and chanted rude war songs.

The real significance of all this unwonted noise and commotion was not at all understood by Cronus, who, in the intervals of his numerous affairs, congratulated himself upon the cunning he had shown to prevent the accomplishment of his father's curse. But all his anxiety and fears were aroused when he suddenly became aware of the fraud practiced upon him, and of young Zeus's continued existence. He immediately tried to devise some plan to get rid of him; but, before he could put it into execution, he found himself attacked, and, after a short but terrible encounter, signally defeated.

Zeus, delighted to have triumphed so quickly, took possession of the supreme power, and aided by Rhea's counsels, and by a nauseous potion prepared by Metis, a daughter of Oceanus, compelled Cronus to produce the unfortunate children he had swallowed; i.e., Poseidon, Hades, Hestia, Demeter and Hera.

Following the example of his predecessor, Zeus gave his brothers and sisters a fair share of his new kingdom. The wisest among the Titans— Mnemosyne, Themis, Oceanus and Hyperion—submitted to the new sovereign without murmur, but the others refused their allegiance; which refusal, of course, occasioned a deadly conflict.

The Giants' War

❧

ZEUS, FROM THE TOP OF MOUNT OLYMPUS, discerned the superior number of his foes, and, quite aware of their might, concluded that reinforcements to his party would not be superfluous. In haste, therefore, he released the Cyclopes from Tartarus, where they had languished so long, stipulating that in exchange for their freedom they should supply him with thunderbolts,—weapons which only they knew how to forge. This new engine caused great terror and dismay in the ranks of the enemy, who, nevertheless, soon rallied, and struggled valiantly to overthrow the usurper and win back the sovereignty of the world.

During ten long years the war raged incessantly, neither party wishing to submit to the dominion of the other, but at the end of that time the rebellious Titans were obliged to yield. Some of them were hurled into Tartarus once more, where they were carefully secured by Poseidon, Zeus' brother, while the young conqueror joyfully proclaimed his victory.

The scene of this mighty conflict was supposed to have been in Thessaly, where the country bears the imprint of some great natural convulsion; for the ancients imagined that the gods, making the most of their gigantic strength and stature, hurled huge rocks at each other, and piled mountain upon mountain to reach the abode of Zeus, the Thunderer.

Cronus, the leader and instigator of the revolt, weary at last of bloodshed and strife, withdrew to Italy, or Hesperia, where he founded a prosperous kingdom, and reigned in peace for many long years.

Zeus, having disposed of all the Titans, now fancied he would enjoy the power so unlawfully obtained; but Gaea, to punish him for depriving her children of their birthright, created a terrible monster, called Typhoeus, or Typhon, which she sent to attack him. He was a giant, from whose trunk one hundred dragon heads arose; flames shot from his eyes, nostrils, and mouths; while he incessantly uttered such blood-curdling screams, that the gods, in terror, fled from Mount Olympus and sought refuge in Egypt. In mortal fear lest this terror-inspiring monster would pursue them, the gods there assumed the forms of different animals; and Zeus became a ram, while Hera, his sister and queen, changed herself into a cow.

The king of the gods, however, soon became ashamed of his cowardly flight, and resolved to return to Mount Olympus to slay Typhoeus with his terrible thunderbolts. A long and fierce struggle ensued, at the end of which, Zeus, again victorious, viewed his fallen foe with boundless pride; but his triumph was very short-lived.

Enceladus, another redoubtable giant, also created by Gaea, now appeared to avenge Typhoeus. He too was signally defeated, and bound with adamantine chains in a burning cave under Mount Aetna. In early times, before he had become accustomed to his prison, he gave vent to his rage by outcries, imprecations, and groans: sometimes he even breathed forth fire and flames, in hopes of injuring his conqueror. But time, it is said, somewhat cooled his resentment; and now he is content with an occasional change of position, which, owing to his huge size, causes the earth to tremble over a space of many miles, producing what is called an earthquake.

Zeus had now conquered all his foes, asserted his right to the throne, and could at last reign over the world undisturbed; but he knew that it would be no small undertaking to rule well heaven, earth, and sea, and resolved to divide the power with his brothers. To avoid quarrels and recriminations, he portioned the world out into lots, allowing each of his brothers the privilege of drawing his own share.

Poseidon thus obtained control over the sea and all the rivers, and immediately expressed his resolve to wear a symbolic crown, composed exclusively of marine shells and aquatic plants, and to abide within the bounds of his watery realm.

Hades, the most taciturn of the brothers, received for his portion the sceptre of Tartarus and all the Lower World, where no beam of sunlight was ever allowed to find its way; while Zeus reserved for himself the general supervision of his brothers' estates, and the direct management of Heaven and Earth.

Peace now reigned throughout all the world. Not a murmur was heard, except from the Titans, who at length, seeing that further opposition would be useless, grew reconciled to their fate.

In the days of their prosperity, the Titans had intermarried. Cronus had taken Rhea "for better or for worse;" and Iapetus had seen, loved, and wedded the fair Clymene, one of the ocean nymphs, or Oceanides, daughters of Oceanus. The latter pair became the proud parents of four gigantic sons,— Atlas, Menetius, Prometheus (Forethought), and Epimetheus (Afterthought),— who were destined to play prominent parts in Grecian mythology.

Prometheus

A T THE TIME OF THE CREATION, after covering the new-born Earth with luxuriant vegetation, and peopling it with living creatures of all kinds, Eros perceived that it would be necessary to endow them with instincts which would enable them to preserve and enjoy the life they had received. He therefore called the youngest two sons of Iapetus to his aid, and bade them make a judicious distribution of gifts to all living creatures, and create and endow a superior being, called Man, to rule over all the others.

Prometheus' and Epimetheus' first care was, very naturally, to provide for the beings already created. These they endowed with such reckless generosity, that all their favours were soon dispensed, and none remained for the endowment of man. Although they had not the remotest idea how to overcome this difficulty, they proceeded to fashion man from clay.

They first moulded an image similar in form to the gods; bade Eros breathe into its nostrils the spirit of life, and Athene (Pallas) endow it with a soul; whereupon man lived, and moved, and viewed his new domain.

Justly proud of his handiwork, Prometheus observed man, and longed to bestow upon him some great power, unshared by any other creature of mortal birth, which would raise him far above all other living beings and bring him nearer to the perfection of the immortal gods. Fire alone, in his estimation, could effect this; but fire was the special possession and prerogative of the gods, and Prometheus knew they would never willingly share it with man, and that, should any one obtain it by stealth, they would never forgive the thief. Long he pondered the matter, and finally determined to obtain fire, or die in the attempt.

One dark night, therefore, he set out for Olympus, entered unperceived into the gods' abode, seized a lighted brand, hid it in his bosom, and departed unseen, exulting in the success of his enterprise. Arrived upon earth once more, he consigned the stolen treasure to the care of man, who immediately adapted it to various purposes, and eloquently expressed his gratitude to the benevolent deity who had risked his own life to obtain it for him.

From his lofty throne on the topmost peak of Mount Olympus Zeus beheld an unusual light down upon earth. Anxious to ascertain its exact nature, he watched it closely, and before long discovered the larceny. His anger then burst forth, terrible to behold; and the gods all quailed when they heard him solemnly vow he would punish the unhappy Prometheus without mercy. To seize the offender in his mighty grasp, bear him off to the Caucasian Mountains, and bind him fast to a great rock, was but a moment's work. There a voracious vulture was summoned to feast upon his liver, the tearing of which from his side by the bird's cruel beak and talons caused the sufferer intense anguish. All day long the vulture gorged himself; but during the cool night, while the bird slept, Prometheus' suffering abated, and the liver grew again, thus prolonging the torture, which bade fair to have no end.

Disheartened by the prospect of long years of unremitting pain, Prometheus at times could not refrain from pitiful complaints; but generation after generation of men lived on earth, and died, blessing him for the gift he had obtained for them at such a terrible cost. After many centuries of woe,

Hercules, son of Zeus and Alcmene, found Prometheus, killed the vulture, broke the adamantine chains, and liberated the long-suffering god.

The first mortals lived on earth in a state of perfect innocence and bliss. The air was pure and balmy; the sun shone brightly all the year; the earth brought forth delicious fruit in abundance; and beautiful, fragrant flowers bloomed everywhere. Man was content. Extreme cold, hunger, sickness, and death were unknown. Zeus, who justly ascribed a good part of this beatific condition to the gift conferred by Prometheus, was greatly displeased, and tried to devise some means to punish mankind for the acceptance of the heavenly fire.

With this purpose in view, he assembled the gods on Mount Olympus, where, in solemn council, they decided to create woman; and, as soon as she had been artfully fashioned, each one endowed her with some special charm, to make her more attractive.

Their united efforts were crowned with the utmost success. Nothing was lacking, except a name for the peerless creature; and the gods, after due consideration, decreed she should be called Pandora. They then bade Hermes take her to Prometheus as a gift from heaven; but he, knowing only too well that nothing good would come to him from the gods, refused to accept her, and cautioned his brother Epimetheus to follow his example. Unfortunately Epimetheus was of a confiding disposition, and when he beheld the maiden he exclaimed, "Surely so beautiful and gentle a being can bring no evil!" and accepted her most joyfully.

The first days of their union were spent in blissful wanderings, hand in hand, under the cool forest shade; in weaving garlands of fragrant flowers; and in refreshing themselves with the luscious fruit, which hung so temptingly within reach.

Pandora

ONE LOVELY EVENING, while dancing on the green, they saw Hermes, Zeus's messenger, coming towards them. His step was slow and weary, his garments dusty and travel-stained, and he seemed almost to stagger beneath the weight of a huge box which rested upon his shoulders. Pandora immediately ceased dancing, to speculate with feminine curiosity upon the contents of the chest. She nudged Epimetheus, and in a whisper begged him to ask Hermes what brought him thither. Epimetheus complied with her request; but Hermes evaded the question, asked permission to deposit his burden in their dwelling for safekeeping, professing himself too weary to convey it to its destination that day, and promised to call for it shortly. The permission was promptly granted. Hermes, with a sigh of relief, placed the box in one corner, and then departed, refusing all hospitable offers of rest and refreshment.

He had scarcely crossed the threshold, when Pandora expressed a strong desire to have a peep at the contents of the mysterious box; but Epimetheus, surprised and shocked, told her that her curiosity was unseemly, and then, to dispel the frown and pout seen for the first time on the fair face of his beloved, he entreated her to come out into the fresh air and join in the merry games of their companions. For the first time, also, Pandora refused to comply with his request. Dismayed, and very much discouraged, Epimetheus sauntered out alone, thinking she would soon join him, and perhaps by some caress atone for her present willfulness.

Left alone with the mysterious casket, Pandora became more and more inquisitive. Stealthily she drew near, and examined it with great interest, for it was curiously wrought of dark wood, and surmounted by a delicately carved head, of such fine workmanship that it seemed to smile and encourage her. Around the box a glittering golden cord was wound, and fastened on top in an intricate knot. Pandora, who prided herself specially on her deft fingers, felt sure she could unfasten it, and, reasoning that it would not be indiscreet to untie it if she did not raise the lid, she set to work. Long she strove, but all in vain. Ever and anon the laughing voices of Epimetheus and his companions, playing in the luxuriant shade, were wafted in on the summer breeze. Repeatedly she heard them call, and beseech her to join them; yet she persisted in her attempt. She was just on the point of giving it up in despair, when suddenly the refractory knot yielded to her fumbling fingers, and the cord, unrolling, dropped on the floor.

Pandora had repeatedly fancied that sounds like whispers issued from the box. The noise now seemed to increase, and she breathlessly applied her ear to the lid to ascertain whether it really proceeded from within. Imagine, therefore, her surprise when she distinctly heard these words, uttered in the most pitiful accents: "Pandora, dear Pandora, have pity upon us! Free us from this gloomy prison! Open, open, we beseech you!"

Pandora's heart beat so fast and loud, that it seemed for a moment to drown all other sounds. Should she open the box? Just then a familiar step outside made her start guiltily. Epimetheus was coming, and she knew he would urge her again to come out, and would prevent the gratification of her curiosity. Precipitately, therefore, she raised the lid to have one little peep before he came in.

Now, Zeus had malignantly crammed into this box all the diseases, sorrows, vices, and crimes that afflict poor humanity; and the box was no sooner opened, than all these ills flew out, in the guise of horrid little brown-winged creatures, closely resembling moths. These little insects fluttered about, alighting, some upon Epimetheus, who had just entered, and some upon Pandora, pricking and stinging them most unmercifully. Then they flew out through the open door and windows, and fastened upon the merrymakers without, whose shouts of joy were soon changed into wails of pain and anguish.

Epimetheus and Pandora had never before experienced the faintest sensation of pain or anger; but, as soon as these winged evil spirits had stung them, they began to weep, and, alas! quarreled for the first time in their lives. Epimetheus reproached his wife in bitterest terms for her thoughtless action; but in the very midst of his vituperation he suddenly heard a sweet little voice entreat for freedom. The sound proceeded from the unfortunate box, whose cover Pandora had dropped again, in the first moment of her surprise and pain. "Open, open, and I will heal your wounds! Please let me out!" it pleaded.

The tearful couple viewed each other inquiringly, and listened again. Once more they heard the same pitiful accents; and Epimetheus bade his wife open the box and set the speaker free, adding very amiably, that she had already done so much harm by her ill-fated curiosity, that it would be difficult to add materially to its evil consequences, and that, perchance, the box contained some good spirit, whose ministrations might prove beneficial.

It was well for Pandora that she opened the box a second time, for the gods, with a sudden impulse of compassion, had concealed among the evil spirits one kindly creature, Hope, whose mission was to heal the wounds inflicted by her fellow-prisoners.

Lightly fluttering hither and thither on her snowy pinions, Hope touched the punctured places on Pandora's and Epimetheus' creamy skin, and relieved their suffering, then quickly flew out of the open window, to perform the same gentle office for the other victims, and cheer their downcast spirits.

Thus, according to the ancients, evil entered into the world, bringing untold misery; but Hope followed closely in its footsteps, to aid struggling humanity, and point to a happier future.

During many centuries, therefore, Hope continued to be revered, although the other divinities had ceased to be worshiped.

According to another version, Pandora was sent down to man, bearing a vase in which the evil spirits were imprisoned, and on the way, seized by a fit of curiosity, raised the cover, and allowed them all to escape.

The Great Deluge

❧

ITTLE BY LITTLE the world was peopled; and the first years of man's existence upon earth were, as we have seen, years of unalloyed happiness. There was no occasion for labour, for the earth brought forth spontaneously all that was necessary for man's subsistence. "Innocence, virtue, and truth prevailed; neither were there any laws to restrict men, nor judges to punish." This time of bliss has justly borne the title of Golden Age, and the people in Italy then throve under the wise rule of good old Saturn, or Cronus.

Unfortunately, nothing in this world is lasting; and the Golden Age was followed by another, not quite so prosperous, hence called the Silver Age, when the year was first divided into seasons, and men were obliged to toil for their daily bread.

Yet, in spite of these few hardships, the people were happy, far happier than their descendants during the Age of Brass, which speedily followed, when strife became customary, and differences were settled by blows. But by far the worst of all was the Iron Age, when men's passions knew no bounds, and they even dared refuse all homage to the immortal gods.

War was waged incessantly; the earth was saturated with blood; the rights of hospitality were openly violated; and murder, rape, and theft were committed on all sides.

Zeus had kept a close watch over men's actions during all these years; and this evil conduct aroused his wrath to such a point, that he vowed he would annihilate the human race. But the modes of destruction were manifold, and, as he could not decide which would eventually prove most efficacious, he summoned the gods to deliberate and aid him by their counsels. The first suggestion offered, was to destroy the world by fire, kindled by Zeus's much-dreaded thunderbolts; and the king of gods was about to put it into instant execution, when his arm was stayed by the objection that the rising flames might set fire to his own abode, and reduce its magnificence to unsightly ashes. He therefore rejected the plan as impracticable, and bade the gods devise other means of destruction.

After much delay and discussion, the immortals agreed to wash mankind off the face of the earth by a mighty deluge. The winds were instructed to gather together the rain clouds over the earth. Poseidon let loose the waves of the sea, bidding them rise, overflow, and deluge the land. No sooner had the gods spoken, than the elements obeyed: the winds blew; the rain fell in torrents; lakes, seas, rivers, and oceans broke their bonds; and terrified mortals, forgetting their petty quarrels in a common impulse to flee from the death which threatened them, climbed the highest mountains, clung to uprooted trees, and even took refuge in the light skiffs they had constructed in happier days. Their efforts were all in vain, however; for the waters rose higher and higher, overtook them one after another in their ineffectual efforts to escape, closed over the homes where they might have been so happy, and drowned their last despairing cries in their seething depths.

The rain continued to fall, until, after many days, the waves covered all the surface of the earth except the summit of Mount Parnassus, the highest peak in Greece. On this mountain, surrounded by the ever-rising flood, stood the son of Prometheus, Deucalion, with his faithful wife Pyrrha, a daughter of Epimetheus and Pandora. From thence they, the sole survivors, viewed the universal desolation with tear-dimmed eyes.

In spite of the general depravity, the lives of this couple had always been pure and virtuous; and when Zeus saw them there alone, and remembered their piety, he decided not to include them in the general destruction, but to save their lives. He therefore bade the winds return to their cave, and the rain to cease. Poseidon, in accordance with his decree, blew a resounding blast upon his conch shell to recall the wandering waves, which immediately returned within their usual bounds.

Deucalion and Pyrrha followed the receding waves step by step down the steep mountain side, wondering how they should repeople the desolate earth. As they talked, they came to the shrine of Delphi, which alone had been able to resist the force of the waves. There they entered to consult the wishes of the gods. Their surprise and horror were unbounded, however, when a voice exclaimed, "Depart from hence with veiled heads, and cast your mother's bones behind you!" To obey such a command seemed sacrilegious in the extreme; for the dead had always been held in deep veneration by the Greeks, and the desecration of a grave was considered a heinous crime, and punished accordingly. But, they reasoned, the gods' oracles can seldom be accepted in a literal sense; and Deucalion, after due thought, explained to Pyrrha what he conceived to be the meaning of this mysterious command.

"The Earth," said he, "is the mother of all, and the stones may be considered her bones." Husband and wife speedily decided to act upon this premise, and continued their descent, casting stones behind them. All those thrown by Deucalion were immediately changed into men, while those cast by Pyrrha became women.

Thus the earth was peopled for the second time with a blameless race of men, sent to replace the wicked beings slain by Zeus. Deucalion and Pyrrha shortly after became the happy parents of a son named Hellen, who gave his name to all the Hellenic or Greek race; while his sons Aeolus and Dorus, and grandsons Ion and Achaeus, became the ancestors of the Aeolian, Dorian, Ionian, and Achaian nations.

Other mythologists, in treating of the deluvian myths, state that Deucalion and Pyrrha took refuge in an ark, which, after sailing about for many days, was stranded on the top of Mount Parnassus. This version was far less popular with the Greeks, although it betrays still more plainly the common source whence all these myths are derived.

Tales of Troy

THE CITY OF TROY grew on the low hill on the plain near the entrance to the Hellespont, founded by Ilus, a descendant of Zeus, who marked out the boundaries of a city and settled there. Ilus prayed to the gods for good luck and discovered the following morning a large wooden statue, the Palladium, the image that the goddess Athene had made in memory of her friend Pallas. Apollo appeared and begged Ilus to keep sacred the image, to guard and respect it against all invaders. As long as Troy preserved the token of godly esteem, the city would be safe. But men being men, and even then subject to the fates and powers of the gods, events would occur to threaten the sanctity of the beautiful city of Troy. And that city would become the food of legends for aeons to come, the site of a battle which involved the greatest heroes of Greece, the most powerful gods of Olympia, and the most beautiful women in the land. The tales of Troy are the longest and most exciting of all the legends, and they begin with a beautiful woman, and a handsome man, cast from his noble birth...

The Judgement of Paris

❧

THE GOOD NAME OF TROY had been blackened over the years by many of the gods, who had been wronged by her leaders. These gods held a grudge that was relaxed only under the shrewd and swift-footed King Priam, who took over the reins of Troy and allowed her once more to blossom. Now Priam was a superstitious and careful monarch, never erring in order that his command of the lovely land might be released. And when his wise wife Hecuba dreamed that she had borne a firebrand their youngest son was cast away, left to die on the heights of Mount Ida.

This child was Paris, but he did not die. He was suckled by a bear and brought to live with the herdsmen of the mountain, where he grew strong and handsome, proud and respected by his peers. He grew up ignorant of his noble breeding, content to wed and live with an exquisite mountain nymph Oenone in a humble home. He was called Alexander there, the 'helper of men'.

And then one day, as he tended his flocks on the sunlit mountains, surrounded by greenery, and more than content with his simple lot, he was visited by Hermes, messenger of the gods. There had been an altercation he said, looking with awe at the beauty of this mortal, and three of the loveliest goddesses required a judge to ascertain which was the fairest. It had been decreed by Zeus that Paris was a man of great wisdom and fair looks, and that this lowly shepherd should be given the task of judging amongst the goddesses.

'Fear not, Paris,' said Hermes, 'Zeus bids thee judge freely which of the three seems fairest in thine eyes; and the father of gods and men will be thy shield in giving true judgement.'

Paris nodded in amazement, the sanctity of his simple life at once eclipsed by the excitement and shallowness of the deed before him.

The first goddess to appear to him was Hera, Queen of Olympus. She explained to the young shepherd that a wedding had taken place between Peleus and Thetis, to which Eris alone among the immortals had not been included through some oversight. She had appeared nonetheless at the feast, and churning trouble, she threw an apple at the feet of three of the greatest of the goddesses, those who thought themselves the most beautiful in the land – Hera, Athene and Aphrodite. The apple was inscribed with the words: For the Fairest.

And it was to judge that fairest that Paris had been summoned, to put an end to the petty quarrelling. Hera went on to offer him all her queenly gifts, including money and the richest land on earth.

Athene offered him wisdom and success in battle, 'Adjudge the prize to me,' she whispered, 'and thou shall be famed as the wisest and bravest among men.'

The third goddess was Aphrodite, as beautiful certainly as her sisters, but with cunning that matched her looks. 'I am Aphrodite,' she said softly, coyly drawing herself up to the shepherd. 'I can offer thee gifts that are sweeter than any on earth. He who wins my favour needs only love to be loved again. Choose me, and I promise thee the most beautiful daughter of men to be thy wife.'

And although Paris was wed already, he chose Aphrodite without a moment's hesitation, and he gave the golden apple to the goddess of love who thanked him with such a radiant smile that his cheeks were rouged with pleasure.

It was with this glow of gratification that Paris set off the next day to take part in the games arranged each year by King Priam to commemorate the death of his youngest son, Paris. It was his first visit to the city since his birth, and he was anxious to test his strength. He excelled at the games, his strength, his passion and his ambition surpassing even that of his own brothers, the young princes of Troy. And when they, greatly angered by his prowess, took offence, and plotted to have an errant arrow sent in his direction, his sister Cassandra, who had a gift of divination, shouted out, not knowing what she said, 'Do not raise your hand against your brother.'

The princes were aghast, King Priam delighted, and it was with open arms that Paris was reunited with his family and welcomed back to Troy. He was given a great duty to perform for the King, to travel to Greece in order to secure the return of Hesione who had been borne off by Heracles many years before. Cassandra alone was vehemently against this venture, her prophetic vision showing her death and destruction that would lead to a great war against Troy. But her words were ignored, and Paris set off on his voyage, stopping during its course to visit Menelaus, king of Sparta, who was married to Helen, the most beautiful woman in the world.

It was this diversion which led Helen far from her marriage vows, into the arms of another man in an elopement which would excite the world of Greece and begin a battle that would run for ten long, blood-thirsty years.

Helen and Paris

❦

HELEN WAS THE DAUGHTER of Leda and Tyndareus, King of Sparta, and she was undoubtedly the most beautiful woman in all of Greece.

Her beauty caused her to be carried off to Attica by Theseus, and to be worshipped as a goddess at Sparta. As she grew older, she attracted suitors from around the world who swarmed to her side in order that she might receive their attentions.

Men with impeccable records of bravery, with inordinate riches, vied to become Helen's husband, including the wise and cunning Odysseus, Ajax, Diomedes, Philoctetes and Menestheus. Tyndareus did not wish to offend these great men, and he chose the wealthiest of the princes, Menelaus, brother of Agamemnon, lord of Argos, who was married to Helen's half-sister Clytemnestra. Odysseus suggested to Tyndareus that the suitors who had not been chosen to wed Helen should take a vow, swearing to defend to the death the lucky suitor, should anyone or anything appear to strip him of his good fortune. And so it was that Menelaus became King of Sparta, married to the exquisite Helen, who lived with him in harmony and happiness. He was warmly congratulated by the suitors who had not been chosen, and bound by their vow, they returned to their respective homes. Tyndareus marked the occasion by providing an offering to the gods, but it was ill fortune indeed that he omitted Aphrodite in his address, an oversight that would be long remembered and regretted by mortals and gods alike.

Helen gave birth to three children, and all was well in the luxurious palace, where food and drink were plentiful, where Menelaus ruled fairly and kindly, and where Helen and Menelaus grew to find a mutual respect and adoration for one another.

And then, one cruel day, the Fates chose to send to Sparta the ship of Paris, who decided, from the moment he set eyes on Helen, that he must have her as his wife. His true wife Oenone was forgotten, lonely on the Mount of Ida, and so too were his sense of honour, his mission, and the commands of his long-lost father. He called to Aphrodite to fulfil the promise she had made to him on the hillside, and when honest Menelaus set out on an expedition, he trusted the lovesick Paris to care for his wife in a manner befitting his status. Before he could return, Paris had eloped with Helen leaving behind Hermione, her daughter by Menelaus.

With treasure they had looted from the palace of Menelaus, Paris and Helen sailed idly, deep in love that blossomed as they travelled. It was only after months of tender lovemaking, and a true, rich affection, that Paris returned home to Troy, to show off his prize. On their journey, however, the sea became suddenly calm, no breath of air rippling her surface. An eerie silence fell upon them, threatened to overwhelm them with its sinister threat of ill-fate. And then, from the sea, rose a creature so fearful, that Paris thrust Helen below the deck, and with his sword ready, moved forward to hear its words. The quiet was deafening. The creature spoke not, but laid its dripping trident across the prow of the ship and leant forward, its mighty weight dipping the vessel dangerously close to the edge of the sea. And then it uttered words that chilled the heart of Paris.

'I am Nereus, god of the sea. Ill omens guide thy course, robber of another's goods. The Greeks will come across this sea, vowed to redress the wrong done by thee and to overthrow the towers of Priam. How many men, how many horses I see there, dead for thy misdeed, how many Trojans murdered for thy sins, how many Trojans laid low about the ruin of their city!' And with that he cast his trident high into the sky, and disappeared beneath the mirrored sea.

But the deed was done, and fate had cast the die. Paris had been weak in mind and body, and for those sins he would bring about the disgrace and disintegration of Troy and her people. Head down, he surged across the waves that swelled up to greet them, breathed in the air that began to circulate once more. In the name of love, and on the wings of pride, he continued on to Troy, determined to build a life there with his lady love.

The Seeds of War

❧

T HE ELOPEMENT OF PARIS AND HELEN sent waves of shock through the land. Menelaus, his trusting soul rent by sadness, gathered together those men who had pledged an oath to aid him in times of trouble. He called upon all the great rulers from other lands, men who would take up their arms to recover his beloved wife, and to punish the violator of his home. He and his brother Agamemnon were the greatest and most powerful lords of the Peloponnese, and together they summoned the finest leaders of the land to bring their ships and their most courageous warriors for war against Troy, and ever respectful of these two great men, all but two answered the call and set out for Troy.

One of these men was Odysseus, a crafty and highly regarded leader of the small island of Ithaca. Odysseus had recently married his great love Penelope, who had given birth to their son Telemachus. He had found great happiness with his family, and was loath to quit it for a war which had been predicted as long and painful. An Oracle had confirmed to him that he risked twenty years of separation from his home and his wife if he travelled to Troy, and he was not inclined to respond to the summons. Instead, he feigned madness, and when he was visited in person by Menelaus and Palamedes, he put on a rustic cap and ploughed salt into the furrows of his rocky land, with an ox and an ass yoked together. But Palamedes was not fooled by this show, and he laid down the infant Telemachus, in the path of the plough, at which Odysseus was forced to admit his deceit, pull up the team, and rescue his son from certain danger. And so it was that Odysseus travelled reluctantly to Troy, where the oracle proved true, but where he made his name as the most distinguished warrior of all time.

Achilles was also summoned, but had defied the call on the advice of his mother Thetis, who had dressed him in the garb of a maiden and hidden him among the daughters of the King of Scyros. He was the son of Peleus, a mortal who had married the goddess Thetis. Achilles was the youngest of many children born to Thetis, but all had died as she attempted to immortalize them by holding them over a fire. When Achilles was born, she wished once more to make him immortal, but cleverly ignored the murderous flames which promised such status and hung him instead over the waters of the River Styx, making him invulnerable by dipping him into the waters. The heel by which she held him remained the one vulnerable part of his body, and he was brought up with other heroes by Cherion, who fed him on the hearts of lions and the marrow of bears. He was a popular boy, endowed with great prowess and skill in war.

His mother knew that the Trojan War would lead to his certain death, and it was she who hatched the plan to hide him from Menelaus and his men. But it was crafty Odysseus who found him, and revealed him by disguising himself as a purveyor of fine fabrics and jewellery, which provided great excitement to the other young women, but which failed to interest the young hero. When cunning Odysseus laid out a dagger and shield they were leapt upon by Achilles, who disclosed himself, and came readily with Odysseus.

When King Priam heard news of Paris's activities at Sparta, he sank back in disbelief. Odysseus had journeyed to Troy with Palamedes and Menelaus, to demand that Priam return Helen, but Paris had not yet returned to the island and Priam was loath to judge a man before he'd had his say. He responded with courtesy to the requests of these great men who had appeared on his shores with such an urgent mission, but he put them off. And when Paris did finally appear with Helen, King Priam and his sons were so besotted by her, so taken by her beauty that they forgave Paris all his weakness and swore that Helen should remain in Troy for ever. Helen confirmed that she had eloped of her own free will, and that her love for Paris was greater than any known to man or god before them.

However, the people of Troy were less kindly disposed to their new mistress, for with her she brought the threat of war, which would draw into action its many men, and rob them of their freedom and good name. And when Paris stalked the streets of Troy, his new bride on his arm, he was followed by muttered curses. The men of Troy gathered together their troops, led by the great Hector, and Priam's son-in-law, Aeneas, prince of the Dardanians and son of Aphrodite herself.

Many years had passed since Menelaus had put out that first call for assistance, but the impressive collection of warriors grouped now at Aulis, a harbour on the Ruipus, where more than a thousand ships were gathered. But as they prepared to set forth for Troy, their sails were met by calm that disallowed even a breath of wind to set them on their course.

And so it transpired that Artemis was behind the deathly stillness, for Agamemnon had unwittingly hurt her pride by slaying one of her sacred hind, and she now demanded the death of Agamemnon's own daughter Iphigenia in return.

Agamemnon was torn by the command and refused to consider it, while the men of Greece became surly and impatient to begin a war which threatened to be long and hard. So the great lord listened to his men, and encouraged by his brother Menelaus, he called his wife to bring Iphigenia to the site, where he promised her Achilles as a husband. And for that reason alone, Iphigenia was brought to the ships, and when she greeted her father with excitement and love, he cast her aside, daring not to meet her glances. Seeing his unhappiness, Menelaus swallowed his own sadness and forbade his brother to kill the young girl, but this sympathy and pity hardened the heart of Agamemnon and he prepared for the sacrifice.

Clytemnestra was Agamemnon's wife, and she grew suspicious when she saw him shirk the embraces of his favourite daughter. She took herself to the tent of Achilles, who professed no knowledge of an impending wedding, and finally admitted the real purpose of Iphigenia's visit to the camp. In a fiery rage and distress, Clytemnestra flew back to her husband, and found her daughter begging for mercy at his feet.

And then, as Agamemnon struggled again to make a decision that would calm his angry men, console his desperate wife, Iphigenia drew herself up, and wiping away her tears, proclaimed, 'Since so it must be, I am willing to die; then shall I be called the honour of Greek maidenhood, who have given my life for the motherland. Let the fall of Troy be my marriage feast, and my monument.' And the brave young woman cast herself down on the sacrificial table at the altar of Artemis, gazing heavenward as her peaceful expression filled her family with woe anew.

The seer Calchas unsheathed the knife, having been given this painful duty, but as he lifted his arm to strike a blow, Iphigenia vanished, taken by Artemis herself who had pitied the lovely maiden, and borne her away to become a priestess of her temple at Tauris, to live in eternal maidenhood. In her place on the table lay a snow-white fawn, sprinkled with virgin blood, and with a great roar of gladness, Calchas proclaimed Artemis to be appeased. His words were carried away on the whisper of wind that grew until it became a mighty gale, pulling at the idle ships and filling her crew with anticipation and joy.

The winds carried them to Lesbos, and then on to the island of Tenedos, from where the distant walls of Troy could be seen glowing in the light of dawn. The war would begin.

The Trojan War

❧

THE WAR BEGAN BADLY, with the death of Tenes, the son of Apollo, before the invaders had reached the shores of Troy. Achilles had been warned never to take the life of any child of Apollo, but when he saw a figure hurling rocks at the ships of the Greeks, who were approaching the walled city of Troy, he struck him down with one swoop of his mighty sword. Tenes was dead before Achilles could be cautioned, and gloom was cast over the ships as they waited warily for Apollo to strike his revenge.

Then the excellent marksman Philtoctetes was bitten by a snake, causing a wound so stagnant with infection that the Greeks had no choice but to leave the warrior on the rocky island off Lemnos, where he was abandoned and forced to live alone for many years. And while the sombre army struggled to come to terms with the loss of one of their greatest men, Protesilaus, a youth of determination and valour, leapt on to the beaches of Troy where he was slain instantly by Troy's champion Hector, Priam's eldest son. The war had begun. It had been decreed by Zeus himself that mankind must be depleted, and so it was that the gods themselves became involved in a war that had been sparked by one single mortal woman.

For nine years the Greeks fought the impenetrable walls of Troy, guarded zealously by fine men of battle, including Hector, who led King Priam's other forty-nine sons in war. Paris joined their ranks, although the fury at this selfish man was ill-concealed by many. Antenor and Aeneas were men of wisdom and justice, and they too fought for Troy, although peace was their ultimate goal. The walls of the city had been built by Apollo and Poseidon themselves, and could not be damaged or scaled, despite the best efforts of Agamemnon's army. So the men of Greece attacked the allies of Troy instead, burning and looting their cities, and ravishing their women. It was at one such rape that a quarrel occurred which would change forever the course of the battle, drawing it to a fiery close that had been nearly a decade in coming.

Achilles and his men had attacked the city of Lyrnessus, taking as their prize two beautiful young women, Cryseis, who was chosen by Agamemnon, and Briseis, who became Achilles's. When it was discovered that the maiden Cryseis was a priestess of Apollo, a plague struck the camp, and Agamemnon was forced to return her to the temple. This he did, but upon his return, he stealthily lured Briseis from the camp of Achilles, and took her as his own. Achilles was so enraged and disgusted by this act that he threw down his armour and swore that he would no longer fight for such men, no better than pigs as they were.

Achilles was a fighter beyond compare and his absence pressed upon the Trojans an unexpected advantage. But the years of war had taken their toll, and the warriors on both sides had grown tired of the hostility. A peaceful end was sought, and Hector appeared, bravely suggesting that Menelaus and Paris fight a dual in order to decide the fate of Helen. This course was considered fair, and the two men engaged in a battle. Swords clashed, and many maidens fainted at the sight of two such glorious men tempting death so readily, so easily. They were well matched, but Menelaus had the power of a grudge that had festered for many years, and with this advantage, he pinned Paris to the walls of his city, determined to take his self-seeking life.

But Aphrodite could stand the battle no longer, and Paris's life was a sacrifice she would not allow. With flowing locks and gowns, she descended on the fighters, her beauty lighting their faces, filling their hearts with surprise and calm. And then she struck, hiding her beloved behind a cloud and pulling him to safety behind the city walls. Menelaus looked on in amazement, so close had he come after all these years to reclaiming his bride, and here the gods took them as their playthings, changing the course of fate, of mortal lives, on a whim. He cried out in rage, a call that was heard by the rest of the gods, and which opened up a wound that would not be healed until the end of the war was in sight.

Thetis screamed for justice for her son Achilles, and Apollo fell in with the defenders, making them strong. Zeus had taken the side of the invaders, who in their eager fury wounded both Ares and Aphrodite, spilling their immortal blood. The Greeks continued to fight, and in a night raid managed to take the life of Rhesus, capturing the white horses which he was taking to the Trojans under the cover of darkness. Apollo swooped down to encourage the Trojan forces, and they repaid this travesty by burning some of the Greek ships, which had been moored in the harbour. And as the fleet burned and threatened the lives of the Greek army, Patroclus, the great friend of Achilles, appeared in his friend's armour, and frightened the Trojans into retreat.

Forgetting himself, and confident in the armour of Greece's greatest warrior, Patroclus leapt to the top of the Trojan walls, sending their army into panic that was calmed only by Apollo. Once more this great god took the side of the Trojans, and knowing that this brave warrior was none other than Patroclus, he winded him, knocking from his body the sword and shield which protected him. Patroclus called out in anguish, begging for mercy, his bravado shorn from him along with the armour, but Hector stepped in and killed Patroclus with one single blow.

The roar of the Greeks wakened the slumbering Achilles, who had thrust from his mind all thought of the battle. Word of the death of his dear friend soon reached him, and he sprang into action, crying out for revenge which struck terror in the hearts of all who heard him. He trembled with rage, his blood coursing through his veins as he flexed his mighty muscles. New armour was summoned and he dressed quickly, making his way to Troy without delay.

And again the gods chose to intervene. As the terrified Trojans retreated into their city, the river god of the Scamander produced a wall of water that held back the murderous aggressor. This act was met by Hephaestus, who immediately stepped in to dry the waters with a flaming torch. And with a lust for revenge more invincible than the brave Achilles himself, he fought on, searching out the unfortunate Hector and slaying all who crossed his path. Sweat gleamed on his brow, which was furrowed with determination. Achilles presented a picture of such manly beauty that many of his opponents were stopped in their tracks, transfixed by this vision of glorious power. And when Hector saw Achilles, he too stopped dead, and bowed down, determined to fight him hand to hand until he saw that fiery gleam in Achilles' eye and knew that this marauder and his army meant his own certain death. He turned on his heels, and tried to run, but Achilles was stronger, more powerful. Three times they ran round the walls of the city, Hector becoming weaker, more frightened as they ran. And then Achilles caught him, and pinning him like a rabbit to the wall with his sword, howled a mighty cry then thrust his sword through Hector and killed him at once.

The Trojans moaned and wailed for their lost leader, stopping the battle briefly to mourn before swearing vengeance and carrying on more furiously than before. Achilles was unstoppable. When Penthesileia brought her Amazon women to help the Trojans, Achilles killed her mercilessly. And then Thersites, the nasty politician was struck down by Achilles' powerful fist. The invincible Achilles fought on and on, never tiring, never losing his composure, his cunning. Then Memnon arrived with a troop of Ethiopians, putting the favour of the gods once more with the Trojans, who allowed their forces to be increased so heavily. But Achilles, enraged and irreverent, called upon Zeus to judge between himself and Memnon, to reverse the damage done by these visiting troops.

Memnon was out of favour with the king of gods, and Achilles was presented with a sword with which to slay the Ethiopian. And when he died, his followers turned immediately to birds, and followed him to his rocky tomb on the neck of the island.

Achilles continued on, more boastful than ever, never losing a battle, never missing a stroke with his mighty sword. And then the gods lost patience, and irritated by his show of pride, they stepped in once again. Apollo had not yet repaid Achilles for the death of Tenes. Now was his chance. Guiding the hand of Paris, an arrow was directed to the heel of Achilles, the only part on his body which was not invincible. He died immediately.

For a time, the Greeks were weakened by the death of their hero, their determination dwindling, their lust for battle dead. But as they mourned their forsaken leader, a new resolve grew in their hearts, and after a solemn funeral, at which Achilles was awarded the highest honours of any warrior, they regrouped to plan their revenge. If their heart had been cut from them, their mind still functioned. They were supremely competent strategists, extremely confident aggressors. Menelaus appeared to remind them once again of the reason for their battle, and thus inspired they set about deciding whom should take on the arms of Achilles. Agamemnon chose Odysseus, for his intelligence and courage, but Ajax the Greater was steeped in jealousy, knowing his strength was greater than that of Odysseus, beyond all doubt. He swore to avenge himself against Odysseus, but Athene, always a friend to Odysseus, persuaded him in another direction, and thinking he was murdering Odysseus and his troops, he slaughtered instead a flock of sheep. Convinced of his own madness, Ajax took his own life, another untimely and worrying loss to the Greeks.

The war had gone on too long. Zeus had planned it from beginning to end, but now he stopped to appraise, to ensure that the balance was correct. Troy must fall, he decreed, but it could not be achieved without the bow and arrows from the quiver of Heracles, and without the presence of Achilles' son, far away in Scyros. The Greeks moved swiftly. And as they set about summoning Neoptolemus, the son of Achilles, from his home, they were warned of one final condition, without which the war could not be won. The Palladium must be removed from the city, for she guarded the gates and protected her from all invaders. Odysseus began to plan.

Philoctetes was rescued from his terrible ordeal on Lemnos, his wounds long since cleared. He had trained his mind and his muscles while he waited impatiently to be saved, and he was anxious to fight, to use the bow of the great Heracles in battle. He lifted it now, spitting on his palms as he did so, and feeding a poisoned arrow into the string of the bow. With a shriek that released the years of tortuous loneliness and pain, he sent the arrow straight to its mark at the neck of the handsome Paris, who was felled at once. And so Neoptolemus was dressed in his father's armour, a shaking, frightened youth with no knowledge of war, no interest in fighting, but he took courage from the dress of his father, and he rose to the challenge, calmly leading his restored army towards the gates of Troy.

Odysseus was busy elsewhere. Dressed as a miserly beggar, with the help of Athene and Diomedes, he talked himself through the gates of the great city, where he fell upon the sleeping guards of the Palladium with such speed and grace that not one person in the entire city knew of his treachery. And on his stomach, he crawled from the city, dragging the Palladium with him, through a vermin-ridden drain where he struggled through sewage and mud to reach his army on the other side, the Palladium drawn triumphantly behind him.

Troy was on the verge of defeat. The Palladium no longer cast its splendid power over the city, and without that advantage, and with the minds of such cunning men as Odysseus to contend, there was no hope. But still she stood firm against the invaders, until Odysseus, with the help of Athene once again, came up with a final plan.

The craftsman Epeius was commissioned to build an enormous wooden horse, the inside of which was hollowed to hold fifty warriors. Agamemnon chose his greatest men to ride in its belly, and then gathering up the remainder of his fleet, he made as if to sail away, leaving the bay at Troy, but travelling only round the bend of the land, where he waited with anticipation and many prayers. Sinon was left behind on land, and as expected, he was taken prisoner by the Trojans, who wondered at their sudden luck. Sinon feigned fury at his colleagues who had left him behind, and taking the side of the Trojans, he wormed his way into their affections, into their grace, so that when he suggested they take into their walls the wooden horse, they did so, marvelling at its inscription:

A thank-offering to Athene for our safe return home.

Again, it was Cassandra who spoke out against the enemy's soldier, proclaiming that the horse brought nothing but death and final disaster for the city. The prophet Laocoon agreed with her, but as he made his way to the palace to warn the king, he was strangled by two serpents who leapt from the sea, and disappeared once they had finished their deadly task. And the great horse was dragged into the city, into the temple of Athene, where it was wreathed with ribbons and festooned with garlands of herbs.

The Trojans feasted that night, revelling and celebrating the end of a war that had taken quite small toll, despite its very long duration. Inside the wooden horse, the men of Greece laid quietly, waiting for darkness to fall, for their opportunity to strike. Helen alone remained suspicious, knowing that the Greeks were too clever, too ambitious to give in before the bitter end, and she held a grudging admiration for their daring, whatever it may be. She suspected the horse, and late in the evening, she slipped into the darkened temple and called out in the voices of the wives of the men inside, tempting them to come out and be reunited. Only the shrewd Odysseus guessed her trick, and holding his hand over the mouth of each hero who was addressed in false voice, he kept them quiet and soon Helen went away.

The Trojan men were drunk and sleepy when the men slid from the horse on ropes they had prepared earlier. And it was by moonlight, when the city was glowing with a numbing slumber, that the massacre of the Trojans began. King Priam was murdered as he crossed his courtyard, Menelaus went straight to the chambers of his errant wife, who bowed her head and spoke words of such regret, such honest remorse, that the determination in Menelaus was stilled, and he reached out to her and held her again in his arms, transfixed by her beauty, a slave to her love once more.

All was forgiven, and he carried Helen to his ship where she was welcomed into the arms of the Greeks, her fair face disarming them.

The plundering of Troy continued. Women were taken as prizes by the men of Greece who had for so long been starved of female companionship. Cassandra was taken by Agamemnon, and Neoptolemus who had grown in his weeks with the army to become a noble youth, took Hector's widow Andromache. Polyxena was sacrificed at the tomb of Achilles, to appease his ghost. Aeneas was wounded fatally, but the gods swooped to him and healed him. Apollo urged him to challenge the marauders, but Poseidon spoke softly to him, prophesying a day when he would rule Troy. And so Aeneas left the burning city, losing his wife in the escape, his subsequent travels becoming the subject of Roman legends, and Virgil's flawless *Aeneid*.

Queen Hecabe sat in her tower window watching the massacre, the deaths of her family, her colleagues, her servants and their children. And when Odysseus took her as his own, her howls of pure despair reached to the heavens and she was transformed magically into a dog, whose barks could be heard on the shores of Troy for all eternity.

Troy was broken, its streets steeped in the blood of generations of warriors, its walls finally scaled and broken, pouring out the good will and good luck that had been held in her embrace since the very beginning. She was set alight by zealous Greeks, a blazing beacon to all who knew her, her heart beating no longer.

So it was that Helen returned to Sparta with Menelaus, where they were reunited. Other great heroes went their separate ways, many returning to glory, carrying the spoils of their victory in treasure-laden ships. Still others met with disaster on their voyage home, but those are other stories, legends which were spawned by the war of Troy. And the great city of Troy was dead, her fires glowing for all to see, a warning to lovers and to the men of war which would live in their memories for the rest of time.

The Wanderings of Odysseus

FLUSHED WITH THE GLORY of his victory at Troy, the brave and clever Odysseus gathered together the men of Ithaca into twelve ships, and headed across the perilous seas to their homeland. Odysseus was the grandson of the Autolycus, a thief of great artfulness and notoriety. That same cunning lay deep within the breast of Odysseus and it would, said the Oracle before Odysseus set off for Troy, bring about his solitary survival. For Odysseus alone would return from Troy, beaten and infinitely weary, having battled the great gods of the sea and sky and winds, having faced temptations and fears which would bring about the certain death of a lesser man. The journey would take ten years, and its cost would be Odysseus's men and very nearly his soul.

The Cicones

🦋

TEN YEARS HAD PASSED since brave Odysseus had last set eyes on
his faithful wife Penelope, and their son Telemachus. The victory
at Troy had been a sweet one, and sated by the triumph, the lean
and weathered warrior made plans to return his men to their homeland.
Twelve ships were prepared for the voyage, laden with the spoils of their
warfare and leaving the wretched and burning city of Troy a blazing
beacon behind them.

Odysseus and his men were filled with rumbustuous excitement at the
prospect of seeing home once more; they leapt and frolicked aboard the
mighty vessels, unable to leave behind the boisterous energy nurtured in
them by ten years' war. The sea lay calm and welcoming. The journey had
begun, and the ships groaned with booty.

But greed is a fatal human trait, and not content with the plunder they
had foraged at Troy, Odysseus and his men sought new bounty, landing
first on the island of the Cicones. A mass of carousing warriors, they swept
onshore, taking the city of Ismarus, sending its inhabitants to their deaths,
and feasting on the carcasses of their sheep and cattle. Only the priest of
Apollo was spared from the carnage.

This priest was a clever man, and he sank to his knees in gratitude,
bowing his head in respectful silence as he supplied the marauders with
skins of powerful wine. While the men feasted and celebrated the newest
of their victories, Odysseus grew increasingly uneasy. Although he shared
the piratical spirit of his men, he had an ingrown prudence which argued
against the excesses of their plundering. He implored his men to return
to their ships, doubting now the wisdom of their attack. Soon enough his
worries were confirmed.

As the men of Ithaca lay spent and drunk on wine and rich foods, the
Cicones appeared on the hilltops, eager for revenge and accompanied by
troops they had rallied from the islands around their country. Odysseus
tried to rouse his men, but his efforts were futile. The Cicones attacked,
driving the disoriented travellers back to their ship, mercilessly slaying

those who lagged behind. The carnage took tremendous toll on the crews of each ship, and lamed by defeat they limped out of the harbour and back to sea. Back aboard ship, the surviving men worked quietly, bewildered by the proof of their humanity, their weakness. Home lay just round the Cape at the point of the Peloponnese. But as anticipation rose within them, so did the savage gales of the north-east winds. Zeus, king of the gods, would wreak his vengeance.

The Lotus-Eaters

T HE POWERFUL WINDS wrenched and buffeted the wretched ships, carrying them and their dispirited crew far from the point of the Cape, ever further from the welcoming shores of Ithaca. The sails were torn, and desperation clung to the men as they struggled against the most powerful of enemies – the sea and the winds themselves. And then, on the tenth day, there was peace. Just beyond the curve of the gentle waves lay land, a southern island from which a pervading and sweet perfume rose languorously into the air.

Ever watchful, Odysseus dared send ashore only three men from his depleted crew, and the men prepared the boat, their hearts beating. As their oars cut softly through the waves, an eerie and disquieting lassitude overwhelmed the men. Their trembling hands were warmed and stilled, their hearts were calmed in their breasts. And there, in front of them, appeared a remarkable being, whose serenity and stillness relaxed the anxious sailors. With a smile the creature beckoned them forth, holding out to them as he signalled, a large and purple flower.

The perfume of the flower snaked around the men, entrancing them and drawing them forth.

'The lotus flower,' the creature whispered softly. 'Sip its nectar. It is our food and drink here on the island of the lotus-eaters. It brings peace.' With that the lotus-eater raised the flower to the mouths of the men, who one by one drank deeply from its cup. Expressions of pure joy crossed their faces and their minds and memories were cleared of all but the rich and overwhelming pleasures of the nectar.

'It is the food of forgetfulness,' smiled the lotus-eater. 'Come, join us in the land of indolence. We have no worries here.'

Odysseus stood on the prow of his ship, a shadow of concern crossing his noble brow. 'Remain here,' he ordered his men, his voice unusually curt. His senses were buzzing with anticipation. He could feel an uneasy melancholy touching at the corners of his mind, and he angrily shrugged it away. All was not well on the island. He could sense no violence here, but danger lurked in a different cloak. He made his way to shore.

There was no sign of his sailors, and he strode purposefully in the direction he'd seen them take. He fought the growing ease which threatened to fill his mind, the strength of his character, his cunning forcefully keeping the invading sensations at bay. His men lolled by the fire of a group of beautiful beings. There was no anger or fear among them. They smiled a beatific welcome and signalled that he was to join them.

A lotus flower was held up for him to drink, and as he softened, a bell of fear rang in his brain. He curled back his lips and with renewed resolve, thrust the flower away. He drew from his pocket a length of rope, and hastily tied it to the scabbards of his men. He ignored their weak protests, and with his sword in their bags, forced them back to shore, and to the ship.

Their eyes were vague, their smiles bloodless. Odysseus and his men were as strangers to them, but they went aboard ship where they were lashed to the masts until the ship could sail on. The enchantment raised the heads of every man aboard Odysseus's ships. He roared at them to keep their heads down, to pierce their longing with good clean thoughts.

'Think of home, men,' he shouted. 'Forget it not, for it is what fires us onwards.'

And so they were to escape the fruit of the lotus-eaters, and the life of ease that threatened to overcome them. Odysseus and his men, weakened but still alive, sailed on.

The Cyclopes

ODYSSEUS AND HIS MEN sailed until they were forced to stop for food and fresh water. A small island appeared in the distance, and as they drew nigh, they saw that it was inhabited only by goats, who fed on the succulent, sweet grass which grew plentifully across the terrain. Fresh water cascaded from moss-carpeted rocks, and tumbled through the leafy country. The men's lips grew wet in anticipation of its cold purity.

As they clambered aboard shore, the fresh air filling their lungs, the men felt whole once more, and when they discovered, in their travels, an inviting cave filled with goats' milk and cheese, they settled down to feast. Their bellies groaning, and faces pink with pleasure, Odysseus and his men settled back to sleep on the smooth face of the cave, warmed by the hot spring that pooled in its centre, and sated by their sumptuous meal.

They were woken abruptly by heavy footfall, which shook the ground with each step. Eyeing one another warily, the tired men stayed silent, barely alert, but overwhelmingly fearful. Into the cave burst a flock of snow-white sheep and behind them the frightful giant Polyphemus, a Cyclops with one eye in the centre of his face. Polyphemus was the son of Poseidon, and he lived on the island with his fellow Cyclopes, existing peacefully in seclusion. He had not seen man for many years, and his single eyebrow raised in anticipation when he came upon his visitors. Odysseus took charge.

'Sire, in the name of Zeus, I beg your hospitality for the night. I've weary men who ...'

His words were cut off. The Cyclops laughed with outrage and reaching over, plucked up several of Odysseus's men and ate them whole. The others cowered in fear, but Odysseus stood firm, his stance betraying none of the fear that surged through his noble blood.

'I ask you again,' he began. But Polyphemus merely grunted and turned to roll a boulder across the opening to the cave. He settled down to sleep, his snores lifting the men from the stone floor of the cave, and forbidding them sleep. They huddled round Odysseus, who pondered their plight.

When he woke, Polyphemus ate two more men, and with his sheep, left the cave, carefully closing the door on the anxious men. They moved around their prison with agitation, wretched with fear. It was many hours before the Cyclops returned, but the men could not sleep. They waited for the sound of footsteps, they sickened at the thought of their inescapable death.

But the brave Odysseus feared not. His cunning led him through the maze of their predicament, and carefully and calmly he formed a plan. He was waiting when Polyphemus returned, and sidled up to the weary Cyclops with his goatskin of wine.

'Have a drink, ease your fatigue,' he said quietly, and with surprise the giant accepted. Unused to wine, he fell quickly into confusion, and laid himself unsteadily on the floor of the cave.

'Who are you, generous benefactor,' he slurred, clutching at the goatskin.

'My name is No one,' said Odysseus, a satisfied smile fleeting across his face.

'No one ...' the giant repeated the name and slipped into a deep slumber, his snores jolting the men once more.

Odysseus leapt into action. Reaching for a heavy bough of olive-wood, he plunged in into the fire and moulded its end to a barbed point. He lifted it from the fire, and with every ounce of strength and versatility left in his depleted body, he thrust it into Polyphemus' single eye, and stepped back, out of harm's way.

The Cyclops' roar propelled him through the air, momentarily deafening him. The men shuddered in the corner, shrieking with terror as the giant fumbled wildly for his torturers, grunting and shrieking with the intense pain. Soon his friends came running, and when they enquired the nature of his troubles, he could only cry, 'No one has blinded me' at which they returned, perplexed to their homes.

The morning came, cool and inviting, and hearing his sheep scrabbling at the door to get out to pasture, Polyphemus rose, and feeling along the walls, he found his boulder, and moved it. A smug look crossed his tortured features, and he stood outside the cave, his hands moving across the sheep as they left.

'You cannot leave this cave,' he taunted. 'You cannot escape me now.' He giggled with mirth at his cleverness, but his smile faded to confusion and then anger when he realized that the sheep had exited, and the cave was now empty. The men were gone.

Odysseus and his men laughed out loud as they unstrapped themselves from the bellies of the sheep, and racing towards their ships, Odysseus called out, 'Cyclops. It was not No one who blinded you. It was Odysseus of Ithaca,' and with that he lifted their mooring and set out for sea.

The torment of the giant rose in a deluge of sound and fury, echoing across the island and wakening his friends. Tearing off slabs of the mountainside, Polyphemus hurled them towards the escaping voice, which continued to taunt him. He roared a prayer to his father Poseidon, begging for vengeance, and struggled across the grass towards the sea.

But Odysseus had left, his ship surging across the sea to join with the rest of the fleet. Odysseus had escaped once more, and the sea opened up to him and his men, and they continued homewards, unaware that Poseidon had heard the cries of his son, and had answered them. Vengeance would be his.

The Island of Aeolus

O DYSSEUS AND THE REST OF HIS FLEET were carried out to sea by the swell of water which spread from the rocks which Polyphemus had plunged into the waters. His cries echoed across the waters, growing louder as he realized the full measure of Odysseus's treachery, for as he and his men left they had robbed him of most of his flock, which they now cooked on spits over roaring fires in the galley.

They sailed to the Island of Aeolus, the guardian of winds, who lived with his six sons and six daughters in great comfort. Here, Odysseus and his men were entertained and feted, fed with sumptuous buffets which boasted unusual delicacies, their thirst slaked by fine wines and exotic nectars. They remained there for thirty days, convincing Aeolus that the gods must detest these men for unfounded reasons., for they were perfect guests, and Odysseus was a fair man, and an eloquent spokesman and orator.

But at last Odysseus grew restless, eager once more to set sail for Ithaca. The generosity of Aeolus had calmed his men, and well-nourished they were ready to do battle with the elements which were bound to hamper their return. But Aeolus had a gift for Odysseus, which he presented as the men prepared to leave the island. With great solemnity he passed to the warrior a bag, carefully bound with golden lace, and knotted many times over. In it were secured all the winds, except the gentle winds of the west, which would blow them to Ithaca. It was a sacred gift, and a token of Aeolus's regard for his visitor.

The men set off at last, their bellies filled, their minds alert, all maladies relieved. They sailed, blown by the west wind, for nine days, until the bright shores of Ithaca shone, a brilliant beacon in the distance. And so it was that Odysseus, greatly fatigued by the journey, and by the excitement of reaching his native shores once more, allowed himself to rest, to fall into a deep slumber that would prepare him for the festivities about to greet him.

But several of the men who sailed under his command begrudged their gracious leader, and envious of his favour with Aeolus, decided to take for themselves some of the gift presented to Odysseus. It must contain treasure, they thought, so large and unwieldy a parcel it was, and the men encouraged one another, fantasizing about what that bag might contain.

And so it was that the men tiptoed to Odysseus's chambers, and eased the bag from his side, careful not to disturb his slumber. And it was with greedy smiles, and anxious, fumbling hands that the bag was opened and the fierce winds released. They swirled around them, tossing and plunging the ships into waves higher than the mountains of the gods. In no time they were returned to the Island of Aeolus, helpless and frightened by nature's angry howls.

Odysseus was roughly awakened, and pushed forward to greet the displeased Aeolus. Aeolus cursed himself for humouring such foolish men, and understood at last the antipathy felt towards them by the great powers of Greece.

'Be gone, ill-starred wretch,' he snarled, and turned away from the unhappy seamen, towards the confines of his palace.

And so there was nothing for it but to return to the merciless seas, where the winds played havoc in their renewed freedom, where Poseidon waited for his chance to strike.

The Laestrygonians

🕊

THE SHIPS OF ODYSSEUS and his men were buffeted for many days before the winds exhausted their breath. And so they abandoned the ill-fated travellers, and left them in a dreadful calm. The ships sat still, mired in the stagnant waters, sunburnt and parched by the fiery sun. For a week they struggled with the heavy oars, seeming to move no further across the waveless sea. And then, on the eighth day, their ships limped into the rocky harbour of the Laestrygonians, where they moored themselves in an untidy row and made their way to shore. Odysseus was more cautious. Their travels had made him wiser than ever, and he tied his boat beyond the others, to a rocky outcrop in the open water. He signalled the men aboard to hold back, and climbed up the mast to get a better view.

Three of his men had rowed ashore, and Odysseus watched them as they spoke to two lovely young maidens, drawing water from a clear spring. The men stopped to take a drink before pressing on in the direction pointed out to them by the maidens. They looked calm and assured. Odysseus felt no such conviction, and he remained where he was, chewing his lower lip with concern. His men could see the others, and pestered Odysseus to allow them ashore, to drink of the cool fresh water, but he bade them to be silent and returned to his look-out.

The three men were easily visible from his post and Odysseus could see them reaching the walls of a magnificent castle, gilded and festooned with jewels. They hesitated at the gates. And it was then that the Laestrygonians attacked. Great, heaving giants plummeted through the gates on to the hapless men, racing towards shore and wailing a terrible cry, a battle song that tweaked at Odysseus's memory. These were the the evil cannibals who brought overwhelming fear to the heart of every traveller. Their shores were the most dangerous in Greece, their fearsome appetite for violence and unwitting seamen legendary.

They stampeded to shore, flocking in crowds to crush the ships under a deluge of rocks and spears. The sailors were skewered like lambs, and plucked from the waters, swallowed whole or sectioned and dipped into a bath of melted sheep's fat which lay bubbling in a cauldron beside the shores. The Laestrygonians had received word of Odysseus's ships and were prepared for the feast. They splashed and howled, laughing and eating until every one of Odysseus's comrade's ships was destroyed, emptied of its human cargo which presented such a cruel breakfast.

Odysseus had long since cut the ropes which anchored him to the rocks, and he and his crew raced for the deep sea, rowing faster than any mortal before them. Flushed with fear, their hearts pounding, they rowed for two days, one single crew saved from the tortures of the Laestrygonians by the wit of their captain. They rowed until they reached the shores of another island, where they collapsed, unable to lift their weary heads, caring not if in their refuge they courted danger.

Circe and the Island of Aeaea

❧

FOR NEARLY TWO DAYS the men slept on the shores of the unknown island, drinking in the peacefulness which covered them like a blanket, coming to terms with the loss of their comrades in their dreams. They woke freshened, but wary, eager to explore the land, but made prudent by their misadventures. In the distance, smoke curled lethargically into the windless sky. The island was inhabited, but by whom?

Odysseus divided the group into two camps, one taken by himself, the other led by his lieutenant, the courageous and loyal warrior Eurylochus. They drew lots from a helmet, and so it was decreed that Eurylochus would lead his party into the forest, towards the signs of life. His men gathered themselves up, and brushed off their clothes, trembling with anticipation and fear. They moved off.

The path wound its way through the tree-clad island, drawing the men into the bosom of the hills. There, at its centre, was a roughly hewn cottage, chimney smoking, and no sign of danger. Its fine stone walls were guarded by wolves and lions, but they leapt playfully towards the explorers, licking them and wagging their tails. Confused but comforted by the welcome, the men drew forward, and soon were enticed by the exquisite melody which drifted from the cottage. A woman's voice rang out, pure and sweet, calming their hearts, and drying the sweat on their brows. They moved forward confidently, only Eurylochus hanging back in caution.

They were greeted by the figure of a beautiful woman, whose hair tumbled to her heels, whose eyes were two green jewels in an ivory facade. Her smile was benevolent, welcoming, her arms outstretched. The men stumbled over one another to greet her, and were led into the cavernous depths of the cottage, where tables groaned with luxurious morsels of food – candied fruits, roasted spiced meats, plump vegetables and glazed breads, tumbling from platters of silver and gold. Wines and juices glistened in frosted glasses, and a barrel of fine brandy dripped into platinum goblets. It was a feast beyond compare, and the aroma enveloped the men, drawing them forward. They ate and drank while Eurylochus waited uncomfortably, outside the gates. And after many hours, when the men had taken their fill, they sat back with smiles of contentment, of satisfied gluttony, and raised their eyes in gratitude to their hostess.

'Who are you, fine woman?' slurred one of the crewman, made bold by the spirits.

'I am Circe,' she whispered back. And with a broad sweep of her hand, and a cry of laughter which startled her guests, drawing them from their stupor, she shouted, ' And you are but swine, like all men.'

Circe was a great and beautiful enchantress, living alone on this magical island where all visitors were pampered and fed with a charmed repast until Circe grew bored with them. And then, stroking their stupid heads, Circe would make them beasts. Now, she raised her mighty hands and laid them down upon the heads of Eurylochus's men and turned them to swine, corralling them snuffling and grunting through the door. Eurylochus peered round a tree in dismay. Ten men had entered, and now ten pigs left. The enchantress followed them, penning them in sties and stopping to speak gently to the other beasts, who had once been men. Happily she returned to her cottage and took up her loom once more.

Eurylochus sprinted through the forest, breathless with fear and disbelief as he rejoined Odysseus and the crew. Odysseus drew himself up, and a determined look transformed his distinguished features. He reached for his sword, and thrusting a dagger in his belt he set off to rescue his men, turning his head heavenwards and praying for assistance from the very gods who had spurned him. Odysseus had suffered the insults of war, and the tortures of their perilous journey. He would fight for his men, for his depleted crew. No woman, enchantress or not, would outwit him, would take from him his few remaining men.

As he struggled through the forest, a youth stumbled across his path.

'Here,' he whispered. 'Take this.' And he thrust into the hands of Odysseus a divine herb known as Moly, a plant with black roots and a snow white flower so beautiful that only those with celestial hands had the strength to pluck it. Moly was an antidote against the spells of Circe, and with this in his possession, Odysseus would be safe. The boy, who was really the god Hermes, sent by the goddess Athene, warned Odysseus of Circe's magical powers, and offered him a plan.

And so it was that Odysseus reached the cottage of Circe, and entered its welcoming gates. There the same feast greeted him, and he partook of the food until he lay sleepy and sated. Circe could hardly disguise her glee at the ease with which she had trapped this new traveller, and as she waved her wand to change him into a pig, Odysseus rose and spoke.

'Your magic has no power over me,' he said, and he thrust her to the ground at the point of his sword. She trembled with fear, and with longing.

'You,' she breathed, 'you must be the brave Odysseus, come from far to be my loving friend.' And she threw down her wand and took the soldier into her warm embrace. They lay together for a night of love, and in the morning, spent yet invigorated by their carnal feast they rose to set free Odysseus's men.

And there, on the enchanted island of Circe, Odysseus and his men spent days which stretched into golden weeks and then years, fed from the platters laden with food, their glasses poured over with drink, resting and growing fat, until they had forgotten the tortures of their journey. Odysseus was charmed by the lovely Circe, and all thoughts of Penelope and Telemachus were chased from his mind. His body was numbed by the pleasures inflicted upon it.

But the great Odysseus was a supreme leader, and even pure indulgence could not blunt his keen mind forever. As his senses gradually cleared, as Circe's powers over his body, over his soul began to wane, he felt the first rush of homesickness, of longing for Ithaca and his family. And in his heart he began to feel the weight of his responsibilities, the burden of his obligations to his country, to his men and to the gods.

With that, he made secret plans for their escape, and as the enchantment began also to wear at the sanity of his men, as they grew tired of the hedonism which filled their every waking hour, they became party to his strategy. With that, he went in search of Circe.

The House of Hades

ODYSSEUS FOUND THE ENCHANTRESS CIRCE in a calm and equable mood. She loved Odysseus, who had warmed her heart and her bed, but she had known since first setting eyes on the great warrior that he could never be completely hers. This day had been long in coming, but now that it was upon her, she gave him her blessing.

There were, however, tasks to be undertaken before Odysseus could be freed. He and his men could not voyage to Ithaca until they had met with the ghost of the blind prophet Tiresias, wiser than any dead or alive. They must travel to him at Hades, bringing gifts to sacrifice to the powers of the Underworld. Whitened by fear the men agreed to journey with Odysseus, to learn their fate and to receive instructions for their return to Ithaca.

All his men, spare one, prepared themselves for the voyage, but Elpenor, the youngest of the crew, lay sleeping on the roof of the cottage, where he'd stumbled in a drunken stupor the previous night. He woke to see the ship and his comrades setting sail from the island of Circe, and forgetting himself, he tumbled to the ground where he met an instant and silent death.

The men pressed on, unaware that one of their lot was missing. They sailed through a fair wind, raised by Circe, and as darkness drew itself around them, they entered the deep waters of Oceanus, where the Cimmerians lived in eternal night. There the rivers Phlegethon, Cocytus and Styx converged beneath a great rock, and Odysseus and his men drew aground. Following Circe's instructions, they dug a deep well in the earth beside the rock, then they cut the throats of a ram and a ewe, allowing their virgin blood to fill the trough.

The ghosts of the departed began to gather round the blood, some in battle-stained garb, others lost and confused; they struggled up to the pit and fought for a drink. Odysseus drew his sword to hold back the swelling crowd, startled as Elpenor, pale and blood-spattered, greeted his former master. He pressed forward, moaning and reaching greedily for the mortals.

'I have no grave,' he uttered. 'I cannot rest.' He clung to Odysseus whose cold stare belied the anxiety that pressed down on his heart. He was too close to the wretched creatures of the Underworld, near enough to be dragged down with them. He shook Elpenor loose.

'I will build you a grave,' he said gruffly. 'A fine grave with a tomb. There your ashes will lay and you shall have peace.'

Elpenor pulled back at once, a bemused expression crossing his pale face. He slid away, as reaching arms grappled into the space he left. Faces blended together in a grotesque dance of the macabre, writhing bodies struggling to catch a glimpse of mortals, of the other side. Familiar features appeared and then disappeared, as Odysseus fought to keep control of his senses.

'Odysseus,' the voice was soft, crooning. How often he'd heard it, sheltered in the tender arms of its bearer, rocked, adored. Mother.

Anticleia had been alive when he'd sailed for Troy and until this moment he knew not of her death. He longed to reach out for her, to take her pale and withered body against his own, to provide her with the comfort she had so tenderly invested in him.

But his duties prodded at his conscience, and he pricked his sword at her, edging her away from him, searching the tumultuous mass for Tiresias. At last he appeared from the shadowy depths, stopping to drink deeply from the bloody sacrifice. He leaned against his golden staff, and spoke slowly, in a language mellowed with age.

'Odysseus,' Tiresias said. 'Thy homecoming will not be easy. Poseidon bears spite against thee for blinding his Cyclops son Polyphemus. Yet you have guardians, and all may go well still, if, when you reach the hallowed shores of Trinacrian, ye harm not the herds of the Sun that pasture there. Control thy men, Odysseus. Allow not the greed that has tainted their hearts, that has led you astray, to shadow your journey.'

He paused, drinking again from the trenches and shrugging aside the groping arms of his comrades. He spat into the pool of blood.

'If you slay them, Odysseus, you will bring death upon your men, wreckage to your ships, and if you do escape, you will find thy house in trouble, no glory in your homecoming. And in the end, death will come to thee from the sea, from the great Poseidon.' With that, Tiresias leaned heavily on his staff and stumbled away, calling out as he left, 'Mark my words, brave Odysseus. My sight is not hampered by the darkness.'

Odysseus sat down and pondered the blind man's words. Anticleia appeared once again and he beckoned her closer, coaxed her to drink, and with the power invested in her by the blood, she drew a deep breath and spoke. She asked eagerly of his news, and told of her own, how she had died of grief thinking him dead at Troy. But his father, Laertes, she said, was still alive, though weakened by despair and feeble in his old age. Penelope his wife waited for him, loyal despite the attentions of many suitors. And Telemachus had become a man, grown tall and strong like his father.

Odysseus was torn by the sight of his mother, knowing not when he would set eyes on her again. He reached out to touch her, but she shrank from his embrace, a vision only, no substance, no warm blood coursing through her veins. He stood abruptly and was thronged by the clambering dead, as his mother drifted from his sight. He called after her, but she had gone.

Many of his comrades from Troy appeared now, eager to see the fine Odysseus, curious about his presence in Hades without having suffered the indignity of death. There was Agamemnon, and again, Achilles, whose stature was diminished, whose glory had tarnished. Ajax was there, and Tantalus and Sisyphus reached out to him, howling with anguish. And then there was Minos, and Orion, and Heracles, great men once, ghostly spectres now. They circled him and he felt chilled by their emptiness, by their singleness, by their determination to possess him. He turned away and strode from the group, shaking with the effort.

And his men joined him there, as they rowed away from that perilous island, down the Ocean river and back to the open sea. The friendly winds tossed them back to Circe's island, where the enchantress awaited them. Their belongings were ready, and she had resigned herself to the loss of her great love. She pulled Odysseus to one side, stroking him until he stiffened with pleasure, tempted as always to remain with her, enjoyed and enjoying.

She whispered in his ear, warning him of the hazards which stood between Aeaea and Ithaca, the perils of his course. And he kissed her deeply and with a great surge of confidence, pushed her aside and went to meet his men.

Together they uncovered the body of poor Elpenor, and burned it with great ceremony, placing his ashes in a grand and sturdy tomb. Their duty done, they looked towards home.

And so it was that Odysseus escaped the fires of Hades, and the clutches of the shrewd Circe, and found himself heading once more towards Ithaca and home, the warnings of Circe and Tiresias echoing in his ears. As chance would have it, the first of the dangers lay just across the shimmering sea.

The Sirens

THE AIR WAS HOT AND HEAVY around the vessel; the sunlight glinted on her bow as she cut through the silent sea. The men were restless. The silence held the threat of ill fate and they looked to Odysseus with wary eyes, seeking his wisdom, begging him wordlessly for comfort.

Odysseus stood tall alongside the mast, his noble profile chiselled against the airless horizon. He looked troubled, his head cocked to one side as he heard the first whispers of a beautiful melody.

It stung and tore at his sanity, dredging up a memory, a warning, but lulling him somehow away from his men, from his responsibilities, from the course of his voyage. He struggled against the growing sound, alert to the knowledge that his men had not yet heard its seductive strains but every fibre of his being ached to find its source, to touch its creator.

The Sirens. The words leapt to his troubled mind, and with great effort he drew himself from the reverie.

'Lash me to the mast,' he cried suddenly. Something in his voice caused his astonished men to obey.

'But captain, sir ...' one of the younger seamen ventured to express his amazement.

'Now!' Odysseus felt the bewildered hurt of his men. He also heard the growing symphony of the Sirens. He felt himself being drawn back, their melody licking at his mind like the hottest of fires, burning his resolve and his sanity.

'The candles,' he mouthed groggily. 'Melt the candles.' He could barely choke out the words. 'The wax ... in your ears.'

A startled silence was filled by the roaring of Odysseus's first mate: 'Do as he says, men. We have never had cause to question the wisdom of Odysseus. He has the strength and the cunning of ten men. He sees what we cannot see. We must put our faith in him.'

The ears of each man were carefully plugged by the wax of forty candles. As the last man turned his head, a swell of sound filled the air. Odysseus gave himself to it, wrestling with the lashings that restrained his strong frame. The sweet song of death called him, beckoned him from his lofty post.

The Sirens. The birds of death, temptresses of darkness – their sensuous melody played on the chords of his mind, calling him to a blackness which would envelope him forever. They appeared around him, luxuriant hair tumbling about angelic faces. He was trapped in a swarm of soaring wings and resplendent feathers. Women of the birds, with voices to lull even the hardiest warrior to certain death.

The deafened crew of his ship watched in amazement as the elegant creatures swooped among them, their eyes gleaming with secret knowledge, their voices capturing Odysseus in a cloud of passionate yearning.

Befuddled by the play on his senses, Odysseus signalled to his men to begin to row, then he sank back against the mast, spent and sickened by longing. The mighty vessel collected speed, ploughing through the sea that rippled with the thrust of the Sirens and the power of their music.

The sound increased, their music tortuously alluring as the Sirens fought for the spirit of Odysseus. The men battled with their oars, churning the water aside, sensing the danger that had hewn such fear on the face of their leader.

The music of the Sirens took on a rising note of mirth, and then, as the ship surged away from their grips, they laughed aloud.

'You will be ours again,' they sang together, laughing and diving around the fallen man. 'Ours to the end.'

They rose in a cluster of discord and light and disappeared, a painful silence filling the cacophony of sound that was no more. Odysseus rose again. He looked to the east, to the island of the Sirens, and he signalled to his men to clear their ears. He'd had to hear it. Circe had warned him of the Sirens, and although he trusted not the weak natures of his men, he had relished the chance to tempt his own resolve. But it was a bitter triumph, for he'd very nearly been lost to them, tugged so close to the edge of his mind, to madness and the darkness beneath.

A sweet wind caught the main sail and the ship plunged forward. Their small victory raised a smile on the weather-beaten faces of the seamen, and then they turned their faces to waters new.

Scylla and Charybdis

CIRCE HAD WARNED ODYSSEUS of the dangers that would beset him and his crew should they choose to ignore the words of wise Tiresias. The next part of their journey would take them though a narrow strait, peopled by some of the most fearsome monsters in all the lands. Odysseus was to guide the ship through the narrow passage, through fierce and rolling waters, looking neither up nor down, embodying all humility.

But the pride of Odysseus was more deeply rooted than his fear, and ignoring Circe's words, he took a stand on the prow of his ship, heavily armoured and emboldened by the support of his men. Here he stood as they passed the rocks of Charybdis, the hateful daughter of Poseidon, who came to the surface three times each day in order to belch out a powerful whirlpool, drawing into her frothing gut all that came back with it. There was no sign of her now, the waters suspiciously stilled. Ahead lay an island, drenched in warm sunlight, beckoning to the weary sailors. They must just make it through.

Odysseus had kept the details of this fearsome strait from his men. They had been weakened by battle, and by the horrific sights which had met their

·yes since leaving Troy. They were so close to Ithaca, he dared not cast their ropes and anticipation into shadow. And so it was that only Odysseus knew of the next monster who was to be thrust upon them in that dangerous channel, only Odysseus who knew that she was capable of tasks more gruesome than any of them had seen in all their travels.

For Scylla was a gluttonous and evil creature that haunted the strait, making her home in a gore-splattered den where she feasted on the remains of luckless sailors. She was, they said, a nymph who had been the object of Glaucus's attentions. Glaucus was a sea-god who had been turned into a merman by a strange herb he had unwittingly swallowed. And as much as he adored Scylla, so he was loved by Circe who, in a jealous rage, had turned Scylla into a terrible sea-monster with six dog's heads around her waist. She lived there in the cliff face in the straits of Messina, and devoured sailors who passed. She moved silently. Odysseus was loath to admit it, but the silent danger she represented placed more fear in his heart than the bravest of enemies.

Odysseus and his men passed further into the quiet strait, their mouths dry with fear. A silence hung over them like a shroud. And then it was broken by a tiny splash, and tinkle of water dripping, and up, with a mighty roar, came Scylla, the mouths on each head gaping open, their lethal jaws sprung for one purpose alone. Smoothly she leaned forward and in a flash of colour, of torn clothing and hellish screams, six of his best men were plucked from their posts aboard ship and drawn into the mouth of her cave. Their cries rent at the heart, at the conscience of Odysseus, and he turned helplessly to his remaining crew who looked at him with genuine fear, distrust and anger. A mutinous fever bubbled at the edges of their loyalty, and Odysseus knew he had lost them. He looked back at the cave where Scylla had silenced his hapless men, and signalled the others to row faster. A repeat of her attack would leave him with too few men to carry on. They rowed towards the shores of the great three-cornered island, Thrinacie, where the herds of the Sun-god Helios grazed peacefully on the hilltops.

The Flock of Helios

❧

SHAKEN BY THE TORTURE of his men, Odysseus proclaimed that they would make no further stops until they reached the shores of Ithaca. But the mutiny that had been brooding was thrust forward in the form of an insolent Eurylochus, who insisted that they set down their anchors, and have a night of rest. Tiresias and Circe had warned him of this flock of sheep, and Odysseus ordered his men to touch them not, to ignore their bleatings, their succulent fat which spoke of years of grazing on tender grasses, nurtured by Helios himself. The sailors took a solemn oath and Odysseus grudgingly allowed them to moor the ship to the rocky coast. They set about preparing a fire, and after a silent meal, fell into a deep sleep.

When morning broke, the skyline was littered with heavy clouds, tugging on the reins of a prevailing wind. And with it came a tempest which blew over the island for thirty days, prohibiting the safe voyage of the men, trapping them on an island that was empty of nourishment. And so it was that for thirty days the crew dined meagrely on corn and wine which the lovely Circe had provided, and when that was devoured, they took up their harpoons and fished the swirling waters for sustenance. And as hunger grew wild within their bodies, so did their minds wander a seditious path, along which their loyalty was cast and their oaths forgotten.

One night as Odysseus slept, weakened by hunger like his men, the errant sailors slaughtered several of Helios's sacred cows, dedicating some to the god, but gorging themselves on the carcasses of many more, till they sat, fattened and slovenly, rebelliously content. The cows were enchanted, and lowed while impaled on a spit over the fire, their empty carcasses rising to trample the ground around the men, but they repented not and continued to eat until soon their treachery was brought to the attention of Helios himself. Odysseus woke to discover the travesty and corralled his men aboard ship, urging them to escape before vengeance could be sprung upon them. But it was too late.

As Helios cried out to Zeus, imploring the king of gods to take divine retribution, Poseidon reached up his powerful staff and stirred up a tempest so violent that the ship was immediately cast to pieces in the furious waters. And Zeus sent storms and thunderbolts which broke the ship and its men into tiny pieces, crashing down the mast upon the sailors and killing them all. Only Odysseus who had remained true to the gods, was saved, and he clung to the wreckage, which formed a makeshift raft. For nine days he tumbled across waves that were larger than the fist of Poseidon himself, but his resolve was strong, his will to live was greater than the anger of the gods.

His men were drowned. Thoughts of Penelope and Telemachus kept him afloat as he fought the turbulent seas, escaping the grasp of an angry Poseidon. He was battered by the storm which drove him back to Charybdis, and as her great whirlpool was spat out, his raft was sucked into the waters that were drawn into her greedy belly. Faint with hunger, with fear, he reached out and held on to the spreading branches of a great fig tree and there he hung, perilously close to the vortex of water, until his raft was thrown out again. And Odysseus dropped into the sea, and paddled and drifted until he spied land once again. And only then did he allow himself to lay down his head, secure in the knowledge that help was at hand. So the noble Odysseus slept, and was washed towards the shores of this secluded island of Ogygia.

Calypso's Island

❧

ODYSSEUS COULD SEE LAND and in the distance a beautiful nymph, the most beautiful woman on whom he had ever laid eyes. Her milk-white skin was gleaming in the moonlight, and the wrathful winds tossed her silken hair. Her voice was soft, inviting above the raging storms.

'Come to me, Odysseus,' she whispered. 'Here you will find love, and eternal life.'

Odysseus struggled for breath, filled with longing and wonder. She reached a slender hand towards him, across the expanse of water, and lifted him from its depths, the strength of her grip, the length of her reach inhuman. He shuddered at her touch.

'You have come to join me,' she said calmly, as Odysseus laid restless and dripping beneath her.

Odysseus nodded, his passion spent. He was alive. The others had been clutched by the revengeful Poseidon. He was grateful to this nymph. He would plan his escape later.

'I have asked for you, and you have come,' she intoned quietly, settling herself at his side. Odysseus felt the first stirring of fear, but dismissed it as the lovely maiden smiled down on him.

She was Calypso, the lovely daughter of Thetis, and like Circe she was an enchantress. She lived alone on the island, in a comfortable cavern overhung by vines and fragrant foliage. She was gentle, and quiet, tending to Odysseus's every need, feeding him with morsels of delicious foods, warming him with handspun garments which clung to his body like a new skin, and she welcomed him in her bed, running his body over with hot hands that explored and relaxed the beaten hero until he grew to love her, and to build his life with her on the idyllic island.

For seven years he lived with Calypso, drunk with luxury and love. She was more beautiful than any he had seen before, and her island was dripping with pleasures. And as his happiness grew deeper, his fire and fervour spent to become a peaceful equilibrium, he felt the jab of conscience, of something untoward eating at the corners of his idyll, and he realized that he was living in a numb oblivion, that his passion to return home, to see his family, to take up the responsibilities of his leadership, were as strong in him as they had ever been and that he must allow them to surge forth, to fill him again with fiery ambition.

And in that seventh year he spent more and more time seated on the banks of the island, gazing towards his own land where time did not stand still and where his wife's suitors were threatening to take over his country, his rule. He came eventually to the notice of Athene, whose favour he had kept despite the outrage of the other gods, and she went at once to Zeus on his behalf. Zeus was fair and kind, and he balanced the sins of Odysseus against his innate good will, and the struggles to keep in check his unruly crews, all of which were lost to him now. Poseidon was away from Olympus and the time seemed right to set Odysseus free, for he had lived long enough in an enchanted purgatory.

Calypso reluctantly agreed to allow him his freedom, and she provided him with the tools to create a sturdy boat, and with provisions of food and drink enough to last the entire journey. She bathed him, dressed him in fine silks and jewels, as befitted a returning warrior, and kissing him gently but with all the fire of her love for him, she bade him go, with a tear-stained farewell. She had provided him with instructions which would see him round the dangers, across the perils that could beset him. He set sail for Ithaca.

Nausicaa and the Phaeacians

WITH THE STARS of the Great Bear twinkling on his left, Odysseus sailed for eighteen days, tossed gently on a calm sea with a favourable wind breathing on the sails which were pulled tight. And then Poseidon, returning to Olympus, noticed this solitary sailor, and filled with all the fury of a wronged god, produced a calamitous wave which struck out at Odysseus and thrust him overboard. And there ensued a storm of gigantic proportions which stirred the sea into a feverish pitch which threatened with each motion to drown the terrified sailor.

But despite his many wrongs, his well-publicized shortcomings, Odysseus had made friends, and inspired awe and respect among many in Greece. And so it was that the sea-goddess Ino-Leucothea took pity on him, and swimming easily to him in the tempestuous sea, cast off his clothes and hung around his waist a magic veil, which would carry him safely to shore. She lingered before swimming away, her eyes lighting on his strong body which splashed powerfully in the waters, and she laid her hand briefly on his skin, warming him through and filling him with a deep and new energy.

Odysseus swam on, the sea calmed by Athene, and landed, exhausted on the shores of the island of the Phaeacians, where he fell into a profound slumber. Athene moved inland, into the chamber of Nausicaa, the lovely daughter of King Alcinous, and into her dreams, urging her to visit the shores of the island, to wash her clothes in the stream that tumbled by the body of the sleeping warrior. And when she woke, Nausicaa encouraged her friends to come with her to the stream, to play there, and to make clean her soiled garments.

Their cries of frivolity woke the sleepy Odysseus and he crawled from under a bush, naked and unruly. His wild appearance sent the friends of Nausicaa running for help, but she stood still, her virgin heart beating with anticipation. His untamed beauty inspired a carnal longing that was new to her, and from that moment she was devoted to him. She listened carefully to his words and taking his hand, led him to see her father.

Now Athene knew that King Alcinous would be less affected by Odysseus's beauty than his daughter, and prepared a healing mist which enshrouded Odysseus, who had been hastily dressed by Nausicaa.

Alcinous lived in a splendid palace, filled with glittering treasures and elegant furnishings. His table was renowned across the lands, delicious fruits soaked in fine liquors, breads veined with rich nuts, succulent meats which swirled in fine juices, glazed vegetables and herbs from the most remote gardens across the world. There were jellies and sweets, baked goods, cheeses and pâtes, fresh figs and luscious olives, all available every day to whomever visited the kind and generous leader. His women were well-versed in the vocabulary of caring for their men, and the palace gleamed with every luxury, with every necessity, to make an intelligent man content.

He listened to Odysseus now, and was struck by the power of his words. Odysseus had the appearance of a stray, but the demeanour of greatness. Alcinous wondered curiously if he was a god in disguise, so eloquent and masterful was their unknown visitor. But Odysseus kept from them his identity knowing not the reception he would receive, and careful not to destroy his chances of borrowing a ship and some men to take him to Ithaca.

And Odysseus was warmly welcomed in the palace, and fed such marvellous foods and drinks, living in such comfortable splendour, that he considered at length the request by King Alcinous and his lovely wife that he stay on to take Nausicaa as his bride. But he was too close to home to give up, and Alcinous, too polite and kind to keep Odysseus against his will, agreed to let him pass on, aided by the Phaeacian ships and hardy sailors.

So it was that on the final night of his stay with the Phaeacians he was made the guest of honour at a luxuriant feast, where the conversation turned to travels, and to war, and finally, to the victory of Troy. Inspired by their talk, a minstrel took up his lute and began to sing of the wars, of the clear skies of Ithaca, the valour of Achilles, and the skill of Odysseus and Epius. So loudly did he extol the virtues of the brave son of Laertes that Odysseus was forced to lower his head in despair, and the tears fell freely to his plate where they glinted and caught the attention of the king and his men.

'Why do you suffer such dismay?' asked Alcinous gently, for he had grown fond of the elegant stranger in their midst.

Odysseus' reply was choked. The burden of the last ten years now threatened to envelope him. He had never pondered long the nature of the trials that had faced him, but as he ordered them in his mind, preparing his story to tell the King, their enormity swamped him, frightened him, made him weak.

'I am Odysseus,' he said quietly, 'son of Laertes.'

The room filled with excited joy – glasses were lifted, toasts offered, Odysseus was carried to the king where he received a long and honourable blessing. Then silence overcame them and they listened to the tales of the illustrious Odysseus who had suffered such misadventure, and overcome all with his cunning and mastery. They gazed in wonderment on the hero. He had long been thought dead, but everyone knew of the devotion, the loyalty of his wife Penelope, who refused to contemplate the idea. They encouraged him to return home. And if the unknown castaway received such glory in their generous household, a warrior of such note received the very bounty of the gods.

Ships were prepared and laden with gifts. The strongest and bravest of the Phaeacians were chosen to set sail with him, and warmed by the love and admiration of his new friends, Odysseus was placed in fine robes at the helm of a new ship, and sent towards home.

Odysseus, worn by troubles, and the relief of reaching his shores, slept deeply on board the ship, and loathe to wake him, the awe-struck sailors lifted him gently to the sands of Ithaca, where they piled his body with all the glorious gifts provided by the King, and then they retreated through the bay of Phorcys. Poseidon had been smouldering with rage at the disloyalty of Athene and Zeus, but realizing that Odysseus had been charmed, and had friends who would not allow his destruction, he allowed the hero to be placed on the sands, turning his wrath instead on the sailors. As they passed from the harbour into the seas, he struck a blow with his mighty staff and turned them all to stone, their ship frozen forever on the silent waters that led to Ithaca. It remained there as a warning to all who thought they could betray Poseidon and his mighty powers.

And so the mighty Odysseus lay once again on the shores of Ithaca, knowing not that ten years' journey had brought him at last to his promised land, or that the glory predicted by the Phaeacians would not yet be his. Battles new lined themselves on the horizon, but Odysseus was home, and from that secure base, could take on all.

Penelope and Telemachus

WHEN BRAVE ODYSSEUS was laid, deep in slumber, on the shores of Ithaca, he knew nothing of the dangers which faced his country. Loyal Penelope was ensconced in their palace, at the mercy of over a hundred suitors, rulers from neighbouring islands who wished to annex Ithaca. Telemachus had left the island in search of his father, and many of the suitors were involved in a plot to murder him upon his return. Laertes was alive, but old and troubled. When Odysseus woke, he knew not where he was. He was visited by Athene, who briefed him on the ills of his homeland, and who dressed him in the guise of a beggar, and led him to the hut of the faithful swineherd Eumaeus. Here Odysseus could plot, and plan, prepare the tools of battle to make Ithaca his once more.

When Odysseus awoke on the sands of Ithaca, a mist had fallen over the majestic land and he knew not where he was. The Phaeacians had vanished from his sight, and he had only a groggy but pleasant memory of his visit to them. He should be at Ithaca now, he thought, but he could see nothing in the steamy air that enshrouded him. From the mists he heard a soft voice – familiar to Odysseus, but he no longer trusted in anything, and he sat back cautiously.

'You are in the land of the great warrior and traveller Odysseus,' said the voice, which belonged to a young and comely shepherd. 'How do you not know it?'

Odysseus lied glibly about his reasons for being there, inventing a fantastic story that was quite different from his actual voyage. At this the shepherd laughed, and changing shape, became Athene.

'So, crafty Odysseus,' she smiled. 'What a rogue you are. The greatest gods would have trouble inventing such tricks.' With that she held out a hand to the weary traveller, and led him across the sands.

'I've hidden you from your countrymen,' she explained, indicating the mists which surrounded them. 'Things are not as you would have hoped. It is not safe for you now. You must tread slowly.'

She helped Odysseus to hide away his treasures, and sat him down to explain to him the matters of his homeland. Penelope was still faithful to him, but time was running out, and she knew that if he did not appear to her within the next months, Penelope would have little recourse but to join herself with another. Telemachus was greatly angered by the insolent suitors who banded themselves at the palace, taking as their own everything that had belonged to his father, and gorging themselves on the food meant for the people of Ithaca. It was an untidy situation, and Telemachus struggled to believe that his father was still alive.

He had left the island for the mainland, desperate for news of Odysseus, never believing that his father could be dead. He'd vowed to allow one year for news, failing which he would agree to the wishes of a stepfather and stand aside.

In Greece Telemachus was greeted with little interest, and his attempts to uncover the whereabouts of his father were useless. Old Nestor, who knew everything about the war at Troy, and had followed the lives of the great men who had made the victory there, had heard nothing of Odysseus. He had disappeared, he said sadly, shaking his head. Determined, Telemachus pressed on to Sparta where Helen welcomed the son of Odysseus, but had little news to impart. Telemachus began to feel the first stirrings of despair, and sat with his head pressed into his hands. When Menelaus returned to his home that evening, he found Telemachus like this, and leaning over the youth, whispered words of comfort.

'I too have wandered,' he said gently.' And news of your father has reached me through the minions of Poseidon.' He went on to warn Telemachus of Poseidon's rage, explaining how Odysseus had blinded his one-eyed son Polyphemus. Menelaus told how Odysseus had been cast upon the shores of Calypso, where he lived a life that was half enchantment and half longing for his past.

Telemachus moved swiftly. His father was alive. A rescue must be planned at once, but most importantly he must warn his mother. The suitors had moved in too closely. They must be disposed of immediately.

At home in Ithaca, Penelope was also filled with a despair that threatened to destroy her. Her loyalty to Odysseus had kept her sane, and filled her with a kind of clever glee which made possible the machinations of keeping the suitors at bay. She'd held her head low with humility, and explained to the suitors who continued to arrive, to take roost in her home, that she must complete work on a cloth she was weaving, before she could contemplate giving herself to another. She worked hours on end in the days, performing for the suitors at her loom, giving them every belief in her excuses for not receiving their attentions. And yet at night she returned to her lonely bedroom and there she sat by torchlight, unpicking the work of the day. And as the years went by, it became established knowledge that Penelope was not free to marry until she had finished her web.

But Penelope was aware that her excuse was wearing thin, that the seeds of suspicion had been sown in the minds of her suitors, and that they were paying inordinate interest in the mechanics of the loom itself. It was only a question of time before they would insist on her hand and she would be forced to make a choice. Her property was being wasted, her lands falling to ruin, her stocks emptied by their marauding parties. She longed for the firm hand of Odysseus to oust them from their adopted home, to renew the sense of vigour that was required by her workers to make things right again. Most importantly, however, she longed for the warm embrace of her husband, the nights of passion, of sweet love. She had resisted the attentions of her suitors, but her body was afire with longing, and she burned at a single look, at a fleeting touch. Penelope was ready for her husband's return. Soon it would be too late.

At the cottage of Eumaeus, Odysseus had been presented with a fine feast of suckling pig by the swineherd, who spoke sadly of his master's absence. He bemoaned the state of the island and explained to Odysseus in his disguise that the suitors visited his cottage regularly, taking their pick of the pigs so that his herd was sorely depleted. He said kindly that a beggarman was as entitled to a feast as were these inappropriate suitors, and he gave Odysseus his own cloak in which to warm himself by the fire. Odysseus told the loyal subject a wild story, but did say that he had heard news of Odysseus and that the great warrior would return to set his house in order within the next year. At this, the swineherd was filled with joy, and produced more food and wine for this bearer of good news. Odysseus settled in for the night.

By this time Telemachus had returned to the island, aided by Athene who had set out to greet him. He was taken to the cottage in darkness, so as not to arouse the suspicions of the suitors, who were plotting his death. Here a tearful reunion was made, away from the eyes of the swineherd who had been sent to the palace for more drink. Odysseus was transformed once more into his old self by Athene, and Telemachus drank in the sight of his father, who he'd hardly known as a child.

They sat together, heads touching, occasionally reaching over to reassure themselves of the other's presence, and the plans were made to restore Ithaca to her former glory, to rid it of the unruly suitors, to reinstate Odysseus and Telemachus at their rightful places at her helm.

The Battle for Ithaca

O DYSSEUS AND TELEMACHUS WERE READY to set their plans into action. Just before Eumaeus returned to his cottage, Odysseus resumed the form of a beggarman and Telemachus slipped away into the night. The following morning dawned cool and clear, and Odysseus felt a renewed vigour coursing through his veins. He longed to appear in his battle garb, the strong and mighty Odysseus returned from the dead to reclaim his palace, but there was too much at stake to set a wrong foot and he knew the plans he had fixed with Telemachus must be followed to the tiniest detail.

Eumaeus accompanied Odysseus to the palace, to see if there was any work available for a willing but poverty-stricken beggar. He was greeted first by the rude and arrogant Antinous, the leader of Penelope's suitors, who had long considered himself the rightful heir to Odysseus's position within Ithaca. He gazed scathingly at Odysseus as he entered the room where the suitors lolled about on cushions, calling out to the over-burdened servants for refreshment and ever greater feasts of food.

'Who dares to trouble us?' he said lazily.

Odysseus introduced himself as a poor traveller, down on his luck after a long voyage in which his crew members had been struck down by Poseidon. To test them, Odysseus begged them for alms, but he was met by a barrage of rotten fruit, after which several of the younger suitors took turns beating him. Bruised and angry, Odysseus stood his ground, requesting menial work of any nature. And it was then that the young local beggar Irus stepped into the fray. Resenting the competition offered by Odysseus, he challenged him to a fight, at which the lazy suitors leapt to their feet, roaring at the impending carnage. For Odysseus had taken the form of an old man, and Irus was young and strong, a beggar only because of his slothful nature.

But the roars turned to silence as Odysseus lifted his robes to show legs as muscular and powerful as the greatest of warriors, and a prowess with a sword that belonged only to the master of the house. He slayed Irus with one fell of his sword. Odysseus was cheered not by the suitors, who suspected a rival for the attentions of Penelope, and they cast him out, kicking and beating him until he howled with pain and restrained anger. He could not show his true colours yet. The time was not ripe for battle. Odysseus made his way from the waiting rooms, into the kitchen where word of his ill-treatment reached Penelope. Knowing well that gods often travelled in disguise, she sent a message that she wished this sailor to be fed and made comfortable for the night. Penelope herself wished to speak to him, for a traveller might have word of the long-lost Odysseus and she yearned for news of him.

But Odysseus claimed to be too weak to see the mistress of the house, and it was agreed that they would speak later that evening. And so it was that Odysseus slipped from his bed in the kitchen and met with his son in the great hall. Quietly they removed the armour and weapons that the suitors had idly laid to one side, piling them outside the palace gates where they were snatched away by village boys. And now, in the darkened hall, Odysseus agreed to see Penelope, who felt a surge of excitement at their meeting which startled and concerned her. Odysseus had been gone too long, she was losing control.

They met by candlelight, and safe in his disguise, Odysseus wove for Penelope a fanciful story about his travels, which had little in common with the true nature of his voyages, but left her with no doubt that the brave Odysseus was on his way home, and would soon return to set things to right. And then Odysseus heard from Penelope the trials of the last twenty years, and hung his head in shame at the thought of his many years with Calypso, and the time lost through the greed and indolence of his men.

Penelope told of the suitors who had been first quietened by her insistence that the Oracle had promised Odysseus's return, but as the years had passed, they had grown insolent and arrogant, demanding her attentions, her hand in marriage. She had fought them off, she said, by claiming to weave the cloth that would shroud Laertes upon his death, and each night she had spent many hours unpicking the day's work. And then, when this trick had been discovered, she could delay her decision no longer and had feigned illness for many months. The next day was the Feast of Apollo and it was on this day that she had agreed to choose a husband. Penelope wept with misery, her fair face more beautiful with age and distress. Odysseus longed to take her in his arms, to warm her body and to ease her pain, but he held himself back from her, knowing that he must use his anger to feed his resolve, to rid his home of these suitors once and for all.

Penelope was grateful for the reassurance and calm understanding of this stranger, and she urged him to take a chamber for the night, sending the aged nurse Eurycleia to bathe his feet and weary legs. Eurycleia had been Odysseus's own nurse as a child, and when she saw his familiar scar, received in a youthful skirmish with a wild boar, she cried out. Odysseus grabbed her throat.

'Speak not, wise woman,' he whispered harshly, 'all will be set right at the dawn of the feast.' Eurycleia nodded, her eyes bulging with fear and concern and she gathered her skirts around her, heading for the servant's quarters.

The next day was the Feast, and the household was abuzz with activity and preparations. Odysseus took a seat amongst the suitors, strategically placed by the door, but he was jeered at and heckled until he was forced to move to a small stool. Penelope eventually appeared in their midst. Then Agelaus gave her an ultimatum. Today a choice must be made. Penelope turned pleadingly to Telemachus, but he nodded his grudging consent, and she announced that a competition would take place. With that she fled to a table, and shut her eyes in despair.

Telemachus took over, producing Odysseus's great bow, and gently explaining that his mother could only consider marriage to someone the equal of his father, someone who could string the bow and shoot an arrow through the rings of twelve axes set in a row. And one by one, the suitors failed to bend the stiff bow, and disgruntled, cast it aside and sat sullenly along the walls of the hall. So it was that the beggarman was the only remaining man, and he begged a chance to test his strength against the bow. He was taunted, and insults fired at him, but he stood his ground and with the permission of Penelope, who nodded a sympathetic assent, he took the bow.

Like a man born to the act, he deftly wired the bow, and taking an arrow, he fired it straight through the rings of the axes. The room was silent. Telemachus rose and strode across to stand by his father.

'The die is cast,' said Odysseus, thrusting aside his disguise. 'And another target presents itself. Prepare to pay for your treachery.' With that he lifted his arrow and shot Antinous clear through the neck. The suitors searched with amazement for their arms and armour, and finding them gone, tried to make due with the short daggers in their belts. They launched themselves on Odysseus and his son, but the two great men fought valiantly, sending arrow after arrow, spear after spear, to their fatal mark. And when Odysseus and Telemachus grew tired, Athene flew across them in the shape of a swallow and filled them with a surge of energy, a new life that saw them through the battle to victory.

The battle won, the suitors dead, the household was now scourged for those who had befriended the suitors, maids who had shared their beds, porters and shepherds who had made available the stocks and stores of Odysseus's palace. And these maids and men were beheaded and burnt in a fire that was seen for many miles.

Finally Odysseus could pause, and greet properly his long-lost wife, who sat wearily by his side, hardly daring to believe that he had returned. And yet, one look at his time and journey-lined face told her it was all true, and she was overwhelmed once again by her love for this brave man who was so long apart from her. With tears of joy they clutched one another, and their union was sweet and tender. And soon afterwards came Laertes, the veil of madness lifted by news of his son's return.

The courageous Odysseus was home at last, his cunning a match for all that the fates had set in his path. There would be more skirmishes before he could call Ithaca his own once more, and Poseidon must be appeased before he could live fearlessly surrounded by that great god's kingdom, but in time all was undertaken. Some say that Odysseus lived to a ripe old age, dying eventually and suitably on the sea. Others say that he died at the hand of his own son, Telegonus, by the enchantress Circe. All agree that Odysseus was beloved by his subjects, the tales of his journey becoming the food for legends which spread around the world.

Jason and the Argonauts

IT IS FORETOLD, 'Beware of a man with one sandal.' At first glance, hardly the most chilling of prophecies. Yet in an age circumscribed by gods and heroes, when the divine and human intertwined, any such prediction had to be viewed with respect. In this case doubly so, for the prophecy referred to none other than the hero Jason, son of Aeson of Iolcus, whose deeds in pursuit of the famous Golden Fleece would ripple throughout time and legend.

Aeson

❧

AESON, KING OF IOLCUS, was forced to fly from his dominions, which had been usurped by his younger brother, Pelias, and with difficulty succeeded in saving the life of his young son, Jason, who was at that time only ten years of age. He entrusted him to the care of the Centaur Chiron, by whom he was carefully trained in company with other noble youths, who, like himself, afterwards signalized themselves by their bravery and heroic exploits. For ten years Jason remained in the cave of the Centaur, by whom he was instructed in all useful and warlike arts. But as he approached manhood he became filled with an unconquerable desire to regain his paternal inheritance. He therefore took leave of his kind friend and preceptor, and set out for Iolcus to demand from his uncle Pelias the kingdom which he had so unjustly usurped.

In the course of his journey he came to a broad and foaming river, on the banks of which he perceived an old woman, who implored him to help her across. At first he hesitated, knowing that even alone he would find some difficulty in stemming the fierce torrent; but, pitying her forlorn condition, he raised her in his arms, and succeeded, with a great effort, in reaching the opposite shore. But as soon as her feet had touched the earth she became transformed into a beautiful woman, who, looking kindly at the bewildered youth, informed him that she was the goddess Hera, and that she would henceforth guide and protect him throughout his career. She then disappeared, and, full of hope and courage at this divine manifestation, Jason pursued his journey. He now perceived that in crossing the river he had lost one of his sandals, but as it could not be recovered he was obliged to proceed without it.

On his arrival at Iolcus he found his uncle in the market-place, offering up a public sacrifice to Poseidon. When the king had concluded his offering, his eye fell upon the distinguished stranger, whose manly beauty and heroic bearing had already attracted the attention of his people. Observing that one foot was unshod, he was reminded of an oracular prediction which foretold to him the loss of his kingdom by a man wearing only one sandal. He, however, disguised his fears, conversed kindly with the youth, and drew from him his name and errand. Then pretending to be highly pleased with his nephew, Pelias entertained him sumptuously for five days, during which time all was festivity and rejoicing. On the sixth, Jason appeared before his uncle, and with manly firmness demanded from him the throne and kingdom which were his by right. Pelias, dissembling his true feelings, smilingly consented to grant his request, provided that, in return, Jason would undertake an expedition for him, which his advanced age prevented him from accomplishing himself. He informed his nephew that the shade of Phryxus had appeared to him in his dreams, and entreated him to bring back from Colchis his mortal remains and the Golden Fleece; and added that if Jason succeeded in obtaining for him these sacred relics, throne, kingdom, and sceptre should be his.

The Golden Fleece

❧

ATHAMAS, KING OF BOEOTIA, had married Nephele, a cloud-nymph, and their children were Helle and Phryxus. The restless and wandering nature of Nephele, however, soon wearied her husband, who, being a mortal, had little sympathy with his ethereal consort; so he divorced her, and married the beautiful but wicked Ino (sister of Semele), who hated her step-children, and even planned their destruction. But the watchful Nephele contrived to circumvent her cruel designs, and succeeded in getting the children out of the palace. She then placed them both on the back of a winged ram, with a fleece of pure gold, which had been given to her by Hermes; and on this wonderful animal brother and sister rode through the air over land and sea; but on the way Helle, becoming seized with giddiness, fell into the sea (called after her the Hellespont) and was drowned.

Phryxus arrived safely at Colchis, where he was hospitably received by king Aëtes, who gave him one of his daughters in marriage. In gratitude to Zeus for the protection accorded him during his flight, Phryxus sacrificed to him the golden ram, whilst the fleece he presented to Aëtes, who nailed it up in the Grove of Ares, and dedicated it to the god of War. An oracle having declared that the life of Aëtes depended on the safe-keeping of the fleece, he carefully guarded the entrance to the grove by placing before it an immense dragon, which never slept.

The Argo Launches

❧

WE WILL NOW RETURN to Jason, who eagerly undertook the perilous expedition proposed to him by his uncle, who, well aware of the dangers attending such an enterprise, hoped by this means to rid himself for ever of the unwelcome intruder.

Jason accordingly began to arrange his plans without delay, and invited the young heroes whose friendship he had formed whilst under the care of Chiron, to join him in the perilous expedition. None refused the invitation, all feeling honoured at being allowed the privilege of taking part in so noble and heroic an undertaking.

Jason now applied to Argos, one of the cleverest ship-builders of his time, who, under the guidance of Pallas-Athene, built for him a splendid fifty-oared galley, which was called the Argo, after the builder. In the upper deck of the vessel the goddess had imbedded a board from the speaking oak of the oracle of Zeus at Dodona, which ever retained its powers of prophecy. The exterior of the ship was ornamented with magnificent carvings, and the whole vessel was so strongly built that it defied the power of the winds and waves, and was, nevertheless, so light that the heroes, when necessary, were able to carry it on their shoulders. When the vessel was completed, the Argonauts (so called after their ship) assembled, and their places were distributed by lot.

Jason was appointed commander-in-chief of the expedition, Tiphys acted as steersman, Lynceus as pilot. In the bow of the vessel sat the renowned hero Heracles; in the stern, Peleus (father of Achilles) and Telamon (the father of Ajax the Great). In the inner space were Castor and Pollux, Neleus (the father of Nestor), Admetus (the husband of Alcestes), Meleager (the slayer of the Calydonian boar), Orpheus (the renowned singer), Menoctius (the father of Patroclus), Theseus (afterwards king of Athens) and his friend Pirithöus (the son of Ixion), Hylas (the adopted son of Heracles), Euphemus (the son of Poseidon), Oileus (father of Ajax the Lesser), Zetes and Calais (the winged sons of Boreas), Idmon the Seer (the son of Apollo), Mopsus (the Thessalian prophet).

Before their departure Jason offered a solemn sacrifice to Poseidon and all the other sea-deities; he also invoked the protection of Zeus and the Fates, and then, Mopsus having taken the auguries, and found them auspicious, the heroes stepped on board. And now a favourable breeze having sprung up, they take their allotted places, the anchor is weighed, and the ship glides like a bird out of the harbour into the waters of the great sea.

The Argo, with her brave crew of fifty heroes, was soon out of sight, and the sea-breeze only wafted to the shore a faint echo of the sweet strains of Orpheus.

For a time all went smoothly, but the vessel was soon driven, by stress of weather, to take refuge in a harbour in the island of Lemnos. This island was inhabited by women only, who, the year before, in a fit of mad jealousy, had killed all the male population of the island, with the exception of the father of their queen, Hypsipyle. As the protection of their island now devolved upon themselves they were always on the look-out for danger. When, therefore, they sighted the Argo from afar they armed themselves and rushed to the shore, determined to repel any invasion of their territory.

On arriving in port the Argonauts, astonished at beholding an armed crowd of women, despatched a herald in one of their boats, bearing the staff of peace and friendship. Hypsipyle, the queen, proposed that food and presents should be sent to the strangers, in order to prevent their landing; but her old nurse, who stood beside her, suggested that this would be a good opportunity to provide themselves with noble husbands, who would act as their defenders, and thus put an end to their constant fears. Hypsipyle listened attentively to the advice of her nurse, and after some consultation, decided to invite the strangers into the city. Robed in his purple mantle, the gift of Pallas-Athene, Jason, accompanied by some of his companions, stepped on shore, where he was met by a deputation consisting of the most beautiful of the Lemnian women, and, as commander of the expedition, was invited into the palace of the queen.

When he appeared before Hypsipyle, she was so struck with his godlike and heroic presence that she presented him with her father's sceptre, and invited him to seat himself on the throne beside her. Jason thereupon took up his residence in the royal castle, whilst his companions scattered themselves through the town, spending their time in feasting and pleasure. Heracles, with a few chosen comrades, alone remained on board.

From day to day their departure was delayed, and the Argonauts, in their new life of dissipation, had almost forgotten the object of the expedition, when Heracles suddenly appeared amongst them, and at last recalled them to a sense of their duty.

Giants and Doliones

❧

THE ARGONAUTS NOW PURSUED their voyage, till contrary winds drove them towards an island, inhabited by the Doliones, whose king Cyzicus received them with great kindness and hospitality. The Doliones were descendants of Poseidon, who protected them against the frequent attacks of their fierce and formidable neighbours, the earthborn Giants—monsters with six arms.

Whilst his companions were attending a banquet given by king Cyzicus, Heracles, who, as usual, had remained behind to guard the ship, observed that these Giants were busy blocking up the harbour with huge rocks. He at once realized the danger, and, attacking them with his arrows, succeeded in considerably thinning their numbers; then, assisted by the heroes, who at length came to his aid, he effectually destroyed the remainder.

The Argo now steered out of the harbour and set sail; but in consequence of a severe storm which arose at night, was driven back once more to the shores of the kindly Doliones. Unfortunately, however, owing to the darkness of the night, the inhabitants failed to recognize their former guests, and, mistaking them for enemies, commenced to attack them. Those who had so recently parted as friends were now engaged in mortal combat, and in the battle which ensued, Jason himself pierced to the heart his friend king Cyzicus; whereupon the Doliones, being deprived of their leader, fled to their city and closed the gates. When morning dawned, and both sides perceived their error, they were filled with the deepest sorrow and remorse; and for three days the heroes remained with the Doliones, celebrating the funereal rites of the slain, with every demonstration of mourning and solemnity.

The Argonauts once more set sail, and after a stormy voyage arrived at Mysia, where they were hospitably received by the inhabitants, who spread before them plentiful banquets and sumptuously regaled them.

While his friends were feasting, Heracles, who had declined to join them, went into the forest to seek a fir-tree which he required for an oar, and was missed by his adopted son Hylas, who set out to seek him. When the youth arrived at a spring, in the most secluded part of the forest, the nymph of the fountain was so struck by his beauty that she drew him down beneath the waters, and he was seen no more. Polyphemus, one of the heroes, who happened to be also in the forest, heard his cry for help, and on meeting Heracles informed him of the circumstance. They at once set out in search of the missing youth, no traces of whom were to be found, and whilst they were engaged looking for him, the Argo set sail and left them behind.

The ship had proceeded some distance before the absence of Heracles was observed. Some of the heroes were in favour of returning for him, others wished to proceed on their journey, when, in the midst of the dispute, the sea-god Glaucus arose from the waves, and informed them that it was the will of Zeus that Heracles, having another mission to perform, should remain behind. The Argonauts continued their voyage without their companions; Heracles returned to Argos, whilst Polyphemus remained with the Mysians, where he founded a city and became its king.

Next morning the Argo touched at the country of the Bebrycians, whose king Amycus was a famous pugilist, and permitted no strangers to leave his shores without matching their strength with his. When the heroes, therefore, demanded permission to land, they were informed that they could only do so provided that one of their number should engage in a boxing-match with the king. Pollux, who was the best pugilist in Greece, was selected as their champion, and a contest took place, which, after a tremendous struggle, proved fatal to Amycus, who had hitherto been victorious in all similar encounters.

Harpies and Stymphalides

THEY NOW PROCEEDED towards Bithynia, where reigned the blind old prophet-king Phineus, son of Agenor. Phineus had been punished by the gods with premature old age and blindness for having abused the gift of prophecy. He was also tormented by the Harpies, who swooped down upon his food, which they either devoured or so defiled as to render it unfit to be eaten. This poor old man, trembling with the weakness of age, and faint with hunger, appeared before the Argonauts, and implored their assistance against his fiendish tormentors, whereupon Zetes and Calais, the winged sons of Boreas, recognizing in him the husband of their sister Cleopatra, affectionately embraced him, and promised to rescue him from his painful position.

The heroes prepared a banquet on the sea-shore, to which they invited Phineus; but no sooner had he taken his place, than the Harpies appeared and devoured all the viands. Zetes and Calais now rose up into the air, drove the Harpies away, and were pursuing them with drawn swords, when Iris, the swift-footed messenger of the gods, appeared, and desired them to desist from their work of vengeance, promising that Phineus should be no longer molested.

Freed at length from his tormentors the old man sat down and enjoyed a plentiful repast with his kind friends the Argonauts, who now informed him of the object of their voyage. In gratitude for his deliverance Phineus gave them much useful information concerning their journey, and not only warned them of the manifold dangers awaiting them, but also instructed them how they might be overcome.

After a fortnight's sojourn in Bithynia the Argonauts once more set sail, but had not proceeded far on their course, when they heard a fearful and tremendous crash. This was caused by the meeting of two great rocky islands, called the Symplegades, which floated about in the sea, and constantly met and separated.

Before leaving Bithynia, the blind old seer, Phineus, had informed them that they would be compelled to pass between these terrible rocks, and he instructed them how to do so with safety. As they now approached the scene of danger they remembered his advice, and acted upon it. Typhus, the steersman, stood at the helm, whilst Euphemus held in his hand a dove ready to be let loose; for Phineus had told them that if the dove ventured to fly through, they might safely follow. Euphemus now despatched the bird, which passed swiftly through the islands, yet not without losing some of the feathers of her tail, so speedily did they reunite. Seizing the moment when the rocks once more separated, the Argonauts worked at their oars with all their might, and achieved the perilous passage in safety.

After the miraculous passage of the Argo, the Symplegades became permanently united, and attached to the bottom of the sea.

The Argo pursued her course along the southern coast of the Pontus, and arrived at the island of Aretias, which was inhabited by birds, who, as they flew through the air, discharged from their wings feathers sharp as arrows.

As the ship was gliding along, Oileus was wounded by one of these birds, whereupon the Argonauts held a council, and by the advice of Amphidamas, an experienced hero, all put on their helmets, and held up their glittering shields, uttering, at the same time, such fearful cries that the birds flew away in terror, and the Argonauts were enabled to land with safety on the island.

Here they found four shipwrecked youths, who proved to be the sons of Phryxus, and were greeted by Jason as his cousins. On ascertaining the object of the expedition they volunteered to accompany the Argo, and to show the heroes the way to Colchis. They also informed them that the Golden Fleece was guarded by a fearful dragon, that king Aëtes was extremely cruel, and, as the son of Apollo, was possessed of superhuman strength.

Arrival at Colchis

T**AKING WITH THEM THE FOUR NEW-COMERS** they journeyed on, and soon came in sight of the snow-capped peaks of the Caucasus, when, towards evening, the loud flapping of wings was heard overhead. It was the giant eagle of Prometheus on his way to torture the noble and long-suffering Titan, whose fearful groans soon afterwards fell upon their ears. That night they reached their journey's end, and anchored in the smooth waters of the river Phases. On the left bank of this river they beheld Ceuta, the capital of Colchis; and on their right a wide field, and the sacred grove of Ares, where the Golden Fleece, suspended from a magnificent oak-tree, was glittering in the sun. Jason now filled a golden cup with wine, and offered a libation to mother-earth, the gods of the country, and the shades of those of the heroes who had died on the voyage.

Next morning a council was held, in which it was decided, that before resorting to forcible measures kind and conciliatory overtures should first be made to king Aëtes in order to induce him to resign the Golden Fleece. It was arranged that Jason, with a few chosen companions, should proceed to the royal castle, leaving the remainder of the crew to guard the Argo. Accompanied, therefore, by Telamon and Augeas, and the four sons of Phryxus, he set out for the palace.

When they arrived in sight of the castle they were struck by the vastness and massiveness of the building, at the entrance to which sparkling fountains played in the midst of luxuriant and park-like gardens. Here the king's daughters, Chalciope and Medea, who were walking in the grounds of the palace, met them. The former, to her great joy, recognized in the youths who accompanied the hero her own long-lost sons, whom she had mourned as dead, whilst the young and lovely Medea was struck with the noble and manly form of Jason.

The news of the return of the sons of Phryxus soon spread through the palace, and brought Aëtes himself to the scene, whereupon the strangers were presented to him, and were invited to a banquet which the king ordered to be prepared in their honour. All the most beautiful ladies of the court were present at this entertainment; but in the eyes of Jason none could compare with the king's daughter, the young and lovely Medea.

When the banquet was ended, Jason related to the king his various adventures, and also the object of his expedition, with the circumstances which had led to his undertaking it. Aëtes listened, in silent indignation, to this recital, and then burst out into a torrent of invectives against the Argonauts and his grand-children, declaring that the Fleece was his rightful property, and that on no consideration would he consent to relinquish it. Jason, however, with mild and persuasive words, contrived so far to conciliate him, that he was induced to promise that if the heroes could succeed in demonstrating their divine origin by the performance of some task requiring superhuman power, the Fleece should be theirs.

The task proposed by Aëtes to Jason was that he should yoke the two brazen-footed, fire-breathing oxen of the king (which had been made for him by Hephaestus) to his ponderous iron plough. Having done this he must till with them the stony field of Ares, and then sow in the furrows the poisonous teeth of a dragon, from which armed men would arise. These he must destroy to a man, or he himself would perish at their hands.

When Jason heard what was expected of him, his heart for a moment sank within him; but he determined, nevertheless, not to flinch from his task, but to trust to the assistance of the gods, and to his own courage and energy.

The Field of Ares

ACCOMPANIED BY his two friends, Telamon and Augeas, and also by Argus, the son of Chalciope, Jason returned to the vessel for the purpose of holding a consultation as to the best means of accomplishing these perilous feats.

Argus explained to Jason all the difficulties of the superhuman task which lay before him, and pronounced it as his opinion that the only means by which success was possible was to enlist the assistance of the Princess Medea, who was a priestess of Hecate, and a great enchantress. His suggestion meeting with approval, he returned to the palace, and by the aid of his mother an interview was arranged between Jason and Medea, which took place, at an early hour next morning, in the temple of Hecate.

A confession of mutual attachment took place, and Medea, trembling for her lover's safety, presented him with a magic salve, which possessed the property of rendering any person anointed with it invulnerable for the space of one day against fire and steel, and invincible against any adversary however powerful. With this salve she instructed him to anoint his spear and shield on the day of his great undertaking. She further added that when, after having ploughed the field and sown the teeth, armed men should arise from the furrows, he must on no account lose heart, but remember to throw among them a huge rock, over the possession of which they would fight among themselves, and their attention being thus diverted he would find it an easy task to destroy them. Overwhelmed with gratitude, Jason thanked her, in the most earnest manner, for her wise counsel and timely aid; at the same time he offered her his hand, and promised her he would not return to Greece without taking her with him as his wife.

Next morning Aëtes, in all the pomp of state, surrounded by his family and the members of his court, repaired to a spot whence a full view of the approaching spectacle could be obtained. Soon Jason appeared in the field of Ares, looking as noble and majestic as the god of war himself. In a distant part of the field the brazen yokes and the massive plough met his view, but as yet the dread animals themselves were nowhere to be seen. He was about to go in quest of them, when they suddenly rushed out from a subterranean cave, breathing flames of fire, and enveloped in a thick smoke.

The friends of Jason trembled; but the undaunted hero, relying on the magic powers with which he was imbued by Medea, seized the oxen, one after the other, by the horns, and forced them to the yoke. Near the plough was a helmet full of dragon's teeth, which he sowed as he ploughed the field, whilst with sharp pricks from his lance he compelled the monstrous creatures to draw the plough over the stony ground, which was thus speedily tilled.

While Jason was engaged sowing the dragon's teeth in the deep furrows of the field, he kept a cautious look-out lest the germinating giant brood might grow too quickly for him, and as soon as the four acres of land had been tilled he unyoked the oxen, and succeeded in frightening them so effectually with his weapons, that they rushed back in terror to their subterranean stables. Meanwhile armed men had sprung up out of the furrows, and the whole field now bristled with lances; but Jason, remembering the instructions of Medea, seized an immense rock and hurled it into the midst of these earth-born warriors, who immediately began to attack each other. Jason then rushed furiously upon them, and after a terrible struggle not one of the giants remained alive.

Furious at seeing his murderous schemes thus defeated, Aëtes not only perfidiously refused to give Jason the Fleece which he had so bravely earned, but, in his anger, determined to destroy all the Argonauts, and to burn their vessel.

Jason Secures the Golden Fleece

BECOMING AWARE OF THE TREACHEROUS DESIGNS of her father, Medea at once took measures to baffle them. In the darkness of night she went on board the Argo, and warned the heroes of their approaching danger. She then advised Jason to accompany her without loss of time to the sacred grove, in order to possess himself of the long-coveted treasure. They set out together, and Medea, followed by Jason, led the way, and advanced boldly into the grove. The tall oak-tree was soon discovered, from the topmost boughs of which hung the beautiful Golden Fleece. At the foot of this tree, keeping his ever-wakeful watch, lay the dreadful, sleepless dragon, who at sight of them bounded forward, opening his huge jaws.

Medea now called into play her magic powers, and quietly approaching the monster, threw over him a few drops of a potion, which soon took effect, and sent him into a deep sleep; whereupon Jason, seizing the opportunity, climbed the tree and secured the Fleece. Their perilous task being now accomplished, Jason and Medea quitted the grove, and hastened on board the Argo, which immediately put to sea.

Meanwhile Aëtes, having discovered the loss of his daughter and the Golden Fleece, despatched a large fleet, under the command of his son Absyrtus, in pursuit of the fugitives. After some days' sail they arrived at an island at the mouth of the river Ister, where they found the Argo at anchor, and surrounded her with their numerous ships. They then despatched a herald on board of her, demanding the surrender of Medea and the Fleece.

Medea now consulted Jason, and, with his consent, carried out the following stratagem. She sent a message to her brother Absyrtus, to the effect that she had been carried off against her will, and promised that if he would meet her, in the darkness of night, in the temple of Artemis, she would assist him in regaining possession of the Golden Fleece. Relying on the good faith of his sister, Absyrtus fell into the snare, and duly appeared at the appointed trysting-place; and whilst Medea kept her brother engaged in conversation, Jason rushed forward and slew him. Then, according to a preconcerted signal, he held aloft a lighted torch, whereupon the Argonauts attacked the Colchians, put them to flight, and entirely defeated them.

The Argonauts now returned to their ship, when the prophetic board from the Dodonean oak thus addressed them: "The cruel murder of Absyrtus was witnessed by the Erinyes, and you will not escape the wrath of Zeus until the goddess Circe has purified you from your crime. Let Castor and Pollux pray to the gods that you may be enabled to find the abode of the sorceress." In obedience to the voice, the twin-brothers invoked divine assistance, and the heroes set out in search of the isle of Circe.

The good ship Argo sped on her way, and, after passing safely through the foaming waters of the river Eridanus, at length arrived in the harbour of the island of Circe, where she cast anchor.

Commanding his companions to remain on board, Jason landed with Medea, and conducted her to the palace of the sorceress. The goddess of charms and magic arts received them kindly, and invited them to be seated; but instead of doing so they assumed a supplicating attitude, and humbly besought her protection. They then informed her of the dreadful crime which they had committed, and implored her to purify them from it. This Circe promised to do. She forthwith commanded her attendant Naiads to kindle the fire on the altar, and to prepare everything necessary for the performance of the mystic rites, after which a dog was sacrificed, and the sacred cakes were burned. Having thus duly purified the criminals, she severely reprimanded them for the horrible murder of which they had been guilty; whereupon Medea, with veiled head, and weeping bitterly, was reconducted by Jason to the Argo.

The Voyage Home

HAVING LEFT THE ISLAND of Circe they were wafted by gentle zephyrs towards the abode of the Sirens, whose enticing strains soon fell upon their ears. The Argonauts, powerfully affected by the melody, were making ready to land, when Orpheus perceived the danger, and, to the accompaniment of his magic lyre, commenced one of his enchanting songs, which so completely absorbed his listeners that they passed the island in safety; but not before Butes, one of their number, lured by the seductive music of the Sirens, had sprung from the vessel into the waves below. Aphrodite, however, in pity for his youth, landed him gently on the island of Libibaon before the Sirens could reach him, and there he remained for many years.

And now the Argonauts approached new dangers, for on one side of them seethed and foamed the whirlpool of Charybdis, whilst on the other towered the mighty rock whence the monster Scylla swooped down upon unfortunate mariners; but here the goddess Hera came to their assistance, and sent to them the sea-nymph Thetis, who guided them safely through these dangerous straits.

The Argo next arrived at the island of the Phaeaces, where they were hospitably entertained by King Alcinous and his queen Arete. But the banquet prepared for them by their kind host was unexpectedly interrupted by the appearance of a large army of Colchians, sent by Aëtes to demand the restoration of his daughter.

Medea threw herself at the feet of the queen, and implored her to save her from the anger of her father, and Arete, in her kindness of heart, promised her her protection. Next morning, in an assembly of the people at which the Colchians were invited to be present, the latter were informed that as Medea was the lawful wife of Jason they could not consent to deliver her up; whereupon the Colchians, seeing that the resolution of the king was not to be shaken, and fearing to face the anger of Aëtes should they return to Colchis without her, sought permission of Alcinous to settle in his kingdom, which request was accorded them.

After these events the Argonauts once more set sail, and steered for Iolcus; but, in the course of a terrible and fearful night, a mighty storm arose, and in the morning they found themselves stranded on the treacherous quicksands of Syrtes, on the shores of Libya. Here all was a waste and barren desert, untenanted by any living creature, save the venomous snakes which had sprung from the blood of the Medusa when borne by Perseus over these arid plains.

They had already passed several days in this abode of desolation, beneath the rays of the scorching sun, and had abandoned themselves to the deepest despair, when the Libyan queen, who was a prophetess of divine origin, appeared to Jason, and informed him that a sea-horse would be sent by the gods to act as his guide.

Scarcely had she departed when a gigantic hippocamp was seen in the distance, making its way towards the Argo. Jason now related to his companions the particulars of his interview with the Libyan prophetess, and after some deliberation it was decided to carry the Argo on their shoulders, and to follow wherever the sea-horse should lead them. They then commenced a long and weary journey through the desert, and at last, after twelve days of severe toil and terrible suffering, the welcome sight of the sea greeted their view. In gratitude for having been saved from their manifold dangers they offered up sacrifices to the gods, and launched their ship once more into the deep waters of the ocean.

With heartfelt joy and gladness they proceeded on their homeward voyage, and after some days arrived at the island of Crete, where they purposed to furnish themselves with fresh provisions and water. Their landing, however, was opposed by a terrible giant who guarded the island against all intruders. This giant, whose name was Talus, was the last of the Brazen race, and being formed of brass, was invulnerable, except in his right ankle, where there was a sinew of flesh and a vein of blood. As he saw the Argo nearing the coast, he hurled huge rocks at her, which would inevitably have sunk the vessel had not the crew beat a hasty retreat. Although sadly in want of food and water, the Argonauts had decided to proceed on their journey rather than face so powerful an opponent, when Medea came forward and assured them that if they would trust to her she would destroy the giant.

Enveloped in the folds of a rich purple mantle, she stepped on deck, and after invoking the aid of the Fates, uttered a magic incantation, which had the effect of throwing Talus into a deep sleep. He stretched himself at full length upon the ground, and in doing so grazed his vulnerable ankle against the point of a sharp rock, whereupon a mighty stream of blood gushed forth from the wound. Awakened by the pain, he tried to rise, but in vain, and with a mighty groan of anguish the giant fell dead, and his enormous body rolled heavily over into the deep. The heroes being now able to land, provisioned their vessel, after which they resumed their homeward voyage.

After a terrible night of storm and darkness they passed the island of Aegina, and at length reached in safety the port of Iolcus, where the recital of their numerous adventures and hair-breadth escapes was listened to with wondering admiration by their fellow-countrymen.

The Argo was consecrated to Poseidon, and was carefully preserved for many generations till no vestige of it remained, when it was placed in the heavens as a brilliant constellation.

On his arrival at Iolcus, Jason conducted his beautiful bride to the palace of his uncle Pelias, taking with him the Golden Fleece, for the sake of which this perilous expedition had been undertaken. But the old king, who had never expected that Jason would return alive, basely refused to fulfil his part of the compact, and declined to abdicate the throne.

Indignant at the wrongs of her husband, Medea avenged them in a most shocking manner. She made friends with the daughters of the king, and feigned great interest in all their concerns. Having gained their confidence, she informed them, that among her numerous magic arts, she possessed the power of restoring to the aged all the vigour and strength of youth, and in order to give them a convincing proof of the truth of her assertion, she cut up an old ram, which she boiled in a cauldron, whereupon, after uttering various mystic incantations, there came forth from the vessel a beautiful young lamb. She then assured them, that in a similar manner they could restore to their old father his former youthful frame and vigour. The fond and credulous daughters of Pelias lent an all too willing ear to the wicked sorceress, and thus the old king perished at the hands of his innocent children.

Medea and Jason now fled to Corinth, where at length they found, for a time, peace and tranquillity, their happiness being completed by the birth of three children.

As time passed on, however, and Medea began to lose the beauty which had won the love of her husband, he grew weary of her, and became attracted by the youthful charms of Glauce, the beautiful daughter of Creon, king of Corinth. Jason had obtained her father's consent to their union, and the wedding-day was already fixed, before he disclosed to Medea the treachery which he meditated against her. He used all his persuasive powers in order to induce her to consent to his union with Glauce, assuring her that his affection had in no way diminished, but that for the sake of the advantages which would thereby accrue to their children, he had decided on forming this alliance with the royal house. Though justly enraged at his deceitful conduct, Medea dissembled her wrath, and, feigning to be satisfied with this explanation, sent, as a wedding-gift to her rival, a magnificent robe of cloth-of-gold. This robe was imbued with a deadly poison which penetrated to the flesh and bone of the wearer, and burned them as though with a consuming fire. Pleased with the beauty and costliness of the garment, the unsuspecting Glauce lost no time in donning it; but no sooner had she done so than the fell poison began to take effect. In vain she tried to tear the robe away; it defied all efforts to be removed, and after horrible and protracted sufferings, she expired.

Maddened at the loss of her husband's love Medea next put to death her three sons, and when Jason, thirsting for revenge, left the chamber of his dead bride, and flew to his own house in search of Medea, the ghastly spectacle of his murdered children met his view. He rushed frantically to seek the murderess, but nowhere could she be found. At length, hearing a sound above his head, he looked up, and beheld Medea gliding through the air in a golden chariot drawn by dragons.

In a fit of despair Jason threw himself on his own sword, and perished on the threshold of his desolate and deserted home.

Tales of Heracles

SON OF ZEUS, father of the Greek Gods, and Alcmene, a human, Heracles was born a mortal who could feel pain, but was possessed with immense strength, courage and intelligence; a man who bridged the gap between mortals and gods. As such, tales of his extraordinary life are legendary and his twelve labours rank as the most incredible of all. As penance for the murder of his children in a fit of insanity brought on by Hera – Zeus' queen who was jealous of Heracles – Heracles was forced to serve his cousin, the spiteful and cowardly King Eurystheus of Argos, for 12 years, performing any tasks that were asked of him, no matter how deadly and perilous. If Heracles could do this, his soul would be purified and he would earn immortality.

Young Heracles

T THE TIME OF HIS BIRTH Alcmene was living at Thebes with her husband Amphitryon, and thus the infant Heracles was born in the palace of his stepfather.

Aware of the animosity with which Hera persecuted all those who rivalled her in the affections of Zeus, Alcmene, fearful lest this hatred should be visited on her innocent child, entrusted him, soon after his birth, to the care of a faithful servant, with instructions to expose him in a certain field, and there leave him, feeling assured that the divine offspring of Zeus would not long remain without the protection of the gods.

Soon after the child had been thus abandoned, Hera and Pallas-Athene happened to pass by the field, and were attracted by its cries. Athene pityingly took up the infant in her arms, and prevailed upon the queen of heaven to put it to her breast; but no sooner had she done so, than the child, causing her pain, she angrily threw him to the ground, and left the spot. Athene, moved with compassion, carried him to Alcmene, and entreated her kind offices on behalf of the poor little foundling. Alcmene at once recognized her child, and joyfully accepted the charge.

Soon afterwards Hera, to her extreme annoyance, discovered whom she had nursed, and became filled with jealous rage. She now sent two venomous snakes into the chamber of Alcmene, which crept, unperceived by the nurses, to the cradle of the sleeping child. He awoke with a cry, and grasping a snake in each hand, strangled them both. Alcmene and her attendants, whom the cry of the child had awakened, rushed to the cradle, where, to their astonishment and terror, they beheld the two reptiles dead in the hands of the infant Heracles. Amphitryon was also attracted to the chamber by the commotion, and when he beheld this astounding proof of supernatural strength, he declared that the child must have been sent to him as a special gift from Zeus. He accordingly consulted the famous seer Tiresias, who now informed him of the divine origin of his stepson, and prognosticated for him a great and distinguished future.

When Amphitryon heard the noble destiny which awaited the child entrusted to his care, he resolved to educate him in a manner worthy of his future career. At a suitable age he himself taught him how to guide a chariot; Eurytus, how to handle the bow; Autolycus, dexterity in wrestling and boxing; and Castor, the art of armed warfare; whilst Linus, the son of Apollo, instructed him in music and letters.

Heracles was an apt pupil; but undue harshness was intolerable to his high spirit, and old Linus, who was not the gentlest of teachers, one day corrected him with blows, whereupon the boy angrily took up his lyre, and, with one stroke of his powerful arm, killed his tutor on the spot.

Apprehensive lest the ungovernable temper of the youth might again involve him in similar acts of violence, Amphitryon sent him into the country, where he placed him under the charge of one of his most trusted herdsmen. Here, as he grew up to manhood, his extraordinary stature and strength became the wonder and admiration of all beholders. His aim, whether with spear, lance, or bow, was unerring, and at the age of eighteen he was considered to be the strongest as well as the most beautiful youth in all Greece.

Heracles felt that the time had now arrived when it became necessary to decide for himself how to make use of the extraordinary powers with which he had been endowed by the gods; and in order to meditate in solitude on this all-important subject, he repaired to a lonely and secluded spot in the heart of the forest.

Here two females of great beauty appeared to him. One was Vice, the other Virtue. The former was full of artificial wiles and fascinating arts, her face painted and her dress gaudy and attractive; whilst the latter was of noble bearing and modest mien, her robes of spotless purity.

Vice stepped forward and thus addressed him: "If you will walk in my paths, and make me your friend, your life shall be one round of pleasure and enjoyment. You shall taste of every delight which can be procured on earth; the choicest viands, the most delicious wines, the most luxuriant of couches shall be ever at your disposal; and all this without any exertion on your part, either physical or mental."

Virtue now spoke in her turn: "If you will follow me and be my friend, I promise you the reward of a good conscience, and the love and respect of your fellowmen. I cannot undertake to smooth your path with roses, or to give you a life of idleness and pleasure; for you must know that the gods grant no good and desirable thing that is not earned by labour; and as you sow, so must you reap."

Heracles listened patiently and attentively to both speakers, and then, after mature deliberation, decided to follow in the paths of virtue, and henceforth to honour the gods, and to devote his life to the service of his country.

Full of these noble resolves he sought once more his rural home, where he was informed that on Mount Cithaeron, at the foot of which the herds of Amphitryon were grazing, a ferocious lion had fixed his lair, and was committing such frightful ravages among the flocks and herds that he had become the scourge and terror of the whole neighbourhood. Heracles at once armed himself and ascended the mountain, where he soon caught sight of the lion, and rushing at him with his sword succeeded in killing him. The hide of the animal he wore ever afterwards over his shoulders, and the head served him as a helmet.

As he was returning from this, his first exploit, he met the heralds of Erginus, king of the Minyans, who were proceeding to Thebes to demand their annual tribute of 100 oxen. Indignant at this humiliation of his native city, Heracles mutilated the heralds, and sent them back, with ropes round their necks, to their royal master.

Erginus was so incensed at the ill-treatment of his messengers that he collected an army and appeared before the gates of Thebes, demanding the surrender of Heracles. Creon, who was at this time king of Thebes, fearing the consequences of a refusal, was about to yield, when the hero, with the assistance of Amphitryon and a band of brave youths, advanced against the Minyans.

Heracles took possession of a narrow defile through which the enemy were compelled to pass, and as they entered the pass the Thebans fell upon them, killed their king Erginus, and completely routed them. In this engagement Amphitryon, the kind friend and foster-father of Heracles, lost his life. The hero now advanced upon Orchomenus, the capital of the Minyans, where he burned the royal castle and sacked the town.

After this signal victory all Greece rang with the fame of the young hero, and Creon, in gratitude for his great services, bestowed upon him his daughter Megara in marriage. The Olympian gods testified their appreciation of his valour by sending him presents; Hermes gave him a sword, Phoebus-Apollo a bundle of arrows, Hephaestus a golden quiver, and Athene a coat of leather.

Heracles and Eurystheus

❦

AND NOW IT WILL BE NECESSARY to retrace our steps. Just before the birth of Heracles, Zeus, in an assembly of the gods, exultingly declared that the child who should be born on that day to the house of Perseus should rule over all his race. When Hera heard her lord's boastful announcement she knew well that it was for the child of the hated Alcmene that this brilliant destiny was designed; and in order to rob the son of her rival of his rights, she called to her aid the goddess Eilithyia, who retarded the birth of Heracles, and caused his cousin Eurystheus (another grandson of Perseus) to precede him into the world. And thus, as the word of the mighty Zeus was irrevocable, Heracles became the subject and servant of his cousin Eurystheus.

When, after his splendid victory over Erginus, the fame of Heracles spread throughout Greece, Eurystheus (who had become king of Mycenae), jealous of the reputation of the young hero, asserted his rights, and commanded him to undertake for him various difficult tasks. But the proud spirit of the hero rebelled against this humiliation, and he was about to refuse compliance, when Zeus appeared to him and desired him not to rebel against the Fates. Heracles now repaired to Delphi in order to consult the oracle, and received the answer that after performing ten tasks for his cousin Eurystheus his servitude would be at an end.

Soon afterwards Heracles fell into a state of the deepest melancholy, and through the influence of his inveterate enemy, the goddess Hera, this despondency developed into raving madness, in which condition he killed his own children. When he at length regained his reason he was so horrified and grieved at what he had done, that he shut himself up in his chamber and avoided all intercourse with men. But in his loneliness and seclusion the conviction that work would be the best means of procuring oblivion of the past decided him to enter, without delay, upon the tasks appointed him by Eurystheus.

12 Tasks: The Nemean Lion

HIS FIRST TASK was to bring to Eurystheus the skin of the much-dreaded Nemean lion, which ravaged the territory between Cleone and Nemea, and whose hide was invulnerable against any mortal weapon.

Heracles proceeded to the forest of Nemea, where, having discovered the lion's lair, he attempted to pierce him with his arrows; but finding these of no avail he felled him to the ground with his club, and before the animal had time to recover from the terrible blow, Heracles seized him by the neck and, with a mighty effort, succeeded in strangling him. He then made himself a coat of mail of the skin, and a new helmet of the head of the animal. Thus attired, he so alarmed Eurystheus by appearing suddenly before him, that the king concealed himself in his palace, and henceforth forbade Heracles to enter his presence, but commanded him to receive his behests, for the future, through his messenger Copreus.

12 Tasks: The Hydra

HIS SECOND TASK was to slay the Hydra, a monster serpent (the offspring of Typhon and Echidna), bristling with nine heads, one of which was immortal. This monster infested the neighbourhood of Lerna, where she committed great depredations among the herds.

Heracles, accompanied by his nephew Iolaus, set out in a chariot for the marsh of Lerna, in the slimy waters of which he found her.

He commenced the attack by assailing her with his fierce arrows, in order to force her to leave her lair, from which she at length emerged, and sought refuge in a wood on a neighbouring hill. Heracles now rushed forward and endeavoured to crush her heads by means of well-directed blows from his tremendous club; but no sooner was one head destroyed than it was immediately replaced by two others. He next seized the monster in his powerful grasp; but at this juncture a giant crab came to the assistance of the Hydra and commenced biting the feet of her assailant. Heracles destroyed this new adversary with his club, and now called upon his nephew to come to his aid. At his command Iolaus set fire to the neighbouring trees, and, with a burning branch, seared the necks of the monster as Heracles cut them off, thus effectually preventing the growth of more. Heracles next struck off the immortal head, which he buried by the road-side, and placed over it a heavy stone. Into the poisonous blood of the monster he then dipped his arrows, which ever afterwards rendered wounds inflicted by them incurable.

12 Tasks: The Horned Hind

THE THIRD LABOUR OF HERACLES was to bring the horned hind Cerunitis alive to Mycenae. This animal, which was sacred to Artemis, had golden antlers and hoofs of brass.

Not wishing to wound the hind Heracles patiently pursued her through many countries for a whole year, and overtook her at last on the banks of the river Ladon; but even there he was compelled, in order to secure her, to wound her with one of his arrows, after which he lifted her on his shoulders and carried her through Arcadia. On his way he met Artemis with her brother Phoebus-Apollo, when the goddess angrily reproved him for wounding her favourite hind; but Heracles succeeded in appeasing her displeasure, whereupon she permitted him to take the animal alive to Mycenae.

12 Tasks: The Erymanthian Boar

THE FOURTH TASK imposed upon Heracles by Eurystheus was to bring alive to Mycenae the Erymanthian boar, which had laid waste the region of Erymantia, and was the scourge of the surrounding neighbourhood.

On his way thither he craved food and shelter of a Centaur named Pholus, who received him with generous hospitality, setting before him a good and plentiful repast. When Heracles expressed his surprise that at such a well-furnished board wine should be wanting, his host explained that the wine cellar was the common property of all the Centaurs, and that it was against the rules for a cask to be broached, except all were present to partake of it. By dint of persuasion, however, Heracles prevailed on his kind host to make an exception in his favour; but the powerful, luscious odour of the good old wine soon spread over the mountains, and brought large numbers of Centaurs to the spot, all armed with huge rocks and fir-trees. Heracles drove them back with fire-brands, and then, following up his victory, pursued them with his arrows as far as Malea, where they took refuge in the cave of the kind old Centaur Chiron. Unfortunately, however, as Heracles was shooting at them with his poisoned darts, one of these pierced the knee of Chiron. When Heracles discovered that it was the friend of his early days that he had wounded, he was overcome with sorrow and regret. He at once extracted the arrow, and anointed the wound with a salve, the virtue of which had been taught him by Chiron himself. But all his efforts were unavailing. The wound, imbued with the deadly poison of the Hydra, was incurable, and so great was the agony of Chiron that, at the intercession of Heracles, death was sent him by the gods; for otherwise, being immortal, he would have been doomed to endless suffering.

Pholus, who had so kindly entertained Heracles, also perished by means of one of these arrows, which he had extracted from the body of a dead Centaur. While he was quietly examining it, astonished that so small and insignificant an object should be productive of such serious results, the arrow fell upon his foot and fatally wounded him. Full of grief at this untoward event, Heracles buried him with due honours, and then set out to chase the boar.

With loud shouts and terrible cries he first drove him out of the thickets into the deep snow-drifts which covered the summit of the mountain, and then, having at length wearied him with his incessant pursuit, he captured the exhausted animal, bound him with a rope, and brought him alive to Mycenae.

12 Tasks: The Augean Stables

AFTER SLAYING the Erymanthian boar Eurystheus commanded Heracles to cleanse in one day the stables of Augeas.

Augeas was a king of Elis who was very rich in herds. Three thousand of his cattle he kept near the royal palace in an enclosure where the refuse had accumulated for many years. When Heracles presented himself before the king, and offered to cleanse his stables in one day, provided he should receive in return a tenth part of the herds, Augeas, thinking the feat impossible, accepted his offer in the presence of his son Phyleus.

Near the palace were the two rivers Peneus and Alpheus, the streams of which Heracles conducted into the stables by means of a trench which he dug for this purpose, and as the waters rushed through the shed, they swept away with them the whole mass of accumulated filth.

But when Augeas heard that this was one of the labours imposed by Eurystheus, he refused the promised guerdon. Heracles brought the matter before a court, and called Phyleus as a witness to the justice of his claim, whereupon Augeas, without waiting for the delivery of the verdict, angrily banished Heracles and his son from his dominions.

12 Tasks: The Stymphalian Birds

THE SIXTH TASK was to chase away the Stymphalides, which were immense birds of prey who, as we have seen (in the legend of the Argonauts), shot from their wings feathers sharp as arrows. The home of these birds was on the shore of the lake Stymphalis, in Arcadia (after which they were called), where they caused great destruction among men and cattle.

On approaching the lake, Heracles observed great numbers of them; and, while hesitating how to commence the attack, he suddenly felt a hand on his shoulder. Looking round he beheld the majestic form of Pallas-Athene, who held in her hand a gigantic pair of brazen clappers made by Hephaestus, with which she presented him; whereupon he ascended to the summit of a neighbouring hill, and commenced to rattle them violently. The shrill noise of these instruments was so intolerable to the birds that they rose into the air in terror, upon which he aimed at them with his arrows, destroying them in great numbers, whilst such as escaped his darts flew away, never to return.

12 Tasks: The Cretan Bull

THE SEVENTH LABOUR of Heracles was to capture the Cretan bull. Minos, king of Crete, having vowed to sacrifice to Poseidon any animal which should first appear out of the sea, the god caused a magnificent bull to emerge from the waves in order to test the sincerity of the Cretan king, who, in making this vow, had alleged that he possessed no animal, among his own herds, worthy the acceptance of the mighty sea-god. Charmed with the splendid animal sent by Poseidon, and eager to possess it, Minos placed it among his herds, and substituted as a sacrifice one of his own bulls. Hereupon Poseidon, in order to punish the cupidity of Minos, caused the animal to become mad, and commit such great havoc in the island as to endanger the safety of the inhabitants. When Heracles, therefore, arrived in Crete for the purpose of capturing the bull, Minos, far from opposing his design, gladly gave him permission to do so.

The hero not only succeeded in securing the animal, but tamed him so effectually that he rode on his back right across the sea as far as the Peloponnesus. He now delivered him up to Eurystheus, who at once set him at liberty, after which he became as ferocious and wild as before, roamed all over Greece into Arcadia, and was eventually killed by Theseus on the plains of Marathon.

12 Tasks: The Mares of Diomedes

THE EIGHTH LABOUR of Heracles was to bring to Eurystheus the mares of Diomedes, a son of Ares, and king of the Bistonians, a warlike Thracian tribe. This king possessed a breed of wild horses of tremendous size and strength, whose food consisted of human flesh, and all strangers who had the misfortune to enter the country were made prisoners and flung before the horses, who devoured them.

When Heracles arrived he first captured the cruel Diomedes himself, and then threw him before his own mares, who, after devouring their master, became perfectly tame and tractable. They were then led by Heracles to the sea-shore, when the Bistonians, enraged at the loss of their king, rushed after the hero and attacked him. He now gave the animals in charge of his friend Abderus, and made such a furious onslaught on his assailants that they turned and fled.

But on his return from this encounter he found, to his great grief, that the mares had torn his friend in pieces and devoured him. After celebrating due funereal rites to the unfortunate Abderus, Heracles built a city in his honour, which he named after him. He then returned to Tiryns, where he delivered up the mares to Eurystheus, who set them loose on Mount Olympus, where they became the prey of wild beasts.

It was after the performance of this task that Heracles joined the Argonauts in their expedition to gain possession of the Golden Fleece, and was left behind at Chios, as already narrated. During his wanderings he undertook his ninth labour, which was to bring to Eurystheus the girdle of Hippolyte, queen of the Amazons.

12 Tasks: The Girdle of Hippolyte

THE AMAZONS, who dwelt on the shores of the Black Sea, near the river Thermodon, were a nation of warlike women, renowned for their strength, courage, and great skill in horsemanship. Their queen, Hippolyte, had received from her father, Ares, a beautiful girdle, which she always wore as a sign of her royal power and authority, and it was this girdle which Heracles was required to place in the hands of Eurystheus, who designed it as a gift for his daughter Admete.

Foreseeing that this would be a task of no ordinary difficulty the hero called to his aid a select band of brave companions, with whom he embarked for the Amazonian town Themiscyra. Here they were met by queen Hippolyte, who was so impressed by the extraordinary stature and noble bearing of Heracles that, on learning his errand, she at once consented to present him with the coveted girdle. But Hera, his implacable enemy, assuming the form of an Amazon, spread the report in the town that a stranger was about to carry off their queen. The Amazons at once flew to arms and mounted their horses, whereupon a battle ensued, in which many of their bravest warriors were killed or wounded. Among the latter was their most skilful leader, Melanippe, whom Heracles afterwards restored to Hippolyte, receiving the girdle in exchange.

On his voyage home the hero stopped at Troy, where a new adventure awaited him.

During the time that Apollo and Poseidon were condemned by Zeus to a temporary servitude on earth, they built for king Laomedon the famous walls of Troy, afterwards so renowned in history; but when their work was completed the king treacherously refused to give them the reward due to them. The incensed deities now combined to punish the offender. Apollo sent a pestilence which decimated the people, and Poseidon a flood, which bore with it a marine monster, who swallowed in his huge jaws all that came within his reach.

In his distress Laomedon consulted an oracle, and was informed that only by the sacrifice of his own daughter Hesione could the anger of the gods be appeased. Yielding at length to the urgent appeals of his people he consented to make the sacrifice, and on the arrival of Heracles the maiden was already chained to a rock in readiness to be devoured by the monster.

When Laomedon beheld the renowned hero, whose marvellous feats of strength and courage had become the wonder and admiration of all mankind, he earnestly implored him to save his daughter from her impending fate, and to rid the country of the monster, holding out to him as a reward the horses which Zeus had presented to his grandfather Tros in compensation for robbing him of his son Ganymede.

Heracles unhesitatingly accepted the offer, and when the monster appeared, opening his terrible jaws to receive his prey, the hero, sword in hand, attacked and slew him. But the perfidious monarch once more broke faith, and Heracles, vowing future vengeance, departed for Mycenae, where he presented the girdle to Eurystheus.

12 Tasks: The Oxen of Geryon

THE TENTH LABOUR of Heracles was the capture of the magnificent oxen belonging to the giant Geryon or Geryones, who dwelt on the island of Erythia in the bay of Gadria (Cadiz). This giant, who was the son of Chrysaor, had three bodies with three heads, six hands, and six feet. He possessed a herd of splendid cattle, which were famous for their size, beauty, and rich red colour. They were guarded by another giant named Eurytion, and a two-headed dog called Orthrus, the offspring of Typhon and Echidna.

In choosing for him a task so replete with danger, Eurystheus was in hopes that he might rid himself for ever of his hated cousin. But the indomitable courage of the hero rose with the prospect of this difficult and dangerous undertaking.

After a long and wearisome journey he at last arrived at the western coast of Africa, where, as a monument of his perilous expedition, he erected the famous "Pillars of Hercules," one of which he placed on each side of the Straits of Gibraltar. Here he found the intense heat so insufferable that he angrily raised his bow towards heaven, and threatened to shoot the sun-god. But Helios, far from being incensed at his audacity, was so struck with admiration at his daring that he lent to him the golden boat with which he accomplished his nocturnal transit from West to East, and thus Heracles crossed over safely to the island of Erythia.

No sooner had he landed than Eurytion, accompanied by his savage dog Orthrus, fiercely attacked him; but Heracles, with a superhuman effort, slew the dog and then his master. Hereupon he collected the herd, and was proceeding to the sea-shore when Geryones himself met him, and a desperate encounter took place, in which the giant perished.

Heracles then drove the cattle into the sea, and seizing one of the oxen by the horns, swam with them over to the opposite coast of Iberia (Spain). Then driving his magnificent prize before him through Gaul, Italy, Illyria, and Thrace, he at length arrived, after many perilous adventures and hair-breadth escapes, at Mycenae, where he delivered them up to Eurystheus, who sacrificed them to Hera.

Heracles had now executed his ten tasks, which had been accomplished in the space of eight years; but Eurystheus refused to include the slaying of the Hydra and the cleansing of the stables of Augeas among the number, alleging as a reason that the one had been performed by the assistance of Iolaus, and that the other had been executed for hire. He therefore insisted on Heracles substituting two more labours in their place.

12 Tasks: The Apples of the Hesperides

THE ELEVENTH TASK imposed by Eurystheus was to bring him the golden apples of the Hesperides, which grew on a tree presented by Gaea to Hera, on the occasion of her marriage with Zeus. This sacred tree was guarded by four maidens, daughters of Night, called the Hesperides, who were assisted in their task by a terrible hundred-headed dragon. This dragon never slept, and out of its hundred throats came a constant hissing sound, which effectually warned off all intruders. But what rendered the undertaking still more difficult was the complete ignorance of the hero as to the locality of the garden, and he was forced, in consequence, to make many fruitless journeys and to undergo many trials before he could find it.

He first travelled through Thessaly and arrived at the river Echedorus, where he met the giant Cycnus, the son of Ares and Pyrene, who challenged him to single combat. In this encounter Heracles completely vanquished his opponent, who was killed in the contest; but now a mightier adversary appeared on the scene, for the war-god himself came to avenge his son. A terrible struggle ensued, which had lasted some time, when Zeus interfered between the brothers, and put an end to the strife by hurling a thunderbolt between them. Heracles proceeded on his journey, and reached the banks of the river Eridanus, where dwelt the Nymphs, daughters of Zeus and Themis. On seeking advice from them as to his route, they directed him to the old sea-god Nereus, who alone knew the way to the Garden of the Hesperides. Heracles found him asleep, and seizing the opportunity, held him so firmly in his powerful grasp that he could not possibly escape, so that notwithstanding his various metamorphoses he was at last compelled to give the information required. The hero then crossed over to Libya, where he engaged in a wrestling-match with king Anteos, son of Poseidon and Gaea, which terminated fatally for his antagonist.

From thence he proceeded to Egypt, where reigned Busiris, another son of Poseidon, who (acting on the advice given by an oracle during a time of great scarcity) sacrificed all strangers to Zeus. When Heracles arrived he was seized and dragged to the altar; but the powerful demi-god burst asunder his bonds, and then slew Busiris and his son.

Resuming his journey he now wandered on through Arabia until he arrived at Mount Caucasus, where Prometheus groaned in unceasing agony. It was at this time that Heracles (as already related) shot the eagle which had so long tortured the noble and devoted friend of mankind. Full of gratitude for his deliverance, Prometheus instructed him how to find his way to that remote region in the far West where Atlas supported the heavens on his shoulders, near which lay the Garden of the Hesperides. He also warned Heracles not to attempt to secure the precious fruit himself, but to assume for a time the duties of Astlas, and to despatch him for the apples.

On arriving at his destination Heracles followed the advice of Prometheus. Atlas, who willingly entered into the arrangement, contrived to put the dragon to sleep, and then, having cunningly outwitted the Hesperides, carried off three of the golden apples, which he now brought to Heracles. But when the latter was prepared to relinquish his burden, Atlas, having once tasted the delights of freedom, declined to resume his post, and announced his intention of being himself the bearer of the apples to Eurystheus, leaving Heracles to fill his place. To this proposal the hero feigned assent, merely begging that Atlas would be kind enough to support the heavens for a few moments whilst he contrived a pad for his head. Atlas good-naturedly threw down the apples and once more resumed his load, upon which Heracles bade him adieu, and departed.

When Heracles conveyed the golden apples to Eurystheus the latter presented them to the hero, whereupon Heracles placed the sacred fruit on the altar of Pallas-Athene, who restored them to the garden of the Hesperides.

12 Tasks: Cerberus

THE TWELFTH AND LAST LABOUR which Eurystheus imposed on Heracles was to bring up Cerberus from the lower world, believing that all his heroic powers would be unavailing in the Realm of Shades, and that in this, his last and most perilous undertaking, the hero must at length succumb and perish.

Cerberus was a monster dog with three heads, out of whose awful jaws dripped poison; the hair of his head and back was formed of venomous snakes, and his body terminated in the tail of a dragon.

After being initiated into the Eleusinian Mysteries, and obtaining from the priests certain information necessary for the accomplishment of his task, Heracles set out for Taenarum in Lacolia, where there was an opening which led to the under-world. Conducted by Hermes, he commenced his descent into the awful gulf, where myriads of shades soon began to appear, all of whom fled in terror at his approach, Meleager and Medusa alone excepted. About to strike the latter with his sword, Hermes interfered and stayed his hand, reminding him that she was but a shadow, and that consequently no weapon could avail against her.

Arrived before the gates of Hades he found Theseus and Pirithöus, who had been fixed to an enchanted rock by Aïdes for their presumption in endeavouring to carry off Persephone. When they saw Heracles they implored him to set them free. The hero succeeded in delivering Theseus, but when he endeavoured to liberate Pirithöus, the earth shook so violently beneath him that he was compelled to relinquish his task.

Proceeding further Heracles recognized Ascalaphus, who, as we have seen in the history of Demeter, had revealed the fact that Persephone had swallowed the seeds of a pomegranate offered to her by her husband, which bound her to Aïdes for ever. Ascalaphus was groaning beneath a huge rock which Demeter in her anger had hurled upon him, and which Heracles now removed, releasing the sufferer.

Before the gates of his palace stood Aïdes the mighty ruler of the lower world, and barred his entrance; but Heracles, aiming at him with one of his unerring darts, shot him in the shoulder, so that for the first time the god experienced the agony of mortal suffering. Heracles then demanded of him permission to take Cerberus to the upper-world, and to this Aïdes consented on condition that he should secure him unarmed. Protected by his breastplate and lion's skin Heracles went in search of the monster, whom he found at the mouth of the river Acheron. Undismayed by the hideous barking which proceeded from his three heads, he seized the throat with one hand and the legs with the other, and although the dragon which served him as a tail bit him severely, he did not relinquish his grasp. In this manner he conducted him to the upper-world, through an opening near Troezen in Argolia.

When Eurystheus beheld Cerberus he stood aghast, and despairing of ever getting rid of his hated rival, he returned the hell-hound to the hero, who restored him to Aïdes, and with this last task the subjection of Heracles to Eurystheus terminated.

Heracles' Freedom

FREE AT LAST Heracles now returned to Thebes; and it being impossible for him to live happily with Megara in consequence of his having murdered her children he, with her own consent, gave her in marriage to his nephew Iolaus. Heracles himself sought the hand of Iole, daughter of Eurytus, king of Oechalia, who had instructed him when a boy in the use of the bow. Hearing that this king had promised to give his daughter to him who could surpass himself and his three sons in shooting with the bow, Heracles lost no time in presenting himself as a competitor. He soon proved that he was no unworthy pupil of Eurytus, for he signally defeated all his opponents. But although the king treated him with marked respect and honour he refused, nevertheless, to give him the hand of his daughter, fearing for her a similar fate to that which had befallen Megara. Iphitus, the eldest son of Eurytus, alone espoused the cause of Heracles, and essayed to induce his father to give his consent to the marriage; but all to no purpose, and at length, stung to the quick at his rejection, the hero angrily took his departure.

Soon afterwards the oxen of the king were stolen by the notorious thief Autolycus, and Heracles was suspected by Eurytus of having committed the theft. But Iphitus loyally defended his absent friend, and proposed to seek out Heracles, and with his assistance to go in search of the missing cattle.

The hero warmly welcomed his staunch young friend, and entered cordially into his plan. They at once set out on their expedition; but their search proved altogether unsuccessful. When they approached the city of Tiryns they mounted a tower in hopes of discovering the missing herd in the surrounding country; but as they stood on the topmost summit of the building, Heracles became suddenly seized with one of his former attacks of madness, and mistaking his friend Iphitus for an enemy, hurled him down into the plain below, and he was killed on the spot.

Heracles now set forth on a weary pilgrimage, begging in vain that someone would purify him from the murder of Iphitus. It was during these wanderings that he arrived at the palace of his friend Admetus, whose beautiful and heroic wife (Alcestes) he restored to her husband after a terrible struggle with Death, as already related.

Soon after this event Heracles was struck with a fearful disease, and betook himself to the temple of Delphi, hoping to obtain from the oracle the means of relief. The priestess, however, refused him a response on the ground of his having murdered Iphitus, whereupon the angry hero seized upon the tripod, which he carried off, declaring that he would construct an oracle for himself. Apollo, who witnessed the sacrilege, came down to defend his sanctuary, and a violent struggle ensued. Zeus once more interfered, and, flashing his lightnings between his two favourite sons, ended the combat. The Pythia now vouchsafed an answer to the prayer of the hero, and commanded him, in expiation of his crime, to allow himself to be sold by Hermes for three years as a slave, the purchase-money to be given to Eurytus in compensation for the loss of his son.

Heracles bowed in submission to the divine will, and was conducted by Hermes to Omphale, queen of Lydia. The three talents which she paid for him were given to Eurytus, who, however, declined to accept the money, which was handed over to the children of Iphitus.

Heracles now regained his former vigour. He rid the territory of Omphale of the robbers which infested it and performed for her various other services requiring strength and courage. It was about this time that he took part in the Calydonian boar-hunt, details of which have already been given.

When Omphale learned that her slave was none other than the renowned Heracles himself she at once gave him his liberty, and offered him her hand and kingdom. In her palace Heracles abandoned himself to all the enervating luxuries of an oriental life, and so completely was the great hero enthralled by the fascination which his mistress exercised over him, that whilst she playfully donned his lion's skin and helmet, he, attired in female garments, sat at her feet spinning wool, and beguiling the time by the relation of his past adventures.

But when at length, his term of bondage having expired, he became master of his own actions, the manly and energetic spirit of the hero reasserted itself, and tearing himself away from the palace of the Maeonian queen, he determined to carry out the revenge he had so long meditated against the treacherous Laomedon and the faithless Augeas.

Gathering round him some of his old brave companions-in-arms, Heracles collected a fleet of vessels and set sail for Troy, where he landed, took the city by storm, and killed Laomedon, who thus met at length the retribution he had so richly deserved.

To Telamon, one of his bravest followers, he gave Hesione, the daughter of the king, in marriage. When Heracles gave her permission to release one of the prisoners of war she chose her own brother Podarces, whereupon she was informed that as he was already a prisoner of war she would be compelled to ransom him. On hearing this Hesione took off her golden diadem, which she joyfully handed to the hero. Owing to this circumstance Podarces henceforth bore the name of Priamus (or Priam), which signifies the "ransomed one."

Heracles now marched against Augeas to execute his vengeance on him also for his perfidious conduct. He stormed the city of Elis and put to death Augeas and his sons, sparing only his brave advocate and staunch defender Phyleus, on whom he bestowed the vacant throne of his father.

Heracles now proceeded to Calydon, where he wooed the beautiful Deianeira, daughter of Oeneus, king of Aetolia; but he encountered a formidable rival in Achelous, the river-god, and it was agreed that their claims should be decided by single combat. Trusting to his power of assuming various forms at will, Achelous felt confident of success; but this availed him nothing, for having at last transformed himself into a bull, his mighty adversary broke off one of his horns, and compelled him to acknowledge himself defeated.

After passing three happy years with Deianeira an unfortunate accident occurred, which for a time marred their felicity. Heracles was one day present at a banquet given by Oeneus, when, by a sudden swing of his hand, he had the misfortune to strike on the head a youth of noble birth, who, according to the custom of the ancients, was serving the guests at table, and so violent was the blow that it caused his death. The father of the unfortunate youth, who had witnessed the occurrence, saw that it was the result of accident, and therefore absolved the hero from blame. But Heracles resolved to act according to the law of the land, banished himself from the country, and bidding farewell to his father-in-law, set out for Trachin to visit his friend King Ceyx, taking with him his wife Deianeira, and his young son Hyllus.

In the course of their journey they arrived at the river Evenus, over which the Centaur Nessus was in the habit of carrying travellers for hire. Heracles, with his little son in his arms, forded the stream unaided, entrusting his wife to the care of the Centaur, who, charmed with the beauty of his fair burden, attempted to carry her off. But her cries were heard by her husband, who without hesitation shot Nessus through the heart with one of his poisoned arrows. Now the dying Centaur was thirsting for revenge. He called Deianeira to his side, and directed her to secure some of the blood which flowed from his wound, assuring her that if, when in danger of losing her husband's affection, she used it in the manner indicated by him, it would act as a charm, and prevent her from being supplanted by a rival. Heracles and Deianeira now pursued their journey, and after several adventures at length arrived at their destination.

Death of Heracles

THE LAST EXPEDITION UNDERTAKEN BY THE GREAT HERO was against Eurytus, king of Oechalia, to revenge himself upon this king and his sons for having refused to bestow upon him the hand of Iole, after having fairly won the maiden. Having collected a large army Heracles set out for Euboea in order to besiege Oechalia, its capital.

Success crowned his arms. He stormed the citadel, slew the king and his three sons, reduced the town to ashes, and carried away captive the young and beautiful Iole.

Returning from his victorious expedition, Heracles halted at Cenoeus in order to offer a sacrifice to Zeus, and sent to Deianeira to Trachin for a sacrificial robe. Deianeira having been informed that the fair Iole was in the train of Heracles was fearful lest her youthful charms might supplant her in the affection of her husband, and calling to mind the advice of the dying Centaur, she determined to test the efficacy of the love-charm which he had given to her. Taking out the phial which she had carefully preserved, she imbued the robe with a portion of the liquid which it contained, and then sent it to Heracles.

The victorious hero clothed himself with the garment, and was about to perform the sacrifice, when the hot flames rising from the altar heated the poison with which it was imbued, and soon every fibre of his body was penetrated by the deadly venom. The unfortunate hero, suffering the most fearful tortures, endeavoured to tear off the robe, but it adhered so closely to the skin that all his efforts to remove it only increased his agonies.

In this pitiable condition he was conveyed to Trachin, where Deianeira, on beholding the terrible suffering of which she was the innocent cause, was overcome with grief and remorse, and hanged herself in despair. The dying hero called his son Hyllus to his side, and desired him to make Iole his wife, and then ordering his followers to erect a funeral pyre, he mounted it and implored the by-standers to set fire to it, and thus in mercy to terminate his insufferable torments. But no one had the courage to obey him, until at last his friend and companion Philoctetes, yielding to his piteous appeal, lighted the pile, and received in return the bow and arrows of the hero.

Soon flames on flames ascended, and amidst vivid flashes of lightning, accompanied by awful peals of thunder, Pallas-Athene descended in a cloud, and bore her favourite hero in a chariot to Olympus.

Heracles became admitted among the immortals; and Hera, in token of her reconciliation, bestowed upon him the hand of her beautiful daughter Hebe, the goddess of eternal youth.

The Heraclidae

A FTER THE APOTHEOSIS of Heracles, his children were so cruelly persecuted by Eurystheus, that they fled for protection to king Ceyx at Trachin, accompanied by the aged Iolaus, the nephew and life-long friend of their father, who constituted himself their guide and protector. But on Eurystheus demanding the surrender of the fugitives, the Heraclidae, knowing that the small force at the disposal of king Ceyx would be altogether inadequate to protect them against the powerful king of Argos, abandoned his territory, and sought refuge at Athens, where they were hospitably received by king Demophoon, the son of the great hero Theseus. He warmly espoused their cause, and determined to protect them at all costs against Eurystheus, who had despatched a numerous force in pursuit of them.

When the Athenians had made all necessary preparations to repel the invaders, an oracle announced that the sacrifice of a maiden of noble birth was necessary to ensure to them victory; whereupon Macaria, the beautiful daughter of Heracles and Deianira, magnanimously offered herself as a sacrifice, and, surrounded by the noblest matrons and maidens of Athens, voluntarily devoted herself to death.

While these events were transpiring in Athens, Hyllus, the eldest son of Heracles and Deianira, had advanced with a large army to the assistance of his brothers, and having sent a messenger to the king announcing his arrival, Demophoon, with his army, joined his forces.

In the thick of the battle which ensued, Iolaus, following a sudden impulse, borrowed the chariot of Hyllus, and earnestly entreated Zeus and Hebe to restore to him, for this one day only, the vigour and strength of his youth. His prayer was heard. A thick cloud descended from heaven and enveloped the chariot, and when it disappeared, Iolaus, in the full plenitude of manly vigour, stood revealed before the astonished gaze of the combatants. He then led on his valiant band of warriors, and soon the enemy was in headlong flight; and Eurystheus, who was taken prisoner, was put to death by the command of king Demophoon.

After gratefully acknowledging the timely aid of the Athenians, Hyllus, accompanied by the faithful Iolaus and his brothers, took leave of king Demophoon, and proceeded to invade the Peloponnesus, which they regarded as their lawful patrimony; for, according to the will of Zeus, it should have been the rightful possession of their father, the great hero Heracles, had not Hera maliciously defeated his plans by causing his cousin Eurystheus to precede him into the world.

For the space of twelve months the Heraclidae contrived to maintain themselves in the Peloponnesus; but at the expiration of that time a pestilence broke out, which spread over the entire peninsula, and compelled the Heraclidae to evacuate the country and return to Attica, where for a time they settled.

After the lapse of three years Hyllus resolved on making another effort to obtain his paternal inheritance. Before setting out on the expedition, however, he consulted the oracle of Delphi, and the response was, that he must wait for the third fruit before the enterprise would prove successful. Interpreting this ambiguous reply to signify the third summer, Hyllus controlled his impatience for three years, when, having collected a powerful army, he once more entered the Peloponnesus.

At the isthmus of Corinth he was opposed by Atreus, the son of Pelops, who at the death of Eurystheus had inherited the kingdom. In order to save bloodshed, Hyllus offered to decide his claims by single combat, the conditions being, that if he were victorious, he and his brothers should obtain undisputed possession of their rights; but if defeated, the Heraclidae were to desist for fifty years from attempting to press their claim.

The challenge was accepted by Echemon, king of Tegea, and Hyllus lost his life in the encounter, whereupon the sons of Heracles, in virtue of their agreement, abandoned the Peloponnesus and retired to Marathon.

Hyllus was succeeded by his son Cleodaeus, who, at the expiration of the appointed time, collected a large army and invaded the Peloponnesus; but he was not more successful than his father had been, and perished there with all his forces.

Twenty years later his son Aristomachus consulted an oracle, which promised him victory if he went by way of the defile. The Heraclidae once more set out, but were again defeated, and Aristomachus shared the fate of his father and grandfather, and fell on the field of battle.

When, at the expiration of thirty years, the sons of Aristomachus, Temenus, Cresphontes, and Aristodemus again consulted the oracle, the answer was still the same; but this time the following explanation accompanied the response: the third fruit signified the third generation, to which they themselves belonged, and not the third fruit of the earth; and by the defile was indicated, not the isthmus of Corinth, but the straits on the right of the isthmus.

Temenus lost no time in collecting an army and building ships of war; but just as all was ready and the fleet about to sail, Aristodemus, the youngest of the brothers, was struck by lightning. To add to their misfortunes, Hippolytes, a descendant of Heracles, who had joined in the expedition, killed a soothsayer whom he mistook for a spy, and the gods, in their displeasure, sent violent tempests, by means of which the entire fleet was destroyed, whilst famine and pestilence decimated the ranks of the army.

The oracle, on being again consulted, advised that Hippolytes, being the offender, should be banished from the country for ten years, and that the command of the troops should be delegated to a man having three eyes. A search was at once instituted by the Heraclidae for a man answering to this description, who was found at length in the person of Oxylus, a descendant of the Aetolian race of kings. In obedience to the command of the oracle, Hippolytes was banished, an army and fleet once more equipped, and Oxylus elected commander-in-chief.

And now success at length crowned the efforts of the long-suffering descendants of the great hero. They obtained possession of the Peloponnesus, which was divided among them by lot. Argos fell to Temenus, Lacedaemon to Aristodemus, and Messene to Cresphontes. In gratitude for the services of their able leader, Oxylus, the kingdom of Elis, was conferred upon him by the Heraclidae.

Myths of Love and Courage

THE GODS AND GODDESSES OF GREECE were the creators of the earth, makers of the universe and rulers thereafter. In their hectic lives, governed by deep-seated jealousies, petty hatreds, overwhelming passion and love, and desperate bids for revenge, there were other beings, mortals who led lives cast in the shadows of these greater entities. But it was also the acts of these mortals which became tools of understanding for the Greeks, for how could they make sense of the world in which they lived without the interaction of mankind with gods? From where came the echo in the deep valleys of Greece; how do you explain the powerful spirits of the woodland, the waters, the winds? These are the tales of mystery and enchantment which form some of the most exquisite allegories in literature worldwide; they speak of love, desire, deceit and trickery; they explain all.

Orpheus and Eurydice

THE MUSIC OF ORPHEUS was known across the lands. With his lyre, he played the sweetest strains which lulled even the fiercest beasts into a peaceful rapture. For his music Orpheus was loved, and he travelled far and wide, issuing forth melodies that were pure, sublime.

Orpheus was the son of Apollo and the muse Calliope. He lived in Thrace and spent his days singing, playing the music that spread his fame still further. One day, Orpheus came across a gentle and very beautiful young nymph, who danced to his music as if she was born to do so. She was called Eurydice, and wings seemed to lift her heels, as she played and frolicked to his music. And then, when their eyes caught, it was clear that it was love at first sight and that their destiny was to be shared.

It was only a few days later that they were joined in marriage, and never before had such an angelic couple existed. As they danced on the eve of their wedding, the very trees and flowers, the winds and rushing streams paused and then shouted their congratulations. The world stopped to watch, to approve, to celebrate.

And then that most sinister of animals, a stealthy viper, made its way into the babbling midst and struck at the ankle of Eurydice, sending her to an icy, instant death. Eurydice sank down in the circle, and all efforts to revive her failed. Time seemed to stop. Certainly there was no music, anywhere.

Orpheus was disconsolate with grief. He could not even bring himself to bury her, and he played on his lyre such tunes that even the rocks, the hardened fabric of the caves, shed tears. After several days he came to a decision which seemed at once as clear and as necessary as anything he had ever undertaken.

Orpheus made his way to the Underworld, determined to rescue his great love. His lyre in hand, his heart pounding with emotion, he reached the river Styx, the black waterway which snakes its way into the Underworld, which divides the other world from our own. There he played his lute so tunefully, so eloquently, that Charon, the ferryman, took him across the river at no charge, granted access to a place into which no mortal must go.

As Orpheus was drawn deeper into the Underworld, grisly, frightening sights greeted his eyes, but he continued to play his soulful tune, filling with tears the eyes of those cast in wretched purgatory, the ghosts of beings who had done ill deeds, the spirits of men who had been cursed. He played on and on, his music seeping into the blackness and creating an effortless light which guided the way.

At the end of his journey King Hades and Queen Persephone sat, entranced by his music. They knew of his mission. They would allow him to take Eurydice. His music had unwound the rigours of their rules, of their laws, and momentarily appeased, temporarily relaxed, they permitted Orpheus to take one of their own.

There was a condition, as there is in all such matters. Orpheus could have his bride returned to him; she would follow him as his shadow. But he must not look back on his trip from their world. The music from Orpheus' lyre picked up the timbre of his pleasure and took on a jaunty character which brought a look of surprise to the stony faces of Hades' guards. Orpheus turned and made his way back to the Styx, to his world, to home and Eurydice.

The gate of the Underworld was in sight when Orpheus felt an overwhelming need to confirm that Eurydice was there. Instinctively, he turned towards his great love, and there she stood, shrouded in a dark cape. As he reached for her, just as he felt the warmth of her skin, her breath on his cheek, she vanished, drawn back into death, into the darkened world of the afterlife.

Orpheus left the Underworld alone, and when he returned to his land, he lay broken and wasted on the shores of the Styx. For the rest of his short life he wandered among the hills, carrying a broken lyre which he would not mend and could not play. He cared for nothing. He was attacked, one day, without the powers to play, to appease his enemy. His attackers were a throng of Thracian women who killed him, and tore him to pieces. His lyre was taken to Lesbos, where it became a shrine, and some years later, his head was washed upon the shores of the island. There it was joined with his sacred lyre, its broken strings representing forever the broken heart of Orpheus.

Echo and Narcissus

ECHO WAS A WOOD NYMPH who danced and sang in the forest. She told engaging stories to anyone who would listen, and although she was adored by the other nymphs her headstrong ways meant that none of her playmates had the last word. Echo would skip and frolic among the trees, charming the small creatures and befriending the forest folk as she played.

Hera was enchanted by the nubile young nymph, and she came daily to hear Echo's tales of adventure, of fairies and of far-off places, stories that grew ever more complicated with each telling. One day Hera left earlier than usual, inspired to see her husband Zeus by Echo's romantic tales. It was on this day that Hera was presented with evidence of her husband's philanderings, and discovered that Echo had been involved in the subterfuge, receiving a wage from Zeus to occupy his lovely wife.

Hera flew into a rage which resounded through the Kingdom, and the victim of her wrath was Echo, who was stripped of her power of speech, able only to echo the last words spoken by any person. Echo fled deep into the forest, tortured by her speechlessness, drained of her life and vitality.

Now in this same forest lived a handsome young man named Narcissus, a Thespian and the son of the blue nymph Leirope and the River-god Cephisus. When Narcissus was but a child, his mother consulted the seer Tiresias to learn of his fortune. Would he live to old age? she longed to know.

'If he never knows himself,' said the wise man.

Tales of Narcissus' beauty had spread far and wide and it was not long before a he grew conceited and self-satisfied. Lovers came and went, but Narcissus' heart grew colder, frosted by the knowledge that none could match his charm and grace.

Echo had been drawn to the youth for many months, and secretly followed him in the forest, begging him silently to speak so she could make her presence known. One day her wish was granted, and Narcissus, who had lost his companions in the forest, called out, 'Is anyone here?"

'Here,' cried the young nymph with delight.

'Come!' replied Narcissus, his face a haughty mask.

'Come!' repeated Echo.

'Why do you avoid me?' asked Narcissus, a surprised look crossing his face.

'Why do you avoid me?' said Echo.

'Let us come together,' he shouted, with careless confidence. He looked purposefully around, his manly brow furrowed with intrigue.

'Let us come together.' And as the words tumbled from Echo's tender lips, she leapt from her hiding place, and threw herself against the comely young man.

He stepped back in horror, roughly detaching himself from her grasp, and snarling, 'I will die before you ever lay with me!' Summoning up the arrogance of his youth, he cast Echo aside and left the clearing, failing to hear her pleading 'Lay with me ...' as he stalked away.

Echo grew cold with misery, and unable to draw breath, she lay still and pined for her lost love, the vessel for her childish hopes and aspirations. There Echo laid until she was no more than her voice, her tiny body becoming one with the woodland floor.

Narcissus quickly forgot this uneasy encounter, and carried on his relentless search for love. One day, deep in the forest, he stopped his hunting in order to take a drink from a pure, clear stream. As he leant over the crystal waters he was caught by such a sight of beauty that his breath escaped in a stunned gasp. There, in this magical current, was a face of such perfect loveliness that Narcissus was unable to move, to call out.

He whispered to the dazzling illusion, but though the lips of this creature moved, too, no sound was uttered. Narcissus was enchanted.

He reached forwards to the elegant face, the princely features, but alas, with every movement the object of his passion disappeared in a kaleidoscope of colour.

Narcissus had fallen in love with his own reflection, and he was held captive by its magnificence. He reclined by the stream, unable to move, and there he laid without food or water until he too pined away, to become one with the forest. The last words to slip from his aristocratic lips were,

'O youth beloved in vain. Farewell.' To which the spirit of the love-sickened nymph Echo replied, 'Farewell.'

Those who had once swooned for Narcissus prepared his funeral pyre, but his body had disappeared. In its place grew a slim and elegant flower with a blood-red heart, which gazed piteously at its reflection as it dipped over the water. Today, this flower can be found by the waters of certain streams, a flower known for its beauty, which gazes eternally at its own reflection.

The spirit of Echo is often heard, for she fled that forest, and wanders far from the shores of that stream, ever searching for her lost love, and, of course, her voice.

Perseus and the Gorgon

❦

THERE ONCE WAS A TROUBLED KING who learned, through an Oracle, that he would reach his death through the hand of his own grandson. This king was Acrisius, king of Argos, and he had only one child, the fair Danae. Acrisius shut her away in a cave, in order to keep her unwedded, and there she grew older, and more beautiful, as time passed. No man could reach her, although many tried, and eventually word of her beauty reached the gods, and finally the king of the Gods himself, Zeus.

He entered her prison in a cascade of light, and planted in her womb the seed of the gods, and from this the infant Perseus was spawned. Acrisius heard the infant's cries, and unable to kill him outright, he released Danae from her prison, and with her child she was placed on a raft, and sent out on the stormy seas to meet their death.

Now Poseidon knew of Zeus's child, and calmed the seas, lifting the mother and child carefully to the island of Seriphos, where they washed onto safe shores. They were discovered there by a kind fisherman, who brought them to his home. It was in this humble and peaceful abode that Perseus grew up, a boy of effortless intelligence, cunning and nobility. He was a sportsman beyond compare, and a hero among his playmates. He was visited in his dreams by Athene, the goddess of war, who filled his head with lusty ambition and inspired him to seek danger and excitement.

The fisherman became a father figure to Perseus, but another schemed to take his place. The fisherman's brother Polydectes, chief of the island, was besotted by the beautiful Danae, and longed to have her for his wife.

He showered her with priceless jewels, succulent morsels of food, rich fabrics and furs, but her heart belonged to Perseus, and she refused his attentions. Embittered, he resolved to dispose of the youth, and set Perseus a task at which he could not help but fail, and from which no mortal man could ever return.

The task was to slay the creature Medusa, one of the three Gorgon sisters. Medusa was the only mortal of the Gorgons, with a face so hideous, so repulsive, that any man who laid eyes on her would be turned to stone before he could attack. Her hair was a nest of vipers, which writhed around that flawed and fatal face. Perseus was enthralled by the idea of performing an act of such bravery and that night, as he slept, he summoned again the goddess Athene, who provided him with the tools by which the task could be shouldered.

Athene came to him, a glorious figure of war, and with her she brought Hermes, her brother, who offered the young man powerful charms with which he could make his way. Perseus was provided with Hermes own crooked sword, sturdy enough to cut through even the strongest armour, and Perseus's feet were fitted with winged sandals, by which he could make his escape. From Hades he received a helmet which had the power to make its wearer invisible. Athene offered her mirrored shield, which would allow Perseus to strike Medusa without seeing her horrible face. Finally, he was given a skin bag, to carry the Gorgon's head from the site.

Perseus set out the next morning, his first assignment to find the half-sisters of the Gorgons, in the icy wilderness of the northern steppes of Graiae. They alone could provide him with the whereabouts of Medusa. With the aid of his winged sandals, Perseus flew north, till he came to the frosted mists of the mountains. There the earth was so cold, a fabulous crack was rent across her surface. The land was barren, icy, empty, and although he felt no fear, Perseus had to struggle to carry on, his breath frozen on his lips. There, on the edge of the Hyperborean sea were the Gray Sisters, witches from another era who had come there to end their days, wreaking a wretched existence from the snow-capped mountains, toothless and haggard with age. They had but one eye between them, and one tooth, without which they would surely have died.

Perseus chose his moment carefully, and lunged into their midst, grasping their single eye, and stepping out of reach.

'I require your assistance,' he said firmly. 'I must know the way to the Gorgons. If you cannot help me I shall take your tooth as well, and you shall starve in this wilderness.'

The Gray Sisters swayed and muttered, lolling upon the snow and fumbling across its icy surface towards the awe-inspiring voice.

A cry rose up when they realized that he had their eye, and they threatened and cursed Perseus, their howls echoing in the blackness of the wasteland. Finally, they succumbed, the fear of blindness in that empty place enlivening their tongues, loosening their resolve. Perseus graciously returned their eye, and on a breath of Arctic air, he rose and headed southwards, out of sight of the sisters, who struggled to see their tormentor.

Back through the mists he flew, where the sea sent spirals of spray that lashed at his heels and tried to drag him down. On he went, and the snows melted away into a sea so blue he seemed enveloped in it. The sky grew bright, the grass of the fields green and inviting, and as he flew he grew hotter, his eyes heavy with exhaustion, his perfect skin dripping with effort. The other end of the world rose up, a land and a sea where no human dared enter, a land of burning heat, of fiery hatred and fear, where none lived but the Gorgons themselves, surrounded by the hapless stone statues of man and beast who had dared to look upon them.

He came across the sisters as they slept in the midday sun. Medusa lay between her sisters, who protectively laid their arms across her mass. Her body was scaled and repellent, her limbs clawed and gnarled. Perseus dared look no further, but from the corner of his eye he saw the coiling vipers, and the serpent's tongue which even in sleep darted from her razor-sharp lips. Her fearsome eyes were shut. He was safe.

With one decisive movement he plunged himself and his sword towards this creature, Athene's shield held high. And Medusa's answering howl pierced the air, ripping the breath from his lungs, and dragging him down towards her. He struggled to maintain his composure, shivering and drawn to look at the source of this violent cry. He fell on her, shaking his head to clear it, fighting the temptation to give in. And then the courage that was deep inside him, born within him, the gift of his father Zeus, redeemed him. He lifted his head, and with shield held high, thrust his sword in one wild swoop that lopped off the head of Medusa.

He packed it hastily in his bag, and leapt up, away from the arms of the Sisters Gorgon who had woken abruptly, and now hissed and struck out at him. The Gorgons were not human, and could not, like Medusa, be slain by humans. They rose on wings, like murderous vultures, yowling and gnashing their teeth, screaming of revenge.

But Perseus had disappeared. His helmet took him from their side, enshrouded him with a curtain that protected him from their eyes. He was safe.

For days on end he flew with his booty, across the desert, where the dripping blood of Medusa hit the sand and bred evil vipers and venomous snakes, ever to populate the sunburnt earth. The Gorgons flew behind him, a whirlwind of hatred and revenge, but Perseus soared above them, until he was safe, at the edge of his world.

He came to rest at the home of Atlas, the giant, who held up with great pillars the weight of the sky. He begged for a place to lay his weary head, for sustenance and water. But the giant refused him. Tired and angry, Perseus thrust his hand into his bag and drew out the monstrous head. To this day, Atlas stands, a stone giant holding up the skies, his head frosted with snow, his face frozen with horror.

And Perseus flew on, although it was several months and many more challenges before he was able to present his trophy. But his travels are another story, involving passion, bravery and an ultimate battle. He would meet Polydectes once again, would defend his hostage mother, and face his long-lost grandfather. He would make his own mark at Olympus, and become, eventually, a bright star, a divine beacon which would guide courageous wanderers, as he had once been.

Icarus and Daedalus

❦

IN THE CITY OF ATHENS lived Daedalus, an inventor and artisan renowned across the world for his skill and genius. He loved nothing more than to create masterpieces of invention and wonder, except the recognition and admiration his talents won him. On fearing that his nephew and apprentice would one day surpass his lofty skills, Daedalus murdered the boy in cold blood. He and his family then fled to Crete. It was here that King Minos requested his service for a very special purpose.

The King had a monster living among his household, one that was cursed with insatiable, unnatural appetites. This miscreation was the Minotaur, the half-bull, half-human progeny of Minos's wife, Pasiphae. Pasiphae had been enchanted to fall in love with the bull of Poseidon. Her blood boiling in lust for the magnificent beast, Pasiphae demanded that Daedalus build her a contraption so that the bull could mount her. The resulting offspring was the atrocity that grew into the uncontrollable Minotaur. Seeking advice from the Delphic oracle, Minos was told to build a creation dense and elaborate enough to house the beast safely. For this, Minos needed Daedalus. Eager to test his skills, Daedalus accepted and, taking his son Icarus, he set off to Minos's palace to begin work on the Labyrinth, which would be his most extraordinary work.

The Labyrinth was an immense maze in the ground of Minos's palace. Daedalus used every method he could think of in the formation of his masterpiece; dead ends, winding passages, shadowy corners and pathways that never seemed to end, driving anyone trapped within to the very edge of insanity and beyond. So cunning was the Labyrinth that Daedalus himself was almost doomed among its dark and convoluted corridors. The complex twists and perplexing turns successfully trapped the Minotaur, who was kept contented by annual sacrifices of seven youths and seven maidens for him to hunt down and gorge upon at will.

But Minos did not react as Daedalus expected. Instead of showering him with praise and riches, the king was desperate to ensure that no one would ever discover the secret of the great Labyrinth. He trapped Daedalus and his son in a tall tower to ensure that the dark mystery of the Labyrinth would forever be protected. And so the days passed, but Minos would not release his prisoners. He even took the precaution of having the routes out of Crete by both land and sea guarded. But Daedalus was also crafty, as well as resourceful. The time came when he grew desperately weary of his enforced capture. Never forgetting that his beloved son had been imprisoned because of his ambition and love of fame, Daedalus plotted to win their freedom.

Daedalus began collecting the supplies they would need for their escape. Careful not to arouse suspicion in the King, he knew he would have to use natural objects where possible. He also knew that Minos was watching the roads and sea, which left only one way for escape. They would have to fly.

Daedalus set to work making wings for himself and Icarus. Basing them on the natural curve of a bird's wing, he carefully bound together layers and layers of feathers with cord and sealed the binding with wax, without which the feathers would be pulled out of the cords during flight. He took the utmost care in his creation, placing the wings in order of size from smallest to largest. Finally, the instruments of freedom were ready. Trialling them, Daedalus strapped his wings in place and flapped his arms. The movement caught the wind and lifted him up into the air where he was able to hover above the ground.

Ecstatic with joy at the thought of their approaching freedom, Icarus – a tempestuous boy with little of his father's foresight – wanted immediately to set off for home. Tempering his son's eagerness, Daedalus again impressed upon Icarus how to get home safely. They had to avoid both the spray from the sea that would weigh down the wings and the heat from the sun, which would melt the wax securing the wings together.

Father and son took flight, leaving their tower of captivity forever. As they flew, Crete growing smaller behind them, both grew lighter at heart at the thought of home. Passing landmarks, ever hopeful that they would reach the shores of Athens, Daedalus's heart filled with heady pride at his construction. But he was overconfident. His invention – masterful as it was – was imperfect.

Icarus, his reckless boy, had inherited some of his father's ego. Feeling invincible, all warnings about how to fly safely flew from his mind. As the Aegean sea glittered beneath him, Icarus felt like a king up there in the heavens, so he flew higher and higher so as to fly among the gods. However the blazing sun caused the wax holding his precious wings together to melt. Desperately trying to regain control, Icarus swooped downwards to escape the sun's burning rays. But it was too late. Before his father could even make a move to help him, Icarus – with barely time to give his beloved father one final glance – plummeted to his death. Landing heavily in the deep, dark sea, Icarus breathed his last.

Wracked with grief, Daedalus was almost unable to complete his journey home, the sweet sensation of liberty forever tainted by his tragic loss. In homage to his son, and as a permanent reminder of the grief and loss caused by his pride and arrogance, Daedalus named the land nearest to Icarus's place of death Icaria, which it remains to this day.

Theseus

WHEN YET but a very young man, Aegeus, King of Athens, journeyed off to Troezene, where he fell in love with and married a pretty young princess by the name of Aethra. For some reason, which mythologists do not make known, the king was forced to return alone to Athens; but ere he departed he concealed his sword and sandals beneath a stone, bidding his wife remember, that, as soon as the strength of their son Theseus permitted, he must raise the rock, appropriate sword and sandals, and come and join him in Athens, where he should be introduced to the people as his son and heir. These instructions given, Aegeus bade a fond farewell to his wife and infant son, and returned home.

As the years passed by, they brought strength, beauty, and wisdom to Theseus, whose fame began to be published abroad. At last Aethra deemed him strong enough to raise the rock beneath which his father's trusty weapon lay; and, conducting him to the spot where it was, she told him the whole story, and bade him try his strength.

Theseus immediately obeyed. With a mighty effort he raised the rock, and, to his great satisfaction, found the sword and sandals in a perfect state of preservation. Sword in hand, he then set out for Athens,—a long and dangerous journey. He proceeded slowly and cautiously, for he knew that many dangers lurked along his pathway, and that ere he reached his father's city he would have to encounter both giants and monsters, who would strive to bar his way.

He was not at all mistaken in his previsions; for Troezene was scarcely lost to sight ere he came across the giant Periphetes, son of Vulcan, who stood in the road and attacked with a huge club, whose blows were generally fatal, all who strove to pass. Adroitly evading the giant's first onslaught, Theseus plunged his sword deep into his huge side ere he could renew the attack, and brought him lifeless to the ground.

Theseus then disarmed his fallen foe, and, retaining the club for future use, continued his journey in peace, until he came to the Isthmus of Corinth, where two adventures awaited him. The first was with a cruel giant named Sinis, nicknamed The Pine-bender, whose usual practice was to bend some huge pine until its top touched the ground, and call to any unsuspecting passer-by to seize it and lend him a helping hand for a moment. Then, as soon as the innocent stranger had complied with his request, he would suddenly let go the pine, which, freed from his gigantic grasp, sprang back to its upright position, and hurled the unfortunate traveler way up in the air, to be dashed to pieces against the rocky mountain side.

Theseus, who had already heard of the giant's stratagem, skillfully eluded the danger, and finally caused Sinis to perish by the same cruel death which he had dealt out to so many others.

In one place the Isthmus of Corinth was exceedingly narrow, and the only practicable pathway led along a rocky ledge, guarded by a robber named Sciron, who forced all who tried to pass him to wash his feet. While the traveler was thus engaged, and knelt in the narrow pathway to do his bidding, he would suddenly raise his foot, kick him over the side, and hurl him down into the sea below, where a huge tortoise was ever waiting with gaping jaws to devour the victims.

Instead of yielding to Sciron's exactions, Theseus drew his sword, and by his determined bearing so terrified the robber, that he offered him a free passage. This offer, however, did not satisfy Theseus, who said he would sheathe his sword only on condition that Sciron performed for him the menial office he had imposed upon so many others. Sciron dared not refuse, and obeyed in fear and trembling; but he was doomed never to molest any one again, for Theseus kicked him over the precipice, into the breakers, where the tortoise feasted upon his remains with as keen a relish as upon former victims.

After disposing of another world-renowned robber, Cercyon (The Wrestler), Theseus encountered Procrustes (The Stretcher), a cruel giant, who, under pretext of entertainment, deluded travelers into entering his home, where he had two beds of very different dimensions,—one unusually short, the other unusually long. If the unfortunate traveler were a short man, he was put to bed in the long bedstead, and his limbs were pulled out of joint to make him fit it; but if, on the contrary, he were tall, he was assigned the short bed, and the superfluous length of limb was lopped off under the selfsame pretext. Taking Procrustes quite unawares, Theseus gave him a faint idea of the sufferings he had inflicted upon others by making him try each bed in turn, and then, to avoid his continuing these evil practices, put an end to his wretched existence.

Theseus successfully accomplished a few more exploits of a similar character, and finally reached Athens, where he found that his fame had preceded him.

The first tidings that there reached his ear were that Aegeus had just married Medea, the enchantress; but, although these tidings were very unwelcome, he hastened on to his father's court, to make himself known, and receive the welcome promised so many years before. Medea, seated by Aegeus' side, no sooner saw the young stranger draw near, than she knew him, and foresaw that he had come to demand his rights. To prevent his making known claims which might interfere with the prospects of her future offspring, she hastily mixed a deadly poison in a cup, which she filled with fragrant wine, and bade Aegeus offer it to the stranger.

The monarch was about to execute her apparently hospitable purpose, when his eye suddenly rested upon the sword at Theseus' side, which he immediately recognized. One swift glance into the youth's open face convinced him that Aethra's son stood before him, and he eagerly stretched out his arms to clasp him to his heart. This sudden movement upset the goblet, and the poisonous contents, falling upon a dog lying at the king's feet, caused his almost instantaneous death. Seeing her crime discovered and Theseus recognized, Medea quickly mounted her magic dragon car, and fled to Media, whence she never returned.

One day, some time after his arrival at Athens, Theseus heard a sound of weeping and great lamentation throughout all the city, and in reply to his wondering inquiries was told, that ever since an unfortunate war between the Cretans and Athenians, the latter, who had been vanquished, were obliged to pay a yearly tribute of seven youths and as many maidens, destined to serve as food for the Minotaur. Further questions evolved the fact that the Minotaur was a hideous monster, the property of Minos, King of Crete, who kept it in an intricate labyrinth, constructed for that express purpose by Daedalus, the far-famed architect. This labyrinth was so very intricate, that those who entered could not find their way out.

These varied details kindled Theseus' love of adventure, and still further strengthened him in his sudden resolve to join the mournful convoy, try his strength against the awful Minotaur, and, if possible, save his country from further similar exactions.

Even his father's tears and entreaties were powerless to move him from his purpose, and, the hour having come, he embarked upon the black-sailed vessel which was to bear the yearly tribute to Crete, promising to change the black sails for snowy white ones if he were fortunate enough to return victorious.

Favourable winds soon wafted the galley to distant Crete, and as they sailed along the coast, searching for the port, they were challenged by the brazen giant Talus, who walked daily thrice around the whole island, killing, by contact with his red-hot body, all who had no business to land on that coast. Knowing, however, that the black-sailed galley brought a fresh supply of youths and maidens for the terrible Minotaur, Talus let it pass unharmed; and the victims were brought into the presence of Minos, who personally inspected each new freight-load, to make sure he was not being cheated by the Athenians.

At the monarch's side stood his fair daughter Ariadne, whose tender heart was filled with compassion when she beheld the frail maidens and gallant youths about to perish by such a loathsome death. Theseus, by right of his birth, claimed the precedence, and proffered a request to be the first victim,—a request which the king granted with a sardonic smile, ere he returned unmoved to his interrupted feast.

Unnoticed by all, Ariadne slipped out of the palace, and, under cover of the darkness, entered the prison where Theseus was confined. There she tremblingly offered him a ball of twine and a sharp sword, bidding him tie one end of the twine to the entrance of the labyrinth, and keep the other in his hand as a clew to find the way out again should the sword enable him to kill the dreaded Minotaur. In token of gratitude for this timely assistance, Theseus solemnly promised Ariadne to take her with him to Athens as his bride, were he only successful in his undertaking.

At dawn the next day Theseus was conducted to the entrance of the labyrinth, and there left to await the tender mercies of the Minotaur. Like all heroes, he preferred to meet any danger rather than remain inactive: so, mindful of Ariadne's instructions, he fastened his twine to the entrance, and then boldly penetrated into the intricate ways of the labyrinth, where many whitening bones plainly revealed the fate of all who had preceded him.

He had not gone very far before he encountered the Minotaur,—a creature more hideous than fancy can paint,—and he was obliged to use all his skill and ingenuity to avoid falling a prey to the monster's appetite, and all his strength to lay him low at last. The Minotaur slain, Theseus hastily retraced his footsteps.

Arrived at the place where his ship rode at anchor, he found his companions and Ariadne awaiting him, and, springing on board, bade the sailors weigh anchor as quickly as possible. They were almost out of reach of the Cretan shores, when Talus came into view, and, perceiving that his master's prisoners were about to escape, leaned forward to catch the vessel by its rigging. Theseus, seeing this, sprang forward, and dealt the giant such a blow, that he lost his balance and fell into the deep sea, where he was drowned, and where thermal springs still bear witness to the heat of his brazen body.

The returning vessel, favoured by wind and tide, made but one port, Naxos; and here youths and maidens landed to view the beautiful island. Ariadne strayed apart, and threw herself down upon the ground to rest, where, before she was aware of it, sleep overtook her. Now, although very brave, Theseus was not very constant. He had already grown weary of Ariadne's love; and, when he saw her thus asleep, he basely summoned his companions, embarked with them, and set sail, leaving her alone upon the island, where Bacchus soon came to console her for the loss of her faithless lover.

Theseus, having committed a deed heinous in the eyes of gods and men, was doomed to suffer just punishment. In his preoccupation he entirely forgot his promise to change the black sails for white; and Aegeus, from Attica's rocky shore, seeing the sable sails when the vessel was yet far from land, immediately concluded that his son was dead, and in his grief cast himself into the sea since known as the Aegean, where he perished.

Theseus, on entering the city, heard of his father's death; and when he realized that it had been caused by his carelessness, he was overwhelmed with grief and remorse. All the cares of royalty and the wise measures he introduced for the happiness of his people could not divert his mind from this terrible catastrophe: so he finally resolved to resign his authority and set out again in search of adventures, which might help him forget his woes. He therefore made an excursion into the land of the Amazons, where Hercules had preceded him, and whence he brought back Hippolyte, whom he married. Theseus was now very happy indeed, and soon all his hopes were crowned by the birth of a son, whom he called Hippolytus. Shortly after this joyful event, the Amazons invaded his country under pretext of rescuing their kidnapped queen, and in the battle which ensued Hippolyte was accidentally wounded by an arrow, and breathed her last in Theseus' arms.

Theseus next set out with an Athenian army to fight Pirithous, king of the Lapithae, who had dared to declare war; but when the armies were face to face, the two chiefs, seized with a sudden liking for each other, simultaneously cast down their weapons, and, falling on each other's necks, embraced, and swore an eternal friendship.

To show his devotion to this newly won friend, Theseus consented to accompany him to the court of Adrastus, King of Argos, and witness his marriage to Hippodamia, daughter of the king. Many guests were, of course, present to witness the marriage ceremony, among others Hercules and a number of the Centaurs. The latter, struck with admiration for the bride's unusual beauty, made an attempt to kidnap her, which was frustrated by the Lapithae, seconded by Theseus and Hercules. The terrible struggle which ensued between the conflicting parties has ever been a favourite subject in art, and is popularly known as the "Battle between the Centaurs and Lapithae."

The hotly contested bride did not, however, enjoy a very long life, and Pirithous soon found himself, like Theseus, a disconsolate widower. To avoid similar bereavement in future, they both resolved to secure goddesses, who, being immortal, would share their thrones forever. Aided by Pirithous, Theseus carried off Helen, the daughter of Zeus, and, as she was still but a child, entrusted her to the care of his mother, Aethra, until she attained a suitable age for matrimony. Then, in return for Pirithous' kind offices, he accompanied him to Hades, where they intended to carry off Proserpina.

While they were thus engaged, Helen's twin brothers, Castor and Pollux, came to Athens, delivered her from captivity, and carried her home in triumph. As for Theseus and Pirithous, their treacherous intention was soon discovered by Hades, who set the first on an enchanted rock, from which he could not descend unassisted, and bound the second to the constantly revolving wheel of his father, Ixion.

When Hercules was in Hades in search of Cerberus, he delivered Theseus from his unpleasant position, and thus enabled him to return to his own home, where he now expected to spend the remainder of his life in peace.

Although somewhat aged by this time, Theseus was still anxious to marry, and looked about him for a wife to cheer his loneliness. Suddenly he remembered that Ariadne's younger sister, Phaedra, must be a charming young princess, and sent an embassy to obtain her hand in marriage. The embassy proved successful, and Phaedra came to Athens; but, young and extremely beautiful, she was not at all delighted with her aged husband, and, instead of falling in love with him, bestowed all her affections upon his son, Hippolytus, a virtuous youth, who utterly refused to listen to her proposals to elope. In her anger at finding her advances scorned, Phaedra went to Theseus and accused Hippolytus of attempting to kidnap her. Theseus, greatly incensed at what he deemed his son's shameful actions, implored Poseidon to punish the youth, who was even then riding in his chariot close by the shore. In answer to this prayer, a great wave suddenly arose, dashed over the chariot, and drowned the young charioteer, whose lifeless corpse was finally flung ashore at Phaedra's feet. When the unfortunate queen saw the result of her false accusations, she confessed her crime, and, in her remorse and despair, hung herself.

As for Theseus, soured by these repeated misfortunes, he grew so stern and tyrannical, that he gradually alienated his people's affections, until at last they hated him, and banished him to the Island of Scyros, where, in obedience to a secret order, Lycomedes, the king, treacherously slew him by hurling him from the top of a steep cliff into the sea. As usual, when too late, the Athenians repented of their ingratitude, and in a fit of tardy remorse deified this hero, and built a magnificent temple on the Acropolis in veneration of him. This building, now used as a museum, contains many relics of Greek art. Theseus' bones were piously brought back, and inhumed in Athens, where he was long worshiped as a demigod.

Bellerephon

BELLEREPHON, a brave young prince, the grandson of Sisyphus, King of Corinth, had the great misfortune to kill his own brother while hunting in the forest. His grief was, of course, intense; and the horror he felt for the place where the catastrophe had occurred, added to his fear lest he should incur judicial punishment for his involuntary crime, made him flee to the court of Argos, where he took refuge with Proetus, the king, who was also his kinsman.

He had not sojourned there very long, before Anteia, the queen, fell in love with him; and although her husband, Proetus, treated her with the utmost kindness, she made up her mind to desert him, and tried to induce Bellerophon to elope with her.

Too honest to betray a man who had treated him as a friend, the young prince refused to listen to the queen's proposals. His refusal was to cost him dear, however; for, when Anteia saw that the youth would never yield to her wishes, she became very angry indeed, sought her husband, and accused the young stranger of crimes he had never even dreamed of committing.

Proetus, indignant at what he deemed deep treachery on the part of a guest, yet reluctant to punish him with his own hand as he deserved, sent Bellerophon to Iobates, King of Lycia, with a sealed message bidding him put the bearer to death.

Quite unconscious of the purport of this letter, Bellerophon traveled gayly onward, and presented himself before Iobates, who received him very hospitably, and, without inquiring his name or errand, entertained him royally for many days. After some time, Bellerophon suddenly remembered the sealed message entrusted to his care, and hastened to deliver it to Iobates, with many apologies for his forgetfulness.

With blanched cheeks and every outward sign of horror, the king read the missive, and then fell into a deep reverie. He did not like to take a stranger's life, and still could not refuse to comply with Proetus' urgent request: so, after much thought, he decided to send Bellerophon to attack the Chimaera, a terrible monster with a lion's head, a goat's body, and a dragon's tail.

His principal motive in choosing this difficult task was, that, although many brave men had set forth to slay the monster, none had ever returned, for one and all had perished in the attempt.

Although very courageous, Bellerophon's heart beat fast with fear when told what great deed he must accomplish; and he left Iobates' palace very sorrowfully, for he dearly loved the king's fair daughter, Philonoe, and was afraid he would never see her again.

While thus inwardly bewailing the ill luck which had so persistently dogged his footsteps, Bellerophon suddenly saw Athene appear before him in all her glory, and heard her inquire in gentle tones the cause of his too evident dejection. He had no sooner apprised her of the difficult task appointed him, than she promised him her aid, and before she vanished gave him a beautiful golden bridle, which she bade him use to control Pegasus.

Bridle in hand, Bellerophon stood pondering her words, and gradually remembered that Pegasus was a wonderful winged steed, born from the blood which fell into the foam of the sea from Medusa's severed head. This horse, as white as snow, and gifted with immortal life as well as incredible speed, was the favourite mount of Apollo and the Muses, who delighted in taking aërial flights on his broad back; and Bellerophon knew that from time to time he came down to earth to drink of the cool waters of the Hippocrene (a fountain which had bubbled forth where his hoofs first touched the earth), or to visit the equally limpid spring of Pirene, near Corinth.

Bellerophon now proceeded to the latter fountain, where, after lingering many days in the vain hope of catching even a glimpse of the winged steed, he finally beheld him sailing downward in wide curves, like a bird of prey. From his place of concealment in a nearby thicket, Bellerophon watched his opportunity, and, while the winged steed was grazing, he boldly vaulted upon his back.

Pegasus, who had never before been ridden by a mortal, reared and pranced, and flew up to dizzy heights; but all his efforts failed to unseat the brave rider, who, biding his time, finally thrust Athene's golden bit between his teeth, and immediately he became gentle and tractable. Mounted upon this incomparable steed, Bellerophon now went in search of the winged monster Chimaera, who had given birth to the Nemean lion and to the riddle-loving Sphinx.

From an unclouded sky Bellerophon and Pegasus swooped suddenly and unexpectedly down upon the terrible Chimaera, whose fiery breath and great strength were of no avail; for after a protracted struggle Bellerophon and Pegasus were victorious, and the monster lay lifeless upon the blood-soaked ground.

This mighty deed of bravery accomplished, Bellerophon returned to Iobates, to report the success of his undertaking; and, although the king was heartily glad to know the Chimaera was no more, he was very sorry to see Bellerophon safe and sound, and tried to devise some other plan to get rid of him.

He therefore sent him to fight the Amazons; but the hero, aided by the gods, defeated these warlike women also, and returned to Lycia, where, after escaping from an ambush posted by the king for his destruction, he again appeared victorious at court.

These repeated and narrow escapes from certain death convinced Iobates that the youth was under the special protection of the gods; and this induced the king not only to forego further attempts to slay him, but also to bestow upon the young hero his daughter's hand in marriage.

Bellerophon, having now attained his dearest wishes, might have settled down in peace; but his head had been utterly turned by the many lofty flights he had taken upon Pegasus' back, and, encouraged by the fulsome flattery of his courtiers, he finally fancied himself the equal of the immortal gods, and wished to join them in their celestial abode.

Summoning his faithful Pegasus once more, he rose higher and higher, and would probably have reached Olympus' heights, had not Zeus sent a gadfly, which stung poor Pegasus so cruelly, that he shied viciously, and flung his too confident rider far down to the earth below.

This fall, which would doubtless have killed any one but a mythological hero, merely deprived Bellerophon of his eyesight; and ever after he groped his way disconsolately, thinking of the happy days when he rode along the paths of air, and gazed upon the beautiful earth at his feet.

Bellerophon, mounted upon Pegasus, winging his flight through the air or fighting the Chimaera, is a beloved subject in sculpture and painting, which has frequently been treated by ancient artists, a few of whose most noted works are still extant in various museums.

This story, like many others, is merely a sun myth, in which Bellerophon, the orb of day, rides across the sky on Pegasus, the fleecy white clouds, and slays Chimaera, the dread monster of darkness, which he alone can overcome. Driven from home early in life, Bellerophon wanders throughout the world like his brilliant prototype, and, like it, ends his career in total darkness.

Pelops

PELOPS, the son of the cruel Tantalus, was a pious and virtuous prince. After his father was banished into Tartarus, a war ensued between Pelops and the king of Troy, in which the former was vanquished and forced to fly from his dominions in Phrygia. He emigrated into Greece, where, at the court of Oenomaus, king of Elis, he beheld Hippodamia, the king's daughter, whose beauty won his heart. But an oracle having foretold to Oenomaus that he would die on the day of his daughter's marriage, he threw every obstacle in the way of her suitors, and declared that he would only give her to him who succeeded in vanquishing him in a chariot race, but that all unsuccessful competitors should suffer death at his hands.

The conditions of the contest were as follows: The race was to be run from a given point at Pisa to the altar of Poseidon at Corinth; the suitor was allowed to start on his course whilst Oenomaus performed his sacrifice to Zeus, and only on its completion did the king mount his chariot, guided by the skilful Myrtilus, and drawn by his two famous horses, Phylla and Harpinna, who surpassed in swiftness the winds themselves. In this manner many a gallant young prince had perished; for although a considerable start was given to all competitors, still Oenomaus, with his swift team, always overtook them before they reached the goal, and killed them with his spear. But the love of Pelops for Hippodamia overcame all fears, and, undeterred by the terrible fate of his predecessors, he announced himself to Oenomaus as a suitor for the hand of his daughter.

On the eve of the race, Pelops repaired to the sea-shore and earnestly implored Poseidon to assist him in his perilous undertaking. The sea-god heard his prayer, and sent him out of the deep a chariot drawn by two winged horses.

When Pelops appeared on the course, the king at once recognized the horses of Poseidon; but, nothing daunted, he relied on his own supernatural team, and the contest was allowed to proceed.

Whilst the king was offering his sacrifice to Zeus Pelops set out on the race, and had nearly reached the goal, when, turning round, he beheld Oenomaus, spear in hand, who, with his magic steeds, had nearly overtaken him. But in this emergency Poseidon came to the aid of the son of Tantalus. He caused the wheels of the royal chariot to fly off, whereupon the king was thrown out violently, and killed on the spot, just as Pelops arrived at the altar of Poseidon.

As the hero was about to return to Pisa to claim his bride, he beheld, in the distance, flames issuing from the royal castle, which at that instant had been struck by lightning. With his winged horses he flew to rescue his lovely bride, and succeeded in extricating her uninjured from the burning building. They soon afterwards became united, and Pelops reigned in Pisa for many years in great splendour.

Ion

ION WAS THE SON of Crëusa (the beauteous daughter of Erechtheus, king of Athens) and the sun-god Phoebus-Apollo, to whom she was united without the knowledge of her father.

Fearing the anger of Erechtheus, Crëusa placed her new-born babe in a little wicker basket, and hanging some golden charms round his neck, invoked for him the protection of the gods, and concealed him in a lonely cave. Apollo, pitying his deserted child, sent Hermes to convey him to Delphi, where he deposited his charge on the steps of the temple. Next morning the Delphic priestess discovered the infant, and was so charmed by his engaging appearance that she adopted him as her own son. The young child was carefully tended and reared by his kind foster-mother, and was brought up in the service of the temple, where he was entrusted with some of the minor duties of the holy edifice.

And now to return to Crëusa. During a war with the Euboeans, in which the latter were signally defeated, Xuthus, son of Aeolus, greatly distinguished himself on the side of the Athenians, and as a reward for his valuable services, the hand of Crëusa, the king's daughter, was bestowed upon him in marriage. Their union, however, was not blest with children, and as this was a source of great grief to both of them, they repaired to Delphi in order to consult the oracle. The response was, that Xuthus should regard the first person who met him on leaving the sanctuary as his son. Now it happened that Ion, the young guardian of the temple, was the first to greet his view, and when Xuthus beheld the beautiful youth, he gladly welcomed him as his son, declaring that the gods had sent him to be a blessing and comfort to his old age. Crëusa, however, who concluded that the youth was the offspring of a secret marriage on the part of her husband, was filled with suspicion and jealousy; when an old servant, observing her grief, begged her to be comforted, assuring her that the cause of her distress should be speedily removed.

When, upon the occasion of the public adoption of his son, Xuthus gave a grand banquet, the old servant of Crëusa contrived to mix a strong poison in the wine of the unsuspecting Ion. But the youth—according to the pious custom of the ancients, of offering a libation to the gods before partaking of any repast—poured upon the ground a portion of the wine before putting it to his lips, when suddenly, as if by a miracle, a dove flew into the banquet-hall, and sipped of the wine of the libation; whereupon the poor little creature began to quiver in every limb, and in a few moments expired.

Ion's suspicions at once fell upon the obsequious servant of Crëusa, who with such officious attention had filled his cup. He violently seized the old man, and accused him of his murderous intentions. Unprepared for this sudden attack he admitted his guilt, but pointed to the wife of Xuthus as the instigator of the crime. Ion was about to avenge himself upon Crëusa, when, by means of the divine intervention of Apollo, his foster-mother, the Delphic priestess appeared on the scene, and explained the true relationship which existed between Crëusa and Ion. In order to set all doubts at rest, she produced the charms which she had found round the neck of the infant, and also the wicker basket in which he had been conveyed to Delphi.

Mother and son now became reconciled to each other, and Crëusa revealed to Ion the secret of his divine origin. The priestess of Delphi foretold that he would become the father of a great nation, called after him the Ionians, and also that Xuthus and Crëusa would have a son called Dorus, who would be the progenitor of the Dorian people, both of which predictions were in due time verified.

Philemon and Baucis

THE GREEKS SUPPOSED that the divine ruler of the Universe occasionally assumed a human form, and descended from his celestial abode, in order to visit mankind and observe their proceedings, his aim being generally either to punish the guilty, or to reward the deserving.

On one occasion Zeus, accompanied by Hermes, made a journey through Phrygia, seeking hospitality and shelter wherever they went. But nowhere did they receive a kindly welcome till they came to the humble cottage of an old man and his wife called Philemon and Baucis, who entertained them with the greatest kindness, setting before them what frugal fare their humble means permitted, and bidding them welcome with unaffected cordiality. Observing in the course of their simple repast that the wine bowl was miraculously replenished, the aged couple became convinced of the divine nature of their guests. The gods now informed them that on account of its wickedness their native place was doomed to destruction, and told them to climb the neighbouring hill with them, which overlooked the village where they dwelt. What was their dismay on beholding at their feet, in place of the spot where they had passed so many happy years together, nothing but a watery plain, the only house to be seen being their own little cottage, which suddenly changed itself into a temple before their eyes. Zeus now asked the worthy pair to name any wish they particularly desired and it should be granted. They accordingly begged that they might serve the gods in the temple below, and end life together.

Their wish was granted, for, after spending the remainder of their lives in the worship of the gods, they both died at the same instant, and were transformed by Zeus into trees, remaining for ever side by side.

Loves of the Gods

THE GODS have been seen to be capable of many strong emotions, and they loved no less passionately. They loved and married amongst themselves but were also constantly involving themselves in human affairs where they would fall for mortals too. Zeus was particularly known for his desire of mortal women, much to his wife Hera's displeasure. The love of the gods can also translate into love for family, as seen by Demeter's love for her daughter Persephone which is just as fierce as Hades' love; and in Helios' desire for acceptance by his son which ultimately leaves him grief-stricken.

Eros and Psyche

ONCE THERE WAS A KING AND A QUEEN with three lovely daughters. The youngest daughter, Psyche, was so beautiful, so fair of face that she was revered throughout the land, and the subjects of her father reached out to touch her as she passed. No suitors dared to cross her doorstep, so highly was she worshiped. Psyche was deeply lonely.

Her beauty became legend, far and wide, and it was not long before word of it reached the ears of Aphrodite, the epitome of all beauty, the goddess of love herself. Tales of the young princess enraged the jealous goddess, and she made plans to dispose of her. Aphrodite arranged for Psyche's father to present Psyche as a sacrifice, in order to prevent his kingdom being devoured by a monster, and this he grudgingly did, placing her on a mountaintop, and bidding her a tearful farewell.

Eros, the errant son of Aphrodite, was sent to murder Psyche but he too was entranced by her gentle ways, and implored Zephyr, the West Wind, to lift her and place her down far from the hillside, in a lush and verdant valley. When Psyche opened her eyes, she found herself in front of a sumptuous palace unlike any she had seen before. She called out, and although there was no response, quiet voices simmered just beyond her hearing, comforting her, soothing her, setting her at ease. She stretched and thought briefly of food, at which a platter of succulent morsels was laid, as if by magic, at her disposal. When she grew tired, a soft bed was presented, and she slipped dreamlessly into sleep.

Psyche woke in the night. A presence had stirred her, but she felt no fear. A warmth pervaded the room and she closed her eyes, sinking into its musky perfume. She was joined and embraced by a body so inviting, she gave herself at once, filled by a sense of joy that overwhelmed her.

'Who are you,' she whispered, and a finger was laid firmly to her lips. She said no more, spending the night in tender love. When she woke, she felt gilded, but her bed was empty.

And so the days passed, with Psyche growing ever more peaceful, ever happier. She had clothes and jewels which miraculously appeared – her every comfort was seen to. And the only hole in her happiness was loneliness, for apart from the moonlit visits from her phantom husband, she was entirely alone. She'd tried to learn more about this man who held her each night in passionate embrace, but he'd told her that his identity must remain secret, or their alliance would be no more. She agreed to his wishes because she loved him, because he filled her with a sense of belonging that she had never before experienced.

One day, however, her peaceful idyll was interrupted by the cries of her two sisters. Concerned about her disappearance, they'd spent many weeks searching the hills, and now they stood just beyond the bend of the valley. Shrieking with delight, Psyche raced up the mountain, and drew them back into her new home. And as she toured her sisters around her exquisite palace, she failed to notice their growing silence, their churlish looks. Her sisters were sickened with envy, and they teased their younger sister about her ghostly lover.

'No,' she protested, 'he was real.' She felt him, explored him each night. Held him warm in her arms.

But her sisters taunted and teased until Psyche agreed to seek out his identity. That night, when he came to her once again, she broke her word for the first time, leaning across him to light the oil lamp. As she moved, a drop of the hot liquid fell onto the snow white skin of her lover, and his face was revealed. He was none other than the most beautiful of the gods, Eros, son of Aphrodite. But burned, and bewildered, he rose from her bed and disappeared from her forever.

Psyche's torment was so deep that she tried to take her own life. Eros, still deeply in love with his wife, but now invisible to her, saved her on each occasion, caring for her as she travelled across the kingdom in search of him. He longed to touch her, but the wrath of his mother was more than he could bear. He longed to speak to her, but could use only the trees, the winds, the creatures of the forest, to deliver his words.

Searching far and wide for Eros, Psyche came, by and by, to the home of Aphrodite. Poisoned by her jealousy, Aphrodite resolved to dispose of the young princess, knowing not of her son's attachment, caring only that Psyche was more beautiful than she, and that Psyche had eluded her careful plot to send her to her death. She set the young princess impossible tasks, determined to punish her further.

The first task was to pluck the golden wool from a flock of bloodthirsty sheep. As Psyche stood by the edge of their paddock, she heard the quiet song of the reeds in the wind. As she listened, their words became clear. She was not to pluck the wool from their backs. There, on the gorsebushes which lined their field, was the wool that had been brushed from their hides each time they passed. She crept over and filled her basket. Gleefully she returned to Aphrodite, basket held high, but her mistress's sour expression greeted her, and all hope of freedom vanished.

The goddess sent her out once again, this time to fetch water from the stream which flowed to the Styx, the river of the Underworld. As she neared its banks, Psyche grew frightened. The stream itself cut through a deep gorge, and all her efforts to reach its waters failed. Furthermore, as she caught a glimpse of its shimmering blackness, she became aware of the guard of dragons, who patrolled its shores, boiling the seething waters with their fiery breath. She sank down in despair, her bottle falling to her side.

Suddenly it was snatched up, and into the air, clutched in the grasp of Zeus's Royal Eagle. The winds had told him of Psyche's plight, and enchanted by her loveliness, he vowed to help her. Smoothly he dodged the dragons, filling the flask and returning it to her waiting arms.

Aphrodite was ill pleased by this success. She had imagined Psyche long dead by now, and set all her powers of determination to plot the third task. Psyche was to descend to the Afterworld, and beg Persephone for some of her beauty, which should be returned to Aphrodite. Once again Psyche tried to take her own life, deep in desolation and longing for Eros, and frustrated by the seemingly impossible tasks before her. But yet again, she was plucked from death by Eros, and through his powers realized the way to achieve her task. The tower from which she had attempted to leap confirmed the instructions.

Psyche was to follow the path nearby, which would take her to the Afterworld. She was to take several things along – barley cakes and honey cakes for Cerberus, the three-headed dog who guarded the entry and two coins to pay Charon, the ferryman. She was to ignore the messages of her own kind heart and refuse help to anyone who sought her assistance along the way.

Psyche set off, the words ringing in her ears. As she journeyed she was met by hapless travellers who called out for her help. At every turn lay another trap set by Aphrodite, who was determined for Psyche to remain in the Afterworld once and for all. But Psyche too had determination, fed by love for Eros, to whom she longed to return. She made her way past the pitfalls set out for her, and on to Persephone, who presented her with a box.

As she returned once more to the land of the living, she was struck by curiosity, and opened the box. The box seemed empty. But as she struggled to close it, she felt an overwhelming sleep flower around her, kissing shut her eyes, and drawing from her lungs her final breath. Death clung to the maiden, embracing her lifelessness, waiting for its usurpation to be complete.

Ever vigilant, Eros flew down, brushing the sleep of death from her eyes and placing it back in the box. And so Psyche was revived, fresh and invigorated, and glowing with new life. She returned to Aphrodite, and handed over the deadly box. She waited with anticipation. Surely Aphrodite was finished with her now.

But the goddess had a final task in store for Psyche, and led her to a large shed, full of various grains. Here lay oats, and black beans, millet, lentils, vetch and poppyseeds, wheat and rye, mixed together in an overwhelming pile. Psyche was to sort it, said Aphrodite firmly. And then she could be free.

Psyche crouched down and gingerly picked at the pile. Tears welled in her eyes and she felt the beginnings of despair touching again at her heart. As the first glistening tear fell, a tiny voice woke her from her sorrow. An ant, enchanted by the lovely princess, had moved to her side. He could help, he said, and so it was that hundreds of ants marched to the pile, and within just one hour the pile was sorted.

Aphrodite was enraged, but she was also wise enough to know that Psyche was not going to succumb to her plots. She set her free, and Psyche set off once more in her search for Eros.

Now Eros had been deeply disillusioned by his mother's antics. Her jealousy had sparked in him a rebellion such as he'd never felt before, and with a revelatory burst, he flew at once to Olympus and begged Zeus to offer his advice.

Zeus was the King of gods for many reasons. Throughout his reign, many such sensitive matters were put before him, and his awesome wisdom and sense of justice had always prevailed. On this day, Eros was not disappointed. Zeus examined the goodness of Psyche, her dedication and her exquisite charms. He agreed to allow her marriage to Eros, he agreed to make her immortal. And in return Eros must become reconciled to his mother, and they must share the deep respect of family.

And so it was that Psyche became a daughter to Aphrodite, and entered a union with Eros. She returned once again to her palace in the valley, to a happiness that was enriched by the goodness in her heart and which was, as a result of her tribulations, now complete.

The Rape of Persephone

PERSEPHONE WAS THE DAUGHTER of Zeus and Demeter, a virgin of such remarkable beauty that she was kept hidden from the eyes of wishful suitors for all of her life. She spent her days idyllically, gathering fragrant flowers in the fields which spread as far as the eye could see, and dancing with the wood folk, who doted on the young maiden. Demeter was goddess of the earth, and Persephone whiled away the long summery hours helping her mother to gather seeds, to pollinate, and to sow the fertile earth. She was shielded from the outside world by her doting parents, kept carefully away from the dangers that could befall so fair a creature. They lived in the Vale of Enna, where Persephone blossomed like the flowers which surrounded her sanctuary.

One warm, sun-kissed evening, Persephone lay back in the long grasses by the idle stream which trickled through the paddock at the end of the garden. Bees hummed above the lapping waters, butterflies glided and came to rest beside the serene young woman. An eager toad lapped at the darting dragonflies. Persephone's beauty was accentuated by lush green grass, and by the expression of placid contentment which embraced her exquisite features.

It was no wonder then, that the passionate Hades, king of the Underworld, should stop in his tracks when he spied this graceful vision, should draw back the anarchic horses which lunged and tugged at his fiery chariot. He drew a deep breath. He must have her.

Now Hades and Zeus were brothers, and Hades thought nothing of approaching him to ask for Persephone's hand in marriage. Zeus knew that his daughter would be well cared for by Hades, but he felt saddened by the thought of losing her to the world from which no mortal could return. He wavered, reluctant to displease his brother, but more apprehensive still of the wrath of Demeter, who would never allow such a match to take place. Zeus announced that he could not offer his permission, but neither would he deny it, and encouraged by this response, Hades returned to the peaceful spot where Persephone lay and seized her. A great chasm opened in the earth, and holding Persephone under an arm, Hades and his horses plunged into the dark world beneath.

It was many hours before Demeter realized that Persephone had vanished, and many days before she could come to terms with her loss. She shunned the attentions of Zeus, refused to attend the council of the gods. She dressed herself in the robes of a beggarwoman, and in this disguise, prepared to roam the realm, in search of her missing daughter. The earth grew bare as Demeter ceased to tend it; fruit withered on the vine, plenteous fields grew fallow, the warm western winds ceased to blow. The land grew cold and barren.

Demeter's travels took her across many lands. At each, she stopped, searched, and begged for information. At each she was turned away empty-handed, often snubbed and ill-treated. She grew colder, and famine spread across the earth. At last she came to the land of Eleusis, the kingdom of Celeus and his wife Metaneira. There Demeter, in her disguise, was welcomed and taken in by Queen Metaneira, who instinctively trusted the beggarwoman and asked her to act as nurse to her baby son, the Prince Demaphoon.

Demeter was weakened by her journey, and welcomed the respite. She fell in love with the young prince, and poured out her longing for her daughter in his care. She grew more content, bathing the infant in nectar and holding him daily above the fire in order to burn away his mortality. The greatest gift she could offer him was immortality, and she poured her supreme powers into the process, protecting the child from the flames so that he remained unharmed.

One day, Metaneira paid an unexpected visit to the nursery, and chanced to see this extraordinary sight. She flew into a panic, and the startled Demeter dropped the child in to the fire, where he was burned to death. At once Demeter took on her godly form, and chastised the Queen for causing the death of the child they both loved so deeply. The people of Eleusis paid tribute to the god in their midst, and in return she set up a temple, and showed them how to plant and sow seeds in the arid earth. She blessed them, and as their kindness was repaid by an end to their years of famine, so came the news she had long awaited.

A stranger came to her in her temple one night, as she prepared to retire. He'd been tending his flocks, he said, and he'd seen the ground open up to greet a flaming chariot led by a team of black horses. In the carriage was a screaming girl who'd thrust something into the startled herder's hands, just before the earth closed upon her. He held it out to her now. It was Persephone's girdle.

The wretched Demeter knew at once what had befallen her beloved precious daughter. She returned in haste to Olympus, where she confronted Zeus. And so it was decided that Persephone should be allowed to return to her mother. He sent word to Hades, who reluctantly agreed to part from his young bride. As Persephone prepared to leave, he shyly offered her a pomegranate to eat on the journey, a token of his love, his esteem, he said. Persephone was charmed by the gesture, and breaking the fast she had undertaken while trapped in the Underworld, she nibbled at several seeds.

At once darkness fell upon her. Her mother stood just past the gates to the Underworld, but she was unable to reach her. For any mortal who eats or drinks in the land of Hades has no choice but to remain there forever. A chasm opened between mother and child, one which neither could pass.

But Zeus, ashamed by his part in the matter, and deeply concerned by Demeter's neglect of the land, which refused to flower or bear fruit, stepped in. It was agreed that Persephone would become reunited with her mother, and make her home again on earth. But for three months each year, one month for every seed of the pomegranate she had eaten, she must return to the Underworld, and become Hades' queen.

Their reunion was warmed by the sun, which shone for the first time on the cold land. Birds poked their heads from knotted branches, buds and then leaves thrust their way through the hardened earth. Spring had arrived in all her fecund splendour.

But for the three months each year in which Persephone returns to Hades, Demeter throws her cloak across the earth, bringing sterility and darkness until Persephone breathes once more in the land of the living, bringing Spring.

Zeus' Affairs

🦅

IN ADDITION TO THE SEVEN IMMORTAL WIVES of Zeus, he was also allied to a number of mortal maidens whom he visited under various disguises, as it was supposed that if he revealed himself in his true form as king of heaven the splendour of his glory would cause instant destruction to mortals. The mortal consorts of Zeus have been such a favourite theme with poets, painters, and sculptors, that it is necessary to give some account of their individual history. Those best known are Antiope, Leda, Europa, Callisto, Alcmene, Semele, Io, and Danae. Zeus appeared to Danae under the form of a shower of gold, and more of her story is told under the myth of Perseus.

Antiope, to whom Zeus appeared under the form of a satyr, was the daughter of Nicteus, king of Thebes. To escape the anger of her father she fled to Sicyon, where king Epopeus, enraptured with her wonderful beauty, made her his wife without asking her father's consent. This so enraged Nicteus that he declared war against Epopeus, in order to compel him to restore Antiope. At his death, which took place before he could succeed in his purpose, Nicteus left his kingdom to his brother Lycus, commanding him, at the same time, to carry on the war, and execute his vengeance. Lycus invaded Sicyon, defeated and killed Epopeus, and brought back

Antiope as a prisoner. On the way to Thebes she gave birth to her twin sons, Amphion and Zethus, who, by the orders of Lycus, were at once exposed on Mount Cithaeron, and would have perished but for the kindness of a shepherd, who took pity on them and preserved their lives. Antiope was, for many years, held captive by her uncle Lycus, and compelled to suffer the utmost cruelty at the hands of his wife Dirce. But one day her bonds were miraculously loosened, and she flew for shelter and protection to the humble dwelling of her sons on Mount Cithaeron. During the long period of their mother's captivity the babes had grown into sturdy youths, and, as they listened angrily to the story of her wrongs, they became all impatience to avenge them. Setting off at once to Thebes they succeeded in possessing themselves of the town, and after slaying the cruel Lycus they bound Dirce by the hair to the horns of a wild bull, which dragged her hither and thither until she expired. Her mangled body was cast into the fount near Thebes, which still bears her name. Amphion became king of Thebes in his uncle's stead. He was a friend of the Muses, and devoted to music and poetry. His brother, Zethus, was famous for his skill in archery, and was passionately fond of the chase. It is said that when Amphion wished to enclose the town of Thebes with walls and towers, he had but to play a sweet melody on the lyre, given to him by Hermes, and the huge stones began to move, and obediently fitted themselves together.

Leda, whose affections Zeus won under the form of a swan, was the daughter of Thestius, king of Aetolia. Her twin-sons, Castor and (Polydeuces or) Pollux, were renowned for their tender attachment to each other. They were also famous for their physical accomplishments, Castor being the most expert charioteer of his day, and Pollux the first of pugilists. Their names appear both among the hunters of the Calydonian boar-hunt and the heroes of the Argonautic expedition. The brothers became attached to the daughters of Leucippus, prince of the Messenians, who had been betrothed by their father to Idas and Lynceus, sons of Aphareus. Having persuaded Leucippus to break his promise, the twins carried off the maidens as their brides. Idas and Lynceus, naturally furious at this proceeding, challenged the Dioscuri to mortal combat, in which Castor perished by the hand of Idas, and Lynceus by that of Pollux. Zeus wished to confer the gift of immortality upon Pollux, but he refused to accept it unless allowed to share it with Castor. Zeus gave the desired permission, and the faithful brothers were both allowed to live, but only on alternate days. The Dioscuri received divine honours throughout Greece, and were worshipped with special reverence at Sparta.

Europa was the beautiful daughter of Agenor, king of Phoenicia. She was one day gathering flowers with her companions in a meadow near the sea-shore, when Zeus, charmed with her great beauty, and wishing to win her love, transformed himself into a beautiful white bull, and trotted quietly up to the princess, so as not to alarm her. Surprised at the gentleness of the animal, and admiring its beauty, as it lay placidly on the grass, she caressed it, crowned it with flowers, and, at last, playfully seated herself on its back. Hardly had she done so than the disguised god bounded away with his lovely burden, and swam across the sea with her to the island of Crete.

Europa was the mother of Minos, Aeacus, and Rhadamanthus. Minos, who became king of Crete, was celebrated for his justice and moderation, and after death he was created one of the judges of the lower world, which office he held in conjunction with his brothers.

Callisto, the daughter of Lycaon, king of Arcadia, was a huntress in the train of Artemis, devoted to the pleasures of the chase, who had made a vow never to marry; but Zeus, under the form of the huntress-goddess, succeeded in obtaining her affections. Hera, being extremely jealous of her, changed her into a bear, and caused Artemis (who failed to recognize her attendant under this form) to hunt her in the chase, and put an end to her existence. After her death she was placed by Zeus among the stars as a constellation, under the name of Arctos, or the bear.

Alcmene, the daughter of Electryon, king of Mycenae, was betrothed to her cousin Amphytrion; but, during his absence on a perilous undertaking, Zeus assumed his form, and obtained her affections. Heracles (whose world-renowned exploits will be related among the legends) was the son of Alcmene and Zeus.

Semele, a beautiful princess, the daughter of Cadmus, king of Phoenicia, was greatly beloved by Zeus. Like the unfortunate Callisto, she was hated by Hera with jealous malignity, and the haughty queen of heaven determined to effect her destruction. Disguising herself, therefore, as Beroe, Semele's faithful old nurse, she artfully persuaded her to insist upon Zeus visiting her, as he appeared to Hera, in all his power and glory, well knowing that this would cause her instant death. Semele, suspecting no treachery, followed the advice of her supposed nurse; and the next time Zeus came to her, she earnestly entreated him to grant the favour she was about to ask. Zeus swore by the Styx (which was to the gods an irrevocable oath) to accede to her request whatsoever it might be. Semele, therefore, secure of gaining her petition, begged of Zeus to appear to her in all the glory of his divine power and majesty. As he had sworn to grant whatever she asked of him, he was compelled to comply with her wish; he therefore revealed himself as the mighty lord of the universe, accompanied by thunder and lightning, and she was instantly consumed in the flames.

Io, daughter of Inachus, king of Argos, was a priestess of Hera. She was very beautiful, and Zeus, who was much attached to her, transformed her into a white cow, in order to defeat the jealous intrigues of Hera, who, however, was not to be deceived. Aware of the stratagem, she contrived to obtain the animal from Zeus, and placed her under the watchful care of a man called Argus-Panoptes, who fastened her to an olive-tree in the grove of Hera. He had a hundred eyes, of which, when asleep, he never closed more than two at a time; being thus always on the watch, Hera found him extremely useful in keeping guard over Io. Hermes, however, by the command of Zeus, succeeded in putting all his eyes to sleep with the sound of his magic lyre, and then, taking advantage of his helpless condition, slew him. The story goes, that in commemoration of the services which Argus had rendered her, Hera placed his eyes on the tail of a peacock, as a lasting memorial of her gratitude. Ever fertile in resource, Hera now sent a gadfly to worry and torment the unfortunate Io incessantly, and she wandered all over the world in hopes of escaping from her tormentor. At length she reached Egypt, where she found rest and freedom from the persecutions of her enemy. On the banks of the Nile she resumed her original form and gave birth to a son called Epaphus, who afterwards became king of Egypt, and built the famous city of Memphis.

Helios

❦

HELIOS IS SAID to have loved Clytie, a daughter of Oceanus, who ardently returned his affection; but in the course of time the fickle sun-god transferred his devotion to Leucothea, the daughter of Orchamus, king of the eastern countries, which so angered the forsaken Clytie that she informed Orchamus of his daughter's attachment, and he punished her by inhumanly burying her alive. Helios, overcome with grief, endeavoured, by every means in his power, to recall her to life. At last, finding all his efforts unavailing, he sprinkled her grave with heavenly nectar, and immediately there sprang forth from the spot a shoot of frankincense, which spread around its aromatic perfume.

The jealous Clytie gained nothing by her cruel conduct, for the sun-god came to her no more. Inconsolable at his loss, she threw herself upon the ground, and refused all sustenance. For nine long days she turned her face towards the glorious god of day, as he moved along the heavens, till at length her limbs became rooted in the ground, and she was transformed into a flower, which ever turns towards the sun.

Helios married Perse, daughter of Oceanus, and their children were, Aëtes, king of Colchis (celebrated in the legend of the Argonauts as the possessor of the Golden Fleece), and Circe, the renowned sorceress.

Helios had another son named Phaethon, whose mother was Clymene, one of the Oceanides. The youth was very beautiful, and a great favourite with Aphrodite, who intrusted him with the care of one of her temples, which flattering proof of her regard caused him to become vain and presumptuous. His friend Epaphus, son of Zeus and Io, endeavoured to check his youthful vanity by pretending to disbelieve his assertion that the sun-god was his father. Phaethon, full of resentment, and eager to be able to refute the calumny, hastened to his mother Clymene, and besought her to tell him whether Helios was really his father. Moved by his entreaties, and at the same time angry at the reproach of Epaphus, Clymene pointed to the glorious sun, then shining down upon them, and assured her son that in that bright orb he beheld the author of his being, adding that if he had still any doubt, he might visit the radiant dwelling of the great god of light and inquire for himself. Overjoyed at his mother's reassuring words, and following the directions she gave him, Phaethon quickly wended his way to his father's palace.

As he entered the palace of the sun-god the dazzling rays almost blinded him, and prevented him from approaching the throne on which his father was seated, surrounded by the Hours, Days, Months, Years, and Seasons. Helios, who with his all-seeing eye had watched him from afar, removed his crown of glittering rays, and bade him not to be afraid, but to draw near to his father. Encouraged by this kind reception, Phaethon entreated him to bestow upon him such a proof of his love, that all the world might be convinced that he was indeed his son; whereupon Helios desired him to ask any favour he pleased, and swore by the Styx that it should be granted. The impetuous youth immediately requested permission to drive the chariot of the sun for one whole day. His father listened horror-struck to this presumptuous demand, and by representing the many dangers which would beset his path, endeavoured to dissuade him from so perilous an undertaking; but his son, deaf to all advice, pressed his point with such pertinacity, that Helios was reluctantly compelled to lead him to the chariot. Phaethon paused for a moment to admire the beauty of the glittering equipage, the gift of the god of fire, who had formed it of gold, and ornamented it with precious stones, which reflected the rays of the sun. And now Helios, seeing his sister, the Dawn, opening her doors in the rosy east, ordered the Hours to yoke the horses. The goddesses speedily obeyed the command, and the father then anointed the face of his son with a sacred balm, to enable him to endure the burning flames which issued from the nostrils of the steeds, and sorrowfully placing his crown of rays upon his head, desired him to ascend the chariot.

The eager youth joyfully took his place and grasped the coveted reins, but no sooner did the fiery coursers of the sun feel the inexperienced hand which attempted to guide them, than they became restive and unmanageable. Wildly they rushed out of their accustomed track, now soaring so high as to threaten the heavens with destruction, now descending so low as nearly to set the earth on fire. At last the unfortunate charioteer, blinded with the glare, and terrified at the awful devastation he had caused, dropped the reins from his trembling hands. Mountains and forests were in flames, rivers and streams were dried up, and a general conflagration was imminent. The scorched earth now called on Zeus for help, who hurled his thunderbolt at Phaethon, and with a flash of lightning brought the fiery steeds to a standstill. The lifeless body of the youth fell headlong into the river Eridanus, where it was received and buried by the nymphs of the stream. His sisters mourned so long for him that they were transformed by Zeus into poplars, and the tears they shed, falling into the waters, became drops of clear, transparent amber. Cycnus, the faithful friend of the unhappy Phaethon, felt such overwhelming grief at his terrible fate, that he pined and wasted away. The gods, moved with compassion, transformed him into a swan, which for ever brooded over the fatal spot where the waters had closed over the head of his unfortunate friend.

The chief seat of the worship of Helios was the island of Rhodes, which according to the following myth was his especial territory. At the time of the Titanomachia, when the gods were dividing the world by lot, Helios happened to be absent, and consequently received no share. He, therefore, complained to Zeus, who proposed to have a new allotment, but this Helios would not allow, saying, that as he pursued his daily journey, his penetrating eye had beheld a lovely, fertile island lying beneath the waves of the ocean, and that if the immortals would swear to give him the undisturbed possession of this spot, he would be content to accept it as his share of the universe. The gods took the oath, whereupon the island of Rhodes immediately raised itself above the surface of the waters.

Eos and Tithonus

EOS, THE DAWN, like her brother Helios, whose advent she always announced, was also deified by the early Greeks. She too had her own chariot, which she drove across the vast horizon both morning and night, before and after the sun-god. Hence she is not merely the personification of the rosy morn, but also of twilight, for which reason her palace is placed in the west, on the island Aeaea. The abode of Eos is a magnificent structure, surrounded by flowery meads and velvety lawns, where nymphs and other immortal beings, wind in and out in the mazy figures of the dance, whilst the music of a sweetly-tuned melody accompanies their graceful, gliding movements.

Eos is described by the poets as a beautiful maiden with rosy arms and fingers, and large wings, whose plumage is of an ever-changing hue; she bears a star on her forehead, and a torch in her hand. Wrapping round her the rich folds of her violet-tinged mantle, she leaves her couch before the break of day, and herself yokes her two horses, Lampetus and Phaethon, to her glorious chariot. She then hastens with active cheerfulness to open the gates of heaven, in order to herald the approach of her brother, the god of day, whilst the tender plants and flowers, revived by the morning dew, lift their heads to welcome her as she passes.

Eos first married the Titan Astraeus, and their children were Heosphorus (Hesperus), the evening star, and the winds. She afterwards became united to Tithonus, son of Laomedon, king of Troy, who had won her affection by his unrivalled beauty; and Eos, unhappy at the thought of their being ever separated by death, obtained for him from Zeus the gift of immortality, forgetting, however, to add to it that of eternal youth. The consequence was that when, in the course of time, Tithonus grew old and decrepid, and lost all the beauty which had won her admiration, Eos became disgusted with his infirmities, and at last shut him up in a chamber, where soon little else was left of him but his voice, which had now sunk into a weak, feeble quaver. According to some of the later poets, he became so weary of his cheerless and miserable existence, that he entreated to be allowed to die. This was, however, impossible; but Eos, pitying his unhappy condition, exerted her divine power, and changed him into a grasshopper, which is, as it were, all voice, and whose monotonous, ceaseless chirpings may not inaptly be compared to the meaningless babble of extreme old age.

The Loves of Apollo

IS FIRST LOVE WAS DAPHNE (daughter of Peneus, the river-god), who was so averse to marriage that she entreated her father to allow her to lead a life of celibacy, and devote herself to the chase, which she loved to the exclusion of all other pursuits. But one day, soon after his victory over the Python, Apollo happened to see Eros bending his bow, and proud of his own superior strength and skill, he laughed at the efforts of the little archer, saying that such a weapon was more suited to the one who had just killed the terrible serpent. Eros angrily replied that his arrow should pierce the heart of the mocker himself, and flying off to the summit of Mount Parnassus, he drew from his quiver two darts of different workmanship—one of gold, which had the effect of inspiring love; the other of lead, which created aversion. Taking aim at Apollo, he pierced his breast with the golden shaft, whilst the leaden one he discharged into the bosom of the beautiful Daphne. The son of

Leto instantly felt the most ardent affection for the nymph, who, on her part, evinced the greatest dislike towards her divine lover, and, at his approach, fled from him like a hunted deer. He called upon her in the most endearing accents to stay, but she still sped on, until at length, becoming faint with fatigue, and fearing that she was about to succumb, she called upon the gods to come to her aid. Hardly had she uttered her prayer before a heavy torpor seized her limbs, and just as Apollo threw out his arms to embrace her, she became transformed into a laurel-bush. He sorrowfully crowned his head with its leaves, and declared, that in memory of his love, it should henceforth remain evergreen, and be held sacred to him.

He next sought the love of Marpessa, the daughter of Evenus; but though her father approved his suit, the maiden preferred a youth named Idas, who contrived to carry her off in a winged chariot which he had procured from Poseidon. Apollo pursued the fugitives, whom he quickly overtook, and forcibly seizing the bride, refused to resign her. Zeus then interfered, and declared that Marpessa herself must decide which of her lovers should claim her as his wife. After due reflection she accepted Idas as her husband, judiciously concluding that although the attractions of the divine Apollo were superior to those of her lover, it would be wiser to unite herself to a mortal, who, growing old with herself, would be less likely to forsake her, when advancing years should rob her of her charms.

Cassandra, daughter of Priam, king of Troy, was another object of the love of Apollo. She feigned to return his affection, and promised to marry him, provided he would confer upon her the gift of prophecy; but having received the boon she desired, the treacherous maiden refused to comply with the conditions upon which it had been granted. Incensed at her breach of faith, Apollo, unable to recall the gift he had bestowed, rendered it useless by causing her predictions to fail in obtaining credence. Cassandra became famous in history for her prophetic powers, but her prophecies were never believed. For instance, she warned her brother Paris that if he brought back a wife from Greece he would cause the destruction of his father's house and kingdom; she also warned the Trojans not to admit the wooden horse within the walls of the city, and foretold to Agamemnon all the disasters which afterwards befell him.

Apollo afterwards married Coronis, a nymph of Larissa, and thought himself happy in the possession of her faithful love; but once more he was doomed to disappointment, for one day his favourite bird, the crow, flew to him with the intelligence that his wife had transferred her affections to a youth of Haemonia. Apollo, burning with rage, instantly destroyed her with one of his death-bringing darts. Too late he repented of his rashness, for she had been tenderly beloved by him, and he would fain have recalled her to life; but, although he exerted all his healing powers, his efforts were in vain. He punished the crow for its garrulity by changing the colour of its plumage from pure white to intense black, and forbade it to fly any longer among the other birds.

Coronis left an infant son named Asclepius, who afterwards became god of medicine. His powers were so extraordinary that he could not only cure the sick, but could even restore the dead to life. At last Aïdes complained to Zeus that the number of shades conducted to his dominions was daily decreasing, and the great ruler of Olympus, fearing that mankind, thus protected against sickness and death, would be able to defy the gods themselves, killed Asclepius with one of his thunderbolts. The loss of his highly gifted son so exasperated Apollo that, being unable to vent his anger on Zeus, he destroyed the Cyclops, who had forged the fatal thunderbolts. For this offence, Apollo would have been banished by Zeus to Tartarus, but at the earnest intercession of Leto he partially relented, and contented himself with depriving him of all power and dignity, and imposing on him a temporary servitude in the house of Admetus, king of Thessaly.

Apollo faithfully served his royal master for nine years in the humble capacity of a shepherd, and was treated by him with every kindness and consideration. During the period of his service the king sought the hand of Alcestis, the beautiful daughter of Pelias, son of Poseidon; but her father declared that he would only resign her to the suitor who should succeed in yoking a lion and a wild boar to his chariot. By the aid of his divine herdsman, Admetus accomplished this difficult task, and gained his bride. Nor was this the only favour which the king received from the exiled god, for Apollo obtained from the Fates the gift of immortality for his benefactor, on condition that when his last hour approached, some member of his own family should be willing to die in his stead. When the fatal hour arrived, and Admetus felt that he was at the point of death, he implored his aged parents to yield to him their few remaining days. But "life is sweet" even to old age, and they both refused to make the sacrifice demanded of them. Alcestis, however, who had secretly devoted herself to death for her husband, was seized with a mortal sickness, which kept pace with his rapid recovery. The devoted wife breathed her last in the arms of Admetus, and he had just consigned her to the tomb, when Heracles chanced to come to the palace. Admetus held the rites of hospitality so sacred, that he at first kept silence with regard to his great bereavement; but as soon as his friend heard what had occurred, he bravely descended into the tomb, and when death came to claim his prey, he exerted his marvellous strength, and held him in his arms, until he promised to restore the beautiful and heroic queen to the bosom of her family.

Whilst pursuing the peaceful life of a shepherd, Apollo formed a strong friendship with two youths named Hyacinthus and Cyparissus, but the great favour shown to them by the god did not suffice to shield them from misfortune. The former was one day throwing the discus with Apollo, when, running too eagerly to take up the one thrown by the god, he was struck on the head with it and killed on the spot. Apollo was overcome with grief at the sad end of his young favourite, but being unable to restore him to life, he changed him into the flower called after him the Hyacinth. Cyparissus had the misfortune to kill by accident one of Apollo's favourite stags, which so preyed on his mind that he gradually pined away, and died of a broken heart. He was transformed by the god into a cypress-tree, which owes its name to this story

Dionysus and Ariadne

AN INCIDENT WHICH OCCURRED to Dionysus on one of his travels has been a favourite subject with the classic poets. One day, as some Tyrrhenian pirates approached the shores of Greece, they beheld Dionysus, in the form of a beautiful youth, attired in radiant garments. Thinking to secure a rich prize, they seized him, bound him, and conveyed him on board their vessel, resolved to carry him with them to Asia and there sell him as a slave. But the fetters dropped from his limbs, and the pilot, who was the first to perceive the miracle, called upon his companions to restore the youth carefully to the spot whence they had taken him, assuring them that he was a god, and that adverse winds and storms would, in all probability, result from their impious conduct. But, refusing to part with their prisoner, they set sail for the open sea.

Suddenly, to the alarm of all on board, the ship stood still, masts and sails were covered with clustering vines and wreaths of ivy-leaves, streams of fragrant wine inundated the vessel, and heavenly strains of music were heard around. The terrified crew, too late repentant, crowded round the pilot for protection, and entreated him to steer for the shore. But the hour of retribution had arrived.

Dionysus assumed the form of a lion, whilst beside him appeared a bear, which, with a terrific roar, rushed upon the captain and tore him in pieces; the sailors, in an agony of terror, leaped overboard, and were changed into dolphins. The discreet and pious steersman was alone permitted to escape the fate of his companions, and to him Dionysus, who had resumed his true form, addressed words of kind and affectionate encouragement, and announced his name and dignity. They now set sail, and Dionysus desired the pilot to land him at the island of Naxos, where he found the lovely Ariadne, daughter of Minos, king of Crete. She had been abandoned by Theseus on this lonely spot, and, when Dionysus now beheld her, was lying fast asleep on a rock, worn out with sorrow and weeping. Rapt in admiration, the god stood gazing at the beautiful vision before him, and when she at length unclosed her eyes, he revealed himself to her, and, in gentle tones, sought to banish her grief. Grateful for his kind sympathy, coming as it did at a moment when she had deemed herself forsaken and friendless, she gradually regained her former serenity, and, yielding to his entreaties, consented to become his wife.

Crime and Punishment

THE GODS were nothing if not vengeful, as has been seen repeatedly in the Greek epics, and any suggestion of hubris or irreverence on the mortal side was certainly to be punished. In some cases the Gods can seem to be overly sensitive to our modern sensibilities, but the Greeks did not question the all-powerful deities who had to be properly worshipped and appeased. However undoubtedly some humans were capable of truly wicked deeds and Tartarus was the portion of the Underworld reserved for their ingeniously devised punishments.

Tartarus

❧

ARTARUS WAS A VAST and gloomy expanse, as far below Hades as the earth is distant from the skies. There the Titans, fallen from their high estate, dragged out a dreary and monotonous existence; there also were Otus and Ephialtes, those giant sons of Poseidon, who, with impious hands, had attempted to scale Olympus and dethrone its mighty ruler. Principal among the sufferers in this abode of gloom were Tityus, Tantalus, Sisyphus, Ixion, and the Danaïdes.

Tityus, one of the earth-born giants, had insulted Hera on her way to Peitho, for which offence Zeus flung him into Tartarus, where he suffered dreadful torture, inflicted by two vultures, which perpetually gnawed his liver.

Tantalus was a wise and wealthy king of Lydia, with whom the gods themselves condescended to associate; he was even permitted to sit at table with Zeus, who delighted in his conversation, and listened with interest to the wisdom of his observations. Tantalus, however, elated at these distinguished marks of divine favour, presumed upon his position, and used unbecoming language to Zeus himself; he also stole nectar and ambrosia from the table of the gods, with which he regaled his friends; but his greatest crime consisted in killing his own son, Pelops, and serving him up at one of the banquets to the gods, in order to test their omniscience. For these heinous offences he was condemned by Zeus to eternal punishment in Tartarus, where, tortured with an ever-burning thirst, he was plunged up to the chin in water, which, as he stooped to drink, always receded from his parched lips. Tall trees, with spreading branches laden with delicious fruits, hung temptingly over his head; but no sooner did he raise himself to grasp them, than a wind arose, and carried them beyond his reach.

Sisyphus was a great tyrant who, according to some accounts, barbarously murdered all travellers who came into his dominions, by hurling upon them enormous pieces of rock. In punishment for his crimes he was condemned to roll incessantly a huge block of stone up a steep hill, which, as soon as it reached the summit, always rolled back again to the plain below.

Ixion was a king of Thessaly to whom Zeus accorded the privilege of joining the festive banquets of the gods; but, taking advantage of his exalted position, he presumed to aspire to the favour of Hera, which so greatly incensed Zeus, that he struck him with his thunderbolts, and commanded Hermes to throw him into Tartarus, and bind him to an ever-revolving wheel.

The Danaides were the fifty daughters of Danaus, king of Argos, who had married their fifty cousins, the sons of Aegyptus. By the command of their father, who had been warned by an oracle that his son-in-law would cause his death, they all killed their husbands in one night, Hypermnestra alone excepted. Their punishment in the lower world was to fill with water a vessel full of holes, a never-ending and useless task.

Aïdes is usually represented as a man of mature years and stern majestic mien, bearing a striking resemblance to his brother Zeus; but the gloomy and inexorable expression of the face contrasts forcibly with that peculiar benignity which so characterizes the countenance of the mighty ruler of heaven. He is seated on a throne of ebony, with his queen, the grave and sad Persephone, beside him, and wears a full beard, and long flowing black hair, which hangs straight down over his forehead; in his hand he either bears a two-pronged fork or the keys of the lower world, and at his feet sits Cerberus. He is sometimes seen in a chariot of gold, drawn by four black horses, and wearing on his head a helmet made for him by the Cyclops, which rendered the wearer invisible. This helmet he frequently lent to mortals and immortals.

The Punishments of Apollo

B UT THOUGH APOLLO WAS SO RENOWNED in the art of music, there were two individuals who had the effrontery to consider themselves equal to him in this respect, and, accordingly, each challenged him to compete with them in a musical contest. These were Marsyas and Pan. Marsyas was a satyr, who, having picked up the flute which Athene had thrown away in disgust, discovered, to his great delight and astonishment, that, in consequence of its having touched the lips of a goddess, it played of itself in the most charming manner. Marsyas, who was a great lover of music, and much beloved on this account by all the elf-like denizens of the woods and glens, was so intoxicated with joy at this discovery, that he foolishly challenged Apollo to compete with him in a musical contest. The challenge being accepted, the Muses were chosen umpires, and it was decided that the unsuccessful candidate should suffer the punishment of being flayed alive. For a long time the merits of both claimants remained so equally balanced, that it was impossible to award the palm of victory to either, seeing which, Apollo, resolved to conquer, added the sweet tones of his melodious voice to the strains of his lyre, and this at once turned the scale in his favour. The unhappy Marsyas being defeated, had to undergo the terrible penalty, and his untimely fate was universally lamented; indeed the Satyrs and Dryads, his companions, wept so incessantly at his fate, that their tears, uniting together, formed a river in Phrygia which is still known by the name of Marsyas.

The result of the contest with Pan was by no means of so serious a character. The god of shepherds having affirmed that he could play more skilfully on his flute of seven reeds (the syrinx or Pan's pipe), than Apollo on his world-renowned lyre, a contest ensued, in which Apollo was pronounced the victor by all the judges appointed to decide between the rival candidates. Midas, king of Phrygia, alone demurred at this decision, having the bad taste to prefer the uncouth tones of the Pan's pipe to the refined melodies of Apollo's lyre. Incensed at the obstinacy and stupidity of the Phrygian king, Apollo punished him by giving him the ears of an ass. Midas, horrified at being thus disfigured, determined to hide his disgrace from his subjects by means of a cap; his barber, however, could not be kept in ignorance of the fact, and was therefore bribed with rich gifts never to reveal it. Finding, however, that he could not keep the secret any longer, he dug a hole in the ground into which he whispered it; then closing up the aperture he returned home, feeling greatly relieved at having thus eased his mind of its burden. But after all, this very humiliating secret was revealed to the world, for some reeds which sprung up from the spot murmured incessantly, as they waved to and fro in the wind: "King Midas has the ears of an ass."

In the sad and beautiful story of Niobe, daughter of Tantalus, and wife of Amphion, king of Thebes, we have another instance of the severe punishments meted out by Apollo to those who in any way incurred his displeasure. Niobe was the proud mother of seven sons and seven daughters, and exulting in the number of her children, she, upon one occasion, ridiculed the worship of Leto, because she had but one son and daughter, and desired the Thebans, for the future, to give to her the honours and sacrifices which they had hitherto offered to the mother of Apollo and Artemis. The sacrilegious words had scarcely passed her lips before Apollo called upon his sister Artemis to assist him in avenging the insult offered to their mother, and soon their invisible arrows sped through the air. Apollo slew all the sons, and Artemis had already slain all the daughters save one, the youngest and best beloved, whom Niobe clasped in her arms, when the agonized mother implored the enraged deities to leave her, at least, one out of all her beautiful children; but, even as she prayed, the deadly arrow reached the heart of this child also. Meanwhile the unhappy father, unable to bear the loss of his children, had destroyed himself, and his dead body lay beside the lifeless corpse of his favourite son. Widowed and childless, the heart-broken mother sat among her dead, and the gods, in pity for her unutterable woe, turned her into a stone, which they transferred to Siphylus, her native Phrygian mountain, where it still continues to shed tears.

The Calydonian Boar Hunt

ARTEMIS RESENTED ANY DISREGARD or neglect of her worship; a remarkable instance of this is shown in the story of the Calydonian boar hunt, which is as follows:

Oeneus, king of Calydon in Aetolia, had incurred the displeasure of Artemis by neglecting to include her in a general sacrifice to the gods which he had offered up, out of gratitude for a bountiful harvest. The goddess, enraged at this neglect, sent a wild boar of extraordinary size and prodigious strength, which destroyed the sprouting grain, laid waste the fields, and threatened the inhabitants with famine and death. At this juncture, Meleager, the brave son of Oeneus, returned from the Argonautic expedition, and finding his country ravaged by this dreadful scourge, entreated the assistance of all the celebrated heroes of the age to join him in hunting the ferocious monster. Among the most famous of those who responded to his call were Jason, Castor and Pollux, Idas and Lynceus, Peleus, Telamon, Admetus, Perithous, and Theseus. The brothers of Althea, wife of Oeneus, joined the hunters, and Meleager also enlisted into his service the fleet-footed huntress Atalanta.

The father of this maiden was Schoeneus, an Arcadian, who, disappointed at the birth of a daughter when he had particularly desired a son, had exposed her on the Parthenian Hill, where he left her to perish. Here she was nursed by a she-bear, and at last found by some hunters, who reared her, and gave her the name of Atalanta. As the maiden grew up, she became an ardent lover of the chase, and was alike distinguished for her beauty and courage. Though often wooed, she led a life of strict celibacy, an oracle having predicted that inevitable misfortune awaited her, should she give herself in marriage to any of her numerous suitors.

Many of the heroes objected to hunt in company with a maiden; but Meleager, who loved Atalanta, overcame their opposition, and the valiant band set out on their expedition. Atalanta was the first to wound the boar with her spear, but not before two of the heroes had met their death from his fierce tusks. After a long and desperate encounter, Meleager succeeded in killing the monster, and presented the head and hide to Atalanta, as trophies of the victory. The uncles of Meleager, however, forcibly took the hide from the maiden, claiming their right to the spoil as next of kin, if Meleager resigned it. Artemis, whose anger was still unappeased, caused a violent quarrel to arise between uncles and nephew, and, in the struggle which ensued, Meleager killed his mother's brothers, and then restored the hide to Atalanta. When Althea beheld the dead bodies of the slain heroes, her grief and anger knew no bounds. She swore to revenge the death of her brothers on her own son, and unfortunately for him, the instrument of vengeance lay ready to her hand.

At the birth of Meleager, the Moirae, or Fates, entered the house of Oeneus, and pointing to a piece of wood then burning on the hearth, declared that as soon as it was consumed the babe would surely die. On hearing this, Althea seized the brand, laid it up carefully in a chest, and henceforth preserved it as her most precious possession. But now, love for her son giving place to the resentment she felt against the murderer of her brothers, she threw the fatal brand into the devouring flames. As it consumed, the vigour of Meleager wasted away, and when it was reduced to ashes, he expired. Repenting too late the terrible effects of her rash deed, Althea, in remorse and despair, took away her own life.

The news of the courage and intrepidity displayed by Atalanta in the famous boar hunt, being carried to the ears of her father, caused him to acknowledge his long-lost child. Urged by him to choose one of her numerous suitors, she consented to do so, but made it a condition that he alone, who could outstrip her in the race, should become her husband, whilst those she defeated should be put to death by her, with the lance which she bore in her hand. Thus many suitors had perished, for the maiden was unequalled for swiftness of foot, but at last a beautiful youth, named Hippomenes, who had vainly endeavoured to win her love by his assiduous attentions in the chase, ventured to enter the fatal lists. Knowing that only by stratagem could he hope to be successful, he obtained, by the help of Aphrodite, three golden apples from the garden of the Hesperides, which he threw down at intervals during his course. Atalanta, secure of victory, stooped to pick up the tempting fruit, and, in the meantime, Hippomenes arrived at the goal. He became the husband of the lovely Atalanta, but forgot, in his newly found happiness, the gratitude which he owed to Aphrodite, and the goddess withdrew her favour from the pair. Not long after, the prediction which foretold misfortune to Atalanta, in the event of her marriage, was verified, for she and her husband, having strayed unsanctioned into a sacred grove of Zeus, were both transformed into lions.

The trophies of the ever-memorable boar hunt had been carried by Atalanta into Arcadia, and, for many centuries, the identical hide and enormous tusks of the Calydonian boar hung in the temple of Athene at Tegea. The tusks were afterwards conveyed to Rome, and shown there among other curiosities.

A similar forcible instance of the manner in which Artemis resented any intrusion on her retirement, is seen in the fate which befell the famous hunter Actaeon, who happening one day to see Artemis and her attendants bathing, imprudently ventured to approach the spot. The goddess, incensed at his audacity, sprinkled him with water, and transformed him into a stag, whereupon he was torn in pieces and devoured by his own dogs.

The Cattle of Admetus

❧

HERMES WAS THE SON of Zeus and Maia, the eldest and most beautiful of the seven Pleiades (daughters of Atlas), and was born in a cave of Mount Cyllene in Arcadia. As a mere babe, he exhibited an extraordinary faculty for cunning and dissimulation; in fact, he was a thief from his cradle, for, not many hours after his birth, we find him creeping stealthily out of the cave in which he was born, in order to steal some oxen belonging to his brother Apollo, who was at this time feeding the flocks of Admetus.

But he had not proceeded very far on his expedition before he found a tortoise, which he killed, and, stretching seven strings across the empty shell, invented a lyre, upon which he at once began to play with exquisite skill. When he had sufficiently amused himself with the instrument, he placed it in his cradle, and then resumed his journey to Pieria, where the cattle of Admetus were grazing. Arriving at sunset at his destination, he succeeded in separating fifty oxen from his brother's herd, which he now drove before him, taking the precaution to cover his feet with sandals made of twigs of myrtle, in order to escape detection. But the little rogue was not unobserved, for the theft had been witnessed by an old shepherd named Battus, who was tending the flocks of Neleus, king of Pylos (father of Nestor).

Hermes, frightened at being discovered, bribed him with the finest cow in the herd not to betray him, and Battus promised to keep the secret. But Hermes, astute as he was dishonest, determined to test the shepherd's integrity. Feigning to go away, he assumed the form of Admetus, and then returning to the spot offered the old man two of his best oxen if he would disclose the author of the theft. The ruse succeeded, for the avaricious shepherd, unable to resist the tempting bait, gave the desired information, upon which Hermes, exerting his divine power, changed him into a lump of touchstone, as a punishment for his treachery and avarice. Hermes now killed two of the oxen, which he sacrificed to himself and the other gods, concealing the remainder in the cave. He then carefully extinguished the fire, and, after throwing his twig shoes into the river Alpheus, returned to Cyllene.

Apollo, by means of his all-seeing power, soon discovered who it was that had robbed him, and hastening to Cyllene, demanded restitution of his property. On his complaining to Maia of her son's conduct, she pointed to the innocent babe then lying, apparently fast asleep, in his cradle, whereupon, Apollo angrily aroused the pretended sleeper, and charged him with the theft; but the child stoutly denied all knowledge of it, and so cleverly did he play his part, that he even inquired in the most naive manner what sort of animals cows were. Apollo threatened to throw him into Tartarus if he would not confess the truth, but all to no purpose. At last, he seized the babe in his arms, and brought him into the presence of his august father, who was seated in the council chamber of the gods. Zeus listened to the charge made by Apollo, and then sternly desired Hermes to say where he had hidden the cattle. The child, who was still in swaddling-clothes, looked up bravely into his father's face and said, "Now, do I look capable of driving away a herd of cattle; I, who was only born yesterday, and whose feet are much too soft and tender to tread in rough places? Until this moment, I lay in sweet sleep on my mother's bosom, and have never even crossed the threshold of our dwelling. You know well that I am not guilty; but, if you wish, I will affirm it by the most solemn oaths."

As the child stood before him, looking the picture of innocence, Zeus could not refrain from smiling at his cleverness and cunning, but, being perfectly aware of his guilt, he commanded him to conduct Apollo to the cave where he had concealed the herd, and Hermes, seeing that further subterfuge was useless, unhesitatingly obeyed. But when the divine shepherd was about to drive his cattle back into Pieria, Hermes, as though by chance, touched the chords of his lyre. Hitherto Apollo had heard nothing but the music of his own three-stringed lyre and the syrinx, or Pan's pipe, and, as he listened entranced to the delightful strains of this new instrument, his longing to possess it became so great, that he gladly offered the oxen in exchange, promising at the same time, to give Hermes full dominion over flocks and herds, as well as over horses, and all the wild animals of the woods and forests. The offer was accepted, and, a reconciliation being thus effected between the brothers, Hermes became henceforth god of herdsmen, whilst Apollo devoted himself enthusiastically to the art of music.

They now proceeded together to Olympus, where Apollo introduced Hermes as his chosen friend and companion, and, having made him swear by the Styx, that he would never steal his lyre or bow, nor invade his sanctuary at Delphi, he presented him with the Caduceus, or golden wand. This wand was surmounted by wings, and on presenting it to Hermes, Apollo informed him that it possessed the faculty of uniting in love, all beings divided by hate. Wishing to prove the truth of this assertion, Hermes threw it down between two snakes which were fighting, whereupon the angry combatants clasped each other in a loving embrace, and curling round the staff, remained ever after permanently attached to it. The wand itself typified power; the serpents, wisdom; and the wings, despatch—all qualities characteristic of a trustworthy ambassador.

The young god was now presented by his father with a winged silver cap (Petasus), and also with silver wings for his feet (Talaria), and was forthwith appointed herald of the gods, and conductor of shades to Hades, which office had hitherto been filled by Aïdes.

The Theban Cycle

THE THEBAN CYCLE references stories related to Thebes, of which there are four epics. Sadly these epics are almost entirely lost to us now. The *Oedipodea* which relates the unfortunate story of Oedipus, the *Thebaid* which is the origin of 'The Seven Against Thebes' story, the *Epigoni* and the *Alcmeonis*. These stories by different authors all serve in the same canon of Theban tales, following through several generations and are set before the events of the Trojan War, allowing Homer to reference them in his own epics. We have also included the story of Cadmus and the founding of the city here, which is not always traditionally considered one of the Cycle but is undoubtedly relevant as a pivotal story about Thebes.

Cadmus

T**HE FOLLOWING IS THE LEGENDARY ACCOUNT** of the founding of Thebes. After the abduction of his daughter Europa by Zeus, Agenor, king of Phoenicia, unable to reconcile himself to her loss, dispatched his son Cadmus in search of her, desiring him not to return without his sister.

For many years Cadmus pursued his search through various countries, but without success. Not daring to return home without her, he consulted the oracle of Apollo at Delphi; and the reply was that he must desist from his task, and take upon himself a new duty, i.e. that of founding a city, the site of which would be indicated to him by a heifer which had never borne the yoke, and which would lie down on the spot whereon the city was to be built.

Scarcely had Cadmus left the sacred fane, when he observed a heifer who bore no marks of servitude on her neck, walking slowly in front of him. He followed the animal for a considerable distance, until at length, on the site where Thebes afterwards stood, she looked towards heaven and, gently lowing, lay down in the long grass. Grateful for this mark of divine favour, Cadmus resolved to offer up the animal as a sacrifice, and accordingly sent his followers to fetch water for the libation from a neighbouring spring. This spring, which was sacred to Ares, was situated in a wood, and guarded by a fierce dragon, who, at the approach of the retainers of Cadmus, suddenly pounced upon them and killed them.

After waiting some time for the return of his servants Cadmus grew impatient, and hastily arming himself with his lance and spear, set out to seek them. On reaching the spot, the mangled remains of his unfortunate followers met his view, and near them he beheld the frightful monster, dripping with the blood of his victims. Seizing a huge rock, the hero hurled it with all his might upon the dragon; but protected by his tough black skin and steely scales as by a coat of mail, he remained unhurt. Cadmus now tried his lance, and with more success, for it pierced the side of the beast, who, furious with pain, sprang at his adversary, when Cadmus, leaping aside, succeeded in fixing the point of his spear within his jaws, which final stroke put an end to the encounter.

While Cadmus stood surveying his vanquished foe Pallas-Athene appeared to him, and commanded him to sow the teeth of the dead dragon in the ground. He obeyed; and out of the furrows there arose a band of armed men, who at once commenced to fight with each other, until all except five were killed. These last surviving warriors made peace with each other, and it was with their assistance that Cadmus now built the famous city of Thebes. In later times the noblest Theban families proudly claimed their descent from these mighty earth-born warriors.

Ares was furious with rage when he discovered that Cadmus had slain his dragon, and would have killed him had not Zeus interfered, and induced him to mitigate his punishment to that of servitude for the term of eight years. At the end of that time the god of war became reconciled to Cadmus, and, in token of his forgiveness, bestowed upon him the hand of his daughter Harmonia in marriage. Their nuptials were almost as celebrated as those of Peleus and Thetis. All the gods honoured them with their presence, and offered rich gifts and congratulations. Cadmus himself presented his lovely bride with a splendid necklace fashioned by Hephaestus, which, however, after the death of Harmonia, always proved fatal to its possessor.

The children of Cadmus and Harmonia were one son, Polydorus, and four daughters, Autonoe, Ino, Semele, and Agave. For many years the founder of Thebes reigned happily, but at length a conspiracy was formed against him, and he was deprived of his throne by his grandson Pentheus. Accompanied by his faithful wife Harmonia, he retired into Illyria, and after death they were both changed by Zeus into serpents, and transferred to Elysium.

Oedipus

AIUS AND JOCASTA, King and Queen of Thebes, in Boeotia, were greatly delighted at the birth of a little son. In their joy they sent for the priests of Apollo, and bade them foretell the glorious deeds their heir would perform; but all their joy was turned to grief when told that

the child was destined to kill his father, marry his mother, and bring great misfortunes upon his native city.

To prevent the fulfillment of this dreadful prophecy, Laius bade a servant carry the new-born child out of the city, and end its feeble little life. The king's mandate was obeyed only in part; for the servant, instead of killing the child, hung it up by its ankles to a tree in a remote place, and left it there to perish from hunger and exposure if it were spared by the wild beasts.

When he returned, none questioned how he had performed the appointed task, but all sighed with relief to think that the prophecy could never be accomplished. The child, however, was not dead, as all supposed. A shepherd in quest of a stray lamb had heard his cries, delivered him from his painful position, and carried him to Polybus, King of Corinth, who, lacking an heir of his own, gladly adopted the little stranger. The Queen of Corinth and her handmaidens hastened with tender concern to bathe the swollen ankles, and called the babe Oedipus (swollen-footed).

Years passed by. The young prince grew up in total ignorance of the unfortunate circumstances under which he had made his first appearance at court, until one day at a banquet one of his companions, heated by drink, began to quarrel with him, and taunted him about his origin, declaring that those whom he had been accustomed to call parents were in no way related to him.

These words, coupled with a few meaning glances hastily exchanged by the guests, excited Oedipus' suspicions, and made him question the queen, who, afraid lest he might do himself an injury in the first moment of his despair if the truth were revealed to him, had recourse to prevarication, and quieted him by the assurance that he was her beloved son.

Something in her manner, however, left a lingering doubt in Oedipus' mind, and made him resolve to consult the oracle of Delphi, whose words he knew would reveal the exact truth. He therefore went to this shrine; but, as usual, the oracle answered somewhat ambiguously, and merely warned him that fate had decreed he should kill his father, marry his mother, and cause great woes to his native city.

What! kill Polybus, who had ever been such an indulgent father, and marry the queen, whom he revered as his mother! Never! Rather than perpetrate these awful crimes, and bring destruction upon the people of

Corinth, whom he loved, he would wander away over the face of the earth, and never see city or parents again.

But his heart was filled with intense bitterness, and as he journeyed he did not cease to curse the fate which drove him away from home. After some time, he came to three crossroads; and while he stood there, deliberating which direction to take, a chariot, wherein an aged man was seated, came rapidly toward him.

The herald who preceded it haughtily called to the youth to stand aside and make way for his master; but Oedipus, who, as Polybus' heir, was accustomed to be treated with deference, resented the commanding tone, and refused to obey. Incensed at what seemed unparalleled impudence, the herald struck the youth, who, retaliating, stretched his assailant lifeless at his feet.

This affray attracted the attention of the master and other servants. They immediately attacked the murderer, who slew them all, thus unconsciously accomplishing the first part of the prophecy; for the aged man was Laius, his father, journeying incognito from Thebes to Delphi, where he wished to consult the oracle.

Oedipus then leisurely pursued his way until he came to the gates of Thebes, where he found the whole city in an uproar, "because the king had been found lifeless by the roadside, with all his attendants slain beside him, presumably the work of a band of highway robbers or assassins."

Of course, Oedipus did not connect the murder of such a great personage as the King of Thebes by an unknown band of robbers, with the death he had dealt to an arrogant old man, and he therefore composedly inquired what the second calamity alluded to might be.

With lowered voices, as if afraid of being overheard, the Thebans described the woman's head, bird's wings and claws, and lion's body, which were the outward presentment of a terrible monster called the Sphinx, which had taken up its station without the city gates beside the highway, and would allow none to pass in or out without propounding a difficult riddle. Then, if any hesitated to give the required answer, or failed to give it correctly, they were mercilessly devoured by the terrible Sphinx, which no one dared attack or could drive away.

While listening to these tidings, Oedipus saw a herald pass along the street, proclaiming that the throne and the queen's hand would be the reward of any man who dared encounter the Sphinx, and was fortunate enough to free the country of its terrible presence.

As Oedipus attached no special value to the life made desolate by the oracle's predictions, he resolved to slay the dreaded monster, and, with that purpose in view, advanced slowly, sword in hand, along the road where lurked the Sphinx. He soon found the monster, which from afar propounded the following enigma, warning him, at the same time, that he forfeited his life if he failed to give the right answer:—

Oedipus was not devoid of intelligence, by any manner of means, and soon concluded that the animal could only be man, who in infancy, when too weak to stand, creeps along on hands and knees, in manhood walks erect, and in old age supports his tottering steps with a staff.

This reply, evidently as correct as unexpected, was received by the Sphinx with a hoarse cry of disappointment and rage as it turned to fly; but ere it could effect its purpose, it was stayed by Oedipus, who drove it at his sword's point over the edge of a nearby precipice, where it was killed. On his return to the city, Oedipus was received with cries of joy, placed on a chariot, crowned King of Thebes, and married to his own mother, Jocasta, unwittingly fulfilling the second fearful clause of the prophecy.

A number of happy and moderately uneventful years now passed by, and Oedipus became the father of two manly sons, Eteocles and Polynices, and two beautiful daughters, Ismene and Antigone; but prosperity was not doomed to favour him long.

Just when he fancied himself most happy, and looked forward to a peaceful old age, a terrible scourge visited Thebes, causing the death of many faithful subjects, and filling the hearts of all with great terror. The people now turned to him, beseeching him to aid them, as he had done once before when threatened by the Sphinx; and Oedipus sent messengers to consult the Delphic oracle, who declared the plague would cease only when the former king's murderers had been found and punished.

Messengers were sent in every direction to collect all possible information about the murder committed so long ago, and after a short time they brought unmistakable proofs which convicted Oedipus of the crime. At the same time the guilty servant confessed that he had not

illed the child, but had exposed it on a mountain, whence it was carried
o Corinth's king.

The chain of evidence was complete, and now Oedipus discovered that
ie had involuntarily been guilty of the three crimes to avoid which he
iad fled from Corinth. Tales of these dreadful discoveries soon reached
ocasta, who, in her despair at finding herself an accomplice, committed
uicide.

Oedipus, apprised of her intention, rushed into her apartment too late
o prevent its being carried out, and found her lifeless. This sight was more
han the poor monarch could bear, and in his despair he blinded himself
with one of her ornaments.

Penniless, blind, and on foot, he then left the scene of his awful crimes,
iccompanied by his daughter Antigone, the only one who loved him still,
and who was ready to guide his uncertain footsteps wherever he wished
to go. After many days of weary wandering, father and daughter reached
Colonus, where grew a mighty forest sacred to the avenging deities, the
Furies, or Eumenides.

Here Oedipus expressed his desire to remain, and, after bidding his
faithful daughter an affectionate farewell, he groped his way into the
dark forest alone. The wind rose, the lightning flashed, the thunder
pealed; but although, as soon as the storm was over, a search was made
for Oedipus, no trace of him was ever found, and the ancients fancied that
the Furies had dragged him down to Hades to receive the punishment
of all his crimes.

Antigone, no longer needed by her unhappy father, slowly wended
her way back to Thebes, where she found that the plague had ceased,
but that her brothers had quarreled about the succession to the throne.
A compromise was finally decided upon, whereby it was decreed that
Eteocles, the elder son, should reign one year, and at the end of that
period resign the throne to Polynices for an equal space of time, both
brothers thus exercising the royal authority in turn. This arrangement
seemed satisfactory to Eteocles; but when, at the end of the first year,
Polynices returned from his travels in foreign lands to claim the sceptre,
Eteocles refused to relinquish it, and, making use of his power, drove the
claimant away.

The Seven Against Thebes

P OLYNICES' NATURE WAS NOT ONE TO ENDURE such a slight patiently. He now repaired to Argos, where he arrived in the dead of night. Outside the gates of the royal palace he encountered Tydeus, the son of Oeneus, king of Calydon. Having accidentally killed a relative in the chase, Tydeus was also a fugitive; but being mistaken by Polynices in the darkness for an enemy, a quarrel ensued, which might have ended fatally, had not king Adrastus, aroused by the clamour, appeared on the scene and parted the combatants.

By the light of the torches borne by his attendants Adrastus observed, to his surprise, that on the shield of Polynices a lion was depicted, and on that of Tydeus a boar. The former bore this insignia in honour of the renowned hero Heracles, the latter in memory of the famous Calydonian boar-hunt. This circumstance reminded the king of an extraordinary oracular prediction concerning his two beautiful daughters, Argia and Deipyle, which was to the effect that he would give them in marriage to a lion and a boar. Hailing with delight what he regarded as an auspicious solution of the mysterious prophecy, he invited the strangers into his palace; and when he heard their history, and had convinced himself that they were of noble birth, he bestowed upon Polynices his beautiful daughter Argia, and upon Tydeus the fair Deipyle, promising at the same time that he would assist both his sons-in-law to regain their rightful patrimony.

The first care of Adrastus was to aid Polynices in regaining possession of his lawful share in the government of Thebes. He accordingly invited the most powerful chiefs in his kingdom to join in the expedition, all of whom readily obeyed the call with the exception of the king's brother-in-law, Amphiaraus, the seer. As he foresaw a disastrous termination to the enterprise, and knew that not one of the heroes, save Adrastus himself, would return alive, he earnestly dissuaded the king from carrying out his project, and declined to take any part in the undertaking. But Adrastus, seconded by Polynices and Tydeus, was obstinately bent on the achievement of his purpose, and Amphiaraus, in order to escape from their importunities, concealed himself in a hiding-place known only to his wife Eriphyle.

Now on the occasion of the marriage of Amphiaraus it had been agreed, that if he ever differed in opinion with the king, his wife should decide the question. As the presence of Amphiaraus was indispensable to the success of the undertaking, and, moreover, as Adrastus would not enter upon it without "the eye of the army," as he called his brother-in-law, Polynices, bent on securing his services, determined to bribe Eriphyle to use her influence with her husband and to decide the question in accordance with his wishes. He bethought himself of the beautiful necklace of Harmonia, wife of Cadmus, which he had brought with him in his flight from Thebes. Without loss of time he presented himself before the wife of Amphiaraus, and held up to her admiring gaze the glittering bauble, promising that if she revealed the hiding-place of her husband and induced him to join the expedition, the necklace should be hers. Eriphyle, unable to withstand the tempting bait, accepted the bribe, and thus Amphiaraus was compelled to join the army. But before leaving his home he extorted a solemn promise from his son Alcmaeon that, should he perish on the field of battle, he would avenge his death on his mother, the perfidious Eriphyle.

Seven leaders were now chosen, each at the head of a separate detachment of troops. These were Adrastus the king, his two brothers Hippomedon and Parthenopaeus, Capaneus his nephew, Polynices and Tydeus, and Amphiaraus.

When the army was collected they set out for Nemea, which was at this time governed by king Lycurgus. Here the Argives, being short of water, halted on the outskirts of a forest in order to search for a spring, when they saw a majestic and beautiful woman seated on the trunk of a tree, nursing an infant. They concluded from her noble and queenly appearance that she must be a goddess, but were informed by her that she was Hypsipile, queen of the Lemnians, who had been carried away captive by pirates, and sold as a slave to king Lycurgus, and that she was now acting as nurse to his infant son. When the warriors told her that they were in search of water, she laid the child down in the grass, and led them to a secret spring in the forest, with which she alone was acquainted. But on their return they found, to their grief, that the unfortunate babe had been killed during their absence, by a serpent. They slew the reptile, and then collecting the remains of the infant, they buried them with funereal honours and proceeded on their way.

The warlike host now appeared before the walls of Thebes, and each leader placed himself before one of the seven gates of the city in readiness for the attack. Eteocles, in conjunction with Creon, had made due preparations to repel the invaders, and had stationed troops, under the command of trusty leaders, to guard each of the gates. Then, according to the practice of the ancients of consulting soothsayers before entering upon any undertaking, the blind old seer Tiresias was sent for, who, after carefully taking the auguries from the flight of birds, declared that all efforts to defend the city would prove unavailing, unless the youngest descendant of the house of Cadmus would offer himself as a voluntary sacrifice for the good of the state.

When Creon heard the words of the seer his first thought was of his favourite son Menoeceus, the youngest scion of the royal house, who was present at the interview. He therefore earnestly implored him to leave the city, and to repair for safety to Delphi. But the gallant youth heroically resolved to sacrifice his life for the benefit of his country, and after taking leave of his old father, mounted the city walls, and plunging a dagger into his heart, perished in the sight of the contending hosts.

Adrastus now gave his troops the word of command to storm the city, and they rushed forward to the attack with great valour. The battle raged long and furiously, and after heavy losses on both sides the Argives were routed and put to flight.

After the lapse of some days they reorganized their forces, and again appeared before the gates of Thebes, when Eteocles, grieved to think that there should be such a terrible loss of life on his account, sent a herald into the opposite camp, with a proposition that the fate of the campaign should be decided by single combat between himself and his brother Polynices. The challenge was readily accepted, and in the duel which took place outside the city walls, in the sight of the rival forces, Eteocles and Polynices were both fatally wounded and expired on the field of battle.

Both sides now claimed the day, and the result was that hostilities recommenced, and soon the battle raged with greater fury than ever. But victory at last declared itself for the Thebans. In their flight the Argives lost all their leaders, Adrastus excepted, who owed his safety to the fleetness of his horse Arion.

By the death of the brothers, Creon became once more king of Thebes, and in order to show his abhorrence of the conduct of Polynices in fighting against his country, he strictly forbade any one to bury either his remains or those of his allies. But the faithful Antigone, who had returned to Thebes on the death of her father, could not endure that the body of her brother should remain unburied. She therefore bravely disregarded the orders of the king, and endeavoured to give sepulture to the remains of Polynices.

When Creon discovered that his commands had been set at defiance, he inhumanly condemned the devoted maiden to be entombed alive in a subterranean vault.

But retribution was at hand. His son, Haemon, who was betrothed to Antigone, having contrived to effect an entrance into the vault, was horrified to find that Antigone had hanged herself by her veil. Feeling that life without her would be intolerable, he threw himself in despair on his own sword, and after solemnly invoking the malediction of the gods on the head of his father, expired beside the dead body of his betrothed.

Hardly had the news of the tragic fate of his son reached the king, before another messenger appeared, bearing the tidings that his wife Eurydice, on hearing of the death of Haemon, had put an end to her existence, and thus the king found himself in his old age both widowed and childless.

Nor did he succeed in the execution of his vindictive designs; for Adrastus, who, after his flight from Thebes, had taken refuge at Athens, induced Theseus to lead an army against the Thebans, to compel them to restore the dead bodies of the Argive warriors to their friends, in order that they might perform due funereal rites in honour of the slain. This undertaking was successfully accomplished, and the remains of the fallen heroes were interred with due honours.

The Epigoni

TEN YEARS AFTER THESE EVENTS the sons of the slain heroes, who were called Epigoni, or descendants, resolved to avenge the death of their fathers, and with this object entered upon a new expedition against the city of Thebes.

By the advice of the Delphic oracle the command was entrusted to Alcmaeon, the son of Amphiaraus; but remembering the injunction of his father he hesitated to accept this post before executing vengeance on his mother Eriphyle. Thersander, however, the son of Polynices, adopting similar tactics to those of his father, bribed Eriphyle with the beautiful veil of Harmonia, bequeathed to him by Polynices, to induce her son Alcmaeon and his brother Amphilochus to join in this second war against Thebes.

Now the mother of Alcmaeon was gifted with that rare fascination which renders its possessor irresistible to all who may chance to come within its influence; nor was her own son able to withstand her blandishments. Yielding therefore to her wily representations he accepted the command of the troops, and at the head of a large and powerful army advanced upon Thebes.

Before the gates of the city Alcmaeon encountered the Thebans under the command of Laodamas, the son of Eteocles. A fierce battle ensued, in which the Theban leader, after performing prodigies of valour, perished by the hand of Alcmaeon.

After losing their chief and the flower of their army, the Thebans retreated behind the city walls, and the enemy now pressed them hard on every side. In their distress they appealed to the blind old seer Tiresias, who was over a hundred years old. With trembling lips and in broken accents, he informed them that they could only save their lives by abandoning their native city with their wives and families. Upon this they despatched ambassadors into the enemy's camp; and whilst these were protracting negotiations during the night, the Thebans, with their wives and children, evacuated the city. Next morning the Argives entered Thebes and plundered it, placing Thersander, the son of Polynices (who was a descendant of Cadmus), on the throne which his father had so vainly contested.

Alcmaeon and the Necklace

❦

WHEN ALCMAEON RETURNED from his expedition against the Thebans he determined to fulfil the last injunction of his father Amphiaraus, who had desired him to be revenged on his mother Eriphyle for her perfidy in accepting a bribe to betray him. This resolution was further strengthened by the discovery that his unprincipled mother had urged him also to join the expedition in return for the much-coveted veil of Harmonia. He therefore put her to death; and taking with him the ill-fated necklace and veil, abandoned for ever the home of his fathers.

But the gods, who could not suffer so unnatural a crime to go unpunished, afflicted him with madness, and sent one of the Furies to pursue him unceasingly. In this unhappy condition he wandered about from place to place, until at last having reached Psophis in Arcadia, Phegeus, king of the country, not only purified him of his crime, but also bestowed upon him the hand of his daughter Arsinoë, to whom Alcmaeon presented the necklace and veil, which had already been the cause of so much unhappiness.

Though now released from his mental affliction, the curse which hung over him was not entirely removed, and on his account the country of his adoption was visited with a severe drought. On consulting the oracle of Delphi he was informed that any land which offered him shelter would be cursed by the gods, and that the malediction would continue to follow him till he came to a country which was not in existence at the time he had murdered his mother. Bereft of hope, and resolved no longer to cast the shadow of his dark fate over those he loved, Alcmaeon took a tender leave of his wife and little son, and became once more an outcast and wanderer.

Arrived after a long and painful pilgrimage at the river Achelous, he discovered, to his unspeakable joy, a beautiful and fertile island, which had but lately emerged from beneath the water. Here he took up his abode; and in this haven of rest he was at length freed from his sufferings, and finally purified of his crime by the river-god Achelous. But in his new-found home where prosperity smiled upon him, Alcmaeon soon forgot the loving wife and child he had left behind, and wooed Calirrhoë, the beautiful daughter of the river-god, who became united to him in marriage.

For many years Alcmaeon and Calirrhoë lived happily together, and two sons were born to them. But unfortunately for the peace of her husband, the daughter of Achelous had heard of the celebrated necklace and veil of Harmonia, and became seized with a violent desire to become the possessor of these precious treasures.

Now the necklace and veil were in the safe-keeping of Arsinoë; but as Alcmaeon had carefully concealed the fact of his former marriage from his young wife, he informed her, when no longer able to combat her importunities, that he had concealed them in a cave in his native country, and promised to hasten thither and procure them for her. He accordingly took leave of Calirrhoë and his children, and proceeded to Psophis, where he presented himself before his deserted wife and her father, king Phegeus. To them he excused his absence by the fact of his having suffered from a fresh attack of madness, and added that an oracle had foretold to him that his malady would only be cured when he had deposited the necklace and veil of Harmonia in the temple of Apollo at Delphi. Arsinoë, deceived by his artful representations, unhesitatingly restored to him his bridal gifts, whereupon Alcmaeon set out on his homeward journey, well satisfied with the successful issue of his expedition.

But the fatal necklace and veil were doomed to bring ruin and disaster to all who possessed them. During his sojourn at the court of king Phegeus, one of the servants who had accompanied Alcmaeon betrayed the secret of his union with the daughter of the river-god; and when the king informed his sons of his treacherous conduct, they determined to avenge the wrongs of their sister Arsinoë. They accordingly concealed themselves at a point of the road which Alcmaeon was compelled to pass, and as he neared the spot they suddenly emerged from their place of ambush, fell upon him and despatched him.

When Arsinoë, who still loved her faithless husband, heard of the murder, she bitterly reproached her brothers for the crime which they had perpetrated, at which they were so incensed, that they placed her in a chest, and conveyed her to Agapenor, son of Ancaeus, at Tegea. Here they accused her of the murder of which they themselves were guilty, and she suffered a painful death.

Calirrhoë, on learning the sad fate of Alcmaeon, implored Zeus that her infant sons might grow at once to manhood, and avenge the death of their father. The ruler of Olympus heard the petition of the bereaved wife, and, in answer to her prayer, the children of yesterday became transformed into bearded men, full of strength and courage, and thirsting for revenge.

Hastening to Tegea, they there encountered the sons of Phegeus, who were about to repair to Delphi, in order to deposit the necklace and veil in the sanctuary of Apollo; and before the brothers had time to defend themselves, the stalwart sons of Calirrhoë rushed upon them and slew them. They then proceeded to Psophis, where they killed king Phegeus and his wife, after which they returned to their mother with the necklace and veil, which, by the command of her father Achelous, were deposited as sacred offerings in the temple of Apollo at Delphi.

Roman Myths

Introduction to Roman Myths

THE ROMANS LEAPT upon the pantheon of Greek gods with a vengeance, and they became even further ingrained in the consciousness of the European culture, which eventually spread northwards and across the oceans. Ovid and Virgil gave the myths new meaning and significance, imbibing them with credibility and elevating them to an art form. And with each ensuing generation, writers and readers have been inspired by the myths of the Greeks, and have adopted them as an essential part of their culture, retold, reworked and often redesigned for a new audience, but most importantly continued.

The Birth of Roman Mythology

From around 1500 BC, the Italic peoples began to settle the fertile Italian peninsula. Though mostly farmers, they were forced into almost constant conflict with marauders from the north. Rome had yet to be founded, but the idealized figure of the farmer-soldier – determined, disciplined and dutiful – had its origins here and was to inspire the Romans and the approach they took to their religion throughout their history.

In the eighth century BC, two new groups of people began to settle the Italian peninsula. The Greeks formed colonies (known collectively as Magna Grecia) along the southern coasts, while in central Italy a people of uncertain origin, the Etruscans, emerged.

At around the same time, the Italic Latins and Sabines were living south of the Tiber in the Alban Hills around the site of what was to become the city of Rome. The family and household were the centre of religious activity for these small agricultural communities and unwittingly functioned as the crucible for what was to become the religion of Rome. They clearly, however, did not live in isolation, either from neighbouring Italic tribes or from the more advanced Etruscan and Greek civilizations to their north and south.

Scholars have argued that Roman religion was akin to an early form of animism which in time was overlaid with the more sophisticated beliefs and deities of foreign cultures. Certainly, a vast multitude of deities and spirits pervaded every aspect of life for the nascent citizens of Rome: a Numen, a manifestation of sacred power, was considered to be a part of all phenomena, activities and processes. These manifestations were often faceless, formless and sexless, and most were too vague to receive a name. However, they still required the correct performance of rituals, so that their energies might be renewed and the home and community thrive.

The distinctly Roman ethic of pietas (duty) permeated religious life. What mattered was whether or not a worshipper performed the appropriate ritual correctly; beliefs and morals were inconsequential. This emphasis on orthopraxy (correct practice) rather than orthodoxy (correct belief) persisted in later Roman religion.

Family rituals were supervised by the father of the family: the paterfamilias or household priest. The paterfamilias embodied the Genius (guardian spirit) of the family. He ensured that family members worshipped the gods and tended the household shrine known as the Lararium after the household Lar. Among the most ancient Italic divinities, these Lares seem originally to have been either field deities or divine ancestors. The Penates, with whom the Lares were closely associated, were primarily guardians of the storeroom, who ensured families had enough to eat. Offerings were made to the Penates before each meal. Sometimes these consisted of special cakes, wine or honey and, occasionally, a blood sacrifice.

As Rome emerged as the dominant power in Italy, so Roman religion evolved to serve the political needs of the state. Mars and Jupiter, originally local agricultural deities, became the great god of war and the mighty protector of the state respectively; Venus, the goddess of vegetables and the garden, became the goddess of love and the mother of Rome's founding heroes. But, while some spirits and deities eventually acquired individual, more complex, characteristics, the Romans continued to hold dear the traditions of their farmer-soldier ancestors, and the concept of Numen, of a world suffused with sacred powers, persisted alongside.

The Foundation of Rome

From at least the third century BC the Romans worshipped Aeneas under the name Jupiter Indiges. However, it was not until the reign of the great Emperor Augustus (31 BC–AD 14) that the Roman poet Virgil transformed the story of Aeneas, and his role in founding the settlement from which Rome was to spring, into a great epic.

According to the Greeks, Aeneas fought against them in the Trojan War of the twelfth century BC. Virgil's *Aeneid* tells how, as Troy burns about him, Aeneas is commanded in a vision to flee and to found a great city overseas. Carrying his father Anchises on his back and clutching the household gods of Troy, Aeneas makes his escape with his son Ascanius Iulus at his side. However, in the confusion of leaving the burning city, his wife disappears. Though Aeneas scours the streets for her, he encounters only her ghost, a piteous phantom, who informs him that he is to go to a land where the Tiber River flows and where a kingdom and a royal bride await him.

Aeneas embarks on his long voyage, stopping at, among other places, Thrace, Delos, Crete, Carthage and Sicily before finally reaching the mouth of the River Tiber. Latinus, the king of the region, welcomes him, but others resent the Trojans and war breaks out. The Trojans are victorious. Aeneas marries Lavinia, the daughter of Latinus, and founds Lavinium, the parent town of Alba Longa (which Ascanius comes to rule) and of Rome. Though some traditions say that Aeneas founded Rome itself, Virgil succeeds in marrying the story of Aeneas with the account, already well known, of Rome's foundation in 753 BC by Romulus, who is said to be descended from the royal line of Alba Longa.

Homer's great epics the *Iliad* and *Odyssey* date back to the eighth century BC – the same century in which the Greeks founded colonies in Italy, claiming descent from the Homeric heroes of the Trojan War. The Roman story of Aeneas developed, at least in part, as a way of opposing Greek cultural superiority and endowing Roman land and lineage with ancient tradition. 'The house of Aeneas shall rule the whole world: and their sons' sons and those who shall be born of them,' says the great god Apollo in the opening pages of the *Aeneid*.

Virgil had, during his early years, witnessed the end of the Roman Republic, a period that was riven with civil war and conflict. The *Aeneid* celebrated the arrival of peace under the Emperor Augustus and encouraged a renewed pride in Rome: 'Rule the people with your sway, spare the conquered, and wear down the proud,' says the ghost of Aeneas's father. Rome, hopes Virgil, will bring to the world the gifts of peace, justice, order and law.

The Augustan Age (31 BC–AD 14) was one in which the emperor sought to rekindle the traditional Roman values of duty, self-denial, obedience to the gods, responsibility and family devotion. Pious, heroic, true-hearted, dutiful and persevering, Virgil's Aeneas was the perfect hero to emulate, a prototype of the ideal Roman.

Many great Roman families, including the Julii to which the emperor Augustus as well as Julius Caesar belonged, claimed direct descent from Aeneas. The magnificent Forum of Augustus housed statues not only of Aeneas but also of his son Ascanius and the succeeding kings of Alba Longa.

Many historians think that the Etruscans, from north of the Tiber, conquered the area around Rome in the sixth century BC and that they may have provided the impetus for the development of the early city. However, tradition has it that Rome was founded in 753 BC by a man named Romulus.

The story tells how Numitor, King of Alba Longa (a town south-east of Rome), is overthrown by his younger brother Amulius. Rhea Silvia, Numitor's only child, is forced by Amulius to become a Vestal Virgin but is seduced by the great god Mars and gives birth to twin boys. Amulius immediately orders that they be drowned in the Tiber, but the basket in which they are abandoned floats away, coming to rest at the future site of Rome. A wolf suckles the children until they are found by the shepherd Faustulus.

Romulus and Remus grow up to lead a gang of bandits. When Remus is taken prisoner and dragged before the king, Romulus hastens to his rescue, kills Amulius and restores Numitor to his throne. The young men decide to start a city of their own, at the place where they had been found by the shepherd. Through auspicium, they seek the advice of the gods as to which of them should be the founder. (Auspicium was a means of determining the will of the gods by observing the flight – and sometimes the eating habits – of birds. It was usually overseen by Augurs, men who learned secret rules which were said to enable them to discern the meaning behind the birds' behaviour.) Remus is the first to see an omen (six vultures); Romulus sees 12 vultures. A dispute breaks out as to which of them has won. Romulus kills Remus and gives his name to the new city.

A Multitude of Gods

Augustine of Hippo described the Romans as 'men who loved a multitude of gods'. While the sheer number of Roman deities can indeed be overwhelming, early myths associated with them were remarkably undeveloped. In time, however, a more emotionally engaging mythology was to arise, due largely to the influence of the Greeks.

From their earliest days, the gods of Rome were influenced by Greek, Etruscan and Italic deities. The Romans also imported many deities wholesale, in accordance with their policy of tolerance towards other peoples' gods. Considering, also, that many deities had numerous aspects and names, it is not surprising that the Roman priests kept lengthy catalogues of their gods.

Janus, the god of entrances, is the only deity to appear solely in Roman mythology. Another early god, Saturn, was possibly of Latin origin, while Quirinus (with whom Romulus was later identified), was worshipped by the Sabines. Jupiter, who had his origins in Etruria, formed a very early triad with Quirinus and the Italic god Mars. However, by the start of the Republic in 509 BC, he had become Jupiter Optimus Maximus, chief god of the Roman state and head of the Capitoline Triad, flanked by Juno and Minerva, also from Etruria. Another triad was composed of the grain goddess Ceres together with Liber and Libera. The temple of this group, set on the Aventine Hill, was dedicated in 494/3 BC. Ceres came from southern Italy, though she had been influenced by the Greek Demeter before becoming established in Rome.

The twins Castor and Pollux were the earliest Greek gods officially introduced to Rome, at the very beginning of the fifth century BC. According to legend they had helped Rome to victory in a battle against the Latins. Another early direct import from Greece was Apollo, officially admitted in 431 BC.

As Greek culture strengthened its grip, the Roman deities increasingly came to resemble the Greek gods. The Dii Consentes, corresponding to the 12 Greek Olympians, were especially honoured. Listed by the poet Ennius in the third century BC, they numbered Jupiter, Juno, Neptune, Vesta, Mars, Minerva, Venus, Mercury, Diana, Vulcan, Ceres and Apollo.

It is widely assumed that the Dii Consentes were the 12 gods present at a famous *lectisternium* (banquet of the gods) held in 217 BC. Determined to find favour with the gods following early defeats by the Carthaginian general Hannibal, the Romans celebrated the Greek rite by setting images of their gods around a table laden with food. Although this was not the first lectisternium to be held, the Romans had, until now, insisted that the attendant gods should be invisible. The new development is seen as a huge cultural leap, indicating that the Roman gods now shared fully in the full-blooded mythology of the Greeks.

Twelve years after the *lectisternium*, in 205 BC, the Romans officially introduced the mysteries of the goddess Cybele from Asia Minor. The mystery religions, with their appeal to individualism, threatened official Roman religion as never before. A tolerant, all-embracing approach to foreign deities proved to be at once the strength of Roman religion and its fatal flaw. The golden age of the emperor Augustus, who did much to restore the ancient deities, was yet to come, but the seeds of the downfall of the Roman gods were sown.

Public Religion

The religion of the Roman state was in many ways an extension of family religion and ritual. Just as the paterfamilias was the family priest, so the king (or, from the time of the Republic, the religious leader) was chief priest to the people and responsible for public religious activities.

Tradition credits Numa Pompilius, the second king of Rome, with establishing Roman religious rites. The idea of a contract between the gods and the state, the *pax deorum* (peace of the gods), was developed whereby the gods would ensure the preservation and prosperity of Rome if Rome, through the public performance of rituals, helped to sustain the gods in return.

When the last king, Tarquinius Superbus, was ousted and the Republic instated (509 BC), a new office of Rex Sacrorum (king of rites) was created in order that the former monarch's religious duties might continue to be fulfilled. The Rex Sacrorum was a priest appointed for life from amongst the Roman patricians (the powerful, wealthy class). He was prohibited from holding any other office in order to prevent him gaining undue power. Nonetheless, Roman religion and politics were inextricably entwined: priests were quite often politicians or generals. Julius Caesar was, for example, the Pontifex Maximus or chief priest, though he himself was agnostic.

Priests and other religious professionals were usually elected in a general assembly by male citizens of Rome, then organized into colleges. The most prestigious of these were the College of Pontifices and the College of Augures, both of which had 16 members by the time of Julius Caesar. Priests of the former (which was led by the Pontifex Maximus) were said to have 'authority over the most important matters in the Roman state' and were responsible for sacrifices to the gods. Members of the College of Augures were responsible for establishing the will of the gods by, for example, studying the flight of birds and marking out the sacred space within which sacrifices and important meetings were held and omens taken.

The Flamines were individual priests devoted to individual gods. The three major Flamines participated in rituals for Jupiter, Mars and Quirinus, and were distinguished by the apex, a leather hat which they had to wear in public. The Haruspices were Etruscans rather than élite Romans; their duty was to read the entrails of animals to determine the favour or disfavour of the gods. Many other priesthoods arose, to some extent as occasion demanded. They included the Salii, the Luperci, the Fetiales and the Fratres Arvales, to name but a few.

With the rise of the state, festivals which had originally been a part of family and farming life were adopted and magnified into public spectacles, organized and paid for by the state. The Compitalia (held in December) was, for example, transformed from a private agricultural ritual into a public urban event. Among the more notable festivals were the Aedes Vestae (March) – the lighting of the Vestal fires, the Cerialia (March) – an offering to Ceres, the Lemuria (May) – to chase evil spirits from the home, the Saturnalia (December) – a carnival in honour of Saturn, and the October Horse – in honour of Mars.

While the priesthoods were dominated by the Roman élites – and often used to their advantage – the festivals could be enjoyed by the plebeians (common people). Nonetheless, state religion catered mainly to the upper classes, giving them influence, standing and most important of all, power.

Heroes and Emperors

With the eastward expansion of her territory, Rome encountered many new customs. Among these, the practice of worshipping kings as gods proved to be particularly compelling. Though a useful political tool, the association was sufficiently innovatory for it to be left tentative both in Rome and throughout the West.

The idea that a great man could, on his death, become a god was rooted in the founding myths of Rome: Romulus was worshipped as the god Quirinus and Aeneas as Jupiter Indiges. Roman rituals gave divine attributes to dead ancestors and by the third century BC prominent Romans were claiming that their families were descended from deities. However, the notion of an actual living god did not sit easy with the Western frame of mind and for a long time the military honour of Triumphator was the closest a living Roman came to being honoured as divine.

The Triumph was a religious ceremony of Etruscan origin. In order to receive the honour, a Roman general had to triumph over a foreign enemy and return to Rome with at least a token army. The Senate then decided whether the general was worthy to be granted the accolade.

On the day of his Triumph, the hero, his face painted red and wearing a purple toga, rode in a golden chariot through the streets of Rome, from the Campus Martius to the temple of Jupiter on the Capitoline Hill. A slave would stand behind him, holding a golden crown over his head and whispering in his ear, 'Remember, you are mortal'. The day ended with feasting throughout the city. The troops of Julius Caesar would march ahead of their great Triumphator, carrying placards bearing the words *Veni, Vidi, Vici* (I came, I saw, I conquered) or displaying maps of the territories he had conquered.

It was with Julius Caesar (100–44 BC) that the Romans began the regular practice of deifying their dead leaders. Remarkably, whilst still alive, Caesar was granted the distinction of receiving divine honours in the city of Rome itself: his image was carried next to that of Quirinus in processions and he was allocated his own priest. Such honours set Julius Caesar above all other Romans. On his death, the appearance of a comet in the sky was interpreted as a sign of his ascent to heaven and two years later he became Divus Iulius (the deified Julius), an official god of the Roman state.

Augustus (63 BC–AD 14), the first Roman emperor, never outrightly claimed divine status, but he trod a fine line. At one stage he experimented with claiming Apollo as his father, but later thought better of it; he also promoted himself as a second Romulus and allowed worship of his Genius and Numen. Although every Roman had a Genius (something akin to his generative force), the Numen belonged to the realm of the sacred. In the eastern nations of the empire, however, Augustus allowed himself to be worshipped as a god, largely as a means of integrating the diverse peoples of the region, and usually in association with worship of Roma, the goddess of Rome. After Augustus died, a senator took an oath swearing that he had seen him ascend into Heaven. From then on, it became routine practice for Rome to deify her dead emperors.

Mystery Religions

From the third century BC several so-called mystery religions began to arrive in Rome, mainly from the Middle and Near East. Their appeal seems to have been emotional and spiritual, while some also provided a moral code. They were not, however, always looked on kindly by Roman officials.

The mystery religions offered their followers the possibility of an afterlife and had as a central theme the death and resurrection of a deity. Their teachings were kept secret from all but initiates and, unlike the state religion, they encouraged worshippers to enter into a personal relationship with the deity. In an increasingly complex world, they were a source of identity formation and expression.

The cult of Cybele, the Great Mother or Magna Mater, was introduced to Rome on the instruction of the Cumaean Sibyl, a priestess of Apollo from Cumae, a city founded by the Greeks on the coast of Italy in the eighth century BC. Under threat of invasion from Hannibal's army, the Romans consulted the oracle and were told that their enemy would be driven off if the goddess were brought to Rome from Phyrgia in Asia Minor. A deputation was sent to obtain the black stone, the symbol of the goddess, and on 4 April 204 BC it was placed in Rome's Temple of Victory.

Cybele's priests, the Galli, castrated themselves on entering the priesthood and during the annual celebration of the death and resurrection of her consort, Attis, they slashed themselves and led ecstatic dances. When the Roman officials learned of such activities, they kept the cult of Cybele under strict control and, until the reign of Claudius (AD 41–54), forbade any Roman to become her priest.

Like the cult of Cybele, the cult of Isis was especially popular with women devotees. Worship of the Egyptian mother goddess reached Rome early in the first century BC but was banned by the emperor Augustus who associated the goddess with his arch enemy Cleopatra. However, by the early first century AD the worship of Isis was again flourishing, though the satirist Juvenal (c. AD 60–130) said her priestesses were no more than bawds.

About two decades after the Magna Mater's grand entry into Rome, the senate acted against another mystery cult, this time from Greece. Bacchus (the Greek Dionysus) was a saviour god and god of the vine. His rites, the Bacchanalia, were notorious for their drunken licentiousness, supposedly an aid to ecstatic religious experience. In 186 BC the senate restricted the cult, believing not only that it gave free rein to untold depravities but that it also provided an opportunity for the lower classes to conspire against the authorities. All secret Bacchic rites were banned throughout Italy and Romans were forbidden to be priests. The punishment was death.

Mithraism, which flourished from the second to fifth centuries AD, differed from the other mystery religions in that it allowed only men into its community. Meetings were held in small underground chapels, hundreds of which have since been found across the Roman Empire. Such was the secrecy surrounding the religion that much about it remains unclear. However, it seems to have been related both to sun worship and to astrology. The most important stage of initiation was the sacrifice of a bull and the application of its blood to the initiate as a symbol of the victory over death. For a long time, Christianity and Mithraism were fierce competitors. When Christianity finally won, it took over many of the underground chapels as Christian prayer rooms.

Adventures of Aeneas

YOU HAVE ALREADY HEARD how the Greeks entered the city of Troy in the dead of night, massacred the inhabitants, and set fire to the beautiful buildings which had been the king's pride and delight. Now you shall hear how Virgil relates the escape of some of the Trojans from general destruction. In the following chapter is a selection of extracts from Virgil's *Aeneid*, which totals twelve books in its entirety, written in the time of emperor Augustus to explain how his ancestor Aeneas led a group of Trojans from the ruins of the city the Greeks had destroyed to find a new home in Italy.

The Sack of Troy

❧

I N THE FIRST BOOK Aeneas' fleet has been blown to North Africa due to Juno's meddling. Those of the Trojans who have made it safely ashore come upon the great city of Carthage, whose queen is Dido. Aeneas' mother Venus intervenes by making Dido fall in love with Aeneas, and as the second book begins, Dido has encouraged the Trojan hero to describe the escape from Troy. In the following extract from Book Two the ghost of Hector appears to Aeneas to encourage him to flee from Troy, whereupon he wakes and goes out to see the destruction of his city:

'It was the time when by the gift of God rest comes stealing first and sweetest on unhappy men. In slumber, lo! before mine eyes Hector seemed to stand by, deep in grief and shedding abundant tears; torn by the chariot, as once of old, and black with gory dust, his swoln feet pierced with the thongs. Ah me! in what guise was he! how changed from the Hector who returns from putting on Achilles' spoils, or launching the fires of Phrygia on the Grecian ships! with ragged beard and tresses clotted with blood, and all the many wounds upon him that he received around his ancestral walls. Myself too weeping I seemed to accost him ere he spoke, and utter forth mournful accents: "O light of Dardania, O surest hope of the Trojans, what long delay is this hath held thee? from what borders comest thou, Hector our desire? with what weary eyes we see thee, after many deaths of thy kin, after divers woes of people and city! What indignity hath marred thy serene visage? or why discern I these wounds?"

He replies naught, nor regards my idle questioning; but heavily drawing a heart-deep groan, "Ah, fly, goddess-born," he says, "and rescue thyself from these flames. The foe holds our walls; from her high ridges Troy is toppling down. Thy country and Priam ask no more. If Troy towers might be defended by strength of hand, this hand too had been their defence. Troy commends to thee her holy things and household gods; take them to accompany thy fate; seek for them a city, which, after all the seas have known thy wanderings, thou shalt at last establish in might." So speaks he, and carries forth in his hands from their inner shrine the chaplets and strength of Vesta, and the everlasting fire.

'Meanwhile the city is stirred with mingled agony; and more and more, though my father Anchises' house lay deep withdrawn and screened by trees, the noises grow clearer and the clash of armour swells. I shake myself from sleep and mount over the sloping roof, and stand there with ears attent: even as when flame catches a corn-field while south winds are furious, or the racing torrent of a mountain stream sweeps the fields, sweeps the smiling crops and labours of the oxen, and hurls the forest with it headlong; the shepherd in witless amaze hears the roar from the cliff-top.

hen indeed proof is clear, and the treachery of the Grecians opens out. Already the house of Deïphobus hath crashed down in wide ruin amid the overpowering flames; already our neighbour Ucalegon is ablaze: the broad Sigean bay is lit with the fire. Cries of men and blare of trumpets rise up. Madly I seize my arms, nor is there so much purpose in arms; but my spirit is on fire to gather a band for fighting and charge for the citadel with my comrades. Fury and wrath drive me headlong, and I think how noble is death in arms.

'And lo! Panthus, eluding the Achaean weapons, Panthus son of Othrys, priest of Phoebus in the citadel, comes hurrying with the sacred vessels and conquered gods and his little grandchild in his hand, and runs distractedly towards my gates. "How stands the state, O Panthus? what stronghold are we to occupy?" Scarcely had I said so, when groaning he thus returns: "The crowning day is come, the irreversible time of the Dardanian land. No more are we a Trojan people; Ilium and the great glory of the Teucrians is no more. Angry Jupiter hath cast all into the scale of Argos. The Grecians are lords of the burning town. The horse, standing high amid the city, pours forth armed men, and Sinon scatters fire, insolent in victory. Some are at the wide-flung gates, all the thousands that ever came from populous Mycenae. Others have beset the narrow streets with lowered weapons; edge and glittering point of steel stand drawn, ready for the slaughter; scarcely at the entry do the guards of the gates essay battle, and hold out in the blind fight."

'Heaven's will thus declared by the son of Othrys drives me amid flames and arms, where the baleful Fury calls, and tumult of shouting rises up. Rhipeus and Epytus, most mighty in arms, join company with me; Hypanis and Dymas meet us in the moonlight and attach themselves to our side, and young Coroebus son of Mygdon. In those days it was he had come to Troy, fired with mad passion for Cassandra, and bore a son's aid to Priam and the Phrygians: hapless, that he listened not to his raving bride's counsels. . . . Seeing them close-ranked and daring for battle, I therewith began thus: "Men, hearts of supreme and useless bravery, if your desire be fixed to follow one who dares the utmost; you see what is the fortune of our state: all the gods by whom this empire was upheld have gone forth, abandoning shrine and altar; your aid comes to a burning city. Let us die, and rush on their encircling weapons. The conquered have one safety, to hope for none."

'So their spirit is heightened to fury. Then, like wolves ravening in a black fog, whom mad malice of hunger hath driven blindly forth, and their cubs left behind await with throats unslaked; through the weapons of the enemy we march to certain death, and hold our way straight into the town. Night's sheltering shadow flutters dark around us. Who may unfold in speech that night's horror and death-agony, or measure its woes in weeping? The ancient city falls with her long years of sovereignty; corpses lie stretched stiff all about the streets and houses and awful courts of the gods. Nor do Teucrians alone pay forfeit of their blood; once and again valour returns even in conquered hearts, and the victorious Grecians fall. Everywhere is cruel agony, everywhere terror, and the sight of death at every turn.

'First, with a great troop of Grecians attending him, Androgeus meets us, taking us in ignorance for an allied band, and opens on us with friendly words: "Hasten, my men; why idly linger so late? others plunder and harry the burning citadel; are you but now on your march from the tall ships?" He spoke, and immediately (for no answer of any assurance was offered) knew he was fallen among the foe. In amazement, he checked foot and voice; even as one who struggling through rough briers hath trodden a snake on the ground unwarned, and suddenly shrinks fluttering back as it rises in anger and puffs its green throat out; even thus Androgeus drew away, startled at the sight. We rush in and encircle them with serried arms, and cut them down dispersedly in their ignorance of the ground and seizure of panic. Fortune speeds our first labour. And here Coroebus, flushed with success and spirit, cries: "O comrades, follow me where fortune points before us the path of safety, and shews her favour. Let us exchange shields, and accoutre ourselves in Grecian suits; whether craft or courage, who will ask of an enemy? the foe shall arm our hands."

'Thus speaking, he next dons the plumed helmet and beautifully blazoned shield of Androgeus, and fits the Argive sword to his side. So does Rhipeus, so Dymas in like wise, and all our men in delight arm themselves one by one in the fresh spoils. We advance, mingling with the Grecians, under a protection not our own, and join many a battle with those we meet amid the blind night; many a Greek we send down to hell. Some scatter to the ships and run for the safety of the shore; some in craven fear again climb the huge horse, and hide in the belly they knew. Alas that none may trust at all to estranged gods!

'Lo! Cassandra, maiden daughter of Priam, was being dragged with disordered tresses from the temple and sanctuary of Minerva, straining to heaven her blazing eyes in vain; her eyes, for fetters locked her delicate hands. At this sight Coroebus burst forth infuriate, and flung himself on death amid their columns. We all follow him up, and charge with massed arms. Here first from the high temple roof we are overwhelmed with our own people's weapons, and a most pitiful slaughter begins through the fashion of our armour and the mistaken Greek crests; then the Grecians, with angry cries at the maiden's rescue, gather from every side and fall on us; Ajax in all his valour, and the two sons of Atreus, and the whole Dolopian army: as oft when bursting in whirlwind West and South clash with adverse blasts, and the East wind exultant on the coursers of the Dawn; the forests cry, and fierce in foam Nereus with his trident stirs the seas from their lowest depth. Those too appear, whom our stratagem routed through the darkness of dim night and drove all about the town; at once they know the shields and lying weapons, and mark the alien tone on our lips.

'We go down, overwhelmed by numbers. First Coroebus is stretched by Peneleus' hand at the altar of the goddess armipotent; and Rhipeus falls, the one man who was most righteous and steadfast in justice among the Teucrians: the gods' ways are not as ours: Hypanis and Dymas perish, pierced by friendly hands; nor did all thy goodness, O Panthus, nor Apollo's fillet protect thy fall. O ashes of Ilium and death flames of my people! you I call to witness that in your ruin I shunned no Grecian weapon or encounter, and my hand earned my fall, had destiny been thus. We tear ourselves away, I and Iphitus and Pelias, Iphitus now stricken in age, Pelias halting too under the wound of Ulysses, called forward by the clamour to Priam's house.

'Here indeed the battle is fiercest, as if all the rest of the fighting were nowhere, and no slaughter but here throughout the city, so do we descry the war in full fury, the Grecians rushing on the building, and their shielded column driving up against the beleaguered threshold. Ladders cling to the walls; and hard by the doors and planted on the rungs they hold up their shields in the left hand to ward off our weapons, and with their right clutch the battlements. The Dardanians tear down turrets and the covering of the house roof against them; with these for weapons, since they see the end is come, they prepare to defend themselves even in death's extremity: and hurl down gilded beams, the stately decorations of their fathers of old. Others with drawn swords have beset the doorway below and keep it in crowded column. We renew our courage, to aid the royal dwelling, to support them with our succour, and swell the force of the conquered.

Dido and Aeneas

🕊

AENEAS RELATES how he managed to lead a group of Trojans away from their burning city and the swords of the Greeks, including his father – who dies before they arrive at Carthage – and his young son, but sadly his wife did not make it out of Troy. Thinking that Crete might be the location of their new home, the Trojans sail there, however Aeneas receives a vision which shows him that the Italian shores and not Crete are where they should be heading. Book Four then takes us back to the present, where Aeneas is at Dido's court. Aeneas spends a year with the Carthaginian queen, until the gods remind him of his duty. To avoid Dido's tears and recriminations, he keeps his preparations for departure a complete secret, and finally sets sail whilst Dido is asleep. Dido is grief-stricken and ultimately commits suicide as seen in the following extract from Book Four.

But the Queen—who may delude a lover?—foreknew his devices, and at once caught the presaging stir. Safety's self was fear; to her likewise had evil Rumour borne the maddening news that they equip the fleet and prepare for passage. Helpless at heart, she reels aflame with rage throughout the city, even as the startled Thyiad in her frenzied triennial orgies, when the holy vessels move forth and the cry of Bacchus re-echoes, and Cithaeron calls her with nightlong din. Thus at last she opens out upon Aeneas:

'And thou didst hope, traitor, to mask the crime, and slip away in silence from my land? Our love holds thee not, nor the hand thou once gavest, nor the bitter death that is left for Dido's portion? Nay, under the wintry star thou labourest on thy fleet, and hastenest to launch into the deep amid northern gales; ah, cruel! Why, were thy quest not of alien fields and unknown dwellings, did thine ancient Troy remain, should Troy be sought in voyages over tossing seas?

'Fliest thou from me? me who by these tears and thine own hand beseech thee, since naught else, alas! have I kept mine own—by our union and the marriage rites preparing; if I have done thee any grace, or aught of mine hath once been sweet in thy sight,—pity our sinking house, and if there yet be room for prayers, put off this purpose of thine. For thy sake Libyan tribes and Nomad kings are hostile; my Tyrians are estranged; for thy sake, thine, is mine honour perished, and the former fame, my one title to the skies. How leavest thou me to die, O my guest? since to this the name of husband is dwindled down. For what do I wait? till Pygmalion overthrow his sister's city, or Gaetulian Iarbas lead me to captivity? At least if before thy flight a child of thine had been clasped in my arms,—if a tiny Aeneas were playing in my hall, whose face might yet image thine,—I would not think myself ensnared and deserted utterly.'

She ended; he by counsel of Jove held his gaze unstirred, and kept his distress hard down in his heart. At last he briefly answers:

'Never, O Queen, will I deny that thy goodness hath gone high as thy words can swell the reckoning; nor will my memory of Elissa be ungracious while I remember myself, and breath sways this body. Little will I say in this. I never hoped to slip away in stealthy flight; fancy not that; nor did I ever hold out the marriage torch or enter thus into alliance. Did fate allow me to guide my life by mine own government, and calm my sorrows as I would, my first duty were to the Trojan city and the dear remnant of my kindred; the high house of Priam should abide, and my hand had set up Troy towers anew for a conquered people. But now for broad Italy hath Apollo of Grynos bidden me steer, for Italy the oracles of Lycia. Here is my desire; this is my native country. If thy Phoenician eyes are stayed on Carthage towers and thy Libyan city, what wrong is it, I pray, that we Trojans find our rest on Ausonian land? We too may seek a foreign realm unforbidden. In my sleep, often as the dank shades of night veil the earth, often as the stars lift their fires, the troubled phantom of my father Anchises comes in warning and dread; my boy Ascanius, how I wrong one so dear in cheating him of an Hesperian kingdom and destined fields. Now even the gods' interpreter, sent straight from Jove—I call both to witness—hath borne down his commands through the fleet air. Myself in broad daylight I saw the deity passing within the walls, and these ears drank his utterance. Cease to madden me and thyself alike with plaints. Not of my will do I follow Italy. . . .'

Long ere he ended she gazes on him askance, turning her eyes from side to side and perusing him with silent glances; then thus wrathfully speaks:

'No goddess was thy mother, nor Dardanus founder of thy line, traitor! but rough Caucasus bore thee on his iron crags, and Hyrcanian tigresses gave thee suck. For why do I conceal it? For what further outrage do I wait? Hath our weeping cost him a sigh, or a lowered glance? Hath he broken into tears, or had pity on his lover? Where, where shall I begin? Now neither doth Queen Juno nor our Saturnian lord regard us with righteous eyes. Nowhere is trust safe. Cast ashore and destitute I welcomed him, and madly gave him place and portion in my kingdom; I found him his lost fleet and drew his crews from death.

Alas, the fire of madness speeds me on. Now prophetic Apollo, now oracles of Lycia, now the very gods' interpreter sent straight from Jove through the air carries these rude commands! Truly that is work for the gods, that a care to vex their peace! I detain thee not, nor gainsay thy words: go, follow thine Italy down the wind; seek thy realm overseas. Yet midway my hope is, if righteous gods can do aught at all, thou wilt drain the cup of vengeance on the rocks, and re-echo calls on Dido's name. In murky fires I will follow far away, and when chill death hath severed body from soul, my ghost will haunt thee in every region. Wretch, thou shalt repay! I will hear; and the rumour of it shall reach me deep in the under world.'

Even on these words she breaks off her speech unfinished, and, sick at heart, escapes out of the air and sweeps round and away out of sight, leaving him in fear and much hesitance, and with much on his mind to say.

Her women catch her in their arms, and carry her swooning to her marble chamber and lay her on her bed.

But good Aeneas, though he would fain soothe and comfort her grief, and talk away her distress, with many a sigh, and melted in soul by his great love, yet fulfils the divine commands and returns to his fleet. Then indeed the Teucrians set to work, and haul down their tall ships all along the shore. The hulls are oiled and afloat; they carry from the woodland green boughs for oars and massy logs unhewn, in hot haste to go. . . . One might descry them shifting their quarters and pouring out of all the town: even as ants, mindful of winter, plunder a great heap of wheat and store it in their house; a black column advances on the plain as they carry home their spoil on a narrow track through the grass.

Some shove and strain with their shoulders at big grains, some marshal the ranks and chastise delay; all the path is aswarm with work. What then were thy thoughts, O Dido, as thou sawest it? What sighs didst thou utter, viewing from the fortress roof the broad beach aswarm, and seeing before thine eyes the whole sea stirred with their noisy din? Injurious Love, to what dost thou not compel mortal hearts! Again, she must needs break into tears, again essay entreaty, and bow her spirit down to love, not to leave aught untried and go to death in vain.

'Anna, thou seest the bustle that fills the shore. They have gathered round from every quarter; already their canvas woos the breezes, and the merry sailors have garlanded the sterns. This great pain, my sister, I shall have strength to bear, as I have had strength to foresee. Yet this one thing, Anna, for love and pity's sake—for of thee alone was the traitor fain, to thee even his secret thoughts were confided, alone thou knewest his moods and tender fits—go, my sister, and humbly accost the haughty stranger: I did not take the Grecian oath in Aulis to root out the race of Troy; I sent no fleet against her fortresses; neither have I disentombed his father Anchises' ashes and ghost, that he should refuse my words entrance to his stubborn ears. Whither does he run? let him grant this grace—alas, the last!—to his lover, and await fair winds and an easy passage. No more do I pray for the old delusive marriage, nor that he give up fair Latium and abandon a kingdom. A breathing-space I ask, to give my madness rest and room, till my very fortune teach my grief submission. This last favour I implore: sister, be pitiful; grant this to me, and I will restore it in full measure when I die.'

So she pleaded, and so her sister carries and recarries the piteous tale of weeping. But by no weeping is he stirred, inflexible to all the words he hears. Fate withstands, and lays divine bars on unmoved mortal ears. Even as when the eddying blasts of northern Alpine winds are emulous to uproot the secular strength of a mighty oak, it wails on, and the trunk quivers and the high foliage strews the ground; the tree clings fast on the rocks, and high as her top soars into heaven, so deep strike her roots to hell; even thus is the hero buffeted with changeful perpetual accents, and distress thrills his mighty breast, while his purpose stays unstirred, and tears fall in vain.

Then indeed, hapless and dismayed by doom, Dido prays for death, and is weary of gazing on the arch of heaven. The more to make her fulfil her purpose and quit the light, she saw, when she laid her gifts on the altars alight with incense, awful to tell, the holy streams blacken, and the wine turn as it poured into ghastly blood. Of this sight she spoke to none—no, not to her sister.

Likewise there was within the house a marble temple of her ancient lord, kept of her in marvellous honour, and fastened with snowy fleeces and festal boughs. Forth of it she seemed to hear her husband's voice crying and calling when night was dim upon earth, and alone on the house-tops the screech-owl often made moan with funeral note and long-drawn sobbing cry. Therewithal many a warning of wizards of old terrifies her with appalling presage. In her sleep fierce Aeneas drives her wildly, and ever she seems being left by herself alone, ever going uncompanioned on a weary way, and seeking her Tyrians in a solitary land: even as frantic Pentheus sees the arrayed Furies and a double sun, and Thebes shows herself twofold to his eyes: or Agamemnonian Orestes, renowned in tragedy, when his mother pursues him armed with torches and dark serpents, and the Fatal Sisters crouch avenging in the doorway.

So when, overcome by her pangs, she caught the madness and resolved to die, she works out secretly the time and fashion, and accosts her sorrowing sister with mien hiding her design and hope calm on her brow.

'I have found a way, mine own—wish me joy, sisterlike—to restore him to me or release me of my love for him. Hard by the ocean limit and the set of sun is the extreme Aethiopian land, where ancient Atlas turns on his shoulders the starred burning axletree of heaven. Out of it hath been shown to me a priestess of Massylian race, warder of the temple of the Hesperides, even she who gave the dragon his food, and kept the holy boughs on the tree, sprinkling clammy honey and slumberous poppy-seed. She professes with her spells to relax the purposes of whom she will, but on others to bring passion and pain; to stay the river-waters and turn the stars backward: she calls up ghosts by night; thou shalt see earth moaning under foot and mountain-ashes descending from the hills. I take heaven, sweet, to witness, and thee, mine own darling sister, I do not willingly arm myself with the arts of magic.

Do thou secretly raise a pyre in the inner court, and let them lay on it the arms that the accursed one left hanging in our chamber, and all the dress he wore, and the bridal bed where I fell. It is good to wipe out all the wretch's traces, and the priestess orders thus.' So speaks she, and is silent, while pallor overruns her face. Yet Anna deems not her sister veils death behind these strange rites, and grasps not her wild purpose, nor fears aught deeper than at Sychaeus' death. So she makes ready as bidden. . . .

The Underworld

❦

OOK 6 OF THE AENEID RECOUNTS HOW THE TROJANS make it to Cumae in Italy, where there is a famous Sibyl. She tells Aeneas of the many trials he has yet to face, but urges him to continue. He makes known his wish to visit Hades, and entreats her to serve as his guide in that perilous journey. She consents, but at the same time informs him that he must first obtain a golden twig, which grows in a dark forest. Having done so, Aeneas descends into the Underworld where he sees Dido on the way to finding his father Anchises. In this extract from Book 6 Anchises points out the future heroes of Rome waiting to be born, who include amongst them Romulus and the emperor Augustus:

But lord Anchises, deep in the green valley, was musing in earnest survey over the imprisoned souls destined to the daylight above, and haply reviewing his beloved children and all the tale of his people, them and their fates and fortunes, their works and ways. And he, when he saw Aeneas advancing to meet him over the greensward, stretched forth both hands eagerly, while tears rolled over his cheeks, and his lips parted in a cry: 'Art thou come at last, and hath thy love, O child of my desire, conquered the difficult road? Is it granted, O my son, to gaze on thy face and hear and answer in familiar tones? Thus indeed I forecast in spirit, counting the days between; nor hath my care misled me. What lands, what space of seas hast thou traversed to reach me, through what surge of perils, O my son! How I dreaded the realm of Libya might work thee harm!'

And he: 'Thy melancholy phantom, thine, O my father, came before me often and often, and drove me to steer to these portals. My fleet is anchored on the Tyrrhenian brine. Give thine hand to clasp, O my father, give it, and withdraw not from our embrace.'

So spoke he, his face wet with abundant weeping. Thrice there did he essay to fling his arms about his neck; thrice the phantom vainly grasped fled out of his hands even as light wind, and most like to fluttering sleep.

Meanwhile Aeneas sees deep withdrawn in the covert of the vale a woodland and rustling forest thickets, and the river of Lethe that floats past their peaceful dwellings. Around it flitted nations and peoples innumerable; even as in the meadows when in clear summer weather bees settle on the variegated flowers and stream round the snow-white lilies, all the plain is murmurous with their humming. Aeneas starts at the sudden view, and asks the reason he knows not; what are those spreading streams, or who are they whose vast train fills the banks?

Then lord Anchises: 'Souls, for whom second bodies are destined and due, drink at the wave of the Lethean stream the heedless water of long forgetfulness. These of a truth have I long desired to tell and shew thee face to face, and number all the generation of thy children, that so thou mayest the more rejoice with me in finding Italy.'—'O father, must we think that any souls travel hence into upper air, and return again to bodily fetters? why this their strange sad longing for the light?' 'I will tell,' rejoins Anchises, 'nor will I hold thee in suspense, my son.' And he unfolds all things in order one by one.

'First of all, heaven and earth and the liquid fields, the shining orb of the moon and the Titanian star, doth a spirit sustain inly, and a soul shed abroad in them sways all their members and mingles in the mighty frame. Thence is the generation of man and beast, the life of winged things, and the monstrous forms that ocean breeds under his glittering floor. Those seeds have fiery force and divine birth, so far as they are not clogged by taint of the body and dulled by earthy frames and limbs ready to die. Hence is it they fear and desire, sorrow and rejoice; nor can they pierce the air while barred in the blind darkness of their prison-house. Nay, and when the last ray of life is gone, not yet, alas! does all their woe, nor do all the plagues of the body wholly leave them free; and needs must be that many a long ingrained evil should take root marvellously deep.

Therefore they are schooled in punishment, and pay all the forfeit of a lifelong ill; some are hung stretched to the viewless winds; some have the taint of guilt washed out beneath the dreary deep, or burned away in fire. We suffer, each a several ghost; thereafter we are sent to the broad spaces of Elysium, some few of us to possess the happy fields; till length of days completing time's circle takes out the ingrained soilure and leaves untainted the ethereal sense and pure spiritual flame. All these before thee, when the wheel of a thousand years hath come fully round, a God summons in vast train to the river of Lethe, that so they may regain in forgetfulness the slopes of upper earth, and begin to desire to return again into the body.'

Anchises ceased, and leads his son and the Sibyl likewise amid the assembled murmurous throng, and mounts a hillock whence he might scan all the long ranks and learn their countenances as they came.

'Now come, the glory hereafter to follow our Dardanian progeny, the posterity to abide in our Italian people, illustrious souls and inheritors of our name to be, these will I rehearse, and instruct thee of thy destinies. He yonder, seest thou? the warrior leaning on his pointless spear, holds the nearest place allotted in our groves, and shall rise first into the air of heaven from the mingling blood of Italy, Silvius of Alban name, the child of thine age, whom late in thy length of days thy wife Lavinia shall nurture in the woodland, king and father of kings; from him in Alba the Long shall our house have dominion. He next him is Procas, glory of the Trojan race; and Capys and Numitor; and he who shall renew thy name, Silvius Aeneas, eminent alike in goodness or in arms, if ever he shall receive his kingdom in Alba. Men of men! see what strength they display, and wear the civic oak shading their brows.

'They shall establish Nomentum and Gabii and Fidena city, they the Collatine hill-fortress, Pometii and the Fort of Inuus, Bola and Cora: these shall be names that are now nameless lands. Nay, Romulus likewise, seed of Mavors, shall join his grandsire's company, from his mother Ilia's nurture and Assaracus' blood. Seest thou how the twin plumes straighten on his crest, and his father's own emblazonment already marks him for upper air? Behold, O son! by his augury shall Rome the renowned fill earth with her empire and heaven with her pride, and gird about seven fortresses with her single wall, prosperous mother of men; even as our lady of Berecyntus rides in her chariot turret-crowned through the Phrygian cities, glad in the gods she hath borne, clasping an hundred of her children's children, all habitants of heaven, all dwellers on the upper heights.

'Hither now bend thy twin-eyed gaze; behold this people, the Romans that are thine. Here is Caesar and all Iülus' posterity that shall arise under the mighty cope of heaven. Here is he, he of whose promise once and again thou hearest, Caesar Augustus, a god's son, who shall again establish the ages of gold in Latium over the fields that once were Saturn's realm, and carry his empire afar to Garamant and Indian, to the land that lies beyond our stars, beyond the sun's yearlong ways, where Atlas the sky-bearer wheels on his shoulder the glittering star-spangled pole. Before his coming even now the kingdoms of the Caspian shudder at oracular answers, and the Maeotic land and the mouths of sevenfold Nile flutter in alarm. Nor indeed did Alcides traverse such spaces of earth, though he pierced the brazen-footed deer, or though he stilled the Erymanthian woodlands and made Lerna tremble at his bow: nor he who sways his team with reins of vine, Liber the conqueror, when he drives his tigers from Nysa's lofty crest. And do we yet hesitate to give valour scope in deeds, or shrink in fear from setting foot on Ausonian land?

'Ah, and who is he apart, marked out with sprays of olive, offering sacrifice? I know the locks and hoary chin of the king of Rome who shall establish the infant city in his laws, sent from little Cures' sterile land to the majesty of empire. To him Tullus shall next succeed, who shall break the peace of his country and stir to arms men rusted from war and armies now disused to triumphs; and hard on him over-vaunting Ancus follows, even now too elate in popular breath. Wilt thou see also the Tarquin kings, and the haughty soul of Brutus the Avenger, and the fasces regained? He shall first receive a consul's power and the merciless axes, and when his children would stir fresh war, the father, for fair freedom's sake, shall summon them to doom. Unhappy! yet howsoever posterity shall take the deed, love of country and limitless passion for honour shall prevail.

'Nay, behold apart the Decii and the Drusi, Torquatus with his cruel axe, and Camillus returning with the standards. Yonder souls likewise, whom thou discernest gleaming in equal arms, at one now, while shut in Night, ah me! what mutual war, what battle-lines and bloodshed shall they arouse, so they attain the light of the living! father-in-law descending from the Alpine barriers and the fortress of the Dweller Alone, son-in-law facing him with the embattled East. Nay, O my children, harden not your hearts to such warfare, neither turn upon her own heart the mastering might of your country; and thou, be thou first to forgive, who drawest thy descent from heaven; cast down the weapons from thy hand, O blood of mine. . . . He shall drive his conquering chariot to the Capitoline height triumphant over Corinth, glorious in Achaean slaughter. He shall uproot Argos and Agamemnonian Mycenae, and the Aeacid's own heir, the seed of Achilles mighty in arms, avenging his ancestors in Troy and Minerva's polluted temple.

'Who might leave thee, lordly Cato, or thee, Cossus, to silence? who the Gracchan family, or these two sons of the Scipios, a double thunderbolt of war, Libya's bale? and Fabricius potent in poverty, or thee, Serranus, sowing in the furrow? Whither whirl you me all breathless, O Fabii? thou art he, the most mighty, the one man whose lingering retrieves our State. Others shall beat out the breathing bronze to softer lines, I believe it well; shall draw living lineaments from the marble; the cause shall be more eloquent on their lips; their pencil shall portray the pathways of heaven, and tell the stars in their arising: be thy charge, O Roman, to rule the nations in thine empire; this shall be thine art, to lay down the law of peace, to be merciful to the conquered and beat the haughty down.'

Thus lord Anchises, and as they marvel, he so pursues: 'Look how Marcellus the conqueror marches glorious in the splendid spoils, towering high above them all! He shall stay the Roman State, reeling beneath the invading shock, shall ride down Carthaginian and insurgent Gaul, and a third time hang up the captured armour before lord Quirinus.'

And at this Aeneas, for he saw going by his side one excellent in beauty and glittering in arms, but his brow had little cheer, and his eyes looked down:

'Who, O my father, is he who thus attends him on his way? son, or other of his children's princely race? How his comrades murmur around him! how goodly of presence he is! but dark Night flutters round his head with melancholy shade.'

Then lord Anchises with welling tears began: 'O my son, ask not of the great sorrow of thy people. Him shall fate but shew to earth, and suffer not to stay further. Too mighty, lords of heaven, did you deem the brood of Rome, had this your gift been abiding. What moaning of men shall arise from the Field of Mavors by the imperial city! what a funeral train shalt thou see, O Tiber, as thou flowest by the new-made grave! Neither shall the boyhood of any of Ilian race raise his Latin forefathers' hope so high; nor shall the land of Romulus ever boast of any fosterling like this.

'Alas his goodness, alas his antique honour, and right hand invincible in war! none had faced him unscathed in armed shock, whether he met the foe on foot, or ran his spurs into the flanks of his foaming horse. Ah me, the pity of thee, O boy! if in any wise thou breakest the grim bar of fate, thou shalt be Marcellus. Give me lilies in full hands; let me strew bright blossoms, and these gifts at least let me lavish on my descendant's soul, and do the unavailing service.'

Thus they wander up and down over the whole region of broad vaporous plains, and scan all the scene. And when Anchises had led his son over it, each point by each, and kindled his spirit with passion for the glories on their way, he tells him thereafter of the war he next must wage, and instructs him of the Laurentine peoples and the city of Latinus, and in what wise each task may be turned aside or borne.

Embassy to Evander

❧

AFTER A PROLONGED CONVERSATION with his father, Aeneas returned to his companions, and led them to the mouth of the Tiber, whose course they followed until they reached Latium, where their wanderings were to cease. Latinus, king of the country, received them hospitably, and promised the hand of his daughter

Lavinia in marriage to Aeneas. Lavinia was very beautiful, and had already had many suitors, among whom Turnus, a prince, boasted of the most exalted rank. The queen, Amata, specially favoured this youth's suit; and the king would gladly have received him for a son-in-law, had he not twice been warned by the gods to reserve his daughter for a foreign prince, who had now appeared. Juno had not yet forgotten her hatred of the Trojan race, and conspired to meddle once more, stirring up Turnus' hostility against Aeneas and his men. In this extract from Book Eight, Aeneas seeks help from Evander, who has a settlement on the future site of Rome:

When Turnus ran up the flag of war on the towers of Laurentum, and the trumpets blared with harsh music, when he spurred his fiery steeds and clashed his armour, straightway men's hearts are in tumult; all Latium at once flutters in banded uprisal, and her warriors rage furiously. Their chiefs, Messapus, and Ufens, and Mezentius, scorner of the gods, begin to enrol forces on all sides, and dispeople the wide fields of husbandmen.

Venulus too is sent to the town of mighty Diomede to seek succour, to instruct him that Teucrians set foot in Latium; that Aeneas in his fleet invades them with the vanquished gods of his home, and proclaims himself the King summoned of fate; that many tribes join the Dardanian, and his name swells high in Latium. What he will rear on these foundations, what issue of battle he desires, if Fortune attend him, lies clearer to his own sight than to King Turnus or King Latinus.

Thus was it in Latium. And the hero of Laomedon's blood, seeing it all, tosses on a heavy surge of care, and throws his mind rapidly this way and that, and turns it on all hands in swift change of thought: even as when the quivering light of water brimming in brass, struck back from the sunlight or the moon's glittering reflection, flickers abroad over all the room, and now mounts aloft and strikes the high panelled roof. Night fell, and over all lands weary creatures were fast in deep slumber, the race of fowl and of cattle; when lord Aeneas, sick at heart of the dismal warfare, stretched him on the river bank under the cope of the cold sky, and let sleep, though late, overspread his limbs. To him the very god of the ground, the pleasant Tiber stream, seemed to raise his aged form among the poplar boughs; thin lawn veiled him with its gray covering, and shadowy reeds hid his hair. Thereon he addressed him thus, and with these words allayed his distresses:

'O born of the family of the gods, thou who bearest back our Trojan city from hostile hands, and keepest Troy towers in eternal life; O long looked for on Laurentine ground and Latin fields! here is thine assured home, thine home's assured gods. Draw not thou back, nor be alarmed by menace of war. All the anger and wrath of the gods is passed away . . . And even now for thine assurance, that thou think not this the idle fashioning of sleep, a great sow shall be found lying under the oaks on the shore, with her new-born litter of thirty head: white she couches on the ground, and the brood about her teats is white. By this token in thirty revolving years shall Ascanius found a city, Alba of bright name. My prophecy is sure.

'Now hearken, and I will briefly instruct thee how thou mayest unravel and overcome thy present task. An Arcadian people sprung of Pallas, following in their king Evander's company beneath his banners, have chosen a place in these coasts, and set a city on the hills, called Pallanteum after Pallas their forefather. These wage perpetual war with the Latin race; these do thou take to thy camp's alliance, and join with them in league. Myself I will lead thee by my banks and straight along my stream, that thou mayest oar thy way upward against the river. Up and arise, goddess-born, and even with the setting stars address thy prayers to Juno as is meet, and vanquish her wrath and menaces with humble vows. To me thou shalt pay a conqueror's sacrifice. I am he whom thou seest washing the banks with full flood and severing the rich tilth, glassy Tiber, best beloved by heaven of rivers. Here is my stately home; my fountain-head is among high cities.'

Thus spoke the River, and sank in the depth of the pool: night and sleep left Aeneas. He arises, and, looking towards the radiant sky of the sunrising, holds up water from the river in fitly-hollowed palms, and pours to heaven these accents:

'Nymphs, Laurentine Nymphs, from whom is the generation of rivers, and thou, O father Tiber, with thine holy flood, receive Aeneas and deign to save him out of danger. What pool soever holds thy source, who pitiest our discomforts, from whatsoever soil thou dost spring excellent in beauty, ever shall my worship, ever my gifts frequent thee, the hornèd river lord of Hesperian waters. Ah, be thou only by me, and graciously confirm thy will.'

So speaks he, and chooses two galleys from his fleet, and mans them with rowers, and withal equips a crew with arms.

And lo! suddenly, ominous and wonderful to tell, the milk-white sow, of one colour with her white brood, is espied through the forest couched on the green brink; whom to thee, yes to thee, queenly Juno, good Aeneas offers in sacrifice, and sets with her offspring before thine altar. All that night long Tiber assuaged his swelling stream, and silently stayed his refluent wave, smoothing the surface of his waters to the fashion of still pool and quiet mere, to spare labour to the oar.

So they set out and speed on their way with prosperous cries; the painted fir slides along the waterway; the waves and unwonted woods marvel at their far-gleaming shields, and the gay hulls afloat on the river. They outwear a night and a day in rowing, ascend the long reaches, and pass under the chequered shadows of the trees, and cut through the green woodland in the calm water. The fiery sun had climbed midway in the circle of the sky when they see afar fortress walls and scattered house roofs, where now the might of Rome hath risen high as heaven; then Evander held a slender state. Quickly they turn their prows to land and draw near the town.

It chanced on that day the Arcadian king paid his accustomed sacrifice to the great son of Amphitryon and all the gods in a grove before the city. With him his son Pallas, with him all the chief of his people and his poor senate were offering incense, and the blood steamed warm at their altars. When they saw the high ships, saw them glide up between the shady woodlands and rest on their silent oars, the sudden sight appals them, and all at once they rise and stop the banquet. Pallas courageously forbids them to break off the rites; snatching up a spear, he flies forward, and from a hillock cries afar: 'O men, what cause hath driven you to explore these unknown ways? or whither do you steer? What is your kin, whence your habitation? Is it peace or arms you carry hither?' Then from the lofty stern lord Aeneas thus speaks, stretching forth in his hand an olive bough of peace-bearing:

'Thou seest men born of Troy and arms hostile to the Latins, who have driven us to flight in insolent warfare. We seek Evander; carry this message, and tell him that chosen men of the Dardanian captains are come pleading for an armed alliance.'

Pallas stood amazed at the august name. 'Descend,' he cries, 'whoso thou art, and speak with my father face to face, and enter our home and hospitality.' And giving him the grasp of welcome, he caught and clung to his hand.

Advancing, they enter the grove and leave the river. Then Aeneas in courteous words addresses the King:

'Best of the Grecian race, thou whom fortune hath willed that I supplicate, holding before me boughs dressed in fillets, no fear stayed me because thou wert a Grecian chief and an Arcadian, or allied by descent to the twin sons of Atreus. Nay, mine own prowess and the sanctity of divine oracles, our ancestral kinship, and the fame of thee that is spread abroad over the earth, have allied me to thee and led me willingly on the path of fate. Dardanus, who sailed to the Teucrian land, the first father and founder of the Ilian city, was born, as Greeks relate, of Electra the Atlantid; Electra's sire is ancient Atlas, whose shoulder sustains the heavenly spheres. Your father is Mercury, whom white Maia conceived and bore on the cold summit of Cyllene; but Maia, if we give any credence to report, is daughter of Atlas, that same Atlas who bears up the starry heavens; so both our families branch from a single blood.

'In this confidence I sent no embassy, I framed no crafty overtures; myself I have presented mine own person, and come a suppliant to thy courts. The same Daunian race pursues us and thee in merciless warfare; we once expelled, they trust nothing will withhold them from laying all Hesperia wholly beneath their yoke, and holding the seas that wash it above and below. Accept and return our friendship. We can give brave hearts in war, high souls and men approved in deeds.'

Aeneas ended. The other ere now scanned in a long gaze the face and eyes and all the form of the speaker; then thus briefly returns:

'How gladly, bravest of the Teucrians, do I hail and own thee! how I recall thy father's words and the very tone and glance of great Anchises! For I remember how Priam son of Laomedon, when he sought Salamis on his way to the realm of his sister Hesione, went on to visit the cold borders of Arcadia. Then early youth clad my cheeks with bloom. I admired the Teucrian captains, admired their lord, the son of Laomedon; but Anchises moved high above them all. My heart burned with youthful passion to accost him and clasp hand in hand; I made my way to him, and led him eagerly to Pheneus' high town.

'Departing he gave me an adorned quiver and Lycian arrows, a scarf inwoven with gold, and a pair of golden bits that now my Pallas possesses. Therefore my hand is already joined in the alliance you seek, and soon as to-morrow's dawn rises again over earth, I will send you away rejoicing in mine aid, and supply you from my store. Meanwhile, since you are come hither in friendship, solemnise with us these yearly rites which we may not defer, and even now learn to be familiar at your comrades' board.'

The Death of Pallas

🦅

ENEAS AND HIS TUSCAN ALLIES ARRIVE on the battle scene just in time to give the necessary support to the almost exhausted Trojans; and now the fight rages more fiercely than ever, with deeds of great valour accomplished on both sides. Finally Evander's brave young son Pallas is killed by Turnus, who grabs his sword belt as spoils. When aware of the death of this promising young prince, Aeneas' heart is filled with grief, as he imagines the sorrow of Evander when he brings his son's body home for burial. Aeneas then and there registers a solemn vow to avenge Pallas' death by slaying Turnus, and immediately hastens forth to keep his word. It is foreshadowed in the extract from Book 10 below that Turnus will come to rue taking Pallas' sword belt, as from this point his destiny is sealed:

Meanwhile Turnus' gracious sister bids him take Lausus' room, and his fleet chariot parts the ranks. When he saw his comrades, 'It is time,' he cried, 'to stay from battle. I alone must assail Pallas; to me and none other Pallas is due; I would his father himself were here to see.' So speaks he, and his Rutulians draw back from a level space at his bidding. But then as they withdrew, he, wondering at the haughty command, stands in amaze at Turnus, his eyes scanning the vast frame, and his fierce glance perusing him from afar. And with these words he returns the words of the monarch: 'For me, my praise shall even now be in the lordly spoils I win, or in illustrious death: my father will bear calmly either lot: away with menaces.' He speaks, and advances into the level ring.

The Arcadians' blood gathers chill about their hearts. Turnus leaps from his chariot and prepares to close with him. And as a lion sees from some lofty outlook a bull stand far off on the plain revolving battle, and flies at him, even such to see is Turnus' coming. When Pallas deemed him within reach of a spear-throw, he advances, if so chance may assist the daring of his overmatched strength, and thus cries into the depth of sky: 'By my father's hospitality and the board whereto thou camest a wanderer, on thee I call, Alcides; be favourable to my high emprise; let Turnus even in death discern me stripping his blood-stained armour, and his swooning eyes endure the sight of his conqueror.'

Alcides heard him, and deep in his heart he stifled a heavy sigh, and let idle tears fall. Then with kindly words the father accosts his son: 'Each hath his own appointed day; short and irrecoverable is the span of life for all: but to spread renown by deeds is the task of valour. Under high Troy town many and many a god's son fell; nay, mine own child Sarpedon likewise perished. Turnus too his own fate summons, and his allotted period hath reached the goal.' So speaks he, and turns his eyes away from the Rutulian fields. But Pallas hurls his spear with all his strength, and pulls his sword flashing out of the hollow scabbard.

The flying spear lights where the armour rises high above the shoulder, and, forcing a way through the shield's rim, ceased not till it drew blood from mighty Turnus. At this Turnus long poises the spear-shaft with its sharp steel head, and hurls it on Pallas with these words: See thou if our weapon have not a keener point. He ended; but for all the shield's plating of iron and brass, for all the bull-hide that covers it round about, the quivering spear-head smashes it fair through and through, passes the guard of the corslet, and pierces the breast with a gaping hole. He tears the warm weapon from the wound; in vain; together and at once life-blood and sense follow it. He falls heavily on the ground, his armour clashes over him, and his bloodstained face sinks in death on the hostile soil. And Turnus standing over him . . .: 'Arcadians,' he cries, 'remember these my words, and bear them to Evander. I send him back his Pallas as was due. All the meed of the tomb, all the solace of sepulture, I give freely. Dearly must he pay his welcome to Aeneas.'

And with these words, planting his left foot on the dead, he tore away the broad heavy sword-belt engraven with a tale of crime, the array of grooms foully slain together on their bridal night, and the nuptial chambers dabbled with blood, which Clonus, son of Eurytus, had wrought richly in gold. Now Turnus exults in spoiling him of it, and rejoices at his prize. Ah spirit of man, ignorant of fate and the allotted future, or to keep bounds when elate with prosperity!—the day will come when Turnus shall desire to have bought Pallas' safety at a great ransom, and curse the spoils of this fatal day. But with many safety at a great ransom, and curse the spoils of this fatal day. But with many moans and tears Pallas' comrades lay him on his shield and bear him away amid their ranks. O grief and glory and grace of the father to whom thou shalt return! This one day sent thee first to war, this one day takes thee away, while yet thou leavest heaped high thy Rutulian dead.

And now no rumour of the dreadful loss, but a surer messenger flies to Aeneas, telling him his troops are on the thin edge of doom; it is time to succour the routed Teucrians. He mows down all that meets him, and hews a broad path through their columns with furious sword, as he seeks thee, O Turnus, in thy fresh pride of slaughter. Pallas, Evander, all flash before his eyes; the board whereto but then he had first come a wanderer, and the clasped hands. Here four of Sulmo's children, as many more of Ufens' nurture, are taken by him alive to slaughter in sacrifice to the shade below, and slake the flames of the pyre with captive blood.

Next he levelled his spear full on Magus from far. He stoops cunningly; the spear flies quivering over him; and, clasping his knees, he speaks thus beseechingly: 'By thy father's ghost, by Iülus thy growing hope, I entreat thee, save this life for a child and a parent. My house is stately; deep in it lies buried wealth of engraven silver; I have masses of wrought and unwrought gold. The victory of Troy does not turn on this, nor will a single life make so great a difference.' He ended; to him Aeneas thus returns answer: 'All the wealth of silver and gold thou tellest of, spare thou for thy children. Turnus hath broken off this thy trafficking in war, even then when Pallas fell. Thus judges the ghost of my father Anchises, thus Iülus.' So speaking, he grasps his helmet with his left hand, and, bending back his neck, drives his sword up to the hilt in the suppliant.

The Slaying of Turnus

❧

A S WE COME TO THE LAST BOOK of the *Aeneid*, there have been losses on both sides. We know that Pallas has been slain by Turnus and Aeneas has vowed to avenge him. In his grief-stricken rage Aeneas slays many warriors, among others Lausus and his aged father Mezentius, two allies of Latinus, who had specially distinguished themselves by their great

Turnus is defeated. With the death of Turnus the war comes to an end. A lasting peace is made with Latinus; and the brave Trojan hero, whose woes are now over, is united in marriage with Lavinia.

In concert with Latinus, Aeneas goes on to rule the Latins, and found a city, which he calls Lavinia in honour of his bride, and which becomes for a time the capital of Latium. Aeneas, as the gods had predicted, becomes the father of a son named Aeneas Silvia, who founds Alba Longa, where his descendants reign for many a year, and where one of his race, the Vestal Virgin Ilia, after marrying Mars, gives birth to Remus and Romulus, the founders of Rome. But let us return now to the climactic end of Book 12:

Meanwhile the King of Heaven's omnipotence accosts Juno as she gazes on the battle from a sunlit cloud. 'What yet shall be the end, O wife? what remains at the last? Heaven claims Aeneas as his country's god, thou thyself knowest and avowest to know, and fate lifts him to the stars. With what device or in what hope hangest thou chill in cloudland? Was it well that a deity should be sullied by a mortal's wound? or that the lost sword—for what without thee could Juturna avail?—should be restored to Turnus and swell the force of the vanquished? Forbear now, I pray, and bend to our entreaties; let not the pain thus devour thee in silence, and distress so often flood back on me from thy sweet lips. The end is come. Thou hast had power to hunt the Trojans over land or wave, to kindle accursed war, to put the house in mourning, and plunge the bridal in grief: further attempt I forbid thee.' Thus Jupiter began: thus the goddess, daughter of Saturn, returned with looks cast down:

'Even because this thy will, great Jupiter, is known to me for thine, have I left, though loth, Turnus alone on earth; nor else wouldst thou see me now, alone on this skyey seat, enduring good and bad; but girt in flame I were standing by their very lines, and dragging the Teucrians into the deadly battle. I counselled Juturna, I confess it, to succour her hapless brother, and for his life's sake favoured a greater daring; yet not the arrow-shot, not the bending of the bow, I swear by the merciless well-head of the Stygian spring, the single ordained dread of the gods in heaven. And now I retire, and leave the battle in loathing.

This thing I beseech thee, that is bound by no fatal law, for Latium and for the majesty of thy kindred. When now they shall plight peace with prosperous marriages (be it so!), when now they shall join in laws and treaties, bid thou not the native Latins change their name of old, nor become Trojans and take the Teucrian name, or change their language, or alter their attire: let Latium be, let Alban kings endure through ages, let Italian valour be potent in the race of Rome. Troy is fallen; let her and her name lie where they fell.'

To her smilingly the designer of men and things:

'Jove's own sister thou art, and second seed of Saturn, such surge of wrath tosses within thy breast! But come, allay this madness so vainly stirred. I give thee thy will, and yield thee ungrudged victory. Ausonia shall keep her native speech and usage, and as her name is, it shall be. The Trojans shall sink mingling into their blood; I will add their sacred law and ritual, and make all Latins and of a single speech. Hence shall spring a race of tempered Ausonian blood, whom thou shalt see outdo men and gods in duty; nor shall any nation so observe thy worship.' To this Juno assented, and in gladness withdrew her purpose; meanwhile she quits her cloud, and retires out of the sky.

This done, the Father revolves inly another counsel, and prepares to separate Juturna from her brother's arms. Twin monsters there are, called the Dirae by their name, whom with infernal Megaera the dead of night bore at one single birth, and wreathed them in like serpent coils, and clothed them in windy wings. They appear at Jove's throne and in the courts of the grim king, and quicken the terrors of wretched men whensoever the lord of heaven deals sicknesses and dreadful death, or sends terror of war upon guilty cities. One of these Jupiter sent swiftly down from heaven's height, and bade her meet Juturna for a sign. She wings her way, and darts in a whirlwind to earth. Even as an arrow through a cloud, darting from the string when Parthian hath poisoned it with bitter gall, Parthian or Cydonian, and sped the immedicable shaft, leaps through the swift shadow whistling and unknown; so sprung and swept to earth the daughter of Night.

When she espies the Ilian ranks and Turnus' columns, suddenly shrinking to the shape of a small bird that often sits late by night on tombs or ruinous roofs, and vexes the darkness with her cry, in such change of likeness the monster shrilly passes and repasses before Turnus' face, and her wings beat restlessly on his shield. A strange numbing terror unnerves his limbs, his hair thrills up, and the accents falter on his tongue. But when his hapless sister knew afar the whistling wings of the Fury, Juturna unbinds and tears her tresses, with rent face and smitten bosom. 'How, O Turnus, can thine own sister help thee now? or what more is there if I break not under this? What art of mine can lengthen out thy day? can I contend with this ominous thing? Now, now I quit the field. Dismay not my terrors, disastrous birds; I know these beating wings, and the sound of death, nor do I miss high-hearted Jove's haughty ordinance. Is this his repayment for my maidenhood? what good is his gift of life for ever? why have I forfeited a mortal's lot? Now assuredly could I make all this pain cease, and go with my unhappy brother side by side into the dark. Alas mine immortality! will aught of mine be sweet to me without thee, my brother? Ah, how may Earth yawn deep enough for me, and plunge my godhead in the under world!'

So spoke she, and wrapping her head in her gray vesture, the goddess moaning sore sank in the river depth.

But Aeneas presses on, brandishing his vast tree-like spear, and fiercely speaks thus: 'What more delay is there now? or why, Turnus, dost thou yet shrink away? Not in speed of foot, in grim arms, hand to hand, must be the conflict. Transform thyself as thou wilt, and collect what strength of courage or skill is thine; pray that thou mayest wing thy flight to the stars on high, or that sheltering earth may shut thee in.' The other, shaking his head: 'Thy fierce words dismay me not, insolent! the gods dismay me, and Jupiter's enmity.'

And no more said, his eyes light on a vast stone, a stone ancient and vast that haply lay upon the plain, set for a landmark to divide contested fields: scarcely might twelve chosen men lift it on their shoulders, of such frame as now earth brings to birth: then the hero caught it up with trembling hand and whirled it at the foe, rising higher and quickening his speed. But he knows not his own self running nor going nor lifting his hands or moving the mighty stone; his knees totter, his blood freezes cold; the very stone he hurls, spinning through the empty void, neither wholly reached its distance nor carried its blow home. And as in sleep, when nightly rest weighs down our languorous eyes, we seem vainly to will to run eagerly on, and sink faint amidst our struggles; the tongue is powerless, the familiar strength fails the body, nor will words or utterance follow: so the disastrous goddess brings to naught all Turnus' valour as he presses on. His heart wavers in shifting emotion; he gazes on his Rutulians and on the city, and falters in terror, and shudders at the imminent spear; neither sees he whither he may escape nor how rush violently on the enemy, and nowhere his chariot or his sister at the reins.

As he wavers Aeneas poises the deadly weapon, and, marking his chance, hurls it in from afar with all his strength of body. Never with such a roar are stones hurled from some engine on ramparts, nor does the thunder burst in so loud a peal. Carrying grim death with it, the spear flies in fashion of some dark whirlwind, and opens the rim of the corslet and the utmost circles of the sevenfold shield. Right through the thigh it passes hurtling on; under the blow Turnus falls huge to earth with his leg doubled under him. The Rutulians start up with a groan, and all the hill echoes round about, and the width of high woodland returns their cry. Lifting up beseechingly his humbled eyes and suppliant hand: 'I have deserved it,' he says, 'nor do I ask for mercy; use thy fortune. If an unhappy parent's distress may at all touch thee, this I pray; even such a father was Anchises to thee; pity Daunus' old age, and restore to my kindred which thou wilt, me or my body bereft of day. Thou art conqueror, and Ausonia hath seen me stretch conquered hands. Lavinia is thine in marriage; press not thy hatred farther.'

Aeneas stood wrathful in arms, with rolling eyes, and lowered his hand; and now and now yet more the speech began to bend him to waver: when high on his shoulder appeared the sword-belt with the shining bosses that he knew, the luckless belt of the boy Pallas, whom Turnus had struck down with mastering wound, and wore on his shoulders the fatal ornament. The other, as his eyes drank in the plundered record of his fierce grief, kindles to fury, and cries terrible in anger: 'Mayest thou, thou clad in the spoils of my dearest, escape mine hands? Pallas it is, Pallas who now strikes the sacrifice, and exacts vengeance in thy guilty blood.' So saying, he fiercely plunges the steel full in his breast. But his limbs grow slack and chill, and the life with a moan flies indignantly into the dark.

The Founding of Rome

THE ROMANS, like all peoples, were interested in their own origins. The *Aeneid* gave them their roots back to the times of the Trojan War and a hero founder. The following stories depict how the actual city of Rome came to be, and traces it through its original legendary kings to the founding of the Roman Republic which is told through the story of Lucretia – the ultimate paragon of womanly purity and virtue. The Romans liked to use tales of virtue and courage as didactic examples for the morals they should uphold.

Romulus and Remus

❧

ALTHOUGH SUCH A PARTISAN of strife, Mars was not impervious to softer emotions. He fell in love with a beautiful young Vestal named Ilia, a descendant of Aeneas, who, in spite of the solemn pledge not to listen to a lover's pleadings until her time of service at the goddess Vesta's altar was accomplished, yielded to Mars' impetuous wooing, and consented to a clandestine union.

Although secretly married, Ilia continued to dwell in the temple until the birth of her twin sons Romulus and Remus. Her parents, hearing she had broken her vows, commanded that she should suffer the prescribed punishment of being buried alive, and that the children should be exposed to the teeth and claws of the wild beasts of the forest. The double sentence was ruthlessly carried out, and the young mother perished; but, contrary to all previsions, the babes survived, and, after having been suckled for a time by a she-wolf, were found and adopted by a shepherd.

Romulus and Remus throve under this man's kind care, and grew up strong and fearless. When they reached manhood, they longed for a wider sphere for their youthful activity, and, leaving the mountain where they had grown up, journeyed out into the world to seek their fortunes. After some time they came to a beautiful hilly country, where they decided to found a great city, the capital of their future realm. Accordingly the brothers began to trace the outline of their city limits, and, in doing so, quarreled over the name of the prospective town.

Blinded by anger, Romulus suddenly raised the tool he held, and struck Remus such a savage blow that he fell to the ground, slain by his brother in a fit of passion. Alone now, Romulus at first vainly tried to pursue his undertaking, but, being soon joined by a number of adventurers as wicked and unscrupulous as he, they combined their forces, and built the celebrated city of Rome.

As founder of this city, Romulus was its first king, and ruled the people with such an iron hand that his tyranny eventually became unbearable. The senators, weary of his exactions and arbitrary measures, finally resolved to free themselves of his presence. Taking advantage of an eclipse, which plunged the city in sudden darkness at noonday, and which occurred while all were assembled on the Forum, the magistrates slew Romulus, cut his body into pieces, and hid them under their wide togas.

When the light returned, and the terrified and awestruck people, somewhat reassured, looked about them for their king, they were told he had gone, never to return, carried off by the immortal gods, who wished him to share their abode and dignity. The senators further informed the credulous population that Romulus was to be henceforth worshiped as a god under the name of Quirinus, and gave orders for the erection of a temple on one of the seven hills, which since then has been known as Mount Quirinal. Yearly festivals in veneration of Romulus were ever after held in Rome, under the name of Quirinalia.

Well pleased with the new city of Rome and its turbulent, lawless citizens, Mars took it under his special protection; and once, when a plague was raging which threatened to destroy all the people, the Romans rushed in a body to his temple, and clamoured for a sign of his favour and protection.

Even while they prayed, it is said, a shield, Ancile, fell from heaven, and a voice was distinctly heard to declare that Rome would endure as long as this token of the god's good will was preserved. The very same day the plague ceased its frightful ravages, and the Romans, delighted with the result of their petitions, placed the heavenly shield in one of their principal temples.

Then, in constant dread lest some of their enemies should succeed in stealing it, they caused eleven other shields to be made, so exactly like the heaven-sent Ancile, that none but the guardian priests, the Salii, who kept continual watch over them, could detect the original from the facsimiles. During the month of March, which, owing to its blustery weather, was dedicated to Mars and bore his name, the ancilae were carried in a procession all through the city, the Salii chanting their rude war songs, and executing intricate war dances.

The Sabine Women

ONE OF ROMULUS'S FIRST DEEDS on founding the city was to offer asylum to people in trouble in other communities. Though Rome initially flourishes, a lack of women means that it is likely to die out after a single generation. At his wits' end, Romulus invited the neighbouring Sabines to a magnificent festival. In the famous Rape of the Sabine Women, his bandits seize the Sabines' womenfolk (the most beautiful reserved for the senators) and drive off the men. Romulus promises the young girls that they will have the status of wives and the men cajole them with protestations of love.

War broke out between the Romans and the Sabines, led by their king Titus Tatius. Eventually, the women rush into the fray to stop the fighting and a treaty is drawn up whereby Tatius becomes joint king with Romulus. A few years later, Tatius is killed by a mob, leaving Romulus sole king again. After a long rule he mysteriously disappears in a storm. He later came to be identified with the god Quirinus.

Lucretia

ACCORDING TO TRADITION there were only seven kings between the founding of Rome and the establishment of the Roman Republic. The sixth king was Servius Tullius, originally, by tradition, a slave. Servius Tullius succeeded Tarquinius Priscus, an Etruscan. The story tells of how Servius's daughter persuaded her husband, the son of Tarquinius Priscus, to murder her father whereupon the young man assumed the throne, becoming known as Tarquinius Superbus (the arrogant). While the king was away at war, his son Sextus raped the beautiful and virtuous Lucretia, the wife of a relative. After exacting an oath of vengeance against the Tarquins from her father and her husband, Lucretia plunged a dagger into her heart and died. Her family then led a revolt against the king, driving the Etruscan Tarquins from Rome and founded the Roman republic. The event is traditionally dated to 509 BC.